GEMSICUTED!

2436-JOSE

GEMSICUTED!

Julian Robov

To order additional copies of this book, contact:
Xlibris Corporation
1-888-7-XLIBRIS
www.Xlibris.com
Orders@Xlibris.com

B(u)y the book

To judge by the contents of the shelves in local bookstores, every expat who has ever set foot in Thailand believes (rightly often wrongly) that he or she has a Great Bangkok Novel inside, just begging to be read.

We're not big fans of the genre, purely as a matter of personal taste. In fact, a case could be made for prosecution on grounds of cruelty to trees where some examples of the GBN are concerned. An environmentally responsible author, then, is someone worthy of encouragement.

Step forward, Julian Robov, who is publishing his GBN online—you can check at <www.xlibris.com>. Perhaps if the e-book finds a market, a paper version will follow. And maybe even a movie, but we're getting ahead of ourselves.

The title Gemsicuted! , and if that throws you, the author counsels that the work itself is..........well.............experimental, according to a pitch received by a colleague. The blurb being circulated suggests that the work could earn its place among the finer exemplars of the GBN:

" After brilliantly masterminding a successful copper deal in London, Ris Rubyhall, the self-anointed king of rubies who had always craved for wealth, recognition, and virtual ruby monopoly discover quickly that a 37carat ruby has appeared in the Bangkok gem market without reaching his office for that first look."

" And things start to change quickly and violently with the arrival of new gamblers who are prepared to risk everything in their strong pursuit to buy the most beautiful red stone on earth. In Bangkok! Here, in a promised city awash with multicolored saints, secret lovers, gem scams and scoundrels, Rubyhall is waiting for the ruby-and into the hands of a killer."

The novel portrays a kind of gem trade life baptized with black humor and raunchy dialogue, along with a cast of nineties impresarios, bozos, lust-driven wives, gangsters and plain Joe Does, all swept in this tornado of a plot.

A minor quibble, but Mr Robov seems to have forgotten to include " diplomats, journalists and the women they buy for the night," three elements without which no book can achieve GBN status.

There are people to whom he can turn on this score............and oops, we're out of space.

Bangkok Post

"Intrigue! Thrills, romance, mystery are just a few words to describe this book by Julian Robov.

Whether you have knowledge of the world of colored stones is immaterial as the author reveals the characters and landmarks of the gem trade of Bangkok. If you have visited the Silom, Mahesak or Surawong Roads of the city, your imagination will let you identify some of the 'characters portrayed' in this revealing story.

No other book incorporates the centuries old culture of the gem business, which the author has been an active participant in both on the African continent and the small Kingdom of Thailand.

A 'must read' book for those who want to explore a different environment of gems from the glossy advertisement of the jewelry industry."

Margaret Magnussen

"The first spiritual want of barbarous man is decoration."

Thomas Carlyle

ONE

BANGKOK, 1997

Winston Lord was lounging upon the sofa dressed casually in an opennecked shirt warming his hands as to what had gone wrong while in London to close a lucrative copper deal. He remembered the conversation and laughter with his friends in London, as the deal was about to work in the syndicate's favor. There had been a longstanding gentleman's agreement between him and Ris Rubyhall for many years not to rock the boat. Stiff and sore from the betrayal, he drank the cup of tea with Rubyhall's agents for the last time. He refused to join them for a light supper.

As the bewildering high voltage thermal shock began to burn inside him against Rubyhall, a one time friend and partner, he began to ponder at himself what a fool he had been for having trusted Rubyhall and his agents for so long. The several parcels of uncut and cut rubies in front of him looked blurred and less colorful. He threw them onto the floor in anger and frustration. He was alone in his office.

The fluorescent and incandescent lights in his office fired on him. Several irregular shaped beads of sweat accumulated on his forehead and his cheeks kept moving and creating a tube-like landscape resembling the unusual fingerprint inclusions of a heat-treated natural ruby from Burma. His body and soul were boiling to the melting point.

2200°C!

He switched on his mobile phone to call Tito Mathews, a gemstone dealer. The line was busy. He tried again to call Miko

Francis, Tito's partner. There was no reply. He switched off his mobile and went into a deep thought. Some new ideas began to emerge from his subconscious mind.

Lo and behold, there was a Bible sitting right on Ben's table among several office files. An avid Bible buff it was his beloved wife and third arm. The Bible happened to be a gift from one of his clients. He flicked through the pages while trying to call either Tito or Miko, and then opened one page randomly, and read the following chapter.

"He who touches pitch blackens his hand; he who associates with an impious man learns his way.

Bear no burden too heavy for you; go with no one greater or wealthier than yourself.

How can the earthen pot go with the metal cauldron? When they knock together, the pot will be smashed: the rich man does it wrong and boasts of it, the poor man is wronged and begs forgiveness."

He switched off his mobile. He couldn't stop reading.

"As long as the rich man can use you he will enslave you, but when you are exhausted, he will abandon you.

As long as you have anything he will speak fair words to you, and with smiles he will win your confidence; when he needs something from you he will cajole you, then without regret he will impoverish you.

While it serves his purpose he will beguile you, then twice or three times he will terrify you; when later he sees you will pass by, and shakes his head over you.

Guard against being presumptuous; be not as those who lack sense.

When invited by a man of influence, keep your distance; then he will urge you all the more."

The telephone rang again. He was in no mood to answer the call, instead deciding to continue reading the chapter.

"Be not bold with him lest you be rebuffed, but keep not too far away lest you be forgotten.

Engage not freely in discussion with him, trust not his many words; for by prolonged talk he till test you, and though smiling he will probe you.

Mercilessly he will make of you a laughingstock, and will not refrain from injury or chains.

Be on your guard and take care never to accompany men of violence.

Every living things loves its own kind every man a man like himself.

Every being is drawn to its own kind; with his own kind every man associates.

Is a wolf ever allied with a lamb? So it is with the sinner and the just.

Can there be peace between the hyena and the dog? Or between the rich and poor can there be peace?

Lions prey are the wild asses of the desert; so too the poor are feeding grounds for the rich.

A proud man abhors lowliness; so does the rich man abhor the poor.

When a rich man stumbles he is supported by a friend; when a poor man trips he is pushed down by a friend.

Many are the supporters for a rich man when he speaks; though what he says is odious, it wins approval.

When a poor man speaks they make sport of him; he speaks wisely and no attention is paid to him.

A rich man speaks and all are silent, his wisdom they extol to the clouds.

A poor man speaks and they say: 'Who is that?'

If he slips they cast him down.

Wealth is good when there is no sin; but poverty is evil by the standards of the proud.

The heart of a man changes his countenance, either for good or for evil.

The sign of a good heart is a cheerful countenance; withdrawn and perplexed is the laborious schemer."

Sirach 13: 1-25

"Quite meaningful," Lord said thoughtfully tossing aside the Bible.

His mobile phone rang twice. His feet were numb as if he had climbed the rocky slopes of the Himalayas. He writhed on the ground shoving his frozen feet. He couldn't believe his eyes. He wiped off the beads of sweat with a handkerchief and slumped in a chair.

Lord closed his eyes to hide his fear. Slowly he slapped his legs trying to bring back the sensation, as the rubies both, uncut and cut, lying on the carpet began smiling at him. He took up a few rubies and held them against the light gazing with that unnerving, unblinking stare that babies bestow on objects of curiosity. He leaned over and counted all the rubies on the carpet, depositing them in his safe deposit vault.

Lord walked down through the crowded street of Mahesak, and he was beginning to feel exhausted. He reached his favorite restaurant, Window-on-Silom, overlooking Silom Road.

"Sawadee Khrap, Khun Lord," the waiter said, bowing low. "Nice to see you again."

"Thank you, Binny."

The short, fat waiter with a toothbrush mustache presented him with a menu.

"Give me my regular stuff, Binny," Lord said.

By the time Binny placed a napkin on Lord's lap his mobile phone rang. Lord stared out of the window remembering the past events. Binny knew Lord too well. He poured a glass of his favorite champagne, and then waited.

"Thank you, Binny." Lord then switched off his mobile.

To Binny's surprise, Lord took a quick gulp and waited for a second time. Lord knew only his friends would be able to fix Rubyhall and salvage his reputation in the gem trade.

Lord picked up the spoon in front of him, and began to scoop up the ice cream in a rapid movement. Gem traders at surrounding tables turned to glance in his direction and whispered to their friends.

"He's fuckedup," a gem trader was telling the mia noi (mistress) he was taking out for the first time. She laughed loudly. Normally Lord would have shot the asshole if he had a gun. But tonight he pretended he didn't even notice the asshole. His mind had moved on to the copper deal, Ris Rubyhall and the Swiss bank, where the final decision had been taken to nail him—and all for a few millions.

The waiter knew immediately that Lord wasn't in a good mood, as he whisked away the ice cream bowl. Lord shook his head.

Binny returned a few minutes later. "Shall I bring you a cup of tea?"

"Nay, just the bill," Lord answered.

Lord pushed back his chair, and walked out of the restaurant. His thoughts were elsewhere, with his wife and friends.

TWO

The ruby capital of the world! The city of the rich and famous, and the pathetic poor. The penultimate reward. The transaction and relationship capital where everyone borrowed and spent their success, vicariously, living and transmitting their fame in women, Ferraris, jewelry and gemstones, or anything in your face they could put their hands on. When it came to the most precious gems, the big ones, everyone became desperate to own one special gemstone, a ruby. This darling gemstone, for centuries, had the allure to captivate the rich and famous and the ones who wanted glimpse one, came to one place on earth. BANGKOK!

At Ris Rubyhall Towers! The city also became the most convenient stopover for the elite to poach and swap their success and love stories.

A late July, Saturday afternoon, under the gray sky, Tito Mathews and his business partner, Miko Francis to seek relief from the pathetic weekend business transactions took their usual corner seat at The Redd's Bar and Restaurant behind the Central Department Store on Silom Road. The Redd's owners, Mike and his wife Nikki, entertained patrons by swapping interesting stories of the day often joined by their two daughters, San and Tan.

There were a few bankers, sales reps from the top jewelry companies, brokers, fashion designers, giggling and swapping their seats, either to talk loudly and share a silly joke or to seek new friends, for the weekend bedroom ritual. And to add further, the big losers of the week arrived at the Redd's special table willing to share their miscalculations either in numbers or forecasts as trade for a quickie. The bar became a refuge for the winners and losers to live and share for a few precious hours, to recharge themselves for the unpredictable opening new day. Tito and Miko were no exception.

Tito & Miko Gems Company, a partnership business in operation for the past ten years in Bangkok, specialized in rubies from 2carat to 8carats. Sometimes they consigned from others, if they had a customer for above 8carat rubies. The market trusted them. Business boomed, as merchants and collectors came from all over the world, looking for those special rubies. The ones, who knew the landscape, got what they wanted, at a cost. Tito's and Miko's specialty in rubies, and the skillful way of penetrating even the top dealers, who specialized in 10carat and above, had made for themselves a name among a small number of elite dealers, who preferred to stay low profile.

In Bangkok, the top dealers took decisions instinctively, and the Thainese (Thai Chinese) dealers believed superstitiously in faces. A make or break gem deal depended on those factors, and the ones who did make never had to look back. For those who were trusted, the right type of rubies became available when requested. Tito and Miko had other sources for gems too.

GEMSTONES FROM THE URAL (Russia)!

Roman Pavlov became their prime contact in Moscow. He knew every in and out of the bureaucracy. The partnership worked well and was mutually beneficial. It all started in Bangkok, during a gala dinner at the famed Oriental hotel. It was a happy accident.

Tito and Miko arrived at The Redd for a drink. There were several dealers and foreigners busy watching the world cup soccer replay yelling and betting on their favorite country. Brazil stood at the top of the list.

"You shouldn't have done that to Reema," Tito continued. "You just blew it up. We could have sold the chick a nice stone. You know what? It's costing our business dearly. Look at the numbers. What have we done so far? All bloody postdated and dud checks. Two months, four months, nine months, and the fucking cash? Up in the gray sky. What a bloody week!" Tito unleashed his frustrations on to Miko.

"Nikki, two more please," Miko said.

"Two more what?" Mike asked jokingly.

"The same, you know, chardonnay!" Miko replied.

"Cheers!"

"Now, listen. I want to say something. I bloody like you. Not your mouth, but your heart. Don't corrupt that. Then we are finished-no more partnership. I go my way and you go to hell. This week is over. If you want to tally the numbers in our favor, we have to steal from someone. By the way, I've some good news from one of my acquaintances. If we are lucky, the money we are going to make, will be more than enough for both of us to retire early. Now, you watch the women in the streets," Tito explained.

Miko loved women. He had a way of comparing women to rubies. At times when he got carried away, the result was quite obvious. LOST SALE!

"Okay. I'll cool down. It's over. It's me again. Your good partner. Let's talk business. What's that big deal you talked about just a few minutes ago? I did listen." Miko became alert.

"This one is a ruby, big one, 37carat, Mogok, Burmese! The bloody red one is in Bangkok, the best of the best. The buyer, if we're lucky, is Polly Win. The woman loves rubies. She will eat, sleep and drink the stone. Money no problem. She wants a big one, and a big one is already in town. You know her husband, don't you?" Tito commented.

"No. I don't," Miko replied.

"You know him. Phil Win the business tycoon. He can very well afford pieces like this. The problem is, whether we can afford to buy the piece to sell it to them. We have other commitments to honor, and our reserve money is tied up with those deals," Tito said reluctantly.

"Well, we need a good plan," Miko added. "It takes time. But we can do it."

"Maybe Melvine Sanders, can help us, cut a deal with him, we have done it before," Tito recalled.

"But not for any stones of this size and quality," Miko said. "He may want a big cut. Different deal, perhaps."

"How big?" Tito asked.

"First we talk and negotiate with him, and then you know, a deal can be made. He knows us," Miko said.

"Well, only time will tell. One thing I've known in this business is there is no permanent friendship or enmity. It's all for bloody Money, and money talks here; not us, nor the stones," Tito added.

"Well, you have…" Miko looked a bit confused.

"I'm not talking about you, Miko. About others." There was a compromise.

"Oh, yeah?" Miko asked.

"Well, let it cool down for a while. Something very interesting will turn up. Who knows? Life has always given me surprises." Tito felt confident.

"Well, in that case, let's believe in surprises. We have nothing to lose, right?" Miko said.

"Oh, right!" There was a mutual understanding, as they dipped into their wine-glasses gazing at each other's eyes.

"Nikki, check please. How are you going back?" Tito asked.

"I'll walk the streets. I want to feel, smell and enjoy the streets. They have a different taste during the weekends. Hey, Tito, my regards to Chichi," Miko said.

"Oh, thanks, anyway. Take care, Miko. Goodnight! You know what?" Tito commented.

"What?" Miko asked.

"I bloody like you," Tito continued. "We'll get the money. I don't know how. But it will come."

They both hugged each other, a ritual since they became buddies.

"We'll see. Night, buddy."

THREE

The strongly built granite building on Surawong Road a family run institution; secretively accommodated Ris Rubyhall. Two generations of accumulated experience and assets had been magnets of their own merit driving away potential competitors.
THE GREAT WALL OF SURAWONG!
Due to their forceful acquisition and money power, the nickname ' Shark ' and Ris Rubyhall had become synonymous in the minerals trading circle. Any potential stocks worth the money and risk would rarely slip their notice. Working with this conservative close-knit family organization always became difficult, but for Jay Lam it was like manna fallen from heaven, when he was picked out of obscurity from Minerals Trading Limited. It was a classic poaching.
Minerals Trading Limited was a relatively small operation run by a Hong Kong Chinese family based in Bangkok, but for Lam it became a cliché. He built his colorful career from office assistant, climbing the ladder of opportunity in less than ten years, to reach the prestigious position of vice president. His other perks included a posh condo at the President Park, Sukhumvit Road, and a Mercedes. Marla his faithful wife, and two little girls, April and May, became his ultimate refuge after work. The power and freedom, which came with the title, had at times forced him to reflect on his childhood, which was cursed with hunger and poverty. If it had not been for the mercy of the Catholic run orphanage downtown, he would have ended up like other street bums with guaranteed casualties. He was that accumulated luck boy who outsmarted those genetically defective housemates who were still stuck

in that same black hole of misfortune. No one had told him who his parents were and where they lived. The nuns and priests became his parents, taking care of him and others as best as they could. His only family now was his wife Marla, and two girls.

It all started by a chance introduction, while studying at the Assumption University. The company was looking for someone fresh with the ability to learn, adapt and grow. From an ordinary office assistant, he rose to become the vice president. He desperately missed the chance to share his glory with his parents if they had been alive. Now cruising into his late thirties, he had been with the Mineral Trading Limited for ten years. Then, that fateful day came for him to quit. The Rubyhall's became desparate to poach him, because of his cutthroat abilities in winning contracts and obtaining the best of the best gems from Southeast Asia, especially Burma. He happened to be the best collector for one of their several operations-special acquisitions for collectors. He outsmarted the Harvard and Stanford elite with his simple practical tactics of ease and friendliness; a lesson evidently not learned at prestigious schools.

Ris Rubyhall, a smart oldie, in his early seventies from New York, had been living in Bangkok all these years with his Thainese (Thai Chinese) wife Wim, and was still in good health. He had a hawkish tradition of eliminating deadwood from his organization, mercilessly, with a tattoo scribbled in Khmer. Only God and he knew the meaning. He was well protected by the establishment and politicians. He had a tradition of donating this permanent scar to the employees, and no one dared to question him. He was too powerful and strong to be challenged.

THE GREAT MAN OF BANGKOK!

Lam heard about this stoneage practice in horror and disbelief. But as long as he remained a moneymaker for the establishment that was more than enough to avoid getting tattooed. His benefits were five times better than Mineral Trading Limited. He was elevated to a position like a virtual king without a crown, but powerful. The only spare time he had with his family was after midnight when they were all asleep. He had to keep his loyalty. Otherwise, he knew his fate.

A GRAND TATTOO!

He had to keep on making bundles of money for them. They were watching over his shoulders, all his work and the profits. At times he got the scare of his life when things didn't work his way. But he knew for all those missed opportunities and deals, there would always be a fool coming his way from somewhere.

FOUR

Meljeb Towers, the ultimate dream-come-true-one-stop business center on Silom Road became available for many gemstone dealers from around the world.

RUBIES AND CONTACTS!

Melvine Sanders chose the seventh floor permanently for one reason. He believed in number seven. Several brokers waited outside patiently for his attention. The commission was good and consistent. Sanders had a loyal following, and he made sure they came to his office first, before going elsewhere.

Born in New York, Sanders made Bangkok his second home for convenience, pleasure and business, specializing in rubies from various localities in the world. He never had any taste for religion nor the rituals demanded by the tradition in his country of birth, instead he fled New York, and Thailand became his adopted country. Competition was there, but a very few players controlled the market.

Ruby mines in Burma, Cambodia and Vietnam were primitive and very few good rubies reached the market. He developed a relationship among the miners and traders in and around the ruby producing countries of South Asia, Southeast Asia, and Africa, thus becoming a privileged trader among the few elite. It took a lot of patience and perseverance working with these traders who had their own rules and tradition. The ones who adapted succeeded in getting a foothold in the land of rubies and he was one of them.

"What way can I help you Miko? Now if I understand you properly, you need access to two million to buy the Burmese ruby, right? It's a lot today, you know that, don't you?" Sanders said frankly, motioning Miko to take his seat.

Miko had several ideas.

"Sure I do," Miko replied, thanking Sanders for the Darjeeling tea, his favorite.

"Why is this deal so important to you Miko, if I may ask? Remember, we haven't gotten into business this high. I would like to know complete details, and how are you gonna pay back?" Sanders kept rolling a cabochon ruby in his hand, while listening to Miko.

"We want you to become a partner in this one deal," Miko continued. "We do not have the money to buy this piece on our own. That way your interests would also be protected. Our money is tied up with other acquisitions."

"I can see what you mean. What's so interesting about this ruby?" Sanders asked eagerly.

"This ruby? It's a 37carat piece from the Mogok Stone Tract, Burma, not from Mong Hsu, the new source. Anyone who is familiar with its color would never doubt it. It's a rare piece altogether, the mother of all color. There is that origin report from the Swiss laboratory stating its quality," Miko added, watching Sanders's reaction.

"Well, so far so good. You must know that the Swiss laboratory doesn't mention about grading or quality in their reports. They just identify and give an opinion on their origin, right?" Sanders replied as if he knew everything.

"You're right," Miko said firmly.

"Is it untreated?" Sanders asked anxiously.

"It's natural, untreated. The color is good, exceptionally good. I've seen similar qualities before. So, I remember. No one ever forgets the color of a good quality stone. This piece is top red with a very slight tint of pink in it. That's all," Miko said confidently.

"I see. How about clarity and cut?" Sanders asked.

"Very lightly included. Enough to prove it's natural. A few liquid fingerprints on the pavilion. You need to magnify the stone to see those fingerprints. Cut, I should say fair to good. Like all previous stones they still keep that tradition. Cut slightly imperfectly for weight retention. But overall it has that aesthetic appeal, not at all ugly like the bottoms of a Sumo. Eye catching personality, I must say," Miko answered, proving his knowledge.

"Now, where is the stone? Could it be possible to see the stone before I decide?" Sanders asked.

"I can arrange that. Remember this is a good offer we can't afford to lose. Now, where in the world today can you buy a 37carat ruby for two million? You don't have to go out of Bangkok. Just check the recent catalogues of Sotheby's and Christie's. This is a good bargain. The guy wants privacy and safe passage of his money to a numbered account in Switzerland," Miko pleaded.

"Maybe, I'm interested, but at the moment, I can't make any decisions due to other commitments. But the door is still open for further discussion." Sanders began to test Miko's patience and caliber.

"Sanders, you know this trade too well. It takes a split-second to go this way or the other way. We are dealing with people, not stones. We have to talk to them or others may also have an interest in it. We can't afford to lose this. It's a once in a lifetime deal," Miko said.

"I know that too well, Miko. It's the two million issue. I've got to consult with my partners. They will also have a say in my decisions," Sanders said, playing his game.

"So, when will I know your decision? It shouldn't be that long," Miko argued.

"I'll call you as soon as possible. But, I must see the stone first. When can I see that?" Sanders reminded repeatedly.

"Let's say, tomorrow morning eight o'clock!" Miko answered.

"No. Bring it between twelve and two. For me, light is important. I would like to see how the ruby is going to look like during midday. The rest, I already know," Sanders said plainly.

"As you wish. It will be here tomorrow, say around one o'clock. I'll call you first." Miko assured.

"Thanks, Miko."

They shook hands and Miko left the office.

FIVE

Lam had all the reasons to worry about himself. The rain-maker touch, his bull's-eye started to look like it was turning into a hailstorm. The money and contracts were taking more time than usual to stack up. Rubyhall's telescope and microscope magnification now zoomed to its maximum. He saw Lam's hollow brain.

Rubyhall's piggy face started to expand in accumulated despair, like the foam in a cappuccino. Something had to be done. There were no big stones coming to his office. He always liked big stones. That's where the money took its comfortable residence.

Some Bangkok ladies loved big ones. Just like their husband's big balls. They loved to roll them with their aging fingers so with big stones. Lam wondered why the big ones, rubies, his favorite, and his bosses too, were not coming to his office. He knew who the major and minor players were, and their limitations. His competitors like Melvine Sanders and others were in no way an immediate threat to his position.

With the addition of few Asian newcomers, who lacked the inside information and the knack to pin down the socialites of Bangkok, he had no reason to worry about his prestigious position for the forseeable future. Now that luxurious thought looked threatened by a new invisible group. They were skimming the rubies right from the source with amazing speed and precision. He just couldn't figure out this group's exact operation in Bangkok. The huge market potential in dealing with the more than 10carat stones, which brought millions each week, had now shrunk to the lowest record in Rubyhall's memory.

Lam too had a lot to worry about the unusual twist to his

fortune and of his organization. He could now be tattooed and fired, anytime, if he didn't manage to find the source. Even the regulars who used to bring stones to his marbled office were just not in a mood to see him. He had only one way to know the skimmers. Join them and destroy their roots, once and for all. He had known few chickens like Mark Cleavage, Christian Pinpoint, and David Feather during several trading floor encounters. They all kept their careful distance, as to not to get too attached in order to keep their secret contacts and personal interests away from poachers.

Tito and Miko were too small for Lam to worry about but he still kept an eye on them. They had an occasional chat, just for the sake of avoiding their competitors, but all these players knew their strengths and weaknesses. When Miko called Rubyhall at his office to let him know that he was about to acquire a 37carat ruby of the best quality, that alarmed the old man. He saw Lam's ability to track the source of rubies disappearing right in front of his eyes. He couldn't understand why Miko had to tell Ris that he had a 37carat ruby coming soon for sale. Usually dealers kept quiet until after the sale, because of the presence of powerful brokers and dealers who might thwart the sale if the piece wasn't in the right hands.

But the ones who knew the game of hide and sell always had the advantage no matter how strong the competition was in this dog eat dog market. He didn't know what to do. It looked like the whole world was crumbling under his feet. The tattooing day was approaching faster.

Miko was born to an American father and a Thai mother. He began learning the ropes of ruby trade working with different brokers, dealers, and miners as an intern, first in Chantaburi, and then in Mae Sot and Mae Sai. His mother introduced him to this wild trade at a very early age after his father divorced her for reasons only they knew. He didn't want to know either. She later found another rich American for good and helped Miko quietly till he learned the ropes of the ruby trade. Her second husband didn't like Miko, and the gem trade. But Miko got hooked to the ruby trade with the help of his mother, Suwanee, who happened to be a one-time gem broker. She taught him the secrets of bargaining and how to compete with other brokers, especially women in the gem market. When it came to a certain quality, they were more persuasive, reasoning and aggressive than men. Overall, when it came to making money, everyone competed against each other for survival.

He liked the unpredictable nature of the ruby trade and loved meeting and learning from the crooks and bimbos of the trade, because there were many in all colors, shapes and disguises. With time, he learned fast to spot a potential ruby and cut a deal profitably benefiting both sides.

He had only one problem. His brain remained active only for a few hours a day. That was the time when his concentration peaked and profits then churned out countless amounts of money.

THAT WAS HIS BULL'S EYE!

Tito, his partner, also had an unusual upbringing. He grew up in Australia working for his father in the opal mines in Lightning Ridge. He couldn't stand his father's rigid discipline, and later decided to go his own way. He took his flight to Bangkok, because the air ticket and the cost of living were so cheap, he never bothered to return. Tito met Miko through an acquaintance in Mae Sai, and that brief introduction brought them together like die-hard twins. Tito had a reason to like Miko. A rainmaker in his own way! He had a heart, which no one saw, the heart of a saint.

That was the reason why Tito liked Miko. Tito later met Chichi, a gem broker from Chantaburi. They found a chemical match in their relationship both, business and personal. She later gave birth to a son, Timo. Though Miko remained single, he liked women, if they had beauty inside and outside, and occasionally graded them to see if they met his standards.

When Lam heard Rubyhall was planning to invite Miko to his office, an unbelievable gesture, he had all the reasons to worry about Miko and his motives. But most important of all what bothered Lam was how on earth did he manage to obtain a 37carat ruby, of top quality, if it was to be believed, now in Miko's or Tito's custody. How come he slipped that precious opportunity? Did someone from his traditional contacts switch sides? Why would they want to do that when they were all making such luxurious profit working with him and Rubyhall? Only a lunatic would kill the goose that laid golden eggs every week.

Now Lam had all the reasons to hate and kill Miko with one bite, if he was anywhere close. The achievement, the hard work, and the ambition to grow in prosperity had now come to a halt with the advent of Miko, the python. The only way to eliminate him was to get closer to him and learn the root of his contacts. Excess exposure to the Rubyhall group in the long run had to be minimized. The thought of Miko taking over his portfolio became unthinkable!

It reminded him of a story told by one of the nuns about a camel and the Bedouin in an oasis during his childhood days at the orphanage. The camel had been accompanying the Bedouin for so long, that one day, as he lay resting under his tent, the camel approached the Bedouin requesting, if he could rest his head under his tent while he was asleep. He couldn't refuse. The first day, the camel slept with his head inside the tent.

The second day, the camel had another request. This time he wanted his belly and head to be accommodated inside the tent when asleep. The next day, when the time came for both of them to sleep, the Bedouin got the shock of his life. The camel had taken over his sleeping area leaving him to sleep outside the tent, as the camel had done for years. He couldn't grasp the analogy behind this simple Arabic tale then, but now he knew precisely what it meant. Miko had become the camel of the Rubyhall group.

When it came to rubies, Miko had the magical combination of putting together several color options in front of his table and selecting the best deal with an instinct only he knew. In that little time when his brain activates in any day, he had already done the work of ten people of similar intelligence. He had a unique talent to remember the best of a ruby color under any sort of light. His eyes had a different genetic makeup of selecting the best colors of a ruby in the worst possible lighting, thus weeding out the unsaleables.

Without a loupe or any sort of magnification, he could judge the clarity of rubies in a split-second. He had a library of information regarding the colors of all known localities. His brain also had the ability to calibrate the hue, saturation (vividness, intensity), and tone (relative lightness or darkness / gray) of rubies from the known localities. Using the Burmese top quality as a master color he had developed a system, only he knew to determine the best of best colors.

ALL MENTALLY!

The best came from Burma. The colors were unmatchable and had all the right geological environment to create the best of all best colors known to mankind, up to this day. Miko was considered the walking spectrophotometer among a small circle of Burmese ruby experts.

Now Rubyhall had collected this pertinent information which would immensely fatten his business prospects, if it worked his way. At the same time, he had to laboriously check the consistency of Lam's abilities to bring in uninterrupted profits with minimum overhead. He wondered why the famous gem merchants in the world hadn't yet discovered this genius. INCLUDING HIM!

For him it turned out to be a happy accident of the day. If he could lure both, Miko and Tito to his net without Lam's help, then that would give him a reason to find a cheaper replacement.

With that and more wicked thoughts, he sat on his nephrite chair, rolling in his hand an oval cut Burmese ruby.

SIX

Chu Linthong, a gem broker, with a few rough rubies from a client accosted Tito on Silom Road, as he was returning to his office in Sita Building. He owed her a lunch. After careful thought, he had a last minute change of mind. He decided to look at a parcel of rubies from Chu at the Silom Restaurant on Silom Road, opposite his office.

After a brief discussion with the waitress, they got a table facing Surasak Road. The skylight was good. Tito saw the colors of rubies better. He wasn't happy with the parcel. Tito saw her icy stare. Later on, she decided to lunch with him on condition that he looked at another parcel of rubies from Vietnam, at his office.

"Today we have something very special." The waitress arrived with the menu.

"Like what?" Tito asked abruptly.

"Would you like to see the special menu?" The waitress reminded gently.

"What's your name? You look beautiful!" Tito became inquisitive.

"Jimbo! That's my nickname," the waitress replied with a cute smile.

"That's a good name. Jimbo!" Tito complimented her.

"Thank you!"

Chu poked fun at him by the way he asked Jimbo the questions. But she knew he didn't mean anything.

"This special menu reads like a novel to me. What do we have? Let me read. Okay give me, poached cod with tomatoes and prunes, salmon in papillote with lime, poached fillet of sea bass with olive oil and lemon. Then......oh, rabbit stuffed with bacon and rosemary with the wine, Lindeman's semillon chardonnay 'bin 77', please." Tito returned the menu to Jimbo.

"And for you madam?" Jimbo asked Chu.

"I think I'll go for asparagus with cracklings and black olive caper vinaigrette, linguine with green beans and lemon sauce, and tagliatelle with prawns. The wine, masi valpolicella classico, red, please," Chu said, looking satisfied.

Chu knew Tito would swear in all dirty words after the lunch for ordering an expensive wine. She saw the rage on his face. Tito later settled quietly without saying much, while glancing at her with a wicked smile.

"The rabbit stuffed with bacon and rosemary, sir." The service was fast.

"Great! How would you like it?" Jimbo asked Chu

"Is it treated?" Chu asked.

"How about simonsig shiraz, sir?" Jimbo asked Tito.

"Oh, the South African, right? I love the wine," Tito replied, knowing the bill was going to wipe out the little profit he had made just a few minutes ago from a quick deal. He cursed himself quietly for taking her to this expensive restaurant. He shouldn't have met her in the first place.

"One masi valpolicellaa classico, red!" Chu reminded.

"Cheers!"

"Tito, how is Miko doing? I hear some rumors," Chu asked, knowing his unpredictable answers.

"Like what?" Tito looked outside the window at a leggy woman cross the road.

"Some big ones orbiting the streets," Chu added.

"Really?" Tito pretended as if he knew nothing.

"Ruby! Don't you understand? You're pretending, aren't you?" Chu shot back at him.

"How do you know that?" Tito asked surprisingly.

"Information! My informant tells me that Rubyhall's are into it. Lam is very upset. It's a lot of money, isn't it?" Chu said.

"Screw, Lam. Business is business. Ruby is innocent. They

will end up with whoever deserves it. If the price is right the stone belongs to them. What's wrong with that?" Tito answered.

"But you don't have the money," Chu said, expecting a rude reply.

"It's not that cheap, but not that expensive. You see the point," Tito reminded her. She was wrong this time.

"Who puts the value?" Chu added. "The food is great, Tito."

Tito wanted to say something about her cunning remark, but swallowed immediately.

"The market, of course, who else? If there is a demand and if the market thinks it appropriate, then that's the price," Tito continued.

"There is a difference between value and price, Tito," Chu countered his suggestion.

"Who cares? For me money is everything, value and price. It's for the experts to define the terms. I'm least bothered," Tito replied.

"You should expect a trap when you approach people like Rubyhall, Sanders and David. They know you guys don't have the balls to handle pieces like that. They will cut your profits and balls at the same time. Are you aware of that?" Chu sounded like his mother.

"I've brought the wine, sir," Jimbo reminded them politely.

"It's for me," Chu thanked Jimbo.

"You'll hear all sort of rumors, there is a lot of chaff. We'll find the right buyer. It's all fenced appropriately," Tito said confidently.

"Do you think Lam will sit quietly and watch his ass and balls getting heat-treated? You must be kidding. His future and reputation are now hanging on this mysterious ruby of 37carat, a Burmese one!" Chu reminded.

"Hell with Lam. I don't care a bit of what he thinks. If his ass and balls are burning because of this piece, then that's his problem. We all have to work to survive. The fittest will survive. The jungle law," Tito replied, like his father. His father used to remind him all the time when he did something stupid. Now he was imitating his father. He hated that, but at times it came out of his mouth spontaneously.

"How about some black pepper with cottage cheese, sir?" Jimbo asked.

"Not now, Jimbo!" Tito replied.

"The linguine with green beans and lemon sauce?" Jimbo reminded.

"Yep. Please get us some more brown bread," Tito said.

"In a few seconds, sir." Jimbo rushed back to the kitchen.

"So what's the hook? Who will buy?" Chu asked.

"You want to know who will buy? The highest bidder that simple," Tito replied in a cool way.

"And the money, where is it coming from for you guys?" Chu asked.

"From heaven! What should I say?" Tito said laughingly. He wasn't so interested in replying to her question.

"Be more realistic, Tito. Melvin Sanders is your bank, where else can the money come from knowing your reputation," Chu said, poking fun at him.

"We've a very small reputation. There are some unwritten rules. We follow that. They know that. We've always kept that tradition, and we'll continue to remain that way," Tito commented.

"So he is going to chip in a million or two, right?" Chu quipped.

"Quite likely, but it is still under negotiation," Tito added.

"How will you be privileged to share the profits from this deal with me?" Chu asked.

"In bricks!" Tito replied sarcastically.

"What do you mean by bricks?" Chu asked eagerly.

"Bricks are bricks. The bricks you see over there for those tower blocks," Tito said, pointing his finger at the new building under construction across Surasak Road.

"That was mean of you, Tito," Chu grinned.

"That's all I can afford at the moment," Tito concluded, giggling intermittently.

"Sir. Can I clear the table? I hope you enjoyed the meal," Jimbo said, awaiting their compliment.

"Delicious, Jimbo!" She felt happy. She was looking for a large tip. Tito read the message in her bulging eyes.

"You know what? The way you have dressed today looks like......." Tito remembered something, but retracted to avoid another explosive debate. He didn't want to make her cry, even though she killed him this time with an expensive lunch.

"Say something, Tito. I know you're good at making fun of me in front of others. Now you have found my dress distasteful, right? It's not that bad. It's a Thai design, a creative one. It's not that cheap," Chu said.

"It's horrifying," Tito answered, and then laughed loudly.

"The poached cod with tomatoes and prunes is ready, sir." Jimbo arrived in time to break up the heated conversation.

"Let me taste it. Delicious, Jimbo!" Tito complimented.

"So where is Miko now?" Chu asked.

"He is busy with his customers. Business! No women! This time dead serious. He can't fool around. It will cost us dearly. Once in a while it is okay. But not everyday," Tito said repeatedly.

"Can I interrupt? We have some special desserts today," Jimbo said politely.

"Okay, give me one almond macaroon!" Tito answered.

"And for you, madam?" Jimbo turned her attention to Chu.

"Blackcomb mountain special, please," Chu replied.

"And also, I forgot. One espresso creme brulee!" Tito reminded Jimbo.

"I would also like to have the same, please," Chu said, glancing at Tito and settled with a crafty smile. Tito knew she had squared him again this time.

After the meal, they sat and discussed the ruby parcel she wanted him to look at it and, if possible, buy so that she could get more, if the price was right. But having known her for quite sometime, he didn't wanted to disappoint her. Sometimes he bought from her, if he had clients lined up for a specific quality, and at times he had to keep them for a while in his custody, and then return them if he couldn't sell. They had a good working relationship and the partnership created good business. She had a knack of meeting the miners and traders from Mae Sot, Mae Sai, Bo Rai and Chantaburi, who had offices in Bangkok. But now she had picked up the news regarding a 37carat ruby, and the ruby had all the reason to be the talk of the town. This scoop gave her a reason to get attention when showing rubies to other dealers and the trade loved gossip.

After paying the bill, they returned to his office.

SEVEN

Rubyhall summoned the directors of his company to the conference room. He had something important to deliver. They knew it wasn't going to be good news. He had a way of starting and finishing a meeting. He would gently ask them to opine and if he found their suggestion stupid, he punished them in front of others in his own vocabulary.

So, Mark Amber, director of mines, reminded Rubyhall of the need to renegotiate the gold deal with the JRO group in Indonesia. Instead, Rubyhall threw the ball into Lam's court.

Lam knew Rubyhall's tactic and was well prepared.

"Jay can handle that. What do you say, Jay?"

"Well, there is a rumor that the Canadian counterpart and their research team did claim the 'mother of all' gold find on earth," Lam continued. "And they want us to be part of that success story. We did, in fact, commit to further considerations only when the scientific facts and the commercial reality are put forward in writing with the factual report, no money is involved, only a mutual understanding. Then we will make our financial commitment."

"Okay, good move," Rubyhall said, complimenting him with a few taps on the desk.

Rubyhall had a special relationship with the Suharto family, and the consultants working on their behalf kept informing him of the commercial viability of the discovered mineral deposits. The gold discovery in BUSANG (Indonesia) was brought to Rubyhall's attention, but somehow his refined instincts never yielded to continue the exploration before it came to be known as the largest fraud on earth. Lam helped Rubyhall identify the fraud, avoiding another financial catastrophe. He was rewarded for this foresight appropriately.

"One more question, Mr Rubyhall!" Philip Coral said, bringing others attention.

"What's that Philip? Is it important?" Rubyhall asked. Philip Coral, the marketing director, relayed his concern regarding the YADANA project in Burma.

"Yes, indeed. We had a deal with the Burmese government, the gas pipeline project. My informant reminds me that the environmental groups based in Bangkok and Kanchanaburi are going to disrupt our project. How do you think we're going to handle the situation? It's pretty serious, and remember the money involved," Philip said grimly.

Rubyhall had an interest in the YADANA gas pipeline project with other investors, and the Thai governments Burma policy didn't look like they were working in his favor. He couldn't understand why all of a sudden the politicians and bureaucrats had become born-again environmentalists. They were talking about trees, forests, birds, animals, worms and all sort of nonsense, when they have been killing, destroying, eating, and profiting from them without the world's knowledge for centuries. He knew the members of parliament and the committee heads employed to study the project and the ones involved with Burma policy. Though controversial, he had a way of extending favors to the politicians, which was always acknowledged.

"I can answer that worry. Having mentioned Burma, I'm closely watching the situation. I'll do everything in my power to make the environmental groups proposal vaporize," Rubyhall interrupted. "It is of terrible concern. To continue further, what I had wanted to bring to your attention is, I've come to know just a few days ago of a ruby, again from Burma, top of the top, in Bangkok, for sale. Now what I want to know is why didn't it come to my office? We have a tradition of entertaining brokers and miners to bring in their best only their best for that first look, which is why we have a name. How did it happen? I want to know the reason. Why did it not reach our office first? Jay!"

Lam paused. He knew Rubyhall expected a convincing answer. "I did hear about this rumor the other day. I'm quite doubtful of its existence. Someone is trying to play poker with us. My informants have gone to penetrate the source, and I'll be able to inform the board in a day or two. Till then, it should be considered as a speculation," Lam said, hoping he had convinced Rubyhall.

"What do others think about Jay's statement?" Rubyhall glanced at everyone in the room. They nodded.

"Having said that," Lam continued. "There is a group to be watched closely, Miko and Tito. The presence of ruby is their tactic to look like they can handle gems of this superior quality. Knowing their traditional market and the quality they deal in, it would take several accumulated rebirths to match the wealth of Rubyhall's today, and the money they would have to raise to buy such qualities. Only Rubyhall's could afford to do that. We have a major investment facility deep inside Burma, and there is no way they would allow such top quality rubies to slip by to wannabe's like Miko and Tito. We have a friendship pact with the Burmese miners and dealers, and they haven't disappointed us so far. I believe they will always love to do business with Rubyhall's for the forseeable future taking into consideration the mutual benefits and concerns."

"So you think it is just speculation, Jay?" Rubyhall asked.

"I think so, for the time being," Lam replied promptly.

Others kept mum. Only Lam knew the ropes of this wild trade. Everyone's attention centered on Lam. Even though he was sweating, the statement he made in the conference room somehow felt convincing. Rubyhall liked that remark.

Rubyhall took the podium and said, "I'll have to remind you all, that we are the exclusive custodians of top quality rubies to major collectors around the world," he continued. "We shouldn't at any cost lose this exclusive privilege. The Rubyhall's will weep for the first time when that happens."

"It will not happen, Mr Rubyhall." Lam promised. Everyone nodded.

"I'm awaiting your report as you promised, it will be here in a day or two. Let's get back to work."

The special meeting was adjourned.

After the meeting, Lam couldn't concentrate on his work. He saw from his office window the almighty traffic jam on Surawong Road, accumulating in rows by the second.

Surawong Road had no breathing space. It was virtually dead. Motorcycles and tuk tuk's sped like crazy bees frightening the people walking on the footpath. School children waited patiently with their parents for the green light to cross the road.

Street beggars too had a field day. He saw one beggar counting his days earning behind a filthy back street. There was a sigh of relief after he hid the money in a cloth bag, wiping the flies from his sweating face.

Another day, more begging. Lam thought for a second. Today he was sitting in a high rise building and looking down at people acting their role on a world stage for survival. Tomorrow, if his calculations went wrong, he would end up like that beggar in the back street doing a similar act in a different way. He had witnessed people make and lose money and gem dealers disappearing altogether with other people's money and gems, never again to be seen in the market resulting in broken homes and suicides. He had consoled several souls in the trade when confronted with a difficult situation but he knew no one understood his real problems, when he had one.

Now a 37carat Burmese ruby had come from nowhere to haunt his life. Avoiding the wrath of Rubyhall was an altogether different story. Rubyhall would never hesitate to obtain this exclusive piece by any means. Rubies were in his blood and losing them looked no different than losing his life.

Tom Chavalith walked into Lam's office with a how do you

do? A close friend and gem dealer, Lam had known Tom for more than five years. He had brought in a few sample rough rubies from Vietnam, for Lam's opinion. The stones all looked of alluvial quality with a lot of blemishes. The heavily oxidized skin made it difficult to judge their true color. The roughs, which resembled the size of a small hen's egg got his curious attention. Altogether, there were five pieces. Transparent to translucent, the rough rubies had some crystal inclusions visible under a fiber optic light. The color never matched the Mogok rubies from Burma, overall, a medium quality.

Rubyhall would never touch rubies of such qualities. He would leave it for others to gamble. In the end, he knew they lost money dearly. But he always wanted that first look to discard if deserved.

And, Lam was the first filter. If he approved the rubies, then the rubies took up their residence in Rubyhall's office for the final say. He was the master negotiator. Lam motioned Tom to a seat by his side. They were good friends. But when doing business, they kept friendship separate.

"The rubies need some enhancement. It will be good after burning (heat-treatment)," Lam echoed his sentiments exactly.

Tom understood Lam's statement. That meant another run to the gem doctors of Chantaburi to treat them. Chantaburi was considered the heat-treatment capital of the world when it came to rubies. Lam was the expert. He could judge by the color whether the ruby needed enhancement or otherwise. Some yielded positive results while others didn't. But heat-treating rubies for color or clarity enhancement was always a gamble. With a little bit of luck and experience, dealers made a good profit if everything had gone well.

"I want to tell you something," Tom continued. "There is a big one out in the market looking for a buyer."

"Really?" Lam pretended that he didn't know anything about it.

"Buddy, 37carat, Burmese. I haven't seen the piece yet. I got the information from Chu," Tom said. "She is quite close to Tito and Miko. I think this one is real. Otherwise, Chu wouldn't carry such stories to sell her chick stones."

Lam started to worry. Tom's information had never gone wrong due to the connections he had in the gem market.

"Someone must be playing the old games," Lam said frantically.

"Game or nor, the ruby is out, and it is Burmese. I think Rubyhall must be aware of it, don't you think? Did he tell you anything about it?" Tom gasped.

"Yeah! Sort of. There was a meeting the other day and he brought up this topic. So if you think it is out, then the story is reliable. In fact, I sent Achy and Sammy to double-check the news. If it all turns out to be true, then I have to say so. Rubyhall won't be happy," Lam said, sniffing the air.

His attention returned to Surawong Road again. The police came from nowhere to stop three Africans, who were walking to the Peninsula hotel with their black briefcases.

Lam was watching. Tom seemed more interested in studying the ruby parcel he had just brought in under a fiber optic light than the event outside the office.

"Hey! Tom, look at this. Come," Lam interrupted.

The shell-shocked Africans stood there not knowing the reason for their apprehension in the middle of a sidewalk.

"They are for their money or something," Tom commented.

"Passport!" Lam whispered to Tom.

The Africans showed the two policemen their passport. Still unconvinced, they asked the Africans to open their briefcase. They opened them obediently knowing the consequences.

GEMSTONES!

One policeman took a few crystals not knowing their identity. The policemen asked them something in a language they couldn't understand. The Africans looked at each other in utter confusion and fear. The two policemen took the Africans briefcase and sped away.

"What would you do if it happened to you, like those poor Africans?" Lam asked gravely.

"Nothing. You can't do anything. The police rule the streets whether you are right or wrong. One thing is sure. The Africans will never see those stones again. They are gone forever," Tom said, puzzled.

The Africans were still standing on the sidewalk crying and yelling at the people. No one seemed to care about their plight. People just ignored them.

"So you think I should go to Chantaburi?" Tom asked Lam. It was back to business.

"Yeah! I think so," Lam continued. "I don't know what's happening to me. I'm not in a good mood today."

The phone interrupted him as he rose. Tom and Lam looked at each other, and then Tom rushed out to the lavatory.

It was Ris Rubyhall. After the brief conversation, Lam began to worry as to how he was going to convince Rubyhall regarding that elusive ruby of 37carat.

Rubyhall had a unique passion to collect untreated rubies of superb color. He never collected treated rubies. The good relationship he had with the specialized laboratories in Switzerland made his business thorough and professional so far. There was no room for mistakes. Lam had instructions only to buy untreated rubies of any sizes above 10 carat. The rest he knew. But quietly Lam entertained friends who came for an opinion and they never returned disappointed. Tom wasn't an exception.

Meanwhile, the incandescent lights in the 'DEEP RED' room of Ris Rubyhall Towers glowed too bright as Tony William, a gemstone dealer, was dragged to a teakwood chair. He was still conscious despite being kidnapped and severely beaten to settle an outstanding score by Rubyhall's henchman, a North Korean nicknamed 'Igneous' Kim.

Kim plastered Tony's mouth first, and then tied both his legs to the chair. After a second thought, he untied one hand and taped

Tony's other hand close to his chest. He placed the right hand on a wooden block for convenience. Without waiting, he swung the cleaver, and cleaved Tony's thumb with one swing. He clipped the thumb from Tony's right hand, and put it straight on the table for him to see.

There was a sudden numbness in Tony's arm, then he screamed. He never expected this swing to come that fast. It was the beginning. He struggled with his right arm to keep it steady, but the oozing blood from the wound wouldn't stop. This time he felt Kim meant business.

Tony had no other choice, but to see the end of this sadistic ritual. He remembered the dark days Kim just mentioned. His wife, Robin, and Billy, the only son flashed in front of him in a split-second. He tried hard to stay put, but the severe pain wouldn't allow him to settle himself.

Another swing with the cleaver clipped Tony's forefinger. This time, it was more precise. Kim lifted the cleaved finger from the wooden block and laid it close to Tony's severed thumb. Tony cried loudly, as the pain became unbearable. Kim stared at Tony, with no compassion, as the situation became tenser.

Like a collapsing mud wall, Tony started to crumble physically and mentally, as his energy and endurance drained beyond the limit. His eyes became blurred sliding him into an unconscious state. Barely able to catch his breath, the passionate desire to live longer looked dim and remote, as the numbness spread across his entire body. He had no strength left to talk, as he closed his eyes and slumped in his chair. He wished it were all over.

As Tony tried to open his eyes, another swing from Kim cleaved his three fingers. This time, the cry emerged from his heart, voiceless. With his mouth open, he cried as hard as he could, but only saliva scattered around, clustering into liquid droplets, creating a landscape of countless shiny beads. The severed fingers were laid orderly on the table. There was a victory smile on Kim's face, as he saw Tony's fingers struggling in vain for life. Blood was flowing from the wooden block, like magma from an angry volcano snaking towards the floor.

Kim walked to the refrigerator, pulled a tray of ice cubes, and swallowed a few pieces, before immersing the severed palm of Tony into it. He felt nothing. His breathing became heavier and desperate as the desire for staying alive emerged into incomprehensible mumbling. Kim glanced at his wristwatch, as he wiped the bloodstains from the cleaver for the next phase. Tears rolled down from Tony's face, as he looked at his executioner. Without showing any signs of emotion, Kim spread the left arm on the wooden table.

"Please don't do this to me. No....no......no," Tony pleaded in a low tone. His voice became so low, only he could hear the meaning of his plea. But, Kim had to do what he had intended right from the beginning.

Tony was paying the price for having sold Ris Rubyhall a parcel of synthetic rubies as natural ones from Burma.

Kim sharpened the edges of the cleaver carefully, and this time, instead of clipping fingers one by one, he decided to do the job in two installments.

With the first swing, the thumb got cleaved. Like a butcher, he carefully clipped the thumb and laid it on the table. It was quick this time. He held the rest of the fingers symmetrically for a final swing.

"Aaaaaaaaaaaaaaaaaaaaaaaaaaaaaaaaaaaaaaaa!!!!!!!!!!!!!!!!!!!!!!!!!!!!" Tony cried with all his strength, as the remaining four fingers, cleaved and separated. His severed palm was immersed into the ice tray for the last crude baptism.

With a sigh of relief, Kim walked to the table, and put the severed fingers in a plastic bag with a green tag, time and date. He took another sticker, and pasted on a special mailing address.

"What's the definition of a synthetic ruby, Tony? Can you hear me?" Kim whispered sarcastically.

Tony had no strength left to answer Kim's question, as he became convinced that his end was nearing by the second. He remembered his good old days in a flash anticipating the next move. He tried in vain to remember who his friends had been in times of trouble. But the pain and shock of this torturous ritual prevented him from seeking a quiet consolance. He started to realize, how unlucky a person can be, if death had to be encountered in a cruel and painful way, like the one he was now going through. He wished it all ended in one gunshot. But in his case it was taking more time than usual. He felt like cursing his parents and the womb, which brought him to the world. But, it was too late.

"Are you there, Tony?" Kim whispered again.

Tony never responded. Instead, he was breathing quietly, showing only the slightest signs of life. His eyes began to bulge out of their socket, stubbornly showing signs of endurance. He now realized the time had come, and it would be all over in a matter of seconds. Even the attempt to remember his loved ones became too difficult, as he started to feel the declining energy level followed by that cruel numbness.

Kim positioned Tony's face in profile one more time. There was no room for pity. He squeezed Tony's head to the wooden block for the next phase.

Tony had no interest in knowing what his executioner was up to. His only wish was to see it all end in time. Like a sacrificial lamb, he yielded to the demand, as his head lay face down on the wooden block. Kim checked the cleaver carefully, and with a forceful and precise swing, the sharp edges dug deep cleaving both, the wooden block and the head. Tony's head was slit from his neck precisely the way Kim intended.

Without fail, he wiped the bloodstains with a piece of cloth, before wrapping it with a plastic sheet. He placed it in a special cardboard box with a note to the recipient.

Later on, the severed fingers were also placed carefully in the box with another note. He didn't wait any longer. He chopped the remaining limbs, and packed them separately in special plastic sheets. The rest was dumped into a larger wooden crate.

His revenge over, Kim went to the kitchen sink to wash his

hands and the cleaver thoroughly to get rid of the stubborn bloodstains. He then placed the clean cleaver in the wooden crate for its final destination. Having slaughtered Tony like a frog, Kim felt nothing.

He walked back again to the kitchen, to grab some sandwiches he had left in the refrigerator, before he decided to leave. There was a conqueror's smile on his face, before he stepped into a deep surface-diffused blue van with his special luggage to be delivered to the destined recipient.

Chichi taking a break from office worries was busy with their only son, Timo, playing hide and seek at their SV City Tower 3 condominium situated on Rama 3 Road.

The telephone rang.

"Chichi! It's me," Miko said hurriedly.

"Where is Tito? What happened? Anything serious?" Chichi asked, while holding Timo.

"Nothing, but good news. Sanders is interested in the deal," Miko said, cheering her up.

"Really? So what's next?" Chichi asked, wanting to know more.

"He had gone to collect the stone from the source to show it to Sanders. He wants to see the piece immediately," Miko replied.

"Is that so? You've got to be careful," Chichi continued. "You know what, Miko? I'm so happy. At last we have done it, the big one. How many years have we had to wait to see a big hot screaming red one in our hand?" She sighed. Timo gave her a warm hug.

"Ten years, precisely! Do you believe in God?" Miko asked, jokingly.

"Sure, I do, when I see the money first. We all can take a good vacation somewhere far way from Bangkok. The city is now boring to me. Same people, same problems, and same everything. We all need a change, don't we?" Chichi commented.

"Tito wanted me to call you first before he left," Miko answered.

"Very nice of him," Chichi said affectionately.

"Were you still awake when I called you?" Miko asked.

"Almost," Chichi continued. " Now hopefully I can sleep with some peace of mind. But I've got to see the money first before I can sleep my way, you know, snoring. We must go somewhere very different from Asia. It should be an interesting place better than rushing in a Ferrari in Bangkok. Perhaps, LESOTHO (South Africa)!"

"Are you sure?" Miko asked.

"That's what Tito promised," Chichi replied.

"In that case, he may be right," Miko opined.

"Okay, Miko. Bye!"

EIGHT

It was ten in the morning. Miko pulled the venetian blinds to check the weather after listening to FM 105 station's news bulletin. THE SMOOTH 105!

"Hi, This is Thomas & Marble!"

"Who?" Chichi answered the call.

"Pierre Themiro!"

"Miko, it's for you. Never heard of them. Could be after the ruby trail?" Chichi alerted.

"Hi, Miko speaking. What can I do for you?"

"We heard from the market that you guys are interested in buying a ruby of 37 carat. We understand that you are looking for partners in buying the piece. It would be interesting if we could talk about it. Our specialization is in diamonds. Mostly roughs from Central and West Africa. Nothing to do with De Beers. We do deal in rubies if they are of good quality and larger sizes. Maybe, I could come to your office or you would be most welcome to visit our office anytime. Just call before you decide to come. We could discuss openly and you're under no obligation, whichever way you like," Themiro replied holding his breath.

"Interesting, how the news spreads so fast," Miko added. "All you just mentioned is correct."

"So when can we talk about it? Confidentiality will be guaranteed, if you want to keep it that way," Themiro assured.

"That's very thoughtful of you," Miko smiled. Meanwhile, Chichi turned her attention to the tax files, a job Miko hated so much.

"Have you approached others for an exclusive partnership?" Themiro asked.

"I can't comment on that. Zippo!" Miko commented reluctantly.

"It's all right, just a friendly remark. Would it be convenient for us to see the piece?" Themiro recognized his fault. He shouldn't have asked so quickly.

"I've to ask my partner," Miko reasoned. "We make decisions together. I can't comment on that at the moment. When conditions and terms are acceptable and practical, I don't see any reason why it shouldn't be possible."

"Which facility would be convenient for you? One of us coming to your office or either of you visiting our office?" Themiro began to dig deeper.

"I'll call you when my partner is back. As I said, we make decisions together. Whatever the decision, we will let you know as soon as possible," Miko reminded him.

"As you know in this stone business, whether it be diamond or ruby, it all takes a split-second to win or lose the deal. One thing we can guarantee you is that we have immediate buyers for the whole lot, and if you have more, that too. It's cash and carry. We are very international, and we do have our own line of collectors, who request big ones either as an investment or just for pleasure. It would all take just a matter of hours to settle. So all that I'm saying is, the quicker the better. We would really like to do business with you." Themiro threw the bait.

"I don't see any problem in that logic. Money takes away all prejudices. We will contact you when decided." Miko while listening flicked through the pages of the Economist magazine curious about the latest scandal rocking Washington.

"How long should we wait for your call? We can call you if you want it that way," Themiro said desperately.

"Let's say, in less than a day or two." Miko closed the magazine and grabbed the rough ruby parcel just brought in by a broker.

"That's fine," Themiro commented.

"Thanks for calling. I very much appreciate that gesture. By the way, where is your office?" Miko asked, as he spread the parcel of rough rubies on his table.

"Wall Street Tower, Surawong Road. Bye for now." Themiro hung up the phone.

"Can you believe this?" Miko turned his attention to Chichi. "How on earth do these people get their information? Amazingly fast, isn't it?" Miko put the rough rubies back into a plastic bag to return it to the broker. MINE RUN (unsorted rough stones)!

"Now make sure they are not Mafia's of any stock. You could be dead in a heartbeat. It's dangerous." Chichi warned. She was still busy sorting out the tax files.

"Bloody yeah, you bet. So, what do we have now? The Rubyhall's, Sanders, and now what was his name? Oh yeah, I remember, Pierre Themiro! That's a bloody French name, isn't it?" Miko said, jokingly.

"Could be Africans, Canadians, you never know," said Chichi. "There are quite a few in Bangkok. You know something? The hunters are after us with their guns and money to grab our stones, and perhaps your balls too." Both laughed.

"You're right, Chichi," answered Miko. "I never thought about it that way. We have opened a new miserable situation for ourselves. You know what? We could have avoided these cold calls if we had the money. You see, how these sharks circle when they know that we are in a cash crunch; do you think they are going to leave us peacefully? If we go to their office talking terms and conditions, begging for money, the mother of all terms will drive us to weep in our pants. They will cut us into several pieces like sausages before a deal is struck. When you get into big ones, sometimes it's easy to sell, and sometimes difficult. Sometimes you won't get the money back in time as they promise. But, we owe Winston Lord a lot." Miko reminded her.

She closed the tax files, and put them back into the filing

cabinet. Meanwhile, Miko graded a few parcels of rubies from Cambodia, and sealed them to be shown to a special client.

"If we manage to sell, how much of a killing do you think we are gonna make out of this deal?" Chichi asked.

"It's quite a lot, if we had our own money. If we get these partners in everything is gonna split. It all depends on the percentage we agree to. It's going to be a tough talk, when we go to these sharks. I hate that, but we have no choice. This deal is a windfall unless a miracle happens. Do you believe in miracles, Chichi?" Miko asked.

"Sure I do," she replied immediately.

"You know what? I've an idea. I don't know whether it will work. It's a fifteen million to one chance," Miko said, hopelessly.

"What's that? There's nothing wrong in trying." Chichi became anxious.

"Lotto!" Miko uttered like a mantra.

"Come on! It doesn't work that way," Chichi answered.

"Now, wait a minute. It might work. Who knows? There is one coming sometime this week. I did see the ad somewhere in a magazine in this office. Chichi, you believe in miracles, don't you?" Miko acted like a desperate soul.

"Yeah, if we have nothing to lose. If we win, we celebrate together. If we don't, we have all the time in the world to cry together and forget about it. All our worries are over," Chichi said.

"But if we hit the jackpot, you got your deal, a trip away from Bangkok. Here it is. THE BRITISH LOTTO! Let's do it. Here's the money. You select the numbers with a good intention. It might work, who knows? If it works in the last minute, hell with the Rubyhall's, Sanders, Pierre Themiro, or whoever comes next," Miko added.

"Done, Miko. When are the results going to come?" Chichi asked.

"The ad says, in a week. Je-ez! Maybe, there is a chance to kill all those sharks. Miracles, miracles, and miracles help us! Chichi, do it before it is too late. The numbers, your choice," Miko said, wrapping the magazine in front of him.

"Okay. I'm going to send them the form and money." She took her handbag and walked to the front door.

"Do it!" Miko reminded her again, as she walked down the stairs.

NINE

Lam hadn't been to Lumpini Park in ages. Green was his favorite color since childhood, and the vivid natural green hue swept his dead brain back to life. If he had found the time to at least make it a ritual once a week, he would have looked much younger. Sucked up with his nerve racking demanding work schedules, and now all of a sudden his entire career looked like it was hanging by a frayed thread. A premature mid-life crisis haunted him like a pack of displaced ghosts deadly serious in taking revenge on him desperate to settle his past life crimes. He saw a totally different landscape from his overly decorated marble office, which was turning him into a hunk.

Rubyhall had a reason to believe in the existence of a 37carat ruby. Lam, at any cost, had to convince him that the rare stone remained only on Surawong Road, in his office, not anywhere else. It looked like the whole drama had molded him into a virtual fool, with Miko leaping from street to street to fetch the highest bidder for his treasure, a 37carat ruby.

The informants had now confirmed him of its existence, and Miko and Tito had both become instant celebrities in this reclusive circle of big dealers like Morakot Barasan and Som Salasan. The next board meeting would be a nightmare for him. All their aging hands would be on his throat and his career would be folded several times, like a tissue paper, and thrown out for recycling. A zillion thought coursed through his mind, but no concrete idea emerged. They all illuminated inside his already frozen brain like the icebergs of Antarctica-all dead white. He thought of only one way out. Search and kill, Miko and Tito, if possible.

But how could he accomplish this task stealthily? The accumulated thoughts built up into frenzy and the next thing he remembered was Tito walking towards him. He rubbed his eyes vigorously to confirm he was not dreaming.

"No. It's him. Tito!" Lam said spontaneously. Several questions rushed to the tip of his tongue like a passing tornado, but eventually settled in silence and became mute. His entire body became lifeless and sculpted instantly. He saw his own epitaph, born at an early age, died as a fool. The dead brown speechless leaves swept across his face like flakes leaving their fingerprints for future identification.

Tito glanced at Lam like a natural Swami, and all the volcanic thoughts settled back to their core. Lam's athletic body shrunk into a paper foil, as Tito took his seat on the bench. They had not seen each other for sometime, and with the recent advent of a 37carat ruby orbiting mysteriously the situation had changed dramatically. Both knew their strengths and weaknesses. With such thoughts at hand, a thought emerged as to who should talk first. They already knew the topic. But neither of them wanted to bring up the issue first. There was an emotional tug of war going on between them, as they struggled in vain to start the conversation.

"I heard that you were looking for me," Tito said, without glancing at Lam directly. There was a tai chi and karate session in full swing.

"Yeah. You have the 37carat Burmese ruby. I was wondering if we could work out a deal," Lam added, "but you don't have the money to buy the piece."

"What do you mean by that? Do you think only Rubyhall's can afford to hold big rubies in Bangkok? Wake-up, Lam. The world has changed and so have the people," Tito said, his hands stuck deep into his pockets.

"People in the market have been saying that you are looking for partners to buy the ruby. I have an offer which you can't refuse." Lam's eyes twinkled, as he looked at Tito.

"People in the market say a lot nowadays, because they are

living in a free country. In what way am I obliged to accept your offer," Tito continued, "when we haven't done any business before? I think you should leave us alone."

Lam leaned back in his bench and then lurched forward. "Think about it, Tito. You know your own limitations, and if your prospects of raising the money to buy such big stones are difficult, why don't you just give up and be more realistic? Let the ones who have the resources handle it appropriately. Big stones are like countries. It must be handled by the ones with experience, otherwise, they could end up with the wrong people."

"Are you preaching the big brother gospel to me? Did Rubyhall teach you to recite the verses you mentioned now to change my mind? I think you had better cut and polish yourself. Anyway, thanks for your time. Don't worry about us. Enjoy the scenic view of Lumpini and breathe in some fresh air to mop up yourself," Tito whispered so that the joggers wouldn't hear.

"Think about it again, Tito," Lam stared at Tito for a long moment. But, Tito had gone from his sight.

Tito was the tough guy and hard to convince given the experience and access he has to the market, not only in Bangkok, but also in the border towns of Mai Sai, Mae Sot, and Bo Rai.

Lam couldn't believe his eyes, all happening in front of him. As he glanced around, all he saw was happy faces, jogging and talking, while others remained relaxed.

Lumpini Park still remained a favored place for gem dealers, not only for meeting their friends and competitors, but also to pick up news regarding the market trends and the mining. He saw some trading gemstones while they were exercising, a very unusual practice. But his mind was roaming elsewhere.

The 37carat ruby! Tito had already spoken his mind. But, Lam remained patient. How long? He had no idea. This deal was quite different from the previous deals.

Rubyhall had put his heart into it and for reasons he couldn't understand, it had slipped through his hand.

TEN

"Pierre Themiro, called?" Miko reminded Tito.

Tito arrived with a parcel of Vietnamese rubies given to him by Chu. She had to leave for another office for a deal after she received a call from Suree, another broker. Meanwhile, Tito decided to take his time studying the gemological properties of the rubies, so that after cutting and polishing he didn't lose any money. But Miko had important news for Tito.

"Who?" Tito asked.

"Thomas & Marble!" Miko replied.

"What? I see," Tito continued. "What did you say?"

"When you are back, we will let them know. They are after the ruby. In fact, they wanted to come here to talk about the deal," Miko reminded.

"Is that what you said?" Tito asked.

"I said, we will call back in a day or two," Miko answered.

"You know what? We're going to play our game. The ruby game." Tito added, thinking of something else. "We are all like the one-eyed king in the land of blind."

"What do you mean?" Miko asked, puzzled.

Tito didn't elaborate. He knew there were several players already in the market wanting to cut them with the mysterious ruby. Some were genuine, while others an obvious bluff. He owed loyalty to only one person, Winston Lord!

And he knew Lord was also playing his game to teach Rubyhall a lesson or two. There was no room for compromise.

Like the Chinese saying, it was the two lions in a cage situation.

"If he calls our office again, tell him to come and see us. Let's see, how serious he is," Tito said, holding a cabochon ruby in his palm.

Miko and Tito had no other choice. When Winston Lord gave them the ruby it was on one condition. They could sell the ruby to anyone on earth, except Rubyhall. On that word they collected the 37carat ruby. Bluffing, Lord meant a certain death or a painful visit to a nearby crocodile farm. He meant real business. Raising two million dollars to buy this exquisite ruby looked easy at first. But as time went by, they realized a careless move meant, not only losing the ruby, but also the money and profit. Trusting friends became more difficult when it came to big rubies, because of the locality. There was no permanent friendship or enmity in the ruby business. Everyone worked for one sure thing.

PROFIT!

In a big city like Bangkok, everyone knew what was going on when a big ruby arrived in the market. Brokers and dealers hired their own men or women as secret service agents to obtain the latest information regarding the status of such a ruby. Using all sort of proxies, killing the deal with an asking price became their first motive.

That's why Tito and Miko became very suspicious when phone calls arrived at their office offering to become a partner to buy first, and sell at their price and terms. The only persons they could trust were Melvine Sanders and Jeb Singthowala. They had done businesses several times before and they had a good working relationship. There was a chemical match. But at the same time, they knew like any businessmen in town, they also worked for profit. Nothing more nothing less.

"How about Sanders?" Miko asked impatiently.

"Yeah. We have a meeting tomorrow at his office. You never know. He may change his mind in the last minute. He is a busy man. After that we will know the true situation," Tito added thoughtfully.

A meeting with Sanders wasn't that easy either. He had a style of his own when it came to bargaining. Somehow he had an instinct to know the cost price of any ruby for sale in advance. Only God knew his secret. Depending on the type of relationship he had with the potential partners, it was he who decided how much profit the partners deserved if he had more investment in the deal. Tito and Miko didn't care. They knew too well their position. Two million dollars was beyond their reach, at present. Lord had given them ample time to sell. The only thing they were afraid of was a last minute kidnapping by other dealers to force a deal. Then, everyone lost.

Meanwhile, Lam knew what Rubyhall had in his mind when he was called into his office. He had to tell the truth.

"It's with them. Miko and Tito have it," Lam replied gently.

Now telling Rubyhall the real truth was difficult. He never believed it in the first place. Rubyhall wasn't wrong. His instincts never let him down. The 37carat ruby had gone out of his hand. Lam had no other choice. After careful thought, he said what Rubyhall didn't want to hear.

"Winston Lord is the source," Lam uttered.

Rubyhall knew too well what it meant when it came to competing with Winston Lord. He was as strong and powerful as him, but in a different way. He had now crossed the border. Rubyhall saw the clear picture.

THE RUBY GAME!

Lord too, was good in that profession. Only Rubyhall had the guts and the thickskin to fight one on one with Lord.

THE COPPER DEAL!

Lord was cut off from the Zambian deal in the last minute by foul play. Rubyhall pulled the strings from behind using proxies to break up the deal when he realized his profit didn't look good. Like in any business, friendship and business went separate ways. Rubyhall's proxies won the deal, leaving Lord's negotiating team thumbsucking for life.

Now, Lord wanted to use the same tactic. Proxy war. Miko and Tito accepted Lord's offer, which they couldn't refuse.

Rubyhall kept staring at Lam. After a while, he told Lam to leave his office.

ELEVEN

Lam quietly walked along the sidewalk.

Tuna's Club and Restaurant on Sukhumvit Road, was a convenient hub for the old-timers and newcomers to Bangkok, to meet and digest where information on food, gems, jewelry, and travel of any sort were available through a wide network of agents at a cost. Her place became an attractive choice for the bankers, architects, engineers, and real estate magnates to unwind their worries along with their pet mia noi's (mistresses) who frequented discreetly for fun and business.

Pamella Chen, nicknamed Tuna, a native of Singapore, cruising in her late thirties got hooked to the vibrant lifestyle and colorful characters of Bangkok by choice. She quit her families commodities business and decided to venture on something new and untried. A place where young men and women felt liberated to express their personal views in their own way contradicting the so-called 'Asian' values.

Bangkok became her final destination where she felt free and independent to live her own life. She collected a lot of friends, and Jay Lam was one among them.

"Give me one regular, Tuna." Lam mumbled, as he took his seat opposite her.

"What's up?" Tuna quipped.

"The usual build up," Lam said, slumping in his chair.

"Come on! That bad," she added.

He looked around to see if anyone was watching them. The club wasn't yet crowded. He had arrived a bit early to talk to her.

"Do I look sexy?" She wanted an opinion from him.

"Sure, you do. Sexy and terrific!" His answer satisfied her.

"You look so uptight," Tuna sensed a degree of uneasiness in him.

"Yeah!" Lam complained.

"Why don't you bring him here? I can take care of him." She said humorously. Lam had described Rubyhall to her in such a way, she kept on insisting that he bring him to her club for some physical testing.

He shrugged off.

"Tell me, what stone is this? Given to me by someone. You haven't bothered giving me one," she said jokingly, approaching him with a pad in hand.

"It looks red," he replied, after an initial observation.

"I know that. What is it?" She asked curiously.

"Possibly ruby, spinel, garnet, tourmaline, glass, or even an assembled gem. This is very light and looks deceptive," he answered like a gem expert.

"Not a diamond? He said this was a red diamond," she said looking unhappy.

"It can't be. It's so bloody rare, there are only a few on this planet. It would cost millions for this size. Again, since it is in a ring, it would be quite difficult. But the cut and shape is very unusual for this stone to be a diamond. I will have to check it more carefully," he answered, without making any further comment.

"You can take it and tell me when you come here next time," she interrupted. "Someone else might feel like giving me another ring. Next time, I will be more careful. Maybe, you should try a different bottle today. I've a very special one, Chateau de Loei!" She took out a new bottle of wine from the cupboard changing the topic.

"Where the hell is this from?" he asked curiously.

"You won't believe this. Thailand! A friend of mine, when she returned from a trip to Loei province, someone gave her this, and that's how it took its residence here. Not for sale, just for special friends. Taste it, how is it?" she asked.

"Tastes good. Very much Australian, its aroma pungent like the French," Lam replied.

"Very close, isn't it?" She opined.

"Thanks, Tuna. It's very nice of you. I appreciate that," he quipped.

"So, back to your work. What's bugging you at the office? Did you lose some deal for the old man?" She got to the real topic. BUSINESS!

"Something very close. It's these two guys, Miko and Tito. They have a 37carat ruby from Burma, and the old man wants it at any cost. As I had told you earlier, all big ones have a tradition showing up first on his table, and from there it goes elsewhere in this country. But this time they have it, and the funny side of the story is that they don't have the money to buy it."

"So then how do they own it?" she asked.

"That's the twist. One of Rubyhall's buddies wants to teach him a lesson. So he is using them as proxies to bring him down. It's now an all out war between friends. That's the dark side of this business. It takes only a split-second to become enemies. Tango is over," he said seriously.

"It's in every business," she replied, regretfully.

"So I'm caught in between. This is the first time, I thought I was going to lose my job for this bloody oversight. But later, when I dug up the truth behind this funny and serious scenario, when I told him, he knew it was beyond my control, but he want me to get the ruby for him. His best friend now wants to play a kind of ruby game on him. I was relieved when he told me that he would personally take over, but I don't trust that statement. It's not over. It's the beginning. My nightmares are just beginning. That's why I had to come here to cool down. I can't tell this to Marla. She would faint, and the kids, they are just too young," he answered.

"So what are you going to do now? What do they look like? If they ever come here for a gulp, I will keep an eye on them," she said plainly.

"Like those MTV tattoo stars. Miko and Tito have tattoos on

their ten fingers. Tabular hexagonal prism, terraced / stepped-like pattern. Guess what?" He grinned.

"What?" she asked.

"Crystal habits of rubies from Burma," Lam said.

"Oh God," said Tuna with a feeling. "Is that the way to identify them?"

"Yeah. Very much so," he replied.

"Tito is a bit tough. But Miko, on the other hand, is a fractured genius," said Lam. "Both are shrewd and intelligent. Otherwise, they wouldn't be in this business."

"In that case, he must be the right guy for me. Target shooting!" Tuna replied quickly.

"You bet," Lam quipped.

"Look over there, I've some guests, listen, take it easy. Something will work out. If you want to stay for a while, do stay. But look, it's already late for you. Marla will be anxious." Her face relaxed, as customers started to walk in with their friends.

"Thanks for reminding me. I think, I better go." Lam announced.

"Good night, Tuna."

"Night, Jay."

TWELVE

Mahesak Road thrived like the famous 47th street of New York, in a discreet way behind the tinted glass windows accommodating the small and big time dealers of every denomination. Foreign buyers in every color, size, and disguise had no other choice but to choose selectively the right brokers in order to get close to the gem dealers in specialty merchandise. Everyone knew someone in this multimillion-dollar transaction street. Anyone entering this sacred street required one magic mantra.

RELATIONSHIP!

A native of New Zealand, brought up in Australia and finally destined to live in Bangkok for the past forty years, Winston Lord became known in the gem district as one of the top gem dealers along with Ris Rubyhall. Like some of his friends in the trade, he settled in Bangkok marrying Ben of Thai Chinese stock, who happened to descend from a gem trading family of Chantaburi province. He worked quietly from his office in TD building, a low profile three-room facility along with the big miners from Burma, Cambodia, and Vietnam.

Private collectors from the Middleeast, Europe, and North America came secretively to his office absorbing the rare and expensive ones as soon as they arrived, never again to be seen in the local market. He enjoyed seeing his rubies emerging in style in famous auctions houses like Christie's, Sotheby's, and Phillips, through third parties or special agents. They all played their own games discreetly in different levels, but Lord was well versed in the games and knew when to accommodate a friend and subdue an enemy.

The telephone rang.

"Lord!"

"Ken speaking!"

"Oh, Ken, where are you?" Lord answered the call, while flicking through the Time magazine cover story on the latest Russian crisis.

"Just arrived from Indonesia," Ken Solby replied jovially.

"Indonesia? What the heck are you doing there? Advising, Suharto?" Lord asked jokingly.

"Not yet," Solby continued. "So how are things with Rubyhall? Have you nailed the sonofabitch?"

He had been seeking a revenge act against Rubyhall for sometime after he was thrown out of a mining deal in Indonesia by the invisible hands of Rubyhall's cronies.

"Nailed? My rubies have already started to bleed his balls, then his hands, the last stop his heart. One more plunge, dead meat," Lord said indignantly. He too had a score to settle. So both, Ken and Lord were in the same boat.

"How are the boys doing? Are they safe?" Ken asked.

"Oh yeah. If they play cat and mouse with me, their meat will end up in one of those special restaurants in Bangkok. I can handle them. Don't worry."

Lord remembered the day when he decided to use Tito and Miko as his proxies to play his game with Rubyhall.

"They must be having a hard time raising the money," Ken recalled.

"Oh, yeah, they have all the time in the world to raise money in whatever partnership they want, except Rubyhall. That's the bait. I know he is already after them. I can afford to lose some money with this 37carat. I want to teach him a lesson. He ratted me like Mobutu Sese Seko in that copper deal. I can't forget that. I know his weakness too well. RUBIES! It's like taking his breath out of his body. He will do anything to lick the ruby. That's what I want to see. How on earth is he going to grab this 37carat piece?" Lord bit his tongue, as he became excited.

"Lot of blood spilling in the coming days, Winston?" Ken said softly.

"Very much so. But if the boys are lucky and raise the money to give me my price, they can have all the profits and retire if they want. This is a once in a lifetime opportunity for them. Like those lottery jackpots. They haven't done anything like this before." Lord glanced at the parcel of rough rubies brought in by Ben for his opinion.

"What happens if they lose?" Ken alerted.

Lord paused.

"Head is worthless, if you can't make money. That simple." Lord gestured Ben to send it back to its owner. JUNK!

"Show time, right?" Ken asked.

"Yeah, it is. Keep watching. Are you in Bangkok?" Lord asked.

"Pattaya!"

THIRTEEN

Den, Ris's only brother, a gem dealer on his own specializing in 5 to 10carat rubies of top quality brought with him a few miners from Kenya who had requested a meeting with Ris. The Kenyan miners stood in awe mesmerized by the lavishly decorated office, and the beautiful women walking in and out from one room to another in their miniskirts. They had never seen anything like this in their country.

Lapis lazuli slabs from Afghanistan scaled the walls while authentic and superior Persian carpets covered the entire office floor of Ris Rubyhall Towers. The nephrite carved tables matched by fossilized wood chairs were there to be occupied by the exclusive and privileged gem dealers from around the world. They had the power to make or break any deal in this little grand palace where handshakes and a simple nod meant a zillion word.

Ris, the real gem, stood quietly behind the opaque lapis lazuli wall inhaling and exhaling each transaction with absolute concentration and humor with no room for mistakes. Each powerful handshake meant real and solid commitment, and he made sure they were practiced without fail. His sharp observant eyes instantly recorded its personality traits, and when settled with a beautiful gemstone, he would not indulge first talking about its value, but about its natural origin, its relationship with the almighty earth. He would talk about the fortunate hands that picked God's gift with a desperate passion for exoticism and adventure. He never traded this privileged exuberance with any other environment. Infrared cameras worked stealthily recording and scanning every passionate transaction, and one of his addictive hobbies was to watch their emotional gestures in privacy, analyzing and extracting the necessary clues for his future acquisitions of collectable and investment grade rubies. As he sat in his chair, he glanced at his simulated grand palace, mentally calibrating asking, bidding, and transaction conversations in different combination and programmed and stored in his three gram brain for an important awaiting deal, 37CARAT RUBY!

Ris was not in a mood to meet the Kenyan miners. Den conveyed the message, as he emerged from Ris's office. The Kenyan miners left the office disappointed. Ris Rubyhall was the king. And they were willing to wait.

"Lot of rumors about you in the trade?" Den sat closer to the window to get a glimpse of the tower block under construction across the road.

"Yeah. A lot, in fact, many. Bloody hell! The fight this time is with Winston," Ris said angrily.

"Winston? Our good friend? What happened? What did he do?" Den asked in utter amazement.

"Ah, that copper deal. I had to cut him off. He hasn't forgiven me. But you know his terms were too unacceptable. I had to do it that way to protect our interests," Ris said bluntly.

"So that's the rumor," Den chuckled.

"No. It's ruby this time. My ruby! It didn't come to my office for the first look. In fact, the Qwah Qwah family asked that I obtain a big one. Now that has slipped through my fingers just like that, because of one man. Winston Lord! He is out this time publicly to declare me for the first time a loser. I am not giving up. I'll nail him on a crucifix, tattoo his hands first, and explode him to eternity with Russian missiles." Ris vented his anger by thumping his foot on the floor.

Ruby epilepsy! Den knew too well his elder brother. On the other hand, cooperation not confrontation was his style. Age and tradition were taking a toll on his family. Ris felt it privileged to portray himself as the John Wayne of the ruby business. Once upon a time he ruled and was still ruling. Ris hated newcomers entering the trade with new ideas to change the age-old tradi-tional landscape. He had many enemies around. But somehow he survived among his enemies due to luck, money and timing. "Good day, Ris," Den continued. "Nothing to say further. If you have decided your course, then make sure you don't regret it sometime later. Good luck to you. Don't disappoint those Kenyan miners again. They had come all the way from Nakuru to talk to you. They don't understand your problems, but I do. So keep your word when they see you in two days."

"Den! Where you are going? Stay with me for a while," Ris pleaded in vain.

Den left the office in an unhappy mood.

FOURTEEN

It was a Friday evening. Some had gone to the Chantaburi gem market in the morning, while others preferred to leave on Saturday morning to carry the stones they couldn't sell. It was the norm. And the ones who had no stones or business remained in Bangkok. So naturally going to The Redd's became a ritual when they had nothingelse to do other than relax and update the latest info.

"Give me one Singha beer, please. How come the bar is crowded today?" Charley Che took his seat glancing at others. Another whining gem dealer from Hong Kong!

"The usual weekend crowd, familiar faces, good business," Mike said smilingly.

"Not us. The business is too bad," Che complained.

"What's the matter, Che?" Mike asked.

"This bloody stone business sucks. We don't know anythingelse. I wish I had learned somethingelse to make a living. This family business crap is reducing us to beggars," Che said frustratingly.

"He is right, Mike. All our friends have the same view. Finish, Finish, Finished! The gavel is on our head and balls, the way business is going," William Sparrow, a Kiwi commented.

"Is it that bad, Sparrow?" Mike Chan asked, waving at the regulars who took their seats in front of the tele to watch world cup soccer play.

"I can tell you, our balls are shrinking like those dried blueberries. The big fish are eating the small too fast. Can't survive with so many choices for women today. We can't compete with them. I mean their prices are fucking crazy. We can't afford to survive if this is gonna be the trend in the coming years. Off to the temple. We all have families for heaven's sake. How are we going to feed them? Just this polluted air and filthy sand?" Che seconded Sparrow, a London dealer.

"This business is cyclic, isn't it? It will turnaround," Mike reasoned, pouring Singha beer into his glass.

"It's not like the old days, Mike. It was so much easier and personal. Now it's all bloody computers, price lists, Harvard, and Stanford nerds. They have changed the whole traditional landscape, you know, into commodities like soybeans and sugar. No more romance and personal relationship! You show a stone today, they want an instant discount of ninety percent and three months fucking credit like buying a stolen car. How are we gonna survive? We all have now turned into some sort of jaded magicians, you know. I'm not kidding. This is an illusion business. What do we have here? And our customers! Women! Now that tells you how damn difficult it is to convince these dames; a good color. Ninety percent of the precious rubies are for women. That's where the money is. Color! Next, does this bloody stone have a good pleasing face? Just like a woman's face. A Virgin Mary or a beautiful woman's face! The stone must have a perfect, colorful face with no reason to bargain. How many of those types exist today? How many Virgin Mary's exist today? They do exist, if you search, as long as people like Rubyhall's, Sanders, and Winston's don't meddle with the price, source, and small folk like us. Their hands have stretched to all known holes in the world where these suckers come, and we can't get anywhere closer. We still can't survive. But look at their greed. They have all sorts of other businesses and we small ones only one hole. The Hole of Bangkok! They have consolidated their position by cutting our limbs like sausages. How can we compete with these living dinosaurs? They are swallowing us with one gulp. Wow! Look at that doll," Sparrow got distracted. "Look at her bottoms, like a perfect cabochon cut ruby. Je-ez, do we have women like this in Bangkok? Mike how come you didn't tell us that there are chicks like the ones over there. You see that one over there. My goodness! Holy shape! What a woman!"

Mike knew more than anyone else the gem dealers who frequented his bar. And he was a good listener. It was good for his business as well as for the relationship. The gem dealers liked it. He had a skill in keeping them under control.

"She is a mom for Christ's sake. That's Lord's wife. The group comes regularly during the weekend just to relax and let it go," Mike said, while gesturing his daughter, Tan, to take care of them.

"Let it go? What the hell that means, uh?" Che asked, quite puzzled.

"Let go the pressures of the week, I mean." Mike responded with a smile.

"I see. I know what you mean. Lucky ones! Look at our boring wives. Only bloody complaints when we get back home. Screaming with bills and what not. No sex, nothing," Sparrow said, rising out his chair.

"How can you think about sex when your business is down every week? Even if she wants a quickie, I'm not ready, know what I mean? It's the workload. But look at those women over there. I've yet to see my wife smiling like that. Is her body real? Too perfect," Che asked meekly.

"Well, it is perfect. Exercise, diet, and good husbands, I suppose," Mike opined.

"Lucky those." Che said bluntly.

"Mike, how is your business?" Sparrow poured Singha beer into Mike's empty glass.

"It's going okay. Surviving like you guys." Mike replied piously.

"Surviving? It's a fucking funny word today," Che quipped. Everyone laughed.

"Have you seen Miko and Tito?" Sparrow asked leaning back.

"Last week they were here, right over there their usual place. Must be busy with their clients." Mike suggested.

"You bet. Funny guys. I like them. Sometimes, the younger chap. What's his name?"

"Miko!" Mike replied.

"Well, Miko, he can be really funny with his bloody tattoo, cocky eyes, and doggy tongue. I like the guy. In fact, I like both of them. Good hearts and a solid team too. Harmless and shrewd! Give them my regards if they turn up any one of these days Mike," Sparrow grinned.

"Sure." Mike nodded.

"Already Mike, time to go. Check, please," Che said. His eyes were still glued on Lord's wife, and other women.

FIFTEEN

Jeb Singthowala, Sanders's partner, a Thai, and a regular buyer from the mines in Vietnam, sat in his office calculating the yield from the roughs he had just bought during a recent trip. He was busy studying the size and irregular shape of the rough, and its external and internal imperfections with a fiber optic light, rubbing and licking to detect potential breaks or other blemishes which might ruin the rough if not taken into account during the lengthy process of fashioning. This was his specialty, and Sanders always left Jeb alone when it came to making decisions regarding rough purchases. Sanders had important information to share with Jeb.

"We have something that has fallen out of heaven in this city. A 37carat Mogok ruby of the top color. Miko and Tito have the piece. They need us to become partners to buy this piece," Sanders interrupted.

"How much is the asking price?" Jeb asked.

"Two million!" Sanders replied.

"That's too cheap for that quality. Is it real?" Jeb said doubtfully.

"We have done business with them before. Only in real stones," Sanders added.

"But the price is crazy. They should be asking more," Jeb suggested. He was still busy studying the rough rubies with the fiber optic light, despite the sudden interruption, which he hated so much.

"There must be a story behind the sale," Sanders continued. "I think. Cash crunch, superstition or power struggle, insiders, perhaps? You never know. The Rubyhall's, I hear have already stretched their hand on this piece."

"Have you seen the piece?" Jeb asked eagerly.

"Not yet. Tito promised he would show it to me today. I called him at his home, no response. He might be on his way. Maybe, tomorrow or day after tomorrow. I don't know," Sanders grinned. "Well, you have a look first. I'll join you soon. If Rubyhall had set his eyes on this piece, then the piece must be too good. We are going to see a lot of fireworks in the coming days, don't you think?" Jeb remarked.

"I guess so. I think they are shopping for the best deal," Sanders opined.

"If you think the ruby is really good, then there is less time to gamble. Just close the deal. Put your stamp to it. There shouldn't be any problem," Jeb said, showing the rough rubies to Sanders. He then returned the rubies without making any comment.

"Okay. How is Baddy doing?" Jeb asked.

"He is in a hot spot again. His wife calls me day and night to check on him. The woman had lost her complete confidence in him. No more sex. One enough. He wants to have more. He loves kids. That is the knot. He tried to reason with her but she is adamant with her stance," Sanders said plainly.

"What's wrong with that? Why do we need more kids today? Can you control them today?" Jeb explained.

"I've one at home, and I think I made a mistake by helping Chin to see her into this world," Sanders added.

"What's wrong with Ruth? She is cute," Jeb said, with a twinkle in his eyes.

"Cute? Did you know what happened last night when I returned home? Ruth, bloody fifteen now, was with her boyfriend in my study room. Guess what? The boy was all over her body, and I had to hit him with a baseball bat to release Ruth from him. Is this what you want to see when you get back home?" Sanders said angrily.

"I'm sorry to hear that. How is Ruth now? Is she repentant?" Jeb asked.

"Repentant? Maybe, pregnant now by the way she looks. She is questioning me now for having beaten her dear boyfriend. She is telling me that I had violated her human rights. Can you believe this? I was speechless. We work like donkeys to make a living, and see what happens when you get back home in search of peace and stability," Sanders said, and moved to the window to view a ruby rough.

"How about Chin?" Jeb asked.

"Chin is fucking useless. She is too busy with her community services when she should be staying home and watching the girl. I'm fed up with her. What can you do? I've thought of divorce, a thousand times. But the girl, I love her, and what will be her fate. Now I'm worrying more and more as days pass by. I'll be hearing sharp cries of illegal babies in front of my door when I wake up. That's life. Sometimes we are lucky, and sometimes not. If it wasn't for this business, I would have run away from Bangkok to some far away place, but the money is too good to quit," Sanders sighed.

"Yeah, money, money, money . . . who cares about home nowadays? Only the poor," Jeb commented.

"You're right in a way. I never thought about it. Look at my home and me. Why do they think they can enjoy life the way they do? Because of my money, and the money is coming too fast and looks like candy to them. They can do whatever they like," Sanders said, looking somber.

"Goldie," Jeb said, lowering his glance, "called me yesterday asking how you were doing?"

"Oh, did she? I would love to, but I can't do that again. She was too good. Not like the whores out there. In fact, she was telling me to make peace with Chin," Sanders answered, giving Jeb an exasperated glance.

"Really? That's very strange. Her husband is finished. Maybe, he will have to swallow several bottles of Viagra before he wants to do his stuff," Jeb quipped. And then both laughed.

"Someone told me there is a possibility of going blind if you swallow too many before a blow job. Is it true?" Sanders asked seriously.

"I don't know buddy. I will check it out for you. Don't worry," Jeb answered, still laughing. They took a break from the Viagra subject to Goldie.

"I must tell you if I had met her twenty years ago, I would have married her instantly," Sanders said, spreading a few rough rubies, and picked one piece for that quick look near the window.

"Why do you say that? You like her, don't you?" Jeb asked.

"She is a goddess, Jeb. I pity her husband. A perfect creation of God for a lucky man! She was in complete control and efficient in bed. I was like a baby lying on top of her. She made it all look easy and comfortable. I had the mother of all fuck in my life. I would love to do that again if she wants. It was fantastic!" Sanders said remembering those special hours like yesterday.

"Lucky you, sonofabitch! Some are fortunate, while others aren't. Look at you. You have a legal wife, and a screwedup daughter. Goldie doesn't have kids, because her husband has technical problems. So she found you, and thinks you are the man of her life. What do you say?" Jeb asked, watching Sanders.

"I can't divorce Chin now. Starting all over again at this age? Forget it. Somehow, I've got to pull on with this relationship. I've no hope with Ruth, even though I love her. I was partly responsible for her arrival. I've got to take care of her at least financially. I can't dump Chin too quickly. Then the whole world knows and, of course, her relatives will be on my throat for money and what not. When she drops dead and Ruth, if she finds her own future, well, then I'm relieved, and a decision can be made," Sanders said grimly.

"Goldie would be old by then, like a dried vegetable," Jeb commented.

"What do you think I would look like by then? No different." They both laughed loudly.

It was back to business when Baddy walked in with his briefcase full of gemstones both, rough and cut. They put aside the topic of Goldie, Chin, and Ruth for the time being as the discussions on whether to buy the rough rubies, MINE RUN (unsorted rough) for the price quoted on the parcels became serious. Jeb was the man who had experience and the right instincts. All eyes focused on Jeb, as Sanders and Baddy stood by. It didn't take much time for Jeb. He nodded. He urged Baddy to bid on the parcels, as there were some good roughs which after cutting yielded nice cut stones.

Baddy took note of Jeb's comment and left the room.

Before they could resume the old topic, the telephone rang. After letting Jeb know that Tito was on the line, Sanders rushed to his private room to converse. They wanted to know if it was safe to bring the ruby to their office.

Sanders thought for a second. He had other ideas.

SIXTEEN

It was a Friday morning. Thanon(street) Srichan looked sleepy. The morning sun ascended gradually moving the clouds to a far away destination. Gem dealers loved a clear sky. Some specialized in buying gems in a bad light and selling in good light. Ignorant buyers and novices were taken advantage of by this natural phenomenon in the open gem market of Chanthaburi. Gemstones were everywhere. But the really good ones never emerged in the open market for anyone to view.

The biblical quote, "DON'T CAST PEARLS BEFORE SWINE," rang the ears of most top quality gem dealers.

It was eleven. The gem market began to warm up. Men, women, and children carrying countless gemstone parcel, mostly rubies, sapphires and, of course, loads of synthetic gemstones crowded the streets. Any buyer or a new face was cordially welcomed by a good quality synthetic gemstone. Judging gems with the unaided eye needed other skills. Price was also an indicator at times, but something more was needed.

EXPERIENCE!

Some arrived on foot from the cutting factories scattered around the town while others sped on their motorbike from place to place. Food vendors always had a good time, because everyone loved to eat. If the brokers had problem finding buyers then the immediate option was to talk about the miserable weekend.

If that wasn't enough, eating remained a possible option, a national sport after boxing. Some weekends were good with too many buyers looking for gems, which they couldn't find in Bangkok. While other weekends remained a sheer waste of time and money.

In the streets, faces and relationships remained more important than money. That's how people made and lost bundles of money and gems, buying and selling the wrong type or qualities or good quality synthetic gems at an attractive price or the ones which they couldn't sell. Anyone with sharp eyes, absolute concentration, and fast calculations succeeded incrementally weeding out the chaff from wheat, which came from around the world looking for a bargain.

Chantaburi was not for the novice, but a good place to learn the ropes of ruby trade and the colorful people that populated the environs. Most important of all was TRUST. Then, FACES. Just like the colors of gemstones, people kept changing their colors when buying or selling. Observing their color temperatures and mood swings meant a lost sale or otherwise. Once trust, recognition, and sincerity were established gems kept coming to the table for that first look. That special look made all the difference in a day.

Ken Solby was one among them. He never missed the weekend ritual for one reason.

NO TWO RUBIES LOOKED ALIKE. He also bought rubies for Lord and sold to his clients on a percentage basis. The money was good. They also had a common enemy.

Ris Rubyhall!

Lord owed Ken a lot. It was he who plucked the 37carat Burmese ruby from a top Chantaburi dealer who was about to sell it to a London collector. They both bought the ruby for a bargain. The dealer wanted to get rid of the ruby because of several deaths. It didn't look auspicious. The owner was a Burmese, and superstitious. And to his dismay, he didn't realize that the very same ruby was out to kill people from the hole where it was discovered. His brother who wanted to sell on his own account killed the miner. No sooner had he arrived in Mandalay a soldier shot him in the street for not stopping at one of the several checkpoints. After plucking the ruby from the corpse, the soldier knew where to sell. It was definitely not in Burma.

He started his journey to the Thai border town of Mae Sai. While negotiating with a Thai dealer in the jungle, the Burmese soldier was shot by a Thai soldier suspecting a drug transaction. But the Thai dealer survived the ambush by fleeing the scene at lightning speed to the nearest Buddhist temple. He knew how to find a buyer. He reached Chantaburi disguised as a Buddhist monk. In Chantaburi, dealers loved to keep the identity of the true owner secret in so many ways. Though the traders were open-minded and humorous, they obviously remained discreet. Just like their Bangkok counterparts. Only a very few knew the inside operation of this multimillion dollar market. So when the 37carat Burmese ruby emerged at one of his contacts table, Ken knew immediately that the ruby was going to disappear soon if he didn't bid. He never regretted that decision.

But now for a very different reason, Lord had put the ruby indirectly through Miko and Tito to take on Rubyhall.

At least that was Ken's prognosis.

SEVENTEEN

Everyone loved to stay at the famed Oriental hotel. The hotel had carved its own history entertaining for several decades dignitaries and heads of states from around the world. Situated on the banks of Chao Phraya River the scenic venue portrayed the lives and sounds of the river people.

Long tailed boats kept cruising up and down the river with people and merchandise adding more color and life to the daily scores. The nights looked more beautiful and enticing, as the high rise buildings and hotels on the banks of the river glittered like shining diamonds.

Rubin Rosenberg checked once again the important appointments of the day on his palm pc. Everything looked perfect and confirmed. Now he wanted to enjoy the evening in its peak, and if possible with a beautiful women. He loved fantasy. He instructed the chauffeur to drive him to Cheers Pub at the Holiday Inn on Silom Road, a place he normally frequented whenever in Bangkok.

Skyscrapers competed in style wanting to emerge as a one-stop unique shopping facility. In fact, there were several on both sides of the street. Hawkers haggled and competed in various tongues to make a sale. Rubin was stuck in the traffic. But the sights and sounds were entertaining. He saw women in all shapes, colors, and disguises, chatting and laughing in amazing postures.

Teen-agers in bell-bottoms and baggy outfits kept babbling on their mobile phones giggling, screaming at times, or just plain-talking on sidewalks uninterruptedly. Construction workers in baggy pants were seen everywhere, even in narrow back streets buying lottery tickets. Food vendors never looked tired, as they kept making noodles and other local delicacies for the busy office workers. Sometimes, just like in New York.

Rubin arrived at the Holiday Inn, and asked the chauffeur whether he would wait for him. He nodded.

He ordered a Singha beer, and took his seat studying the people. There were many foreigners with their girlfriends chatting and drinking. There was a festive mood, and then he spotted a young woman sitting alone drinking orange juice with her palm pc. She wasn't interested at all in what was going on around her. He wondered if she was waiting for someone. But he decided to take a chance and feel the difference. He had done it before. She looked beautiful under the incandescent lights.

"Hi, can I take this seat, please? Rubin is my name," he said, extending his hand.

"Hi, I'm Lim. In fact, July Lim. How do you do?" she answered in a cute way. He liked the way she looked at him, but was watchful.

"A tourist in Bangkok, I suppose?" she asked smilingly.

"Nope. Business! I like this place," he said, glancing at the waitress, and then continued, "Drinks?"

"Oh no, how about you? Shall I order one orange juice for you? It's good for your health," she quipped. He couldn't resist this time.

"What's your business, Ms Lim, if I may ask? Oh, by the way, are you expecting anyone at this moment?" he asked reluctantly.

"Nope. I'm alone today. It was my decision," she added. "And to answer your first question, its business. I too like this place whenever I am in Bangkok. I'm from Singapore, and once again glad to meet you."

"New York. Sorry, I forgot to mention before. I'm in the gem business. I come here quite often," he said, and as if he remembered something, he said, "I think I will go for another orange juice."

She laughed. He too laughed after ordering the drinks.

"I love this trade, you know," he continued, "because you've so much access to people from a variety of cultures, and listening to their stories, swapping their life experiences and ours, I love it, you know. There is a different angle to it, and it isn't boring at all. All you have to do is be a good listener, then it flows like a never ending ocean of tales."

"Why are you in Bangkok? You don't have stones in New York?" she asked thoughtfully.

The music was getting louder and no one seemed to complain about it. When the drinks arrived, he requested that the waitress turn the music lower. She smiled at them saying something in Thai, and then fled the scene. They switched off the music.

Rubin and July laughed without making any further requests.

"My father is from Germany. He moved to New York in 1939 to be more precise. I love Bangkok, because whether be it for stone searching or just for a change, you don't have to go to any exotic destinations. It's all in one city. That's Bangkok! Just take a flight, and you meet virtually all known human species on earth here. It's great, and I love it. I can do both. Buy stones and meet new people," he said plainly.

"If you like gemstones, and you said you came to search for good gemstones, and you said you love to meet all these different people in the world right here, then you must like women too, am I wrong?" July asked cunningly.

"Women? Yes!" Rubin replied, smiling.

"My parents are of Chinese stock, but I grew up in London. They are in the gem business, not me. Now I am graudually kind of liking the trade, because of the good money. My father has other business interests in Malaysia, Indonesia, Thailand and Europe. They don't tell us everything, but one thing I know is that I was well taken care of. Sometimes I accompany my father, because he has a lot of old friends, and in turn, I also learn a lot listening to their experiences, which I think is valuable for me," she said proudly.

"I like your name. Is there anything to do with the month of July?" he asked.

"Yep. July born people are different, and my favorite gem is ruby," she whispered cutely.

"Ruby is for July people. Very hard and tough! Are you like that?" he asked laughingly.

A few Japanese men arrived with their Thai girlfriends. They were talking loud and babbling, inviting everyone's attention. Some of the foreigners who were drinking quietly didn't like the interruption, and gestured at the manager to remind the Japanese men to speak low. The response was quick and precise. Instead of staying, they left the place in disgust. There was a loud applause from everyone. But Rubin had a lot to share. Instead, July took the initiative.

"Not really. But I like the red color so much. It's irresistible. I'm here in Bangkok to buy a big one if possible, because I have a client, a rich lady in Jakarta who wants a 10 plus carat ruby. My father has his old friends, and probably he will introduce them to me before he leaves for China. I'll stay for few more days to see if I can find the piece," she said confidently.

"That's interesting. I know one person, Ris Rubyhall, who is a friend of my dad. We always buy from him when we need big stones anything above 10carat. He is a ruby specialist, probably one of the largest ruby dealer in the world. He has a virtual collection of rubies from around the world, and everyone goes to him if they can't find them elsewhere. That's the reason why I'm in Bangkok to buy stones for our special clients back in New York," Rubin said quickly.

"Maybe, I should mention this Rubyhall's name to my father. He must know him too, I suppose. How come he didn't tell me this before? We could have saved a lot of time," she commented.

Rubin glanced at his watch and said, "Oh, I've got to go. It was such a pleasure talking to you, July. Here is my card. I'm staying at the Oriental hotel." July noted his room number and kept smiling at him.

"I'll call you later. Thanks for introducing Ris Rubyhall. But,

I may need your help," she reminded him. He nodded, and gestured at the waitress for the bill.

    Instead, he got a pleasant surprise. She had already paid the
bill.

EIGHTEEN

The past two days were busy. Sanders looked happy. A lot of rubies of various qualities kept coming to his office from legal and illegal sources. He cared less as long as they were real. The brokers knew his taste and kept feeding him with the type of goods he could sell so that they could get their CUT (commission). Army generals and retired geologists disguised as tourists and academics loved to stop by his office.

Some had swallowed or concealed both, rough and cut gems, throughout their torturous journey from the mountains, while others managed to smuggle hoarding them in their anus, penis, ears, mouth, or in a doctored wound. They loved this job for one reason. MONEY, MONEY, MONEY!

They had the type of rubies Sanders could sell well to the rich and famous socialites in Hong Kong, Indonesia, Malaysia, and Singapore, his traditional market. The Vietnamese merchants too had a similar way of taking rubies out of their country to make a good profit. He loved listening to their tales, and in the end the couriers got their CUT (commission). His partner, Jeb Singthowala, made it all easy for the contacts to get those hard to find rubies to Bangkok. Both had developed a relationship portraying themselves as the kids of the block. Cambodia was another treasure-trove for everyone. Khmer merchants kept bringing them to the Thai border town of Bo Rai for Jeb to pick them up. They also became their trusted bankers. A rare privilege! But now to their surprise a new source became available.

JEGDALEK (Afghanistan)!

A broker brought in to Sanders's office a few Afghani men in their rugged clothes who had something to sell.

RUBIES!

They took a few parcels of rough rubies from their cloth bag to show Sanders. The quality really did surprise him. All the rough rubies were embedded in their matrix. They were heavily fractured, and INCLUDED (internal characteristics), but the color was fair to good.

It reminded him of the rubies from Mogok. After cutting, he knew the color would be gone. They babbled in Persian, which he couldn't understand. But the interpreter, Nawaz Hussain, a Pakistani geologist, made the whole conversation easier to grasp.

He had come to Sanders's office anticipating an advance payment of several thousand dollars so that these tribesmen could return and convince their elders to make available all future rubies mined from Jegdalek for him. Sanders had never exercised such gestures to anyone before. But they seemed confident that he was their right savior.

Sanders took Nawaz to Jeb's room to show the type of rubies he sold to the outside market. As he spread the rough and cut rubies on the table for Hussain to view, Sanders saw the excitement in Hussain's eyes. He had never seen such qualities before, and they were so red and well cut. He was speechless. He had nothing to say other than gaze at Sanders in appreciation. Now he realized the junk quality they were carrying all the way from the mountains of Aghanistan to Bangkok.

He returned to the tribesmen and explained the quality he had just seen versus their rubies. The stone-faced tribesmen became angry getting into a verbal warfare. Sanders knew the outcome. Nawaz apologized to Sanders for wasting his time and promised never again to return to his office with these rough-looking tribesmen.

Another day, more experience.

Before Sanders could relax in his chair, Bobby, his assistant reminded Sanders that there was another visitor for him. All the rubies left on the table for grading were quickly deposited in a hidden safe beneath the table, before the visitor was allowed into his office.

After a brief introduction, Sanders motioned Pierre Themiro to take his seat.

"And your business?" he asked.

"Gems! Rubies, always big ones," Themiro replied.

"Well at the moment, we don't have big ones, but if you can leave me your contact telephone number, maybe I could help you with that. You didn't mention how big, if I may ask?" Sanders asked. A usual practice to check their background.

"You have a nice office out here. Do you work here alone?" Themiro remarked.

"No. I've my partners. They should be back here any moment. Who recommended you to come to our office?" Sanders asked.

"Some friends out in the trade," Themiro added. "You are the specialist in this street. Do you have any big rubies to show me now?"

"I'm afraid not. They don't sit here all the time, you know." But the reply didn't convince Themiro.

"But I've the information that you have the stone I'm looking for," Themiro said.

"That must be misinformation," Sanders commented.

"Nope. My information is always correct," Themiro argued.

"Well, in this case, I'll have to tell you, you are wrong," Sanders said impatiently.

"Why are you hiding the stone from me, Mr Sanders?" Themiro asked.

"Who is hiding whose stone here, uh? Who are you? I don't like people coming to my office telling me what to do, understand? When I say I don't have stones to show, then that's it," Sanders replied angrily.

"You are overreacting, Mr Sanders. We know you have the stone, and you are afraid of showing it to me. Why? I'm a businessman like anyone else in this city. Why are you angry with me?" Themiro reasoned.

"I ain't angry with anyone, but your methodical probing is making me sick and tired. I'll have to leave this office in a few minutes. As I said, you can leave me your contact phone number. If it is available, then I might contact you," Sanders said trying to cool him down.

"No. You're not leaving this office, till you show me the ruby," Themiro reminded.

"Who the fuck are you to tell me that I can't leave my office?" Sanders couldn't control him any more.

"You aren't polite, Mr Sanders. You are refusing to show the ruby for some reason I know," Themiro said, playing his game.

"What are you up to? You come to my office like a walk-in, and declare that I'm hoarding your fucking ruby. What's this, some kind of hocus-pocus? You have to leave my office immediately," Sanders ordered.

Themiro slipped his hairy hand swiftly into his jacket and took out his gun, and pointed it directly at Sanders with no smile on his face.

"This is no hocus-pocus. It's real, Mr Sanders. You can't have both at the same time. Either you show me the ruby or the bullet will go straight into your thickskinned head." He looked at Sanders, straight into his eyes with his right finger on the trigger.

"Hey, hey, take it cool and easy. Are you nuts?" Sanders became instantly oxidized and pleaded with his raised hands, as his brain now started to realize the consequence if he didn't act sensibly.

"What happened to your face, Mr Sanders?" Themiro asked sarcastically.

"What's wrong with my face?" Sanders quipped.

"It turned gray, no blood in your face. Are you sick or weak?" The joke began to hurt him deeply.

"You will look the same if I point a gun to your brain, understand? It's a thermal reaction," Sanders replied, keeping his humor and hot temper under control.

"You can put your hands down and talk to me like a man. Listen, I know too well that you know, Miko and Tito, and the 37carat ruby!" Themiro became serious.

"You bugged the conversation. This is illegal and unforgivable. If you bugged the conversation then your bugging machine is as shitty like my shit. Fucking useless, understand? Tell me Rambo who are you? What's your real name? What's your cover?" Sanders became bold and serious. He couldn't believe how he got the courage to ask such question when he knew he was in danger.

"You are rude, Mr Sanders. I don't shit on anybody. I do only business. You have the ruby, and I want to buy. That's all," Themiro said firmly.

"If you want to buy, why are you pointing your fucking gun at me? There is a civilized way to do business like anywhereelse," Sanders answered, confused.

"Okay. I put my gun back in my jacket as you say. We sit and talk about rubies, right?" Themiro said.

Sanders pulled up a chair and sat across the table, face to face. He looked now more relaxed from the tense moment a few minutes ago.

"Let's talk. First, what's your real name, Themiro? A real businessman doesn't do business with ghosts. You understand that, don't you?" Sanders reminded him.

"Grigory Troublov!" At last he spoke the truth.

"So you are Russian, not french. What are you doing here in Bangkok? Do you really do business in rubies or are you working for someone? Now are you here alone or is someone waiting outside to burst in at your command to blow up this place? You know in this country it is illegal to trespass other's property." Sanders warned.

"I don't want to hear all your bullshit. My people are waiting outside to see the ruby. You have it or not? No more talking," Troublov said angrily.

"Hey, in this country people don't do business with strangers. How can you act like this, Troublov? You don't have the money, and then you want to see the ruby. What kind of a businessman are you? Is this how you do business in your country?" Sanders asked.

"I'll shoot your brain if you continue talking like that to me," Troublov said impatiently.

"What will happen if I say I don't have the rubies? Now listen, you said you heard my conversation with Tito and Miko. Where are they? They own the ruby. You must be shooting them, not me," Sanders said plainly

"They have the ruby? Are you telling the truth?" Troublov asked, shockingly.

"Hey, I want to see the ruby too, just like you," Sanders quipped.

"So you don't have the ruby?" Troublov asked in disbelief.

"Do you make a living threatening the people in this country?" Sanders said repeatedly.

"Mr Sanders, you are talking too much. If you play any games with me, next time when we meet, no talking, just business, the gun talks. I'm leaving now, but I'll come back when……." Troublov glanced at Sanders sternly, as he walked out of the door.

Sanders collapsed in his chair like a folded leaf. He was too scared and weak to go anywhereelse or even call his staff, but he had to somehow convince Tito and Miko how dangerous the situation had turned to their disadvantage. He had to somehow save their lives from these goons. He sat in his chair orbiting with his mind thinking of all possibilities. Never in his life had he been so scared of death like the one he had just managed to survive. Themiro could have pulled the trigger in a split-second splashing his brain into porridge. He got the chill out of hell with the repeated thought of pleading like a child in front of a psychopath and his gun who had only one focused goal, the 37carat ruby, and perhaps, more rubies. Then he remembered why he forgot to act.

Sanders looked under his table for the secret switch, a heavy dose of mace secretly installed on both sides of the wall. He just forgot to switch 'on'. He even forgot to use an assortment of stun guns carefully hidden under his gemstone-grading table. He hit his head several times on the table cursing at his stupidity.

NINETEEN

The children were playing happily in and around the swimming pool. Parents loved watching them exercise their skills in a natural way. They were even comparing those who were smart and those who needed more vitamins to compete. Men and women too followed the kids, playing and allowing the frustrations of the day to dissolve in the water.

A few men were busy pretending to read a novel, while comparing quietly the size of their wives physical shape with the ones already in the pool. One genius was already busy sketching a blonde's private parts on a spare paper carefully hidden behind the novel away from the public's notice. He was desperate. The innocent play among children and the way they settled debates looked more colorful and vibrant.

Marla looked impressed at the progress made by April and May, in the pool as she swam with them teaching the special skills. They looked tired after several trials and Marla recognized the signs.

Lam was already at home watching tele, as Marla opened the front door. She walked to the sofa and planted a soft kiss on his cheek. When she returned after the shower, Lam pretended to be busy. She had been watching him for the past few days. He was hiding something. On the contrary, he was thinking of a way to explain the misery he was going through at the office. He just couldn't find the right words to explain to her. She kissed him again.

Lam switched off the tele, and gazed at her innocent face.

"Why do you need the words to explain to me? You can explain in whatever way you like, and I'm old enough to grasp. But this deceptive silence is dangerous. It hurts everyone in the house. The kids are asking me what's wrong with you. When they need help you are not there. What should I say?" she explained. He knew he had screwedup everything. "It's the old man and his pet rubies. There is a 37carat ruby in Bangkok, and two dealers are holding it. Partly, Lord is responsible. The old man wants the ruby on his table at any cost," Lam added. "He is going crazy like hell when he sees me everyday. He wants me to concentrate only on this one bloody ruby, nothingelse. Other projects are taken hostage, because of this sickening situation. That's the big problem."

"What happened between Lord and Rubyhall?" Marla asked.

"It's an all out bloody cold war with their jaded egos, and I'm caught in between," Lam continued. "I'm fuckedup. That brilliant Jay Lam is now shrinking like a goof. It's a cat and mouse situation. Fucking shit!" He couldn't control himself anymore.

"You never used these unscientific words before in front of me. If the kids hear this." She looked back to see if April and May were around.

"I'm sorry," he grinned. His mind was elsewhere.

"Why is it happening to us now?" she asked.

"You asking me? I wish I had the answer a long time ago. Marla, I'm deeply worried," he said. Lam looked at their wedding portrait, as if he remembered something. Old memories kept coming back, and he smiled at her unknowingly.

"We will survive." She kept consoling him.

"Really? Everyday is like a surviving hell," he added. "Anyway thanks for being a good listener. I feel a bit relieved." They walked to their bedroom quietly.

That brief precious moment they had was interrupted by April and May. Marla joined them preparing food in the kitchen. Lam pretended that he was helping their mother sincerely. But he wasn't. After a while, he put the vegetables and the knife on the table and returned to his bedroom.

April and May looked at Marla in utter confusion and disbelief. The girls knew something was bothering him. They were too afraid to ask. Instead, they relied on Marla. But she too didn't know how to explain the complex situation. She wasn't even sure if he still had a job. It looked bad, and she carried on with the work in the kitchen while the girls kept their deceptive silence. They felt instinctively that it was not the right time to ask anything regarding their dad.

Lam didn't join them at the dining table. Instead, he was plotting his next move in his bedroom. Marla joined Lam after she had finished the work in the kitchen and putting the girls to sleep. It was already eleven. He still remained silent, and kept writing something on a pad. Before she got a glimpse of it, he tore the page and threw it in the dustbin. She saw the emergence of evil character in him, though she didn't know how to explain it in words. And, he looked different.

Marla remained in bed wondering whether to talk or go to sleep. Even if she pretended that she was already asleep, he would have known in a matter of seconds. She too was worrying just like him, as time went by. It took her a lot of courage to say something.

"What's going on Jay? You haven't eaten anything so far. Come let's have something to eat. I have already prepared the dinner for you. I haven't eaten either," she said, expecting a positive reply.

"Oh, really? I'm not in a mood to eat anything. Why don't you help yourself? Don't worry about me. I have many things to do," he said frantically.

"If you are not eating, then I will remain in bed," she answered quickly.

"That's bad," he replied, but continued writing and scratching the paper behaving like a madman.

After watching him for a while, she decided to pick up the papers he kept throwing in the dustbin. He saw her open the folded and torn papers, but decided to remain silent. That was the first time she believed Lam had gone awry. She read the names of Rubyhall, Lord, Tito and Miko written repeatedly on the paper.

"I want to kill them all," Lam said frankly.

"You don't mean it, do you?" she said worriedly.

"I don't know," he said, and then kept writing their names in several rows on another piece of paper.

She returned to bed and kept crying not knowing what to do. Meanwhile, Lam had already made some decisions. And he smiled at her thinking how little she knew about the situation and the consequences.

TWENTY

Ben sat with a bunch of brokers at her office in the TD building, as several parcels of rubies, ovals and cushions (shapes) were shown for her opinion. She had an eye for differentiating Thai from Cambodian rubies by their color.

THE SILENT EXPERT!

She ran the office in the absence of Winston Lord. Brokers and dealers respected her like Lord, not because she was the wife of a big ruby dealer, but due to her disciplined approach. Anyone, big or small, was treated equally when she was in the office. Even though Lord didn't share her views all the time he never disapproved her stance if she made a deal or requested his approval. Usually, she never went wrong, either with price or quality.

THE BRILLIANT GEM!

Ben was his third arm. Her Chinese background also helped at times closing a deal. Lord arrived at his office with Gordon Wong, a Hong Kong buyer, whose specialty also happened to be in rubies, but for the rich Mainland Chinese businesswomen. He only selected rubies of half a million dollars per carat and above. Ben had a few selections, and Lord left Wong in her hands. She provided him a convenient table close to the window so that he viewed the gems in skylight, and moved around the room to check the rubies under fluorescent and incandescent light. As they became busy viewing rubies, Lord settled quietly in his private room for a short nap. He tried to sleep, but couldn't.

After gazing for sometime at his own portrait embedded with rubies and other colored gemstones, he decided to call Den

Rubyhall, his good friend. He checked once again if the mobile was on.

"Den, haven't heard from you for some time. How are you? How is the market?"

"Listen Winston, you know the problem. Ris is mad as a madman. I just don't understand why it all happened. We could have worked it out in a more amicable way rather than hurting each other like wild animals," Den answered.

"You understand that, but not your fucking big brother, Ris," Lord conferred.

"Everyone is getting heat-treated (burned) with this craze, aren't they? Why don't we talk about it at my home?" Den requested.

Both of them knew it was very difficult to tame Ris. The first thing was his ruby craze. At times he would mess up his other lucrative businesses, which have brought him bundles of money in order to fetch a ruby, if he liked it. Lam was supposed to handle the international division. Instead, Ris assigned Lam to concentrate on this one 37carat Burmese ruby, till he saw the gem on his table.

After a pause, Lord asked, "Okay. How?"

"I want you and Ris to sit together, and make the everlasting peace. This feud is not good for the business," Den said. "And after all, aren't we friends?"

Lord had heard these statements countless times before, and the more he remembered he wanted to kill Ris. The way Ris treated him at the London auction, Lord couldn't forget. The humiliation was too much for Lord to succumb.

"Are you there?" Den asked, as the line went into a dead silence.

"Yeah. I'm listening. I'll think about it, Den. It's not that easy to make peace with Ris," Lord said thoughtfully, as he glanced at Ben and Wong.

Wong was running around the room with several rubies to compare their color under different lighting. As the dark clouds outside looked so dense, suddenly there was an interruption of skylight. He insisted Ben switch on the fluorescent light and incandescent light together in order to see the difference. Still, Wong wasn't convinced. There was something wrong. Ben read his face, and she too didn't understand what was going on in his mind, despite her experience with him.

Lord looked at them. "Den, I'll call you back. I've a client in the office, and he needs some help." He hung up the phone, and watched Wong from his private room on a closed circuit TV.

Wong was still in the same hot spot. Somehow he couldn't make a decision. The colors and qualities were too close. Though experienced, at times the ruby colors had always some surprises behind their brilliance flashes. When he got the colors right, then it was the price. But Ben knew the unpredictable mood swings in price and quality, and decided to leave him alone for a while so that he had all the time in the world to reason and come to a realistic decision. After all, when it came to money everyone took care of their interests without hurting each other. Now Wong was convinced with the hues of rubies, and Ben's task was to close the deal at the right price. Lord joined Ben, as she punched the numbers for Wong on a calculator.

Finally, Wong nodded.

TWENTY ONE

Baddy Smith, tall, with a curly mop of dark hair, and fast talking met by chance Jeb Singthowala at the Kilimanjaro hotel lobby during one of his trips to Dar-es-Salaam, Tanzania. Though British by birth, he preferred to be identified as an Asian due to his mother's influence. She was Malaysian.

His father was English. He grew up appreciating gemstones at an early age. His father, Michael Smith worked for a Hatton Garden jewelry store as a gemstone specialist. Though the education from his father helped him tremendously understanding the ropes of buying and selling gemstones, there was something in him, which kept emerging day by day. He wanted a bit more knowledge. Baddy decided to venture on his own.

AFRICA!

As the untapped mineral rich continent of the world, Africa had everything-diamonds, colored stones, and precious metals. The wild continent was not for everyone. Only the thick-skinned and determined survived the landscape and culture shock. Gemstones were everywhere.

The locals just didn't know what to call them. Some became part of their traditional culture, while others were cleverly looted out of the country in several guises by the crooked missionaries, mercenaries and, of course, gem traders without borders. The gemstones of Africa were for grabs, and the knowledgeable ones kept the info close to their chest.

They knew these ugly looking rough gemstones when cut and polished had value in their country. So they kept coming back in

various disguises. Some with religious passion, while others introduced themselves as the liberators of ignorance and poverty.

Every foreigner who had landed in Africa profited from the
local population's ignorance and lack of professional skills. They
were too slow to change. The powerful invaders divided and ruled
several countries, their natural and human resources, and at times
created new problems, if they saw a hidden advantage, pitting an
African against African in the name of tribal cleansing or material
gains. The rugged terrain and lack of communication just worked
in their favor.

Africa was any gem enthusiasts dream. A Pandora's box! Baddy
knew about it and wanted to see and experience the rude awakening by himself. After researching quietly for several months at Oxford
University, he decided to start his journey. Tanzania was his first
stop.

By chance, he met a few Asians, at Bradford (England), who
had migrated to England from Tanzania. That introduction helped
him a lot when he arrived in Arusha. He stayed with them for a
few months studying the landscape and the people. The Asian
traders based in Arusha had a lot to share, and with their help and
guidance, he began to trade in red and green garnets.

Extensive traveling and estimating parcels of rough garnets
became easier and with time. He made money selling them in
London at a bit higher prices. One deal led to another.

This arrangement led to frequent traveling between Tanzania
and London. Through several encounters at the mines, he came to
know about other countries in the region that had gemstones.

The Southern African countries had more colored stones. But
he preferred to stay in Tanzania to further strengthen his connections. Many foreigners both, Asian and Western traders, rushed to
the mines and government offices for special concessions, either
the legal way or paying chai (tea money) out-bidding the rivals.
But a local contact became indispensable to pursue the wild ambition. It was at the Ministry of Energy and Minerals where Baddy

met Jeremy Mbuzi. This young miner introduced Baddy to corundum mining. It was an altogether different ball game.

Another meeting at the Ministry of Energy and Minerals, in Dar-es-Salaam, made all the big difference in a day. Together they worked hard, mining corundum of various qualities. Some were sold in kilos, while others in carats. Several trips to Nairobi once upon a time referred to as the Bangkok of Africa, with good ones generated more money and profits.

Again, one deal led to another. Money began to flow like a river, as good and profitable veins (gem pockets) began to show up wherever they dug a hole in Tunduru.

The red variety of corundum was called ruby. When the blue variety became blue sapphire, other colors in the corundum family were classified as fancy sapphires. Some of the blues and fancy colors were so good the experts had difficulty distinguishing them from other well known localities such as Cambodia, Burma, and Thailand.

Jeremy volunteered as his mentor. He taught Baddy every in and out of the trade in the Tanzanian bush, a very rare gesture among the local Tanzanians. They never trusted a foreigner. They knew that any foreigner who landed in any one of the countries in Africa had only one hidden agenda.

EXPLOITATION!

A rare phenomenon, Jeremy trusted Baddy's face. That privilege and convenience became a blessing in disguise. Tall, wellbuilt, cruising in his late forties, he got sucked into the gemstone trade, when his father discovered several green and red crystals popping out of their onion farm in Tunduru.

With time Jeremy's father, Joshua, realized he was sitting on a huge colored gemstone deposit, and that changed the peasant family's fortunes overnight. Married to Mercy with one son, Jerry, Jeremy never indulged in an extravagant lifestyle like some of his fellow miners. He knew one day the gemstones were going to disappear once and for all. They never grew again like vegetables. If it did, it occurred in several million years, but not at the same spot.

So did the money. He was frugal and conservative. He learnt this trait from his father, as well as from the Asian merchants, who dominated the local and regional economies.

Baddy learned this valuable lesson from Jeremy. As was known in the gem trade, competition, jealousy, and disappearance made people go for broke or even quit the business altogether if things didn't work in their favor.

Relationship and trust became the pillar stone of the trade. Meeting crooks and airhead bimbos were a reality. They had only one ambition. Cheat and kill a friendship when opportunities arose. They were everywhere like jackals in several guises. Even an experienced and well-financed miner would go under when these jackals pulled their powerful strings. That's precisely what happened to Jeremy, as he was traveling from Mombasa to Arusha. He had made so much money with a foreigner as his partner not sharing his wealth or the knowledge to the ignorant locals, they decided to do something about it.

Jeremy was killed with a machete, while traveling back to Arusha in a Land Rover by Osman Ndugu, a jealous miner who wanted to see the partnership with Baddy end. Again, one event led to another.

Baddy knew too well, he was a foreigner in a strange land. Even though he knew the language and the landscape there were several miners and traders not so happy with the unusual alliance of a Tanzanian with a Briton. He had to work out a practical strategy if he wanted to survive in the trade. Otherwise, he knew his fate wouldn't be too different from Jeremy. And the local authorities made his life difficult by putting in a lot of restrictions.

Mercy was least interested in continuing the family tradition. She knew that the mining and gem trade was not for her. Instead, she chose modeling. In the end, she advised Baddy to leave Tanzania for good or get killed by anyone who hated his presence in the region. The revelation became a turning point in his life. Never in his dream had he thought of leaving Tanzania and going elsewhere. His roots were in Tanzania. Baddy realized that if this was how he became a victim the same would have happened even if he went elsewhere in the region.

There were too many dogs in the street. Some had to die for others to survive. And, he was not an African. Even if he claimed to be one, he didn't look like them. It was another rude awakening. In a matter of days, events began to change against him. To his dismay, his house was ransacked during his long absence while he was in London. It was the beginning of the end. He discovered the terrain was getting too difficult. There was no evidence or help from his friends as to who was playing the game. His enemies were well organized. He had a decision to make. Life or gemstones!

The thought became an everyday ritual before sleep. Life was more precious to him than gemstones. He didn't want to relocate to London. Perhaps, Southeast-Asia! He pondered for a while.

He knew there were gemstones in Thailand, Burma, Cambodia, Vietnam, and Laos, but then moving to this untested terrain meant starting all over again. As he was waiting to meet a German client, Baddy bumped into Jeb, who also happened to stay at the Kilimanjaro hotel. One event led to another. A casual introduction at the bar made all the big difference in a day. They became friends, as their mutual interests became pretty obvious.

GEMSTONES!

They discussed in detail the future prospects, and Baddy got the surprise of his life when he got an offer from Jeb to join their company as his partner. This was an offer Baddy couldn't refuse. Jeb had other ideas.

When he was introduced to Sanders in Bangkok, and knowing Baddy's background, Sanders knew instantly, he was talking to the right man.

"Welcome to the city of angles, saints, crooks and bimbos!"

Baddy felt amused and a bit disturbed by the unusual introduction. It didn't take him much time to understand what Sanders meant. They were everywhere, wherever there were gemstones. Sanders was speaking his mind, but in a different way.

Bangkok was very different from Dar-es-Salaam or Arusha. The city was vibrant with action in style and chaos, a city under permanent construction. The smell, food, and the people were so different from Tanzania, it took him a while to absorb, adapt, and realize that he was living in one of the most colorful cities in the world, irrespective of its negative image in other areas. The people were friendlier, clean, and charming. The food was tastier than the local Tanzanian dishes, and the varieties kept watering his mouth everyday, as more and more delicacies were introduced. He loved the chaotic city. No wonder, Baddy thought, people kept coming back again and again.

Baddy got a separate office at the Melvine Sanders Trading Corporation. He was briefed on the way Thais did business which was very different from Tanzania. It didn't take much time for him to adapt, just a slight difference in the language and practice. One thing he knew from his experience was gemstones never cheated. Instead, people cheated. Dealers were more concerned with numbers than accents or nationalities. At the end of the day, everyone wanted to make money like anywhereelse. To achieve that goal they needed a gemstone that smiled like a queen or king. He got the excitement of his life when he saw the most colorful rubies and sapphires behind the closed doors of Jeb's office.

Gradually Baddy began to like the Bangkok gem market.

TWENTY TWO

Sanders hurriedly dialed the phone to call Jeb.

"Jeb! Can I talk to you now?" Sanders interrupted. Jeb was in Chantaburi viewing a few parcels of heat-treated rubies from Cambodia. The gem chef was explaining to him the results after heat treatment. Instead of changing to a good red color, the rubies had become dark. In fact, too dark and after cutting and polishing, they wouldn't look much better either. It was a disheartening comment.

"Yeah, just hold on a sec," said Jeb, but his second mobile buzzed. "It's my wife. Jessy, I will talk to you later. I've a customer on the other line." Jeb explained to Jessy.

"You are always like that when I've something important to say. Is this some kind of setup?" Jessy asked indignantly.

"Jessy, what are you talking about? Wait, wait, wait," Jeb continued. "When I talk to a customer I get business, that's how I make a profit, and feed the family, understand?" Jeb tried to reason with her. She was in a nether world.

"Jessy!" The line was disconnected. "Sanders, are you there?" Jeb shrugged expressively.

"I can hear the fireworks. What's she up to this time?" Sanders asked.

"The same old crap, not enough time at home, and she thinks I'm screwing some blondes in the guise of a customer. Man, what a fucking life? Forget about business, I can't even have a nice fuck with her, she is too religious, can you believe this? She is talking about environment degradation, population control, and save the fucking planet gospel. Fuck them all. This is a normal chaos. Okay, what's up?" Jeb's voice was sober.

"This is fucking serious. I can tell you. I just survived a near death experience," Sanders said dryly.

"Why do you want to die now? You owe me a lot, don't you?" Jeb said humorously.

"It's not that I want to die," Sanders added. "A guy walks into my office, you know, like a normal guy and demands that he wants to do business with me. Okay, I tolerated that part. You know, we don't do business with fucking strangers. Then he tells me I'm hoarding a big ruby, which he desperately wants to see. The fuck, what should I say?"

"You say, Noooooooooo!" Jeb uttered.

"That's precisely what I said. Nooooooo! And then, comes the fucking gun pointed at my aging brain. Either I show him the ruby or I'm a confirmed instant porridge," Sanders said.

"Then what happened?" Jeb became alert.

"Me? That's the first time in my life, I ever thought about death, one shot death. Tak tak tak, boom!" Sanders cried in fear.

"Who is this guy? Was he alone or with someone? Hey Sanders hold on a sec, will you? I'm with Suradej," Jeb interrupted.

Suradej urged Jeb to give the Cambodian rubies one more level of heating to remove the undesirable brown after careful inspection. Jeb weighed his options, and after a careful thought, he decided to go along with Suradej, just to see the results. He didn't care much if the result was negative. This ruby parcel was from a new mine.

"Are you there?" Sanders asked, trying hard to stay steady.

"Go ahead," Jeb uttered holding the line.

"It's a gang for sure," Sanders continued. "But he was alone. Bloody cool and polite."

"What's he like? What tribe?" Jeb asked.

"Russian, with a French name," added Sanders, "A pricking, Pierre Themiro!"

"Why was he exactly after you?" Jeb quipped.

"The guy bugged all my conversation with Miko," answered Sanders. "They are after Miko and Tito for the 37carat ruby. They want it for free. He reminded me that he will come back if the information I gave was wrong."

"What information?" Jeb asked.

"I said that the ruby was not with me, instead with Miko and Tito. They are after them. We have to do something to save their lives. Life is more important than rubies, don't you think?" Sanders cried.

"Oh, yeah, sometimes," Jeb reasoned. "Sure. We can't go to the police. It will become a boomerang. The cure will be worse than the disease. What do you think?"

"Me? My brain is dead, a worthless rock, and heavily oxidized. Can't think of any crap. Can't even remember which day it is today?" Sanders said, hopelessly.

"So, what do you want me to do?" Jeb asked.

"We have to save them and ourselves," Sanders added. "They have spotted us like a valuable gem. They want it for free. They are armed and organized. We need a common strategy to wipe out these assholes with their bones so that they don't resurrect in the coming years. You are good in undercover operations. I want you to think of a practical, inexpensive, and precise execution. These morons should never try this again on anyone else in this territory. That's what I mean. We can't afford to just sit and watch these morons blow up our brains."

"So? You want me to go back to the dark ages?" Jeb uttered.

"For our survival. They will hurt our business to the core. We can't afford to look like we are damn weak. We have to eject them permanently out of our territory so that future morons would have to think twice before they land in Bangkok," Sanders said.

"Oh, yeah?"

Their conversation was interrupted by an unexpected call.

"Daddy, its me Ruth!"

"Ruth? Very unusual, What's the matter? Where is your mother?" Sanders asked surprisingly.

Jeb overheard the conversation, and decided to let Sanders continue his talk with Ruth. He disconnected the line, as Sanders tried in vain to reach him. Jeb switched off his mobile so that he could now concentrate on the problematic Cambodian rubies.

"Mom is not at home," Ruth added. "That's why I felt like calling you."

"Tell me Ruth," Sanders insisted. "Don't beat around the bush. What's the problem?"

"I'm pregnant!" she said.

"What? What did you say?" Sanders repeated several times.

"Dad, I'm pregnant. I don't know what to do. Mom is too busy with her friends. I wanted to talk to her first, but . . . . ." Ruth cried in vain.

Sanders opened his mouth to scream, but couldn't. He froze in his chair, speechless. A premature darkness masked the room and his perplexed mind.

"Dad, are you there?" Ruth asked desperately.

"I'm coming home Ruth," he said angrily. He didn't mean that way.

"Please don't hurt me, Daddy. I'm sorry. It happened, please," she pleaded.

"I'm coming home Ruth," Sanders answered in a harsh tone, which meant trouble. This couldn't have come to him at a worse time, between the devil and deep blue sea. Tears rolled out of his eyes like torrential rain, as the build up peaked to its zenith. He cried loudly, the first time in several years. The walls vibrated in sheer accordance. He looked like he was in the middle of a broken dam. It became louder and louder, as he struggled painstakingly limping out of his chair to stand straight. His eyes were almost out of their socket in rage when he thought of Chin. He wanted to chop Chin's every part including her bones with a meat cleaver, till she turned into a stew. So much disgust and hate accumulated in his mind, and had he had the wings, he would have flown to her club and plucked her to death.

It was too late. What happened has happened, and now what?

He forgot about Troublov, Baddy, Tito, Miko, the rubies, and even death. His only thought now concentrated in putting his house in order. Only he could doctor the situation at home.

As he drove home, he thought at each traffic stoplight of his role as a father, and his partial responsibility in this humiliating reward by his only daughter. He could have read the sign on the wall earlier by being with his only child instead of business. Now the damage was done, and he had no other choice but to accept it as his singular fault.

The whole concept of having kids as an investment for the future had turned out to be a bad strategy for him. Money and social recognition had done enough damage for the rest of his life. He thought of his childhood days, when having three meals a day was a luxury. He never wanted his kids to have that same fate. Instead, he worked harder and harder to make as much money as possible for them so that they wouldn't have to worry about the uncertain future ahead. But what he had forgotten was the social prerequisite, the fatherly presence. When she needed him, he was too busy out in the streets making more money. She never understood why he was out there. Neither did Chin bother to make up for his absence. As time dragged and years passed by, negligence piled up like layers of bricks, establishing the wrong foundation. Money never stayed long in one place at any one time so he had no other choice but to grab it at each and every stop before it disappeared. This profit grab syndrome was visible everywhere like the air. He forgot about home.

Everybody thought like him. Why should he be different? Now he had to worry not only about the little girl, but also about the little creature growing up in her womb like a weed, if it was true. What kind of a monster would that turn out to be when it was ready to scream out of the womb? What would that creature's relationship be in an unfriendly world? Who would be paying the cost for this unwelcome arrival? He was just lost in thoughts, as he madly drove to the garage of his villa on Srinakarin Road.

He opened the door violently and called her loudly, "Ruth! Where are you?"

There was no answer. He called again in that same tone. Still there was no answer. Now he had reasons to worry. Has she done anything crazy? He changed his tone. He walked stealthily, room after room looking for her.

"Ruth, this is your dad. I'll not hurt you. Just tell me where you are. I just want to talk to you. What has happened has happened. We need to talk first before we can help. Ruth, please come out wherever you are. Daddy wants to talk to you."

As his patience ran out of heat, she emerged from the bathroom like a helpless lamb with her head down.

"Ruth!" He walked towards her slowly and gazed in disbelief. He then embraced her affectionately. She fell into his arms and cried loudly.

"What happened to you? How could it have happened?" he asked.

"I'm really sorry, daddy." She kept repeating by rote. He slowly raised her tearful face and looked with a mix of compassion and anger.

"How do you know you are pregnant? Who told you that, Ruth?" he asked.

"My friends at school," she replied reluctantly.

"Your friends? Are they doctors?" He couldn't believe her statement.

"No. But they know the symptoms. I had it," she countered.

"Like?" Sanders felt angry again.

"I can't tell you that, dad," she said persistently.

"I'm your father, Ruth," said Sanders. "Who else should know? Your mother is screwedup with some women's group in Sukhumvit or somewhere. What do you mean by I can't tell you? I want to help you. It's not just you. Everyone is involved and you have to speak the truth, understand?" She nodded.

"And, who is the boy responsible? Where is he?" he asked indignantly.

"He's not saying anything, dad," she replied innocently.

"He is not saying anything?" Sanders said indignantly. "I'll fucking kill him. Where is he living? Why are you so supportive of him? You are having the pain, not him. So, why?" Sanders had all the reasons to bury him alive if the boy was anywhere close. He had no one else to blame, except himself and his wife. He continued, "Listen, we can't trust your friends at school. We have to go to a friendly hospital to confirm this thing. When your mother comes, we will have to discuss this," he said.

"Are you still angry with me daddy?" she pleaded.

"It's too late, Ruth. It's too late, there is no point getting angry at this stage. I love you, Ruth. You are still my daughter. But what you did, I'm still trying to cope with, you know. It's not that easy to forget. As a father I've a lot of responsibility and this one, I can't just ignore. I never expected this from you. Never in my dreams did I ever think of facing a situation like this. But, I've no choice," he said hopelessly.

"I didn't expect it to turn out this way," Ruth reasoned.

"Well, that's how it turned out to be. You could have avoided it. It takes only a split-second to do the wrong thing, you understand? That's what happened. Do you know where your boy lives?"

"No!"

"What?" Sanders said angrily. "You don't know where he lives? How can you be so dumb, Ruth? Now he fucks around you putting his thing into yours and you don't know where he lives? What's wrong with you? Are you out of your mind?" He had to control his spontaneous anger again. Her accomplished stupidity in sleeping with a boy with no nametag and family convinced him there was something wrong with Ruth. The price he had to pay was becoming now worth more than the best ruby in the world.

As he collapsed on the sofa, gazing at Ruth thoughtlessly, he heard the front door open. It was his socialite wife, Chin.

"Hello, everybody home? Ruth, why are you crying?"

Ruth just looked at Chin aimlessly and then at Sanders.

"What happened? Melvine, say something instead of staring at me," Chin said.

The immediate thought, which rushed to his mind was to

first grab her hair and spin her head like a top, till she dropped unconscious. He sat there orbiting with his confused thoughts, as to how to reply sensibly, but then again, he wasn't sure if it would have any results. This time he decided she shouldn't get away like before. He looked at her as if he was under control.

"Why don't you ask Ruth, instead of looking at me, Chin?" he said.

"Why don't you tell me? What's wrong with that? I don't have the time now to probe each and every detail. I have a talk to give tomorrow at the Aging Women's workshop!" she said.

That was it. He had enough of her extra-curricular activities. He had to put a full stop to this nonsense.

"How on earth can you fuck around with your Aging Women's workshop, when you have an aging daughter having pain? Do you understand what I'm trying to say?" he said angrily.

"No!" she said.

"Then you are as dumb as your daughter. How can you do something like that? Are you out of your mind? I work like a donkey twenty hours a day to fill your stomach, right? None of you have known the pain of making money. You thought that this is going to be like this for the rest of your life. And when I'm out trying to make a living, you are out spending the money like a freak, and instead of taking care of the kid and her well being. What have you done? All your fucking activities outside with your bloody friends, has it improved your intelligence one iota? Prove it to me, Chin! If you had all that extra knowl-edge from your activities outside this home, why can't you ap-ply it and make a happy and content home? Instead, what have we got? A brainless kid and a chaotic home! Talk to her, your beloved daughter and, of course, mine too. Talk to her first, and then I'll reply," he explained.

Chin took her seat on the sofa, and then moved closer to Sand-ers. Ruth was still standing looking confused.

"Ruth, come to me." Ruth walked toward Chin, and stood motionless.

"Sit close, and tell me what happened?" She first looked at her nervously, and then uttered, "I'm pregnant!"

"That's all? Is that a big problem? I thought it was something more serious. We can go to the clinic tomorrow and abort the whole thing. That's what everyone does nowadays. What do you say, Melvine?"

"What do I say? This is what I do."

He turned around and slapped her face. Sanders stood stunned, as if he was standing on a pack of explosives. He just couldn't believe his ears. He stood up furiously again, and the next thing Chin could remember, Melvine on top, slapping her face mercilessly. He beat her severely, till he dropped to the floor exhausted. He wished she were dead. She was still breathing like a steam engine. By now Ruth had already disappeared from the room, afraid to be the next target.

"All these years I've worked hard to make a living, you bitch. This is how you talk to your daughter when she becomes pregnant at fifteen? I've never heard such a callous remark from anyone, and instead of being a concerned mother, you have encouraged her to fuck again. You don't deserve this house. I don't care what the fuck you think? If you want the fucking divorce, do it now. I have had enough of your partnership. I wish I had kicked you out of this home a long time ago, you bitch. Who the fuck do you think will pay all the cost of aborting Ruth?" He screamed at her.

She didn't hear anything he said. He couldn't tell whether she was unconscious or dead. He cared less. His immediate thought was to put her in a garbage bag and dump her in the gutter. So much disgust had accumulated with time he was now almost desperate to get rid of her at any cost. It had been a burden to him for so long, her distant and immediate presence would only aggravate the situation, not only hurting himself and his business, but the home itself.

As he gradually settled his thoughts, he anxiously looked around for Ruth. But again, he cared less, as suddenly he felt too tired to care.

TWENTY THREE

Troublov woke up with a vague idea of trapping Tito and Miko indirectly at an entertainment place they usually frequented. Then he wondered how on earth such a notion could have come to him. But he wanted to give it a go, in a different way, the nonviolent way.

As he lay on his cot, face to the wall, his shoulders twitching, he envisioned, his only way would be to become a pseudo-gay, and roam the expensive restaurants in and around World Trade Center, till one of them fell into his trap. He knew one of them had a weakness, but didn't know which one. The thought itself seemed revolting to him, as he buried his face in the pillow to mask the light. It took him several hours to reconcile the thought. When he got out of his bed, he had already made up his mind.

His main worry was whether he could, with confidence, make himself attractive to hook the strange men out on the streets in the pursuit of grabbing the 37carat ruby and more. He rushed over to the mirror to glance at his own body. He looked a bit lean from his torturous workout, but his skin tone was good enough to hook them, as they got accustomed to his assets. His blonde hair, blue eyes, and the charming look seemed more than enough for a good jump off at least.

Troublov dressed hurriedly, and walked slowly out of his hotel to hire a cab to a gay saloon near the World Trade Center. He felt no nervousness at first, but as he looked at the passing men accosting him with their vulgar glances, his confidence index took a bungy dive. At first he thought of running back to his hotel. He felt the exhaustion. Then a tall well dressed man in his early sixties came close and whispered, "Let's go over there; you see that restaurant?"

"All right," replied Troublov.

The old man took Troublov's arm, and led him to an American Restaurant. It wasn't crowded and with ease they secured a table. He had a membership card. The man ordered the drinks. His throat felt dry, and he asked for four Miller beers. They looked at each other silently. Troublov saw the man's eyes scanning his face and body. After much thought he said, "You are a greenhorn in the business, aren't you?"

"How did you know that?" Troublov asked.

"I was observing you, as you passed by," the old man replied smilingly.

"Is there anything wrong with me?" Troublov asked again.

"You look childish and stupid!" The old man answered promptly.

"Really? Why then do you want me? You have a Russian accent," Troublov said.

"Dutch or Russian or whatever, I live here," the old man continued. "You have good looks and a frightened face. It's fun watching and meeting novices trying to desperately inspire a potential victim the wrong way. It's real, painful, and at times rewarding. That's my hobby. I can well afford to spend some time that way. You see!"

"Then, how do you make a living?" Troublov asked thoughtlessly.

"That's none of your business. I'm not desperate, but you are. I can see that on your face and body. You don't have that cool, casual and quick jump off style of the old timers. You are just like those rough gemstones. Do you see them right over there? That jewelry store? You aren't different. You need a lot of painful and expert cut and polishing to make you look brilliant. How long have you been on the streets, son?"

"I started today," Troublov answered.

"No one with you, alone? Just like that," the old man asked curiously.

"Just like that," Troublov said, expecting the next question.

"What's the motivation?" The old man asked again.

"I can't tell you, but I wanted to give it a go," Troublov replied plainly.

"If you can't tell me, you aren't going anywhere, son. You can get killed in the streets by old timers if they think you are stealing their clients, understand? You'd like to live longer, wouldn't you?" The old man reminded.

"Oh, sure," Troublov said quickly.

"How old are you, if you don't mind saying?" The old man asked.

"Thirtytwo!" Troublov replied punctually.

"But you don't look like you come from a broken home. The language of your face and eyes tell me you are out on the streets for some definite reasons. I can help you a lot if you reveal your true identity," the old man said.

"No comments, I can't tell you. If you don't want my services, then why are you wasting your time with me? You can always find someone else," Troublov quipped.

"Listen son, there is nothing wrong in what you're doing if you have the balls to do it, the right way. You don't have it, okay," the old man said quickly. Strange though, the man took out a hundred dollar bill and tossed it in front of Troublov.

"This is the cost of convenience. You're trying to be an old boy, but you aren't. I can well afford that. I'm seventy, and often enjoy meeting strangers like you in the streets. I love to meet mysterious people coming to this city, trying to look like somebody. And I always meet the one who doesn't make it. Isn't it strange? Good day, son!" He took his hand, gave a gentle rub, and then walked in the opposite direction.

Troublov sat agape not knowing what to say. He stood up to say something, but the gravity from within pulled him back to his seat.

"Any more drinks?" The waiter asked gently.

"No thanks."

Troublov began to ponder whether it had been a wise decision working for Boris Luganow and Papov Kuchinsky. They had several business connections both, legal and illegal, in Thailand, Cambodia and Vietnam. At times he loved the job because of money and entertainment. He was trained to kill people when ordered. He needed constant attention, but once focused he had no problem doing the job professionally. His patrons knew his strengths and weaknesses, but still decided to keep him because of his good looks and animal instincts. He had also a brief introductory training in gemstone identification, especially ruby, because of its rarity and value. There were several successful business tycoons in Russia who were pursuaded to vacation in Thailand, and that's where Papov and Boris saw the opportunities.

And Troublov became one of their best conduit to trick and plunder the innocents who knew nothing about rubies or gems in particular other than name and color. His patrons had locals who were acquainted with all the right politicians as fences. It was a lucrative operation, and all they had to do was to find the weak and disturbed rich, both local and foreign, and mop up their hidden wealth. And quite a lot of them hid their ill-gotten wealth in investment quality gemstones, especially rubies due to its portability and liquidity.

After paying the bill, Troublov walked out of the restaurant and hailed a taxi. "Lad Phrao!" he barked. He knew it wasn't going to be that easy to get away from the clutches of Papov and Boris. They were just too strong and well organized, but he had one or two tricks up his sleeves if and when a situation arose for self-defense. He was getting sick and tired of his present job. He had seen more than enough blood and for some strange reasons, he began to think of an escape route once the job was over. But first, he had an assignment, to kidnap Rubyhall, Miko, Tito and Sanders, because of the amount of illicit rubies arriving at a discreet destination. His patrons wanted a share of that illicit wealth.

TWENTY FOUR

It should have been a good day several years ago, when one Pius valued Louis Marty's stock of rubies at five times its cost, assuring Marty that he could sell and get the money at the earliest. But, he was wrong.

Ten years passed, and Marty never saw Pius again. That experience, and the sheer love for rubies fired his passion to know all about rubies and the dubious characters.

He arrived in Bangkok, all the way from the mountains of Switzerland, to make a living working in the gemstone industry, and if he met Pius again, he knew what to do. He loved gemstones only for one reason. Easy money and traveling.

That's what he was told, before he quit his steady job as a banker. Twenty years of hard savings became the seed capital, to test the waters of the gem trade. He traveled to South America and Africa, several times to study the prospect of starting with the locals. But it wasn't that easy. There were no schools teaching prospective aspirants how to make heaps of money buying and selling gemstones.

After considerable thought, he decided Bangkok was the place to start. The city was inexpensive and friendly to foreigners. He loved rubies above all other gemstones, because a lot of money was made if the deal came out right. He saw big rubies going under the hammer at the Christie's and Sotheby's auction houses in Geneva for unbelievable prices. Somebody was making big money somewhere. The learning curve came again when he bought rubies at incredibly inflated prices when was taken on a 'ride' by a clever tout on Silom Road. That's where he heard for the first time the name of a town called Chantaburi. The touts kept mentioning it at their shop in one of the back streets off Silom Road.

One event led to another. He went to Switzerland, to see if he could sell the rubies, which he thought he had bought for a bargain. The reply was shocking. They turned out to be man-made glass. He couldn't differentiate between a good quality red glass and a natural ruby. That rude awakening, and the sensible advice by the jeweler in Geneva, took him to a gem school to learn the basics of how to differentiate real from fake. He was bemused to meet people like him in the school who had lost fifty times more than he had lost. He counted his blessings. As he listened to their tales of how crooked and daring the men and women were, he realized for the first time that making fast money was a joke. If it were that easy then everyone would have been on the bandwagon.

The experience at the school taught him one lesson. Crooks and bimbos were everywhere. They were international and skilled. Also, good product knowledge was essential. He learned one more thing. COLOR AND PRICE!

The price of rubies fluctuated like hell by its color. Some crazy markets even paid high premiums if rubies originated from certain localities. Now armed with that knowledge and confidence, he decided to return to the same den of crooks and bimbos to buy rubies, and if lucky to meet Pius one day in flesh. He knew for sure Pius had to be where there were rubies, and that was in Southeast Asia. The advice given by a fellow student, rung his ears.

Gemstones never cheated, it's the people who cheated all the time. There was another twist. This time a fellow student, Christine Pascal, joined him. She too believed working with gems made people creative and independent. She wanted to become a jewelry designer instead of a trader. To achieve that goal, she required good knowledge of gemstones. Rubies became her specialty, because after seeing people pay unbelievable prices for ruby jewelry, she decided jewelry designing as her destined career. Good durability and high hardness made ruby an ideal choice for both, men and women.

In his late thirties, blonde, tall, and comic in character, Pascal had a reason to like Marty. His blue eyes had an attractive texture. They resembled blue moonstones. She loved his humor, and believed if he had the right ruby selling them in Switzerland wouldn't be that difficult. In fact, she had attended some of his seminars on banking and finance issues. He knew how to finesse a client by his humor and plastic face.

Cruising in her mid thirties, Pascal too had an amazing career switch. The banking career made her into a boring bimbo. She wanted to do something different and productive. Gemstones became a possible alternative, and she chose to specialize in rubies, because big investment stones brought in big money.

The chemical match between Marty and Pascal merged them into a different level of relationship. She needed an anchor in her life, and believed Marty to be the right man. After several visits to the auction houses of Christie's and Sotheby's it became pretty obvious that any money to be made would be on untreated rubies from Burma. Big ones! The risk was worth the try. The specialized laboratories in Switzerland were internationally recognized, when it came to obtaining origin reports for rubies. They returned together to Bangkok for the treasure hunt looking for big but good ones. The trip to Chantaburi on a Friday morning was the best option so that they could stay the whole Friday and Saturday in the market. Communication was a problem.

They were referred to Peninsula Lapidary, a longtime ruby dealer with offices in both Bangkok and Chantaburi.

They were given a copy of the rules and regulations regarding the buying procedures and gem testing facilities. Marty and Pascal rented a table. The customs among gem dealers in Chantaburi were quite fascinating. Dealers preferred to employ middlemen instead of trading directly with each other. They gave their goods to many brokers during the day, after receiving inquiries from other dealers or from foreign buyers. The broker then opened the parcel, sometimes a single piece or otherwise. The buyer either refused to bid if found unsuitable or at times allowed selecting part of it, and rejected the rest. Once the buyer decided to bid, they placed either the single piece or the parcel under a paper wrap quoting their price signed, and then sealed by a cello-tape to avoid tampering. The ritual was done in front of the broker who then took it to the owner for consent.

On a bad day, the brokers were forced to run countless times before the deal went off. While on a good day, in a matter of seconds or at the most before late evening a deal was struck drawing his commission from either side, unless specified.

The company provided one of their assistant's, Kamal, to help interpret asking, bidding, and transactions prices. Marty instructed Kamal to write on a piece of paper the type of rubies they were looking for. It was good quality rubies above 10carat. Several runners (go-between) thronged to their table opening stone packets of rubies of various qualities, or at times single stones.

Marty had a cutout of a 31 plus carat Burmese ruby from a Christie's catalogue to compare the ones arriving on his table. Though unprofessional, he had no other choice. Having a natural ruby of that size as a master stone was difficult to find. If available, he was determined to obtain one. He knew from insider information that big ones brought in huge profits if the specialized laboratories in Switzerland determined the origin of the rubies. Lighting was a problem too, but somehow he calibrated the different color shades of the rubies under a type of fluorescent and incandescent light set up on the table.

To his dismay, several synthetic flux rubies kept arriving indiscriminately. They weren't that lucky this time. The brokers just didn't have the ones that Marty and Pascal was looking for. But they knew from experience that patience was of the utmost importance, when it came to obtaining big ones.

Purposely the real owners of the rubies at times refused to release good quality rubies of big sizes. Creating artificial scarcity was a common ploy among the top dealers of Chantaburi. Like the biblical saying, they just wanted to avoid casting pearls before swine. Once convinced of a serious buyer, the clients were invited to their quiet office for that special look. Marty and Pascal waited.

TWENTY FIVE

The more Lam thought about the 37carat ruby, the greater it became obvious that Lord was out to cut Rubyhall into several pieces. Lord was a master manipulator. He never forgave Rubyhall for what he did to him in the Zambian copper deal at the London auction.

Lord had bait, and that was his 37carat ruby.

Eye clean, untreated, well cut, and a top color Burmese ruby with an origin report from Switzerland. Since the market and the people knew each other's goods, and if they had an exquisite stone out in the market, then everyone knew without doubt the owner of the stone. There were only a few who could afford to buy and sell such qualities.

Lord had a special relationship with Tito and Miko for one simple reason. He just liked them, and they never disappointed him when doing business.

FACE AND TRUST. That's what Lord saw when dealing with people in the Bangkok market, because he could very well afford to sacrifice profit if it brought a future deal.

On the contrary, Lam wanted the same ruby at Rubyhall's terms. Bringing Tito and Miko to his den became difficult as days went by. Whenever he called for a meeting, the reply obviously became familiar. They didn't want to sell, which wasn't true. Due to the wide rift between Rubyhall and Lord, Lam had only one option. Tell Rubyhall to make his peace with Lord. Even though he knew the proposal had a remote possibility to materialize at this stage given the strength and unity among his opponent's camp, the only trump card he had was Rubyhall's preemptive strike with

a peace deal. Though the idea looked simple, putting both fero-
cious lions in a peace cage was the difficult part of the equation.
Despite Tito's refusal to confirm the status of the ruby, Lam kept
calling their office just to remind him that there was a genuine
offer.

The tricky part was the price tag. Lam couldn't figure out
their asking price, even though he had a rough idea about rubies
of similar size. But, Rubyhall had already done his homework. He
was awaiting other players to fall into his orbit so that he could
drag their knees in different directions making the eventual transaction price obviously unaffordable.

Lord had known this tactic well ahead, and Tito and Miko
had all the time in the world to sell it to whichever entity, except
Rubyhall, even if he used proxies. The deal was specific. NO to
Ris Rubyhall!

Time was running out and Lam needed ideas to break the
deadlock. Even though he had broken several hard to crack deals
during the course, this one looked like more time. Money wasn't a
problem. It was the games these big guys played which made issues difficult to solve. Rubyhall and Lord had their egos scaling
sky high while the second level players such as him, Tito, and
Miko had a different game to play to get into the big guy's orbit.

Gradually events began to turn against him. He hated coming
to work at Rubyhall's office, because Ris had taken away all his
assignments and powers. He had only one thing to do; find the
37carat ruby. He was still undecided whether he had been de-
moted to an inactive post. The only difference this time was his
pay and perks remained the same, but for how long, he had no
idea. It was getting boring all the same.

Once upon a time, buying a ruby or the arrival of a parcel of
rubies from the mines was always such big news, and of tremendous joy to hold them in his hand, and rubbing them. There was
special feeling and experience going into it, till it was sold to some
collectors to enjoy their beauty in privacy. Now with this unusual
experience, that emotional feeling was getting sucked out of his

mind forever. He hated rubies and even the mention of them. Like a sitting duck, he kept searching for some kind of divine intervention. He became desperate.

Before friends used to pass by to say hi, but not anymore. He didn't know why. He thought of blaming only two sources.

The ruby and, of course, Lord.

Since Lord was too powerful and influential in the gem community, doing anything crazy only added to the misery, and then the elusive Tito and Miko. They too were playing their games, in fact, a good one.

He couldn't do anything against them. Anyway, the ruby was with them, and he couldn't think of any workable idea to convince them to change their mind. He began to do the same exercise he did at home. Writing the names of Rubyhall, Tito, Miko, and Lord on a piece of paper several times. He couldn't think of anything meaningful other than memorize their names. It was a disgusting experience but the more he wrote he seemed to enjoy reading their names. A kind of madness began to permeate his normal thoughts. Before, he couldn't even think about it, but now that thought began to disappear. It was only a matter of time before he could take anyone's life the way he wanted, but then the question of when began to evolve.

He wrote again and again feverishly like crazy, till he got physically tired. After a few minutes break, he continued the same exercise. Lam was enjoying the experience. A sort of wicked smile rushed to his face, as the victim's faces became transparent.

It was noon, time for lunch. He debated whether to go to Mcdonalds or Sizzler. He couldn't decide.

Rubyhall walked into his office with a serious look. The thought of going for lunch disappeared immediately. He wondered what Rubyhall had under his sleeves this time.

"How long do you think you want me to tolerate this situation?" Rubyhall said without even looking at Lam's face.

"You know the truth. What do you want me to do? All my

efforts seem to bear no result. Now, it's your decision," Lam answered frankly.

Rubyhall sat tight-lipped as to how to handle Lam, and his future position in the company. He had several decisions in his mind, but the timing was important to him.

"Do you want me to set a deadline? This can't go on forever. I am paying you all the benefits when you are doing nothing. Think about it. It's not fair. Tell me now, what's your decision?" Rubyhall said seriously.

"Do you want me to quit? Is that what you mean?" Lam asked, raising his voice.

"I didn't say that. All I want is the ruby. You know what I mean, don't you?" Rubyhall continued. "Okay, I will give you some more time. You have less than a week, and then I will let you know my decision," Rubyhall said angrily, and stormed out of the office.

"That's it," Lam said in disgust.

TWENTY SIX

Marty and Pascal stayed at the K.P.Grand hotel in Chantaburi, patiently waiting for a good ruby to show up. There was nothingelse they could do other than wait. Some brokers even brought their pieces to the hotel to show them, but not the one Marty was looking for.

It was already late evening. They had nothing to do other than drink wine and watch television. Watching the tele became too boring, because they were repeating the same news every half an hour. After drinking more wine, Marty and Pascal, began to drift into a romantic situation generated by the light, mood, and the right environment.

The dim light in the bedroom gave more impetus, as they undressed methodically. Finally they looked at each other's naked bodies. The incandescence in the room glowed their pinkish red skin into a much more saturated level giving it a vivid enhancement, like two glowing rubies.

Marty saw Pascal's full breasts hanging down from her chest, like ripe cantaloupes as she untied her blonde hair. She took his hand and like a sheep dog, herded her sheep to bed. She arranged the pillows to the side so that he could lie straight without unnecessary bulge.

Then she turned her face towards him and whispered, "This is my special gift tonight for you, Marty. Just relax!"

As she started to rub his thigh with her soft thick lips, the hair in his whole body stood up straight, like an army of Swiss soldiers. The instant erection he experienced followed by her rub caught her attention. She incrementally moved upwards, massaging his balls gently to further coax his pressurized erection.

Marty was beyond heaven. She was the specialist. She knew all the hot buttons of a man's eruptive epicenter. He enjoyed her each and every finger play. That was her gift. He was moaning like a buffalo, as she massaged his balls again. His erection was red hot by the time she removed her grip from his balls. She gave a gentle stroke and, lo and behold, the whole thing began to shrink like a folding umbrella.

Now she sat on top of him, and stretched her body symmetrically, sliding slowly so that they both saw each other's face. They transformed into one sculpture completely unified.

"Marty!" she called him in a low tone.

He was in his peak ecstasy, with his eyes closed as if in deep meditation. She knew what he meant. She now swept his face with her tongue, one round, and then slowly entered his mouth. The electricity generated from this oral intercourse could have lit the capital of Laos for a comfortable week. Such was the energy of mind and body, as they intertwined first with regular thrusting, and then moved from one direction to another balancing their weight and positions to excite and extract maximum pleasure. When she felt he was getting tired again, she pressed one of his invisible hot buttons to regenerate his vigor. She made him believe he was twenty years younger. There was a frenzy of pushing, pulling, moaning, laughing, and rolling. Only a massive earthquake could stop them. She controlled each and every move, and the more she worked him, the higher he was in heaven moaning like a buffalo.

She glanced at the alarm clock. It was two o'clock in the morning.

"Thank you, Marty. I enjoyed it so much. Let me kiss you again," she whispered.

"Why should you thank me? You ate me like an artichoke. Thank you," Marty replied, kissing her again.

She then turned around, pulled the bedspread over him, and then switched off the light. "Do you want one more shot?"

"Oh, no, please. I won't be able to see the colors of rubies tomorrow. Remember, we have an appointment with Khun Praphan in the morning." Marty slumped, closed his eyes and exhausted slept like a log.

TWENTY SEVEN

Early one morning after breakfast, Troublov went for a stroll alone in and around Chatuchak area. He cursed himself for being so stupid as to pretend to be a gay in order to meet Miko. The information he got was wrong, plus it was a disgusting experience, he vowed never to repeat.

The scenic greenery eased the anxiety, as he prepared himself mentally for the next mission. Several brainstorming ideas rushed to his mind while sipping iced tea and a few cookies at a coffee shop.

His main target was Tito. If he could get Tito, and the expensive rubies he was hoarding, his job was over. Gracefully, he should be back in Moscow.

The other option, the difficult one, was to kidnap Sanders, as a bargain to get Tito into his net, before it was too late. He had quite a lot of information from his patrons who operated several businesses in Pattaya, as well as in Bangkok, about the private lives of Sanders and Jeb.

Another bait was one Anna Garnetova, nicknamed Goldie, a discreet mistress who often catered to Sander's sexual need.

Tito was too clean. He had only one interest, money and gemstones, especially rubies. The magic combination between Pavlov and Tito was that, they stayed only with their loyal wives. There were several Goldie's from Russia, catering to a variety of needs for the Thais, as well as foreigners. Some made a lot of money, while others just kept losing everything.

But this Goldie was different. A rich and lucky one, having several social and political connections. She had a special taste for

Americans. To make it look natural and homely, she legally married an old rich American millionaire, John Rich, in Cyprus, thus becoming his fifth wife. Occasionally, Rich came to Bangkok in disguise to avoid the undercover agents who were after him for tax evasion and money laundering. They never bothered his first wife, Beryl, who ran hotels and restaurants in his home state of Florida, because her books were clean. At times she flew to Cyprus to satisfy his needs. He had homes in Spain, Cyprus, Bermuda, and Bali, and rarely stayed in Bangkok.

Goldie ran part of his business, which included travel agencies, hotels, and computer software. The Khunyings (a royal title) and other socialites courted her for her lavish contributions to various charitable institutions. She had forgotten her Russian patrons, Boris Luganov and Papov Kuchinsky, who had indirect influence in her present status. Instead she was acting more like a born-again American. A cheap imitation! Armed with this information, Troublov worked out his execution plan.

After paying the bills at the coffee shop, he returned to his hotel.

"Sir, there is a message for you," said the receptionist. He remembered the phone number as he walked to his room. Troublov smiled. He dialed the number and waited.

"Is that you?" Troublov recognized the voice. "Good morning, Mr Papov! What a surprise! So what's the news?"

"Why did you go to that American restaurant dressed as a gay?" Papov asked angrily.

Troublov knew the consequences. He didn't realize how serious it was till the call arrived.

"Sorry for the stupidity. I apologize. It will never happen again," said Troublov. "You almost ruined our plan. The undercover agents were waiting for someoneelse, and you happened to waltz in with an old man in his seventies. What do you think you are doing in Bangkok?" Papov exploded.

Troublov was sweating. He hit his forehead several times with his right hand disgusted at his foolish experiment.

"This is the last warning," said Papov, reminding Troublov of the consequences. He continued, "and now listen to me carefully. A man will be waiting for you in the lounge. You have ten minutes to meet him, and listen to him carefully before you act. After that, I will call you," said Papov. He then hung up the phone.

Troublov dressed hurriedly and walked to the lounge anticipating the man Papov just mentioned. Then he realized how stupid he had been for not asking Papov the identity or description of the person. With that thought, he looked around for a clue. He deliberated whether to call Papov again. There were several tourists arriving and departing with their families. He bit his tongue several times under pressure, while looking for the man.

Troublov glanced at his watch. One more minute to go, and before he could walk to the public telephone, a heavy hand pressed his shoulder gently. He couldn't believe his eyes. It was that very same old man he met at the American restaurant.

"Hi, call me Vladimir. Nice meeting you." He didn't elaborate.

Troublov tried to compose himself, as he walked with Vladimir to a quiet corner seat. He realized he had a lot to learn. The only compliment he received from Papov was after the slaughtering of Roman Pavlov a gemstone dealer and a one time close associate of Tito and Miko with a bank account in Cyprus. With two more heads to go, they were not giving him any more chances to relax. That's what he thought.

Vladimir took out a piece of paper and explained the road map for his second mission. In fact, Troublov wanted to know more about Vladimir and his activities, but he was too scared to ask.

"So the next fish is Tito. Is that right?" Troublov asked quickly.

"Goldie, Melvine, Tito and Miko, this time four people. But it is your choice in which order. All the details are in this briefcase. We want you to leave Bangkok, and be with your family as soon as possible," said Vladimir firmly. "And no more mistakes this time."

"I don't have a family in Moscow," added Troublov. "They are all dead."

Vladimir remained silent. Troublov had no idea what Vladimir meant by family. For reasons he couldn't explain, Vladimir remained a mystery. He remembered like it was only yesterday the way Vladimir handled him at the American restaurant, someone with experience.

"Do you like rubies?" It was an unexpected question.

"Why?" Troublov asked.

"Because they are rare, beautiful, durable and, of course, portable. When you add all these attributes, they become highly valuable. You know something," Vladimir added. "Only a very few had the opportunity to hold them. A very few."

"What does that mean?" Troublov asked, puzzled.

"You are going to be the lucky one to hold them. I have yet to see a big one. You shouldn't forget that," said Vladimir, sniffing the air. Troublov couldn't understand why Vladimir was talking indirectly.

"You never collected any rubies from Pavlov, only his stinking dead body. Do you recollect?" Vladimir continued. "But this time you are going to act different. Once, when you finish the job, all the rubies from Tito and Miko should be in a cloth bag, which is in this briefcase."

He handed over his briefcase to Troublov and whispered. "You shouldn't open it here, in your room. You have all the instructions, and their usual meeting places well detailed. Within one week, you should complete your mission, and return this very same briefcase with rubies to your room. You will be leaving Bangkok for Moscow with your reward just after that. Do you have any further questions?"

Troublov sat motionless pondering the deadline. Several questions came to the tip of his mouth. "What happens if I fail?"

Vladimir smiled. "A good wine matures with time. So don't worry. You are on the right track. Just do the right things. The rest will take care of itself. Remember this," he continued, "absolute concentration. That's all that you need."

Troublov paused. Absolute concentration! He repeated the two words quietly in his mind while gazing at Vladimir.

"I got to go," said Vladimir, and rose from his seat. "Read the instructions and maps carefully. You won't have any questions. Take care. Be yourself."

TWENTY EIGHT

It looked like a bright and sunny day after the rain. The biggest and the most attractive rainbow formation in the blue sky caught Rubin's attention, as he stood watching in awe from his room at The Oriental hotel. "Mr Rubyhall! Rubin speaking."

"Oh, Rubin. Where are you now?" Rubyhall asked. He was busy with the Kenyan miners and their rubies.

"I'm calling from The Oriental hotel. What time is appropriate for you?" Rubin asked quickly.

"Uh, let me check. Why don't you come now?" Rubyhall said, while glancing at the rubies and the Kenyan miners.

"Now? Is that O.K?" Rubin added. "By the way, I met a friend here, and she is from Singapore. I told her about you, and would you mind if she comes along with me?"

"She isn't some kind of a bimbo, is she?" Rubyhall too was direct.

"Oh, no. She might be your client in the future. Talk to her and find out her needs. Who knows? Some good deals might come along." Rubyhall wasn't happy at first with Rubin's suggestion.

"Lots of acquaintances have come and gone, sheer waste of time and energy. You know what we deal in, and the type of customers who take up residence in this office. I've no problems with people like you and your father, you know what I mean?" Rubyhall interrupted. "Anyway bring her here if you want, and I think you will do the briefing intelligently to avoid any disappointments. Okay?"

"Done. Dad asked me to send you his regards," Rubin added quickly.

"Where is David now? Is he still in New York?" Rubyhall asked, recalling the good old days with the Rosenberg family.

"Oh, yes. He is busy with his office worries, and you know the economy. He is a bit worried about it," said Rubin, glancing at his palm pc.

"Okay. Come to my office now. What's the time now?" Rubyhall asked.

"Ten."

Rubyhall paused. The Kenyan miners from Nakuru came to a conclusion after intense discussion that the rubies they were carrying didn't match Rubyhall's quality standards.

Since they arrived at his office on Den's recommendation, Rubyhall had to treat them nicely. Otherwise, he would have sent them directly to Jay, instead of wasting his time.

"Well, in that case, we can have lunch together while doing some business, yeah?" Rubyhall suggested. The miners from Nakuru prepared to leave his office.

"Perfect. Let's say, around ten thirty. I should be in the office." Rubyhall waved his hand at them as a goodwill gesture, while his secretary accompanied the Nakuru miners to the reception area. He wanted to get rid of them.

"Looking forward to see you, Rubin. Bye."

"Bye, Mr Rubyhall." He then hung up the phone.

July stood close to Rubin wondering what he had in mind.

"What did he say?" she asked.

"As I told you before, if you give him a hint of doubt, then you are asking for trouble," Rubin continued. "Don't ask any eruptive questions when he shows the stones. He will read you like a book instantly, and then you are rejected. He doesn't like to have people get excited. He believes that shows lack of tradition and experience, and those dropouts would never understand the price difference between an excellent quality and fine. You know what I'm saying? Subjectivity! It's very difficult to analyze. Guess what? You learn that by observation and experience, that's what he is looking for in his clients."

"This is very tough," she quipped.

Rubin got ready to leave. "Its okay," he said. "At least you can observe the way he does business. Just be vigilant. He can very well afford to broadcast his thoughts in harsh words if he thinks it is appropriate. You know something? This is how you learn the likes and dislikes of these big cats in a very short time. It's an experience, which will mold you to be somebody in the future. Not everyone will be lucky enough to work with people like Rubyhall. He is a billionaire! Anyone who attains that pinnacle must be somebody. It's not that easy to accumulate a billion dollars today."

"Are you scaring me?" she asked.

"Let's get ready for the meeting," he reminded. "Just watch your mouth and eyes. You'll like him. I like him. There are a lot who don't like him, but, then that's world. You can't please everyone."

They left the hotel.

TWENTY NINE

Troublov rushed back to his suite and opened the briefcase eagerly. The contents included a gun, a rope, a map, several gloves, a diary, and a few photographs.

He took the gun first and held it in his hand playfully, and aimed at the vase rehearsing a mock execution. He thought of something, and suddenly put the gun back in the briefcase.

The diary was the next intriguing part. It had several addresses, which didn't concern him. But a few pages were folded to indicate something important. He opened the pages and read the notes.

Page fifty had detailed descriptions of Tito's and Miko's daily schedule. Tito frequented Pathumwan Princess hotel's health club. An exercise freak. The timings were marked in black ink.

While Miko loved to hangout at Taurus club on Sukhumvit Road, his mission was to silence them at these spots. Miko's schedules were marked in green ink. Then his inquisitive mind moved to page sixtytwo. It had a detailed record of the secret meetings between Goldie and Sanders at her SV City condo on Rama 3 Road.

Sanders's business dealing with Tito and Miko too were detailed in red ink. He had a deadline of one week, before being spirited out of the country on a fake passport with a new identity. He had no problems executing Roman Pavlov, but the present mission lacked the same commitment and resolution. There was something missing. He had a contract with Papov, and the job had to be executed before the deadline without fail. Troublov was given a freehand to choose either of his targets, first or last. The only requirement Papov demanded was their confirmed dead bodies.

After the delivery, he was a free man with more than enough cash to start a new life in Russia or Finland. Four heads in one week! He put the diary back in the briefcase, and walked to the window for a view. The same old view of countless cars and motorcycles occupied Lad Phrao Road, and the people seemed to tolerate the chaos. After taking a deep breath, he got back to the serious stuff: the execution plan.

He tore a page from the diary, and wrote the dates and times to start the job. But first, he decided to start with Sanders and Goldie, and then Tito. Troublov preferred Miko to be the last.

It was a dream come true. The money and the freedom to do what he liked the most, becoming a politician had to do with the new change in Moscow. The politicians knew how to fill their stomach at others expense, and Troublov decided politics was the best profession in the country, if other endeavors failed. He had no more interest in geology or gemstones. The passion was gone. The sudden turnaround at his job and the personal relationship among his friends also began to wane with time. But he had never killed a woman before. He was too scared to tell Papov the truth, instead he agreed to the conditions due to the timely pressure.

From the photograph, he realized that she was a real knockout. She was blonde, tall, and packed inside a beautiful body. He wriggled in ecstasy just looking at her photograph. He never had any relationship with a woman in Russia or Thailand. For reasons he couldn't explain, he had no interest indulging in such activities. He had a score to settle on behalf of his comrades, and he went the extra mile to meet the goal. That was over.

But the sudden urge from within, after watching her half-naked photograph at some God forbidden beach tickled his mind. He theorized, if she looked beautiful in the picture, then she was something far beyond description in the flesh. And Sanders loafing with her made him angry and jealous. Thinking of Sanders brought back the memories of Pavlov.

He too had a good time with his blonde wife, Katrina. Papov had shown their pictures before the execution in Pathumthani.

At that time, he was more focused to finish Pavlov at any cost. He had a personal vendetta against Pavlov, but never bothered about their natural sex life. Papov had the best photographer in the world secretly record their bedroom gymnastics for a different reason. Though he was shown the video of one such night, Pavlov having sex with Katrina, it didn't really bother him too much. Instead, Troublov kept drinking vodka to prevent himself from falling asleep.

Now after seeing Goldie's picture, old memories began to flood back like yesterday. He didn't want to kill her. His mind wasn't into it. But he had made a promise to Papov. The more he thought about it, the greater it was apparent the guys in Pattaya meant business whether he agreed or not. They were too powerful and well organized, and he was just a messenger in a unique way. He wiped the photograph several times with his hand to feel her face, as if she was in front of him, a typical Russian woman.

The thought of Miko and Tito just disappeared into thin air. They no longer became his priority, even though his instruction was specific. He wanted her to remain alive.

With that sunken feeling, he slumped into the sofa thinking of rescuing her and living with her forever, if possible. Though the idea looked stupid at first, he got the feeling that the money he had already accumulated in a bank in Cyprus was enough to start a new life, away from the influence of crimes and gangs.

A few moments ago, he was thinking of becoming a politician like Zuganov, the communist or Yavilinsky, the reformer, all in a split-second.

Suddenly a smile began to flash across his face. He returned to the diary and read the details regarding Goldie and Sanders. Troublov couldn't believe his eyes, the way the meetings between Sanders and Goldie were recorded in the logbook. Someone was living in the building watching their movements closely or some insider was feeding the info at cost. But there was no video of their activities inside the condo. He would have loved to watch that erotic experience. That thought itself induced a bulge in his pants instantly. He looked at it first casually, and then laughed repeatedly.

A crazy thought. He couldn't get away with it. Her face began to appear in his mind. He tried to push it aside, but kept coming back. He didn't know why. He thought there must be a reason. What reason? He hadn't a clue.

And there it was. He flicked the pages, and on page 102 there was a detailed account of her business activities in Bangkok. She was a rich woman, but in a different way. Now Troublov realized, he hadn't the remotest chance of living with her. He hated that and out of disappointment and anger, he hit the wall with his fist several times.

No machete! Just the gun! He stuck the photographs of Sanders, Goldie, Tito, and Miko, on the sofa separately for mock execution. Deep in his mind there was a little voice in him moaning in silence about what he was doing. And that little voice kept coming back repeatedly with each gunshot. Instead, he kept chanting 'Papov' steadfast to avoid distraction. And, he wanted to win this time.

THIRTY

The receptionist at Ris Rubyhall Towers was waiting for July Lim and Rubin Rosenberg.

"Mr Rubyhall!" July extended her hand to greet Rubyhall, as he walked towards her in a jovial mood.

"July Lim!" Rubyhall said. "Why don't you pull up a chair and sit comfortably? All right, would you mind me calling you, Ms Lim?"

"July, please!" she said cutely.

"Okay, July, I heard from Rubin that you are a resident of President Park. Is that right?" Rubyhall asked, while closing three stone boxes.

"Yeah. We have a condo. It belongs to my dad," she replied, smiling heartily. She wondered why he was asking such questions.

"How did you meet Rubin?" he asked.

"Happy accident, I must say," she said, glancing at Rubin. He nodded gracefully.

"I believe Rubin had done the introduction," Rubyhall continued. "I have other businesses, but ruby is very special to me, and I keep collecting them from all over the world. I have a special ruby desk, and Jay Lam is the man in control. We work together gathering information regarding demand and supply, and do the best in the interest of the trade to stabilize the market. I don't have any monopoly in this business. It's a free enterprise country, and I work within the rules of my country. People outside might say otherwise, but it is not always true. I respect free speech and thought. So I've no control over their lives. But I do have control in my business, and I believe that's why I'm still here doing what

I like best. I've a line of faithful clients who have stood by me during the good and bad times and Rubin's father, David, is one of them. I know the tastes and likes of my special clients, and they in return respect and reward me with repeat business."

"May I interrupt?" July said. "I'm really impressed. I should have met you a long time ago. I've a client in Indonesia who wants a 15carat ruby, the best. Price is not an issue at all. Rubin told me that you are the right person. But I'm really impressed with everything that you said."

"Thank you," he added. "There shouldn't be a problem with a 15carat or 50carat, I have it all. Let me show you something. Perhaps, you might want to look at it."

Rubyhall walked to his safe deposit vault and removed two black stone boxes, and laid them on his table. He opened them slowly and laid twenty rubies of various shapes on a white tray.

"Wow!" She immediately remembered Rubin's advice and managed to restrain herself.

"Do any of these match your specifications?" Rubyhall asked. Rubin remained silent during the period studying both, Rubyhall and July.

"I think so. The round brilliant cut ruby. What's the weight of that ruby?" she asked curiously.

"Let me weigh it again to confirm," Rubyhall said, switching on the electronic weighing balance. "This piece is 15.01carat. The price is in this envelope. Look first. Do you like it?"

"Beautiful! I think this is it. You've made my day, Mr Rubyhall." July began to get excited. She had never seen anything like this before in such quantity.

"Now if you like it, and if you think this is the color and shape your client requested, the deal is you can take it to Indonesia, and show it to your customer. Give her a chance to romance and feel the stone and then call me. I'll give you other details. The ruby is with you," said Rubyhall, surprising her.

July glanced at Rubin and Rubyhall with disbelief. She had never dreamt of anyone taking her for granted and giving this ex-

clusive privilege. She remembered Rubin's advice again. She had
remained composed but deep inside she wanted to scream, because she had never seen such beauties before. If she had the money,
she wanted to buy the whole two stone boxes and immerse herself
with their color in her privacy. A dream! Who would dare blame
her!

"I'll take it," replied July calmly.

Rubyhall watched her gestures carefully. He purposely extended
this offer to test her confidence and understanding of the tradition
and trust. It was an indirect message as to how influential people
did trade with such beauties sometimes without any documenta-
tion.

"So you like that ruby, don't you? Let me wrap it in a nice
stone box for you. Do you want to carry it with you? Or you can
come and pick it up when you leave Bangkok for Indonesia. Either
way, I want you to make sure the stone is in safe hands. It's up to
you," said Rubyhall, glancing at Rubin. Rubin was totally absorbed by the swift pace at which the whole transaction ended.

"I will take it with me, Mr Rubyhall. Thank you very much.
You saved my time. Here is my card," she answered.

"You see how simple it is when it comes to buying good quality rubies," Rubyhall said. "Connection! That's where your success and spectacular failure is, if you don't have one. You can stay
in Bangkok, or wherever there are rubies, but finding the one you
like is sheer luck and planning. One thing I want to emphasize
here is it's very difficult to find a round brilliant cut ruby due to
weight loss. But one good thing is, I have what others don't have."

"I believe so, Mr Rubyhall," said July, rubbing the stone in
her hand.

Rubin slipped a note to Rubyhall, as he walked to his safe
deposit vault. Rubyhall opened it, and read the content. "Why
don't we have lunch together at my office?"

July glanced at Rubin. He nodded.

"I usually don't eat that much nowadays," Rubyhall continued. "The doctors have been constantly reminding me of this ef-

fect and that effect. Who the hell cares? I'm already seventy. Not that many years left. So today I eat what I like. Probably, you will have to eat what I eat. Just for one day." The nephrite carved dining table stood majestically bringing together his most distinguished client.

Rubin Rosenberg!

"Oh, no problem. We would very much appreciate that," replied July.

"What do we have here? Homemade pizza, hamburger, spaghetti, fish, vegetables and fruits! July, you must be familiar with all these combinations. Help me to arrange them accordingly. At my home, I've a wonderful wife, who takes care of me like a child. I'm lucky, and still am," echoed Rubyhall.

Rubyhall saw her inexperienced hand struggling to put them on to the plate. He looked at Rubin and winked.

"You will be extremely lucky if you can find a good husband someday in your life," he said jokingly. He then continued, "These are all the basics a woman must know no matter how busy you are. I tell this all the time to my friend's daughters, who are good in other crafts, but not at home. Then I remind the women in my office of one thing. No matter how busy you are, home is the place you go back to rest. Both, men and women must know today how to run a home. Times have changed okay no more lecture. Let's have something to fill our hungry stomachs." He motioned Rubin and July to go ahead instead of waiting for him to start.

"Could you please pass that orange juice?" Rubyhall asked, smilingly.

"Sure," said Rubin. "Here it is, Mr Rubyhall."

"Perhaps, you might know my father. He comes regularly to Bangkok," reminded July.

"I think so. Mr Lim, right?" Rubyhall recalled. "Singapore! I think I've met him. Let me remember, yeah, on two occasions. I remember. At the Queen Sirikit Convention Center! You look very much like him."

July's face blushed. Rubin looked at her, and then smiled.

"So you want to be a ruby dealer in Indonesia?" Rubyhall asked, sipping the orange juice.

"Oh, not really," she added. "It was a friend of mine who introduced me to this lady, a Suharto relative and a family friend, let me put it that way. She asked me if I could get a ruby of 15carat, as an anniversary present for her beloved husband. I said I would try. So here I am with the right type of stone out of nowhere. I still can't believe my eyes."

"Well, in this case a lucky husband and lucky you," replied Rubyhall. "How many wives today will think of giving their husband such a memorable and expensive gift? She must be a very special person to do such a thing. The husband also must be a good one to deserve this special gesture. Well, that's the allure of this trade. Romance, illusion, charm, affection, relationship, love, all intertwine to make a sale and ruby stands out as their favorite. And I love to repeat that again. I have what they don't have. I'm quite proud of that privilege, and I love to hear people telling how happy they are after wearing this magnificent piece. It's god's gift. How come you two are deceptively quiet? Eat more of the pizza and vegetables. Don't waste. Finish the whole thing. There's some nice wine in the cupboard. Help yourself. I'll stay with the orange juice. You two finish those two bottles, yeah?" Rubyhall reminded them.

"We would like to listen to your experiences and words of wisdom. Rubin has more than enough experience. I'm just a greenhorn. I have a lot to learn before I buy with full confidence." July said, while pouring the wine into two glasses. There was a clink, and then Rubyhall continued.

"You have to keep buying knowing your priorities," Rubyhall said. "Teaching how to buy is very difficult. You have to learn by observation and planning. You might succeed in coining a few words to explain certain attributes of color, which is very important with rubies, but there is something much deeper. Only a developed mind can absorb and understand, and no words can explain what exactly you are thinking at that particular time. The advantage of working with someone who has access to all different types of top quality stones is that you will never forget the experience, because they don't come out of the ground all the time. Rubies are my specialty. Now you understand somewhat of what I mean by quality? Could you please pass me those vegetables and fruits?" He continued, "Rubin has an angle in doing things like I do. His father was no different. I had no problem working with both of them. Two different generations."

"I believe so," replied July. "I should have known him a long time ago."

Rubin just listened to their conversation allowing them to talk more about themselves.

"Time, time and time. It's so important in this trade, because you just don't know when the time comes. The anticipation is there so what is needed is perseverance. Then all follows in order with a little bit of luck. Today you just can't be an expert of gemstones, but must have an eye on other factors, which directly and indirectly influence the price of the stones. You should know the world you live in updating all the time, very important. There is a lot of chaff out there, which is of no use in any way. INFORMATION! If you have it correctly, then you are ahead of others in every respect. For that you must have that access code, which will save your expensive time. How do you do that?" Rubyhall asked

"How?" July glanced at Rubyhall and Rubin.

"Keep your eyes and ears open with a closed mouth," answered Rubyhall. "That's the unwritten rule of the day, everyday. July, Rubin have you had enough?"

"I think so. Two bottles of Bolla Bardolino Superiore, and all of the food, it was absolutely delicious," Rubin said, tapping his bulging stomach.

"I don't think so. You are trying to please me with these flowery words. Are you sure you had enough?" Rubyhall asked, a bit worried.

"Of course, Mr Rubyhall."

"Okay, leave everything here. The office girls will clear the table," Rubyhall said.

"No, Mr Rubyhall. I'll clean up the table. Just give me fifteen minutes." July replied, as she rushed to the kitchen to pick up the gloves.

"Well, I can join you and cut that fifteen minutes, perhaps, to ten minutes," said Rubin.

"Okay, I'll finally join you guys when I've put all the things in the right place. You see the difference in what I said few minutes ago?" Rubyhall said with a smile.

"I do," replied July. "I now realize how stupid and timid I have been all these days. I feel ashamed of myself. Thank you for that friendly reminder."

"What a wonderful day!"

THIRTY ONE

After July had left for Siam Discovery Center, Rubin moved closer to Rubyhall to discuss the serious stuff. Rubies! Big ones!

"Mr Rubyhall, I had to do it that way. The note, I hope you didn't mind," Rubin said with a grin. He didn't want July to know the number and sizes of the rubies he had intended to buy from Rubyhall. Business and friendship always went separate. A cherished lesson he had learned from his dad.

"No . . . no . . . . no. It's just fine," said Rubyhall, holding Rubin's hand. "That's the way you should do. You don't buy stones to show someone that you know how to buy stones. It's stupid and unwise. You lose money doing it that way just to impress someone. July had gone to do her business or whatever. She is happy. It's like winning a jackpot lottery for her, isn't it?" He continued with a meaningful smile, "I'm giving a loose rope to see how far she can afford to go. The reason I did her favor was when they see she can afford to buy or find such stones these people will contact her again and again to buy bigger ones. It's a self-promotion building up confidence and trust. Where will she go to find such pieces? Ris Rubyhall! She will come here. She wouldn't go elsewhere. I've what others don't have. I took a small risk, which I can afford anyway. Let's see what happens when she comes back. Okay, let's get back to business."

Rubin understood everything, the meaning behind Rubyhall's proud statement. He had heard the statement countless times before when Ris had tamed a novice client.

The ruby whisperer! Rubyhall had the knack, patience, and

the stones to deliver when in time of need. It was such a marvel to watch Rubyhall finesse a client.

"Right," said Rubin, extracting a piece of paper from his pocket. "What I need is five pieces. A merchant banker needs the biggest size. 37carat! He wants to give it to his beloved wife in commemoration of their 37th wedding anniversary as a special present. I need two stones of 20carat each for a rich gay couple in Manhattan. One stone of 25carat for a special lady in the White House, and one stone of 30carat for a rich businessman from Hollywood for his Chinese mistress. All Burmese rubies! What do you say Mr Rubyhall?"

Rubyhall walked to his safe deposit vault, and removed two more brown boxes and laid them on the table. He opened the first box, and removed two 20carat stones and put them aside. "Open the master stone box and check its color, clarity and cut," Rubyhall said. "See if it meets your standard. They are twin stones: ovals cut from the same rough good enough for the gay couple. Is the color good?"

"Yeah," said Rubin, after a quick glance face-up (table-up). "It's good. Perfect! They will like it."

"They have certificates from Switzerland stating origin," Rubyhall added.

"Here is your 25carat piece, again Burmese, oval. Check its color, clarity and cut." He opened the second brown box for Rubin to view.

Rubyhall walked back to his safe deposit vault again remembering another box. He opened it recollecting a certain shape and said softly, "I found your 30carat piece, Burmese, oval. Have a look, before I can find your 37carat piece!"

Rubin put all the stones he had requested on the tray, and looked at each of the pieces, side by side, to see the color shift and the quality of luster. They all glowed like embers, as he looked at them in different positions. A life of their own! He had before him what he had asked for, and more.

"Look son, I'm terribly sorry to disappoint you," said Rubyhall.

"Give me a couple of days to get your biggest piece 37carat. I've bigger sizes, like 40carats and above, but not that precise 37carat piece. I'll get it for you." He apologized.

"One more piece, and then I can leave for New York," replied Rubin. "Dad will be happy. I must call and tell him." He said in a low tone, while writing the details of four stones on the invoice. Rubyhall now had all the reasons to hate Jay like a Satan. "37carat ruby!" He had never in his life sent anyone from his office empty-handed. They always got the pieces they had asked for. He had the entire stock of the best in the world in his safe.

"Are you happy with the four pieces?" Rubyhall asked.

"Perfectly happy!"

"Don't worry about the prices. It will all be taken care of," Rubyhall said, "and once I get that 37carat ruby in place, we will talk about the final numbers."

"Fine with me." Rubin had no problems with that suggestion.

While putting back the stones in his safe deposit vault, Rubyhall thought for a sec. How on earth was he going to find that 37carat ruby? He knew for sure, Tito and Miko had the piece. Lam had become a good for nothing. The custodians were much smarter. If worse comes to worse, he might have to re-cut the 40carat ruby to match the 37carat. That means a loss of 3carat, a lot of money. The worst scenario in two days! IMPOSSIBLE!

"Okay, Mr Rubyhall," said Rubin. "I'll take the 4 pieces, and when should I come to collect the last one?"

"In less than a week," answered Rubyhall, confidently. "It will be here, right here. My word!"

"Your word is my word. The invoices, I've prepared and duly signed." They shook hands like always. Rubyhall kept the rubies selected by Rubin separate in his safe deposit vault.

"Don't worry about that. Trust and word is more than enough," said Rubyhall, accompanying Rubin to the front door.

They shook hands once again, and Rubin left the office with a confident smile.

THIRTY TWO

The doorbell rang at the OPO condo, one among the several condominiums Sanders owned for business and pleasure. Melvine got the scare of his life. He gazed at the closed circuit TV screen, and to his dismay it was a woman. Goldie!

He couldn't believe his eyes. He rushed to the door, and opened it with a hearty smile. "Goldie, what a surprise? How did you manage to find my address? Please come in."

"Thank you," she said. "Your name card, of course. I heard a lot of rumors."

"What rumors?" Sanders asked, puzzled.

"About your wife?" she reminded.

"Please don't talk about her," he added. "Whenever I think about the bitch, I get itchy. She deserved what she got."

"It is inhumane to hit your wife like that, Melvine, especially, in front of your daughter. What will she think about you from now onwards? I was shocked." Goldie pulled up a chair and sat opposite gazing at him intently.

"If you were there when that happened, you wouldn't talk to me like this. I'll never forget what she said at that time, when she was supposed to work out a practical solution." Sanders tried to justify his statement. But she looked unconvinced.

"Whatever the situation may be, it was wrong," she said. "That's why I came to express my anger and condolences."

"What for, Goldie?" Sanders asked with a loud laughter.

"We belong to the same gender, Melvine," she continued. "I'm stuck. I just can't find the right words. Would you do something like that to me?"

"Of course not," Sanders reasoned. "Chin is just the opposite. I still can't believe my eyes why on earth I married her in the first place. And a daughter exactly like her, dumb as dumb. Sorry to say that, but that's the truth. A biological mistake. Instead of arguing about my family and crap like that, let's change the topic. What really brings you here, Goldie? I'm just curious. Pardon me, if I'm too direct."

"To see you first," she answered, "and to know the truth about your wife's fate. My husband is going to India for a few weeks. Business, I guess. So if you have free time, perhaps, you might be interested to come and visit me. The door is open." Sanders couldn't resist the offer.

"Oh, that's a privilege," he said. "Now thank you for that gesture. I should never disappoint you in that respect. But I'm going through a severe crisis at the moment."

"What do you mean?" Goldie asked, confused.

"Business," he said quickly. She didn't understand what he meant.

"That bad? I wish I could have helped somehow," she quipped.

"Forget it, Goldie," Sanders said. "You shouldn't get involved in this murky situation. You might get killed. Home is better for you. You are good at nonviolent activities." She kept gazing at him, and then woke up to give him a meaningful smile.

"I think so," she replied. "I have to leave now. My driver will be at the car park any moment. Anyway, thank you very much for your time, and please don't beat your wife. Try not to disappoint me. You know me too well, don't you?"

"Wait a minute. Don't leave that quickly. I can drop you at your home," he said hurriedly.

"You can't do that. You have already more than enough problems. I think it is better to keep it low profile. That way we both will be safe," said Goldie, as she rose to leave.

"You just came to my room like a flash, and you are leaving me just like that?" Sanders said disappointedly.

"You will be seeing me again anyway," she added. "Once you

are free from all worries, we will have all the time in the world to talk about a lot of things."

"When is that going to happen? Next life?" he pleaded.

"You must make your peace with Chin, Melvine. You may not like her now, but remember, you lived with her for more than fifteen years. Is that right?" Goldie began to talk like his mother.

"So what?" Sanders said. "Everybody does that just a mechanical life. No warmth, love, understanding; instead, just money ruled for fifteen years. I paid bills for that facility, and am still paying. I don't know what for. You are different. You understand me. I've no problem with that. Give me a chance, Goldie. That's what I mean."

"I have to go, Melvine. See you soon and take care." She had already gone.

"What the fuck was that all about?" he uttered spontaneously.

THIRTY THREE

Rubyhall became restless. Now that Rubin had gone to his hotel in peace, the missing 37carat ruby kept haunting him. He had several appointments with various government agencies instead he called his secretary to cancel them all till further notice. His mind was now totally focused on this one piece of 37carat ruby, and at whatever the cost he had to get the piece for Rubin. Otherwise, he would be losing his face. He had never disappointed the Rosenberg family.

He waited patiently for Lam at his office, an unusually rare gesture. He could have called Lam to his office. Instead, Rubyhall sat there weighing several options. As Lam entered his office, he got the surprise of his life.

Ris Rubyhall!

"Where is the beef, Jay?" Rubyhall exploded.

"I'm trying my best, Mr Rubyhall," Lam answered politely knowing Rubyhall's temper.

"If you don't get that 37carat ruby, you are tattooed first, and then fired. My patience has reached its limit. It is exasperated at your incompetence and lack of foresight. I can't tolerate this nonsense anymore. Do you have any idea how much it is costing me to employ you? I don't want to talk about that now. My credibility is on the ropes. You understand that, don't you?" Rubyhall said angrily.

"Mr Rubyhall, it's just one telephone call," Lam reasoned. "That call will make all the difference. He controls the whole situation. Not me nor you."

"What are you talking about?" Rubyhall asked, staring at Lam, puzzled.

"I'm talking about Winston Lord," said Lam, "your one time partner. Just a friendly call, the whole saga will come to an end. The ruby belongs to him. Tito and Miko are just proxies. It's just as simple as that."

"So are you telling me to go and kneel down in front of Winston, and beg for pardon, and the 37carat ruby? Do you think he will just hand it over to me at my request? You are crazy and out of touch. I don't know why I had to ask your help. You are talking like a kid out of school. This is not what I expected from you, Jay. Pathetic performance! I can't believe my ears," cried Rubyhall. He knew something was going wrong and he needed a guinea pig.

"Mr Rubyhall, having said that, I've to remind you of one more thing. You are out of your mind, and out of touch with the real world. I don't care what you think about me. As I said, I don't fucking care about your ruby. Anyone with a developed brain can guess from a distance who is right and who is wrong. You are wrong, Mr Rubyhall. A hundred percent!" Lam swiftly shot back at Rubyhall. He knew the risk of losing his job for such an outburst, but he had no other choice.

"Watch your words, Jay," said Rubyhall. "I've a name, but you haven't. You will pay a hefty price for this arrogance and disrespect," said Rubyhall angrily.

"I don't fucking care about your name and respect. I did respect you once upon a time. I thank you from the bottom of my heart, for giving me the best facilities during the earlier period of my job with you. But now you have dragged my reputation to the level of a street cop, forcing me to chase some stupid ruby dealers. You have an ego problem. I'm sure that the 37carat ruby belong to Winston Lord. You might have done some stupid thing to make him hate you like a Satan. And now, I'm sandwiched between you two giants, for what? Do you want me to kill him and bring the ruby to you? If you guarantee me that you will take care of my family and kids, then I'll do the extreme thing. What do you say, Mr. Rubyhall?" Lam could have done better, but that's all he could say.

Rubyhall sat silently listening to Jay's emotionally charged lecture. He just couldn't answer Jay's torrential questions.

"I may be wrong, but the boss is always right," Rubyhall said bluntly.

"What the hell does that mean? You are not accepting your responsibility by any means. You used me like a donkey to drag the issue for a long time. If you really didn't like me, you should have told me a long time ago, the dignified way. If you have any convincing reasons to prove a lack of confidence in my work, I would have accepted that, but not this way. This is a cheap shot for a man of your status and respect as you claim. You threatened me a few minutes ago that you will tattoo and fire me if I don't bring the 37carat ruby back, right? I'm telling you again if you want me to be a gangster blowing off people's heads in the guise of professionalism, sorry guys wrong number. Maybe, I'll not work in the same business, but I'll do something else which gives me more peace of mind and less of a drag like now. If I find one such job, I'll be happy. So when do you want me to leave? Now? Tell me. I've nothing more to care about. I've had enough. You dragged me to the end it in a rough way. So be it," said Lam unrepentantly. Rubyhall was silent.

You could have heard a pin drop. His mind was elsewhere. He was least interested in Lam's gospel. Rubyhall was brewing with some other ideas.

THIRTY FOUR

As days passed by, raising two million dollars became more difficult than expected. Sanders was taking more time in the guise of technical discussions while his partners remained at least seriously committed to the deal. This is what both, Tito and Miko, couldn't understand. This was a once in a lifetime deal benefiting everyone involved, and pieces such as these needed no further discussions. The profit was already there.

The magic combination of price, quality, and a client was taking more time than usual to make it a reality. But knowing Sanders, Jeb, and Baddy, the only thing Miko and Tito could wish was to wait till their technical discussions were over. Another waiting game!

On the other hand, Lam kept calling Tito to sell the piece only to Rubyhall. Tito didn't know that Lam's future was at stake because of a 37carat ruby. And straying away from the promise they had with Lord was more than enough to remind them that ones word meant honor, and violation or deviation meant guaranteed death. Above all, one Pierre Themiro wanted to become a partner, and he too after the convincing call to his office a few days ago was taking more time. He never bothered to visit Tito's office. When calls such as these arrived, false commitments were obviously expected. Miko and Tito had no problem living with that nuisance. It was just a coincidence that they had to beg Sanders and his partners to become partners in this one time only deal. They had the money, but it was tied up with other deals and canceling them would have done more harms than good. It was a real catch-22 situation.

Tito had done the calculation already. Fifty-fifty! One million each! They chipped in one million, and Tito and Miko took care of the rest. There was already more than five million dollars arriving from the account of a Swiss gem collector to their account in Cyprus, but that would be available for disposal only after four weeks. Tito and Miko couldn't wait any longer knowing the typical nature of the ruby trade. It took only a split-second for anyone to like or dislike a ruby not because of the ruby, but some other important things had arrived to claim the money. They already had a client lined up, and she had only one interest. That was to keep collecting rubies no matter what the price, because she had the kind of money to spare. Very rarely could anyone find clients like Polly Win. If the world requested her to display her collections of rubies, famous museums around the world would gasp for breath just looking at them.

She herself had no clue as to how many rubies she had, and neither did her husband. His only commitment towards her was to keep her happy. So buying rubies became a ritual whenever she requested, knowing that one-day a big business deal was awaiting Phil to justify the millions he had already spent on Polly.

Money meant nothing to Phil Win, because it was flowing to his bank account from all sort of business deals, commodities, stock market, computers, hotels, restaurants and real estate, like the Chao Phraya river, never ending. The only reason he could account for this was not because he was smart or intelligent, but due to Polly's luckcharm. A Buddhist monk revealed the enlightening news to Phil while on a merit making ceremony in the northern province of Chiang Rai, and since then he hadn't looked back. His business prospered tremendously beyond expectation.

Then there was this British Lotto craze. Chichi had already bought the tickets, another stupid thing to do. But they had nothing much to lose. If they won, fine enough. If not, they had no problem. It was just that the dates had arrived in time for a chance situation.

Tito and Miko had only one interest, which was to get the

37carat ruby at two million and by any means. Once the money was transferred to Winston Lord's account in Switzerland, their worries were over. Most important of all, they already had a client willing to pay twice the price Lord was asking for. As always, the timing had to be right and realistic, which in turn was the most unpredictable part of this magic equation. At times it clicked as planned. That was the fun and pain of this ruby trade. No one had the magic formula for a successful buy or sell situation. It just fell into the right place with a right client at the right time. So with this situation both, Miko and Tito, had only one choice. Wait.

THE WAITING GAME!

They knew already that pushing Sanders and his partners too much for a decision meant disaster. Another deal wouldn't be anywhere near the horizon if they were looking for a partnership. After all, they had no problem with money and their business interests and priorities always had to be taken into account anyway.

But the chance of losing a 37carat ruby of good quality meant more to both, Tito and Miko. It had just fallen into their hand, and they didn't want to lose it.

Sanders and Jeb carved their niche in history a few years ago buying a 47carat ruby from a Cambodian tycoon for an undisclosed amount when there were already several buyers from New York, Switzerland, and Tokyo waiting at a hotel in Phnom Penh. No one had a clue how Jeb and Sanders outmaneuvered those giants to convince this tycoon, who happened to be a close associate of the strongman and the Prime Minister of Cambodia, Hun Sen, to change his mind and sell it to them. That news sent shock waves in the ruby circle, the talent, shrewdness, and the money these two guys had to funnel to obtain the ruby out of Cambodia. With such spectacular buying and selling tactics recorded, Tito and Miko had no other choice other than pray, till the whole deal was over.

THIRTY FIVE

The wait at Chantaburi did yield some results, but the rubies were small. Marty and Pascal decided to leave for Bangkok, after being given the address of one Boonchu at Gem Plaza on Mahesak Road. Then came the good news, he was a dealer in big sizes.

Marty and Pascal were shown a parcel of rubies at the Bangkok office of Boonchu, a ruby dealer from Mae Sai. His agents got the information from the gem market that two foreigners were looking for big stones. After learning that money wasn't a big problem for them, he decided to show them good ones, but slowly.

EYE CLEANING!

All the rubies shown were big sizes. There were three rubies, oval shaped, in the 8 to 10carat range. They were red with a slight tint of orange. Overall, the pieces looked good.

Then Boonchu showed them two pieces of rubies from Burma. One was 13carat, and the other, 18carat, cushion shaped beauty. Colors were red with a slight tint of violet. The rubies had visible inclusions face-up (table-up) with a large pavilion bulge. Overall, the color wasn't that bad, an average stone due to the influence of inclusions coupled with a bad cut.

Marty glanced at Pascal for her opinion. She didn't like the rubies. But Marty still had a liking for the three orange red rubies. He put them aside for a while. Boonchu took his time to get a feel of their color taste. He was showing rubies of different qualities incrementally, instead of putting good ones first.

He took another box of rubies from his safe and removed five stone packets. On a white background, he put the rubies face-up (table-up) for them to view. One 20carat, 24 carat, 26carat, 30carat, and 36carat were laid on the table respectively. All were oval shaped with a slight degree of pink and violet overtones. The absence of orange or brown tint face-up (table-up) made them desirable choices.

Marty liked all the rubies. The brilliancy flashes were so good he couldn't differentiate the qualities between the five rubies.

Boonchu smiled at them. He knew they had shown some interest in the rubies after studying their faces. Marty glanced at Pascal. She nodded.

"What are the prices for the 13 and 18carat rubies plus the five rubies?" Marty asked Boonchu.

"You like it, don't you?" he commented.

Instead, he wrote on a piece of paper the stone prices for all the rubies separately. Boonchu waited for their reaction.

"Are these numbers the last price?" Pascal interrupted. Boonchu nodded.

Marty and Pascal glanced at each other finding it hard to make a decision. Knowing their mind, Boonchu intervened to make them feel relaxed and less guilty.

"Take your time. No need to rush for decisions. You can come any day you like within this week," he said. As if he remembered something, he continued, "and if you are interested in viewing a 37carat ruby, you should come tomorrow. A broker has promised to show me the piece. Someone from Pattaya wants to sell. Okay."

"Great," Marty added, "and you have some real nice pieces here. We will come tomorrow. What time is right for you?"

Boonchu glanced at his watch and said, "In the afternoon, say around two."

The next day, Marty and Pascal arrived Boonchu's office at around two fifteen. After careful thought they decided to buy the 30carat and 36carat piece, but the office had a lot of people and Marty wondered what was going on. They waited outside for the crowd to leave.

By two thirty, Boonchu appeared smiling heartily first, and then apologized for the inconvenience.

"The ruby is here," said Boonchu, "I haven't studied the stone very well, so if you want to look, do so."

"That's fine. Thank you," answered Pascal.

He walked to the safe and removed a small plastic box from a cloth bag. He laid the 37carat ruby on a white pad for them to view. "The broker says, it is a clean stone and well cut. I think the ruby has a good color which is very unusual and difficult for rubies nowadays," said Boonchu.

Pascal had never seen Marty's face glow before. He was so captivated by the beauty of this one piece, without even thinking further he took the ruby and laid it on his hand to see the color contrast.

The ruby looked the same red under fluorescent, incandescent, and skylight. He was in an excited mood. Marty didn't even bother asking Pascal's opinion. She noticed his sudden excitement and kept her cool temper.

"Wha, Wha, Wha, What's the price of this ruby?" Marty asked quickly.

"I don't know yet, because the broker just left the piece with me in the morning," said Boonchu, "but he should be back in the office by late evening. Why?"

"I like the piece, and I want to buy it," said Marty.

"Excuse me, Mr Boonchu," Pascal interrupted. Boonchu had to rush to the toilet. She took Marty's hand and walked to the corner angrily.

"What's going on? Are you so screwedup with the stones? How come you are not asking my opinion? Do you think I don't understand the situation?" she cried. There was a quick reconciliation after the brief outburst.

"Oh, I'm sorry. Peace, peace! I understand what you are saying. Peace, peace! I don't want Boonchu to see your angry face. Smile like an angel when you take your seat," said Marty, trying to soothe her.

When Boonchu returned from the lavatory both, Marty and

Pascal, were still glued to the ruby and studying its features. He was talking on his mobile to Chai, who had delivered the ruby at his office.

Chai, seeing an opportunity come from an unexpected corner said to Boonchu to sell the ruby, taking into account his commission and other expenses for $1.25 million.

After hearing the price, Boonchu felt something was wrong with the number or quality. He didn't say anything further, because talking over the phone meant someone was listening all the time. He hated that. Instead, with this deal, he wanted the broker and Marty to negotiate separately, because it was not his ruby.

After a pause, he relayed the news to Marty to wait for the broker to arrive instead. That sounded like a fair deal for Marty and Pascal.

"Ah, one more thing," continued Marty. "I would like to buy the 30carat and 36carat rubies." He hesitated first, but asked, "Do you think this is your last price for the rubies? Sorry to bother you, I know the price, since you wrote it on this piece of paper. Can you just, you know?"

Boonchu knew what they meant. In order to avoid further confusion and distrust, he said firmly the quoted price was his last price. He convinced them that the price was fair.

Marty and Pascal nodded. Before they could ask about the mode of payment, Boonchu said to transfer the money first to his bank account in Hong Kong. Once he had the confirmation of the transfer from his financial consultant, they could pick the ruby. That was the deal.

Pascal sent an electronic mail to her lawyer in Geneva to transfer the money through their Swiss bank to the Hong Kong bank. Boonchu checked the money transfer with his bank and his financial consultant. It was quick and precise.

Boonchu was expecting another question from either of them. They weren't asking. And he decided to leave it like that for the time being. It was the identification report regarding the rubies he had just sold.

"So," Marty hesitated first, and then continued, "the ruby is with me, or I should say with us." He then glanced at Pascal and smiled. "Do you think we should wait here for Chai to come? I'm really interested in that 37carat ruby," Pascal inquired.

"Yep. That's what he said to me on the phone. By the way, if you need any more rubies you know where to come," said Boonchu jokingly.

Marty and Pascal laughed. "Sure."

They waited patiently.

THIRTY SIX

It was Friday evening, and gem dealers thronged at The Redd's to ease the tensions and gossip about the business of the week. A Singha beer became a good starter, as the conversation became intense and lively.

Mike knew how to inspire the gem dealers with a humorous remark, and then the conversation went from one thing to another sparking laughter. There were a few of the regulars missing.

Tito and Miko were nowhere to be seen. But there were others who loved to gossip at the latest blunder or arrival of a new ruby from the best known source, Burma. Everyone loved to hold a Burmese ruby in hand and scream aloud. But they never came. Good ones remained only in lucky hands.

"If Rubyhall is after the ruby, then it is worth giving it a try. He would never touch an ugly duckling. The ruby definitely must be a beautiful swan. If we all dig in together, you know, we could all give him the surprise of his life," Pinto Pin whispered hurriedly at James Carr, another gem dealer from London.

"He is a smart cookie," added James. "His sharp eyes will probably control the price. But, where is the source?"

"No one knows for sure," said Pinto, "but one thing I know is that it is in Bangkok, and someone is holding it to get the best price."

Mike walked to their table and gave them a pat moving to the next table. Just to let them know that he was with them. There was a tele replay of world cup soccer match between Nigeria and Denmark. No one seemed interested. There wasn't enough energy in their play, but still they wanted to be there just to watch.

"You shouldn't forget that Ris has a history of using proxies to kill the price," said Pinto, "and his loyal lieutenants, all some kind of ghosts keep orbiting the dealers offices chasing the ruby. So, how are you gonna handle it? At the end of the day, he will end up owning the ruby for life. That's how he does business. You think we can compete with him this way?"

Tim Song joined the group with his girlfriend. Pinto and James never bothered to ask her name, and waited for Song to do the introduction. A common-play among friends. He was a ruby dealer, but never had the opportunity to hold a big one. All he had were rubies below 5 carat. That was his market. Since he had saved enough money to move to a bigger range, he waited for an opportunity.

"I have one dream in my life," said Song, clearing his throat. "Only one. That's to beat the old man, only one time with a good price. I don't care if I win or lose. Purely for sentimental reasons, I would just love to get a chance to do that. If what you are telling turns out to be true, I want to gamble on that 37 carat ruby. Find out the full details and get back to me."

Everyone laughed. They knew Song was really dreaming. Competing with Ris Rubyhall was an altogether different gem game, and the Bangkok dealers knew it too well.

"What happens if we can't track the gem in time, and the gem ends up in one of those auction houses, like Christie's or Sotheby's?" James aired his concern.

"Find the asshole, and sell his meat to those hungry bushmen of Papua New Guinea. We must prevent this happening at any cost. I want hand to hand combat with Rubyhall. I need all the publicity, which will definitely bring in a lot of media speculation. Confusion and chaos is always good for this kind of business. Use it to its zenith. I want to see that 37 carat ruby in my hand live. I'll end up paying more. Just one last wish. That's all," Song said, in a heroic way.

None of them took it seriously. They knew the beer had gone into his brain too fast.

"I think you are dreaming too much," Pinto answered. "Have realistic goals for yourself, then you will sleep well. By the way, how is your chick Maria doing? She looks a bit fat. Is she pregnant?"

Song's girlfriend looked surprised at first, and then gazed at Song. Since he didn't bother to introduce her, no one dared to ask her name. Instead, he whispered in her ear to say it was a joke.

"Is she? I don't know. How do you know if a woman is pregnant?" he asked, playing innocent.

"Song, don't try to jerk me around," said Pinto. "You are the stud master of this street, and if you don't know, then who else would know?"

That statement frightened Song's girlfriend, and the next thing they saw was the unexpected. She stood up and gave an icy stare to everyone sitting around the table and rushed to the door and fled. She thought he was serious with the relationship.

"I was just kidding," said Song. "I'm somehow getting bored with her. Losing taste for her, you know. My wife is crying everyday to stop this nonsense. Maybe, I should think about it."

It seemed he purposely brought Han, a chick from Vietnam, to the Redd's to get rid of her after using her for the past few days.

"Good for you and for your prick. You have been working too much with your prick. It must look heavily abraded by now. Maybe, you are finished. Did you check with the local docs just to make sure you don't have those weeds?" James asked jokingly.

"I'm all right," answered Song. "But I'm seriously thinking of getting rid of Maria. Too much sex, dance, and booze, I'm getting sick of that. And, of course, the money."

Song had a special relationship with Maria Cinni, an Italian blonde. He just couldn't get rid of her, and she knew how to keep him at bay. A rare gift!

"Only gem dealers could afford these luxuries, right? Easy money! They come easy and go easy," said Pinto Pin.

Quite a lot of gem dealers had this handicap. Women became an easy escape for the ones who were mentally too weak. The temptations were too high to avoid when these women came in to their office or at social places with their friends. Not all were prostitutes some were genuine. But the gem dealers kept changing them just to taste new juices.

"How long? That's the problem. The fuck, when it comes it flows like an ocean, and when it dries up, it's like those famine stricken countries in Africa. It's scary at times," added Song, as if he had an advice for everyone. Like always, no one took his opinion serious, even though at times they did have some meaning.

"But that's how it is," said Pinto, "either you adapt or fucking die."

"Have you ever had any extramarital relationships just for fun?" Song asked. No one understood why he was getting so religious unnecessarily.

"Me?" said Pinto. "The fuck, no. Number one, I can't afford. Number two, too much sex sucks. Number three, disease. I can't stand the pain you have to go through for a few hours of pleasure. You see, I've so much peace of mind staying with one; as long as you know how to keep them happy. If you want to use your wife like a pumping machine, then I'm not surprised if you lose your prick in your sleep. I hate that."

"Quite interesting," answered Song. "Different perspective. Get that info about the 37carat ruby, will you? We will have to do something about it. I'll shore up enough money for its acquisition."

"Did you talk to your wife about what you are doing?" James asked.

"She doesn't understand all these complicated matters," Song said. "She is too slow. But my other one, Maria, she is sharp. She understands every bit of info. It's amazing how the woman learned from zero?"

"Well, you must try explaining your business with your wife, Song. If something goes wrong along the way, they wouldn't have to suffer for the rest of their lives for this slight oversight. Maria is just after your body and money. As long as that is taken care of, you are the sugar daddy. If she smells that your money well is drying up, she will be gone with the wind. No more fuck, understand? But your wife will stay. So talk to her slowly if she takes more time to understand. I think she must be informed of your checks and balances. In the future, it will help a lot to avoid disappointments. Be transparent. After all, she gave you nice kids, right? You need to give something in return. Give your true love buddy," said Pinto firmly.

There was a deep silence around the table. It seemed no one wanted to talk. The topic had gone to unexpected levels with strange philosophical twists. They all stood up and left the table with a high five just to remind them that they were still friends.

THIRTY SEVEN

There were several brokers and buyers urgently wanting to meet Sanders and Jeb, and the crowd kept increasing as time passed by. Sanders gave strict instructions to Tip, his secretary, not to bring in any brokers or buyers for the whole day. Despite her concerted effort, they refused to leave. Instead, they kept coming back asking for an appointment with either Sanders or Jeb.

Meanwhile, Sanders, Jeb, and Baddy were holed up in Sanders's office to plot the next move after the unexpected Grigory Troublov incident. Troublov had already threatened he would come back without giving any details of any sort, and the more they thought about the situation it became clear that he was not acting alone. And bad news about any one of them meant a guaranteed suspicion about their business practice and a baggage of negative publicity. That was the last thing in the world they wanted at this particular juncture, when they were preparing for the purchase of a 37carat ruby.

Baddy had been staying low profile for sometime, just concentrating on the ruby business and traveling between Laos, Cambodia, Vietnam, Burma, Pakistan, and Afghanistan. The experience he had gained from Africa proved to be of tremendous benefit by doing business in chaotic conditions and both, Sanders, and Jeb, were thoroughly enjoying the partnership.

In fact they wanted Baddy to be busy with his rough purchase but after careful thought, Jeb decided to involve Baddy so he would know the whole truth for the sake of transparency.

Misunderstanding and disinformation always existed in any

partnership, and that's exactly what they wanted to avoid. They had to agree to an acceptable profit sharing ratio.

There were several formulas put forward by each of them to sound fair. At last they all agreed to Baddy's suggestion. With thirtyfour percent between Sanders and Jeb, Baddy's thirtytwo percent became a perfect alternative choice.

The next part was the difficult one. Sharing the profit after Miko and Tito had sold the ruby. This was the time when business and friendship went separate ways. Everyone involved meant business. It was logic to split the profit from the deal the same way. They left the idea for the time being, till they had a final round of meeting with both, Tito and Miko. But the most excruciating problem facing them was the threat by Troublov, who also happened to be after the very same ruby. The way he managed to get to Sanders's office meant Troublov was well aware of the security fault. That meant there was someone in the organization who knew the daily schedules of Sanders. Firing anyone under suspicion without solid proof meant more trouble in the long run. Hiring gunmen from the streets of Bangkok was not that expensive for the disgruntled staff, and that's what Sanders, Jeb, and Baddy, wanted to avoid by any means. They needed the staff to survive the situation. And the only man who could do the convincing job of keeping the staff under control was Jeb. He had a knack of his own, even though Sanders was the man in charge of daily operations.

After Jeb had agreed to the assignment, their attention turned to Rubyhall and Baddy. Even though they competed against each other in the international ruby market, Baddy felt the time had come to cooperate with Rubyhall, to keep the international competition at bay. He wanted Bangkok to remain the ruby capital of the world, instead of New York taking over with the recent economic boom. The experiences he had acquired by working in the mines of Tanzania and Kenya taught him one or two lessons. The producing countries always remained poor or disorganized, while the consuming countries prospered uninterruptedly in the name of this or that.

But the political and geological landscape of ruby was quite different from Southeast Asia and Africa. The economy and the infrastructure were a bit better than the facilities in Africa. Bangkok being a convenient stopover for any ruby lovers made it all realistic, if there was a will by the concerned interests. The mining countries surrounding Thailand were politically unstable, a blessing in disguise for Bangkok, and the ruby dealers.

Baddy saw an opportunity to find a formula of cooperation so that instead of killing each other in the same street, it was high time that the Thai dealers fought against the dealers from abroad, who usually exploited the disunity and animosity amongst local ruby dealers.

The result was disastrous. Price cutting and deliberate hoarding of good rubies created an artificial scarcity to benefit a handful of dealers like Rubyhall, and his friends. Some were being forced out of the business in the name of misfits or lacking business logic. Though the idea seemed academically feasible, implementing them in a realistic term meant going the extra mile to build up confidence and stability so that big and small dealers benefited from this unique vision. Baddy wanted to be the architect of this idea encouraging other dealers to make it a reality.

Jeb and Sanders laughed at first, but then retreated to their commonsense approach seeing the benefit if all the parties agreed without any preconditions. But those arguments were open to meaningful discussions eventually creating a fortress of unity and stability for everyone.

Bangkok had all the facilities and the human resources to remain the ruby capital of the world. Rubyhall made it a reality working in his own terms with the right political connections The world was changing with new players coming in for a slice of the action, while oldies remained in their ancient world. The advent of Sanders and Jeb with different skills and specialties, the risk of being eaten away by the big dealers, the magic formula, and the peaceful coexistence among different quality groups avoided any conflict in relationships, and every differing interest kept busy with their clients or new gem territories. They succeeded, but not always. But it was okay.

Rubyhall, Winston, Tito, Miko, Jeb, Sanders, Baddy, Den, and an army of locals, big and small, remained in Bangkok, and in its environs continuing their pursuit to obtain the best of the best rubies from anywhere in the world to make someone happy. And those happy ones kept coming back to Bangkok, to acquire the most beautiful red stone on earth.

In the end, Jeb and Sanders agreed in principle to accommodate Baddy's ideas to be executed at an appropriate time in association with other big Thai dealers such as Prapan, Morakot, and Somkit, but Jeb's immediate concern remained to tackle Troublov and his motives. The 37carat ruby partnership was open for further discussion, when Tito and Miko agreed to the suggestion of a safe place to sort out the final details.

They wanted to avoid at any cost any unexpected casualties. Private eyes and ears were everywhere, and this time they had to fulfill the promise.

THIRTY EIGHT

It was taking him nowhere and for Lam the 37carat ruby experience was leading him to such a hell, he lost all interest in his family and in himself. In two days time he was going to know his fate whether he had a job with Rubyhall. But he had already made up his mind. He wanted to flee Bangkok, whichever way he could. Once a loyal parent and a strong advocate of family values and ethics, all those positive qualities seemed sucked out of his brain. A devilish character began to take root in him. He wanted to destroy everything in front of him. Coming home late became a norm, even though Marla tried her best to reconcile with him in all ways she could. He was going nowhere, and she had no one else to blame other than Jay and Rubyhall.

Tuna's Club & Restaurant became a refuge for Lam, and gradually drinking became habitual. She couldn't understand the sudden shift in his behavior. Yet, she tolerated him in her restaurant. He was nonviolent.

It was Friday, and as usual the crowd began to throng the place for a good time. There was the samba music because of world cup soccer, and the food followed by the arrival of new friends swapping tables for convenience and intimacy cheered up the environment.

Harry Takashi had just arrived from Hong Kong, after losing his job in a finance company from the anticipated meltdown of the regional economies. He became one among the several casualties, when one by one the finance companies began to close down. An American by birth with a Japanese root, he decided to flee Hong Kong for Bangkok. He had known from his friends that

Thailand was a cheap place to stay till he found another job or any job if he liked. But there wasn't any, and as days went by the prospect of finding one became obviously bleak. After hearing from other travelers that Tuna's place had a lot of information on trips to the upcountry and the region, he decided to stop by. He had not told his parents that he had lost his job, because saying so meant breaking their heart and creating more worries. They had known his moonlighting with jobs before, and at least hoped the present one made him stay permanent. But they had no clue of the real economic factors in Southeast Asia, and going back home meant losing his face in front of his family, relatives, and friends.

The introduction was casual, as Takashi approached Jay at his table during one of the several drinking sessions. For him, Jay Lam had something very similar to him. But he didn't know what to ask, instead left it that way. Lam liked Takashi. They talked about jobs, economy, women, travel, money, the list of topics were unending. There was a chemical match between them, as the talk progressed. One thing led to another.

It was like two born losers meeting for the first time in their lives. They had nothing more to lose other than talk about it, and enjoyed soaking up each other's misery. The only difference between Takashi and Lam was their nationality and marital status. Though Takashi was staying at a guesthouse in Khao San Road, Lam took the liberty to invite Takashi to his condo at the President Park. But, Takashi politely refused the friendly gesture. He wanted to make it some other day.

After a noted hesitation, Lam accepted Takashi's stand. Both were drunk, but Takashi was more conscious and alert than Lam. Meanwhile, Tuna was watching them from a distance. She felt sorry for both, but again that was life. No one was perfect.

The world cup fever had captivated everyone's interest, as France played Croatia in the semi-finals. At one corner, there was betting going on, as the match began to warm up after the first half. Tuna and her loyal staff made sure everything was under control because the police were against betting and were on a search with their special squad in and around the entertainment facilities of Bangkok. After a friendly reminder, the guys left the restaurant. There was a sigh of relief. Takashi had already gone, and Jay remained at his table pondering whom to talk to next. His eyes looked blurred from the excessive drinks, and he was too weak to talk.

"Jay, are you okay? You know what time it is now?" she said, watching his mood. Instead, he glanced at her with a smile and then focused his attention elsewhere. She knew he had gone a bit too far, and sending him off in a taxi remained the only alternative, before it was too late.

There was a sudden reaction from the viewers when France missed an opportunity to net another goal. They were now drinking too much, as the play became tense. Everyone was rushing to the lavatory in a dash, and coming back to stay put. It was a sight to watch.

Tuna decided to send Jay home. She called one of her male assistants to hail a taxi, as she herded him to a sidewalk. In a few moments, he was put in a taxi, and as a friendly gesture, she asked her assistant, Jack, to accompany Lam to his condo at the President Park.

When she returned to her counter, Takashi was waiting for her. She was taken aback first, as she saw him leave after paying the bills, and now wondered at the reason for his abrupt return.

"Hi, I saw you sending Jay off. Nice of you," Takashi continued. "I'm Harry Takashi. Do you know him very well?"

"Yeah! He is a friend of mine," she said, "and at present, he is not doing well at his work. He is a bit disturbed." She didn't wanted to talk too much about Lam and the fact was she had no idea why he was taking an interest in Jay in the first place.

"He did talk about it briefly, but got too drunk," said Takashi. He hesitated again, but decided to go further. "Do you have any information on trips to Chantaburi and Trat? I read in a newspaper in Hong Kong that there are a lot of gems in those areas. Is that true?"

"Yep. It's true. Chantaburi is probably the only open ruby market in the world. You can see it for yourself. In fact, you can take an air-conditioned bus from Ekamai. Roughly, three hours journey, and another one hour for Trat. Nothing much to see in Trat, if you are looking for gems. But, Chantaburi is the place where the action is," she said.

Tuna saw the excitement in his eyes, as he took note of the information, and then left the place trigger-happy with some plans.

THIRTY NINE

She did it this time. July sold the ruby for a good profit after paying Rubyhall his price, and had an order for one more.

"Where are you calling from?" Rubyhall asked, while holding the line. He had to motion Lam to return in less than thirty minutes. Privacy became pivotal at this stage.

"Singapore!" July was in a festive mood. Rubyhall sensed it instantly, but he kept his emotions in control, as several problems began to converge on him from all sides.

"What can I do for you now?" he asked.

"I need another big one," she said quickly. "A 30 carat plus. How should I send the money, Mr Rubyhall?"

"Do you have a fax number?" he asked.

"Yes. I do."

"I will write the bank account number, price, and other details," Rubyhall added. "Fax me a copy later. When will you be coming to Bangkok?"

"As soon as possible." The reply pleased him.

"The rubies will be ready," he answered. "It's your selection. So you are learning something step by step." She liked the encouraging touch in his words.

"As you said," July continued. "I can't believe I have that much confidence stored up in me. I've no words to explain that. Your advice did serve my purpose. I'm deeply obliged to you."

"Business and friendship should be kept separate," Rubyhall said. "No ill feelings. When you mix them like a yogurt, it tastes funny and sour. Some people might like it, but most don't. The ball is in your court. You know now what to look for and I have something, which others don't have, simple as that. Then we talk numbers. You can't refuse my offer. It's reasonable and consistent, which includes the cost of convenience. That's how we do business. And you are now becoming part of it."

Rubyhall's glance turned to the ruby bust installed in front of his table. The strong body color and the excellent job done by the German cutters illuminated his thoughts of how important he was, not only to the trade, but also among his competitors. The thought passed in a flash.

"I know," she said happily.

"So, when you are in Bangkok just give me a call. I'll send my people to pick you up from your condo. That way you are safe. No one will be watching you," Rubyhall suggested.

"Already. Thank you!"

The bait he threw did bring in a good fish. He had all the reasons to smile. And he wished more came along, but he was not in a hurry. Selling big stones wasn't that easy and if it did sell, then he knew already the range of profit she had made from the stones.

Rubyhall knew too well the complex emotions and price / quality mood swings when his clients came to visit his office. Most of the time he got his way, and for reasons no one knew, the clients kept coming back and again. That special touch in finding rubies both, rough and cut, and the potential clients after the stones had reached his office, accumulated by luck or chance, no one could match his instincts. By word of mouth or by chance introductions, just like the situation with July now, his keen eye and a calculating mind kept creating happy clients day after day, though sometimes he himself hadn't a clue how long it was going to last. With no apparent successions in the offing, Rubyhall enjoyed the thrill and satisfaction the stones brought both to his life and the clients, and that joy no one could explain.

He sat in his office knowing that a quick replacement of a similar quality was close to an impossible task. Just like losing a child, he sat in front of the picture pondering its next life. At least he had made someone happy and secure. So it was with the rubies sold to July. For that brief moment he forgot about everything, but deep from within he was moaning. He just hadn't a clue, as to how he was going to procure the 37carat ruby in time.

Rubyhall couldn't afford to lose his face with Rubin. Even if he lost some money out of the deal, he couldn't care less. Word was more important than money. Money always kept coming some other way. He didn't want Rubin to wait that long.

And, he was running out of time.

FORTY

He pressed the doorbell. Goldie opened the door and welcomed Sanders with a warm hug.

"Come in, please. Make yourself comfortable. I'll be right back."

Sanders sat on the sofa with that heavy thought of a guilty conscience. He knew what he was doing now was wrong, but he had to do something for a break. He felt complete and relaxed when with her and that feeling always brought him back to see her. She knew that as well. She was just doing the same, the other way around. There she was with a tray of wine. After the clink, they settled for a moment.

"Hmm, tastes good. By the way, you look gorgeous today," he said merrily.

"I've been waiting for this opportunity for so long, I thought it appropriate to call you now. So, how is Chin? Is she okay?" Goldie asked with a caring look.

"I think so," he said. "The doctors are taking care of her well at least. This shouldn't have happened. But somehow all these events point to utter necessity. She started the trouble, and I became part of it. I hope everything will be settled soon. Does anyone else know that I'm here?"

"Nobody," she answered. "Except the two of us. It's our day, Sanders. Just feel relaxed."

She took her wineglass and walked towards him and sat close. Sanders in the meantime put his arm around and kissed her on the head. She put the glass of wine on the table and embraced him so hard he had trouble breathing. Both rolled on the sofa kissing each other, till they fell on the floor.

They laughed loudly, as she lay on top of him.

"I didn't expect this exercise," he whispered, staring at her beautiful face.

"Come, let's go to the bedroom. It's more comfortable and safe," she said, while extending her hand.

Sanders got up and followed her to the bedroom. He remembered how she treated him last time. The music and decorations looked purposely orchestrated to fall in love for that very few precious hours. After that it would all be gone.

Back to reality. He knew that. But he loved her company. She had an aura, which captured his thoughts persistently to be with her. She had a way of doing that and he had a hard time controlling himself.

As she approached him to undress, the doorbell rang. Sanders stood shell-shocked, as he saw her frightened face. "What's going on, Goldie?"

"I just don't know. Now, what am I supposed to do?" She screamed at herself, as the doorbell rang twice.

"Hide somewhere, till I find out who wants to see me this time," she said nervously.

"Are you sure it's not your husband? Do you think he had a change of mind in the last minute to be with you, instead of staying in those poisonous cities in India?" Sanders said, knowing the risk if it was her husband.

"I just don't know. I'm going to the front door to see who it is. Stay under the bed till I come back," she said, and left the bedroom.

He had all the reasons to worry one problem after another. Sanders pondered while holed up under her bed what on earth he did in his past life to undergo this miserable period. As he struggled to stay comfortable under her bed, he started to worry. The thought emerged to kill the intruder with one gunshot if he had the skill.

He thought of Ruth and Chin. Definitely not under the bed like him! Hopefully doing something sensible!

"What's going on?" He shouted at himself, as he banged his head.

"It was my secretary," she said, smiling. "Some important papers needed my signature."

"What an unusual time for a signature? Young or old?" Sanders screamed in anger, as he struggled to come out.

"Young. I know her. She loves to bring papers at odd times. Today wasn't an exception. She does that all the time. I hope no one else turns up when we are busy," Goldie said, in a meaningful way.

They ate dinner, continued their conversation about his family, wineglasses in hand, feeling good.

They both now settled in her bedroom to watch a video drinking now more wine than usual. As the movie ended, Sanders and Goldie sensed something unusual permeating all throughout their bodies. By this time they had reclined on the sofa locked in an extreme passionate embrace. She now broke the kiss and moved her pouting mouth to his neck. She sucked and tongued his sensitive skin, as Sanders threw his head back and forth letting out with a little gasp. He unbuttoned her blouse to expose her flaming and rigid nipples. He gently took a nipple into his mouth and kept nibbling on it. He now took the lead, and laid his head on Goldie's stomach, sucking and nibbling at her flesh.

He slowly descended south. Goldie parted her knees to allow him to navigate her special place. She squirmed and raised her hips, as his tongue slipped in and out of the wet part. Both of them could no longer hold back their excitement, as they frantically continued. She grabbed his head and plunged it deeper into her dark universe. He had by now zeroed in on her hot clit. He sucked it harder which sent her orbiting beyond the atmospheric thickness of silence into an epileptic-like seizure of orgasms beyond experience. As they reached the pinnacle of their ecstasy, both collapsed into euphoric state. There was complete silence in the room as their eyes locked in passionate hunger.

Both were now fully naked. "How about another drink?"

She poured the remaining wine into his glass. He was now breathing like a hippo not knowing how to slow down. His heartbeat was beyond the accepted limit, and looked afraid of having an instant heart attack from this experience. He took a quick gulp, and they were locked again in a passionate kiss. She let out with a scream when his erection started to rub her hot thighs.

"Come in," she said hurriedly. She slowly drifted downward licking his balls. He let his erection slip into her mouth, until he couldn't control the thermal inertia any longer.

"Melvine, don't give up. Come in to me again." She pleaded with her wet mouth. He now turned his erection back into her pinkish red clit and thrust over and over again, as their passion reached the melting point. He now had to grab several pillows for balance.

After a few minutes of phosphorescence, Goldie started to cry softly. Sanders, still breathing heavily didn't understand what was going on. It took him a while, as he moved closer again to give her a soft kiss. "Are you all right? What happened?"

As he wiped her tears, she said nothing and instead replied with a meaningful smile. They began to make love again leaving behind her fears and tears. Then it was all over again with high and low moans, as they rolled over the bed. In the accumulated build up, she moved on top of him and became more demanding. She cruised his manhood into her and pumped like a bush priestess. Tracks of wetness strolled down her thighs as she thrust, which made him almost speechless.

Completely spent, they got up and went to the lavatory for a clean up. She washed and dried him like a babe. It reminded him of his early school days when his mother had done the bathing for him before leaving school, but she wasn't anywhere close.

They laid quietly in the bed holding each other in silence for several hours.

"You did a good job," said Goldie, breaking the silence.
"What do you mean?" Sanders glanced at her quite puzzled.
"My husband would never do such things," she said quietly,
satisfied.
"You weren't that bad either," he continued. "It wasn't boring.
I needed this desperately."
"Me too. My husband always has only one thing in his mind,"
she added. "Money, money, and money. Nothingelse! Of course,
he takes care of me like a queen, but what's this money to me? I
can't have kids. He doesn't want to have kids. He hates kids. What
am I supposed to do? Tell me, I don't understand."
"Take it easy," Sanders interrupted. "We all have problems.
You know the hell I'm going through. But at least we have found
refuge in each other's limitations, which I think, is a blessing in
disguise. Somehow this relationship continues to keep us happy,
even though the road towards complete happiness is miles and
miles away. So let's be happy with what we have in hand at the
moment, and for the rest, there is nothing wrong claiming to be
an optimist. That gives some relief from the hell. But how long do
you think we can go on like this? Just look at the mismatches we
have. To tell you the truth, I would have grabbed you instantly, if
I had met you before. But now look at my fate. I'm holed up with
a stupid wife, who can't tell the difference between a rabbit and a
ram. I'm also blessed with a stupid daughter just like her mother,
who is just her photocopy. When I've all these burdens hanging
on my neck, what am I supposed to do? Blame it on destiny? No
way! I've to carry on with my work. But I'm a human being too. I
need some life to keep me moving. I should be thankful to your
husband for introducing you to me. Look how it all changed. Am
I lucky or privileged, Goldie?"
"Both, I would say," Goldie said. "Is this relationship affecting
your business?"
"No. Not at all! In fact, it helps me to concentrate in what I'm
doing. I'm happy, even though I have problems. They keep coming back punctually anyway. But I'm worried about you. What

would happen if he finds out one day that I'm fooling around with you? What do you think? Would he able to stand that sight?" Sanders asked, knowing the consequences.

"What can he do? He knows his own weaknesses. I've my needs, and I've got to satisfy them from somewhere. You came in to fill that emptiness. I'm happy, as long as you fill that gap. The rest is history. Even if he comes to know the truth, he will have no choice but to live with it. I'm not to be blamed. It's he who is having problems. Maybe, one day he will have to accept it as a reality. Then, I hope he will adapt and won't do anything crazy. If he were like you giving me what I want, I wouldn't be having this steamy relationship with you. Just as simple as that." She reasoned.

"Poetic coincidence!" Sanders said, not knowing what to say next.

"Oh, what's that? Do you have another relationship other than me and your wife?" Goldie asked frantically.

"Oh, no, no. I'm not talking about that. This is about business. I'm after a 37carat ruby, Goldie. I have to go now," said Sanders.

"Do you think I can be of any help?" she asked.

"I think you should stay out of this game," he said. "There are a lot of thugs involved. Some foreign gangs are also involved, I mean, Russian Mafia!"

"Are you going to fight them alone without the help of the police?" Goldie asked innocently.

"The police are too weak and legal to handle a crisis like this," Sanders answered. "It will drag out the whole situation. I've friends who can do a better job. But they need my presence when action is involved."

"I'm really scared, Melvine, will I be able to see you again? You know, in case you...." Goldie began to cry.

"Nothing like that will happen," he said. "Everything is well taken care of. I'll see you again in a few days time. I hope I'll be able to settle everything and we can have a good time again."

"One more thing," reminded Goldie. "Take care of Chin and Ruth. They need your loving presence."

"I'll try."

FORTY ONE

The trip by July to Indonesia turned out to be good. Now she needed a big one, a 42carat piece, a birthday gift not for the Suharto family, but another member. It was a common trend among the rich in Indonesia. They competed with each other to outdo other families. Now, she was back in Bangkok again for the precious gem.

"I got your fax," July said. "The money is in your account, as you requested. This is a copy of the transfer."

"I already received the statement from the bank. Thanks, anyway," Rubyhall answered.

"That fast?" July echoed her surprise.

"Nothing is impossible today, when you keep that cordial relationship," Rubyhall added. "When I take care of them, they take care of me. That's all. Let me show you the box, and see for yourself."

Rubyhall walked to his safe deposit vault, and removed two large stone boxes. One he kept under the drawer, he opened for her to view.

"Wow! Isn't that beautiful?" July stood agape. Rubyhall moved swiftly and picked another black box.

"Look, this is yours," he said. "42carat piece! Follow the ritual. Go and look under all the lights available in this room, and see whether it will look the same way in your country. For ruby it is extremely important to have a pleasant light. So, go and check. If the ruby looks red in that fluorescent light, the stone has already passed the test."

"I think it will look okay," July said. "All of your stones will pass the light test, anyway." Rubyhall was flattered.

In fact, July was telling the truth. He had already done several tests before by his experienced eyes and the spectrophotometer, the most advanced color measurement device used by the color experts. The insatiable interests in color theory took him beyond the level of knowing about the causes of color in a ruby, because he knew this subject was the least understood by the majority. Color had the power to manipulate emotions and a colorless world was unthinkable.

"Why do you say that?" Rubyhall became curious, even though he knew the answer.

"Because they are all good. Simple! Period." July smiled.

He could only imagine what the miners would have thought if they heard the statement. The 42carat ruby, oval shaped, was cut from a 142carat rough from Mogok, Burma. In order to improve its color, clarity, and brilliance, he had to suffer a huge weight loss just to get the cut ruby in shape. No one understood the significance of the pain he took to make it look beautiful and desirable. Now the ruby was holding the power and glory to mystify and enhance the custodians for the rest of their lives.

"Is the stone okay for you? Are you convinced?" Rubyhall asked once again.

"Yep," she continued. "I don't want to carry the stone back to my condo. Keep it in your safe. I'll collect it when I leave Bangkok."

"No problem. What are your plans for today?" Rubyhall knew she had some surprises under her sleeve.

"I think I'll give Rubin the surprise of his life," she said smilingly. "He must be staying in the same room, right? I hope he will be free for the evening."

"I think so," recalled Rubyhall. "Enjoy your day. Just give me a call in advance before you come to pick up the ruby. I'll have the details ready."

"Thank you, Mr Rubyhall!"

July could hardly explain her joy after seeing the 42carat ruby. She hailed a taxi from Surawong Road to the Oriental hotel. The taxi moved a few meters and then halted.

Surawong was jam packed with cars, tuk tuks, and buses. There was no way the taxi could move. Neither the taxi driver nor she could do anything. She began pondering whether to walk or just sit in the taxi. She glanced at her watch. Walking seemed the best alternative, and that's precisely what she did. The meter read thirtyfive baht. She gave him a fifty baht bill and decided to walk the street.

While walking on the footpath, her thought was glued to the 42carat ruby, and the profit she would be making from the deal. If she could sell one piece a month that was enough to keep her comfortable. With no excessive overheads, this arrangement with Rubyhall became a perfect source for putting the profit back into the business without bothering her parents. Indonesia was her perfect market, because of the high concentration of ethnic Chinese businessmen and their wealth. And the ruling elite used their connections to keep at bay accusations from the local Indonesians, regarding their accumulation of profit through various government projects and foundations they created to manipulate the situation using a very few friends to run their business interests. Rubies were one such safe haven. The ruling elite competed against each other for status, especially their wives and children. Ruby became a perfect candidate to parade their wealth. Creating more ruby collectors became July's goal after the success in persuading one of the richest Chinese business tycoon's wives. She was a close friend of Suharto's family. And there were many to be sold, if she did it the right way. With Rubyhall's help, she knew she could achieve her goals in a matter of time. The money was great.

The traffic was the same. Not a single vehicle was moving. There were red stoplights at each junction, and she had no idea what was going on. She crossed New Road, knowing it was just another few minutes walk to the Oriental.

School kids thronged the small back streets from the Assumption School, not too far away from the Oriental hotel. It was a sight she could have hardly missed. She loved children. July saw their innocent smiles, street fights, arguments, loud laughter for no reasons, and the sight preoccupied her memories back to her school days in Singapore. Their white and blue uniform with black handbags was visible at all stoplight junctions of New Road. They were arriving from different back streets with their parents and housemaids to cross the street. She forgot about the rubies and Indonesian connections for those few minutes to watch the kids from a sidewalk. It was irresistible.

Even the tourists coming out of the Oriental lane were doing exactly the same. They laughed at each other. The traffic policemen looked helpless at the dead-end situation and he too herded the children to the opposite lane to make sure no motorcycle taxis over ran them knowing their notoriety for speed and carelessness.

FORTY TWO

The receptionist had to call the security guards for help, as the ruby brokers demanded to see the managers: Sanders and Jeb. They couldn't believe that both, Sanders and Jeb, weren't in.

But Jeb and Sanders were already busy with Baddy, Tito, and Miko, at Sanders's Trairong Tower condo on Pattanakarn Road, Klongton. This arrangement was to avoid any last minute surprise moves by Troublov and his accomplices. The discussions kept going, despite the fact that they had come to gentlemen's agreement regarding the profit from the deal. Jeb and Baddy remained quiet, giving Sanders the full authority to finalize the deal. They had no second thoughts regarding the quality of the ruby. After the drinks they got back to business. Tito decided to take the initiative first.

"Speak your mind, Sanders. Don't beat around the bush. We had a deal. Remember, when you called me?" Tito said emphatically.

Miko remained silent giving Tito the opportunity to speak out, as the friendly number game took over the discussions.

"Yeah, I very well remember," Tito continued. "You wanted to know whether we would be interested in getting into a partnership. That's right. That's what I asked for. What's your stance now? Do you want to stick with the deal?"

"Tito, what's the deal? You want me to put up the money to buy the ruby, right? How much are we talking about here?" Sanders asked.

"I have to remind you again that this piece belongs to Lord," said Tito. "He gave it to us for a reason, not that he doesn't know how to sell, but purposely to vent his anger against Rubyhall. So we got the piece and quietly shopped around, till we hit a jackpot."

"THE BRITISH LOTTO, right?" Sanders interrupted. Both, Tito and Miko glanced at Sanders in absolute shock. "How did you know that?"

"I was listening to your phone conversation with Chichi just before this meeting," said Sanders, smiling. "You are a millionaire today, Tito. Congratulations! Now getting back to our main point, you have now the money to buy. Do we have a deal?"

"Here's the deal," Miko answered. "We go fifty-fifty, just this piece. Whatever profit we make we share. A word is a word. No change, whatever the situation. You have been good to us, and we want to continue that relationship, irrespective of the fact that we have the money. Thank God, what a lucky stroke! I've already a customer who will be willing to buy this piece. Now what Lord agreed upon was, we need to give him two million dollars for the piece. We will have to transfer the money to a numbered account, which he has already given to me in advance. Once that money is deposited, the stone belongs to us. That's the whole story."

"Fifty-fifty, right? I chip in one million and you guys one million. Then when you sell the piece, whatever profit we make, we share fifty-fifty. Am I correct?" Sanders asked.

"Absolutely right. Is that a deal?" Tito conferred.

"Deal!"

"Then let's shake hands on it. We have done deals before. But this one is special." They toasted their new partnership with high five and body slams.

"Now what?" Miko asked, as they settled on the couch.

"Before Lord changes his mind, I think we will have to deposit his two million dollars into his Swiss account as early as possible. I believe for this size, this is a good bargain and we cannot afford to lose this opportunity at any cost, know what I mean? There might be those big arms of Rubyhall or whoever, those thugs and bugs they could all be after us. But first, settle the account with Lord, then all this chasing will slow down," said Tito quickly.

"So, why don't we do it now?" Miko added. "Transfer the money now, and give Lord a call. It will be too late for him to change his mind."

"I'll transfer the money now for you guys. The rest you pay me, when your money is in," Sanders reminded.

"Fine, Sanders. Do you have anything to eat? I'm hungry," Miko complained.

"Sure. There's corned beef and pastrami, straight from the Sheraton Grande. Go to the kitchen and help yourself," Jeb replied.

Sanders had to do the money transfer fast, and the best way he could achieve that was to call Hong Kong. His financial consultant, Ricky Hu, did all the money transfers when requested.

The fax machine focused everyone's attention. Sanders rushed to read the incoming fax.

"It's done. The money had gone to Lord's account. We have the copy of the transfer. Now Tito, it is your turn. Give Lord a call," said Sanders happily.

After a pause, Tito telephoned Winston Lord's office.

"Winston Lord!"

"Tito!"

"Where the hell have you been? Now listen, I've an urgent reminder. Where is that ruby, my 37carat piece? I want it back. Now! I'll be in the office," said Winston without elaborating much.

"Are you in the office right now? I'm sending a fax. Read the contents carefully," answered Tito.

"What does that mean?" Lord looked puzzled, as his fax machine went on.

"Please read the message, Mr Lord. It's coming now," said Tito. "I'm holding the line. After you have read, then I'm ready to listen."

"Oh, my God," uttered Lord in disbelief. "You did it. Je-ez, what am I going to tell Ris?"

"I kept my word," said Tito. "Your money is in your account. Now the stone belongs to me."

"Why so quick? How am I gonna face him?" Lord said bluntly. He knew there was no room for further negotiation. The 37carat ruby were gone, and the money was in his account, in Switzerland.

"Are you talking about Ris Rubyhall?" Tito asked, looking at Sanders and Miko. They were listening to him, while munching the goodies from Sheraton Grande.

"It's a long story," said Lord, as if he had another idea to turn around the situation. "Okay, now where are you? How can I contact you?"

"I'll call you back," replied Tito, without going into much detail. In fact, there wasn't much to talk about. There was no way the ruby was going to be returned to Lord.

Lord tried to make one more effort to see if they could sell the ruby indirectly to Rubyhall. It was just a thought, which wasn't his idea in the first place after their brief animosity. It ran against his business logic. But the peace deal came in too late to diffuse the tension.

"I just don't know what to say," said Lord. "Anyway thanks for the transfer. I'll have to eat my pride now."

FORTY THREE

The next day, Winston Lord arrived at his office quite early with some decisions. He wasn't sure if it worked, but he was willing to give it a try. He decided to meet Den personally after a quick confirmation.

Winston called Den on his mobile. Den was having his breakfast at the Holiday Inn. It was a perfect timing for Lord to do some business or just listen to Den's advice, if he had any.

As he walked into the restaurant, Winston saw Den talking with a stranger. He had never seen the person before, and wondered why Den had to call him, when he was with a stranger. As Winston approached Den's table pretending to be unaware of anything, suddenly both, Den and the stranger shook hands, and then the stranger was gone. Winston wondered how to start the conversation, and at the same time to get to the point knowing Den's personality. He hated it when people beat around the bush, when discussing a problem.

"I lost the piece and peace at the same time?" Winston said reluctantly.

"What are you talking about?" Den stared at Winston.

"I'm talking about that 37carat ruby," said Winston, spreading his arm on the table.

"They put the money in my account, very smart and clever. I've no way of negotiating a deal. There is nothing to negotiate when there is no deal. The money is in, and the stone is gone. The problem is how am I gonna tell Ris? I'm sure he will listen to the whole story with that deceptive silence and anger. I just couldn't help him this time."

The waitress arrived with the menu. Winston ordered a cup of tea. He was in no mood for a heavy breakfast like Den. Even after Den's insistence to have the same breakfast Winston stuck to his decision. For him the ruby deal was more important and he needed a way out to save his face, and Ris's too.

"You must find a way to present your case," said Den thoughtfully. "We all do a deal for money. That means profit. So give them another of your pieces."

"But he wants that precise 37carat piece," replied Winston. "Rubin is waiting for that last piece. Ris can't bluff him anymore."

The tea arrived.

"So what is left is to buy back the stone from Miko and Tito," commented Den. "If Ris has no problem paying your price for the sake of keeping a friendship, pay three million and get the stone back. You sell it for four million to Ris, if he is that desperate. In this case, time and word is more important than money. That's when you make your money. There is nothing wrong with that. I would do the same thing if I were in your shoes. Friendship and business should be separate. Give Tito and Miko another offer, which they can't refuse. Don't delay. We all make and lose deals around the clock. So this one shouldn't be an exception. What are you thinking about?"

That really surprised Winston. He understood the logic behind Den's statement, but what he needed was a practical solution.

"Miko and Tito! How am I gonna convince them? I can't even call them back," replied Winston questioningly. "That can be from now till anytime of the year, right? You just can't wait that long. I'm just stuck like a pig in a hole. I've Ris pulling from one side for the ruby, and Tito and Miko feeling relaxed and laid back on the other end of the spectrum. But why this 37carat piece?"

"Someone must have a reason to be so persistent," said Den bluntly. "But, then it's none of your concern. Your job is to find the ruby for them at a marginal cost, right? Can you do it?"

Winston had no immediate answer. He felt the discussion was getting nowhere. The fact was no one had an immediate replacement for that 37carat ruby. Recutting a big ruby to replace the 37carat ruby was the last thing in the world the dealers wanted to do, unless and until they got their price. But this was a unique moment in Winston's, Tito's, and Miko's life. They had never come across a situation like this before. All that Winston wanted at this particular juncture was to find an alternative source.

He knew Den had several pieces of rubies uncut in his inventory from a reliable source and the problem was how to tell him the truth. If he did ask directly it was going to hurt Den knowing his business style. Lord didn't want to embarrass Den at this particular situation. Also, Den was keeping his deceptive silence.

Lord thought otherwise. Den should have said something realistic after listening to his side of the story, and pushing further meant losing a friend. He was in a dilemma. Instead, Lord decided to talk to Ris direct and get it over with. He didn't care what Ris thought about him. He wanted to just clear the misunderstanding after the peace talk they had with Den.

Now the brothers were back to their same old game, and he didn't want to create another reason for continued hatred. It was making him sick and tired. Den was not at all helpful. It didn't take much time for him to understand that.

Without elaborating, he thanked Den for the tea, and walked straight to his office once again for that final meeting with Ris.

FORTY FOUR

The telephone rang. Rubin rushed to the phone wondering, who it might be.

"Who is calling?"

"July!"

That voice really surprised him. There was a rather stunned silence, as he stood holding the phone. "July! Are you back? I was just thinking about you. Where are you now?"

"At the Oriental," she said quickly.

"What? I can't believe this. You are here? I know now. Ris told you, right?" he commented.

"Yeah," she answered. "Sort of. Can I come to your room?"

"Of course," Rubin said. "I've been preparing some business documents. I'm just out of the shower. But, sure you will be always welcome. The door is open."

"Thank you. I'm on my way."

July checked with the bellhop and rushed to the elevator. Before she could knock, the door opened. "Come in, please," he stared at her.

"Oh, thank you. Just out of the shower?" she asked, looking down at his body.

"Yeah, kind of," he added. "A quick one. Usually, it's half an hour. Since you have arrived, I decided to make it short."

"Really? Where is the dirt for a half an hour wash? I would have loved to watch you in the shower if it took that long. Just kidding," she said, sounding a bit friendlier.

"It's all right. So, you're back again for the ruby, right? Lucky you. You managed to sell that piece. What's the surprise this time?

Bigger one?" Rubin decided to change the subject. He motioned to her to take her seat opposite him so that they sat face to face.

"Yeah," she said. "I got it already. It's in his office. I'll be going back in a couple of days. My dad is not with me this time. I'm alone. I thought, well, why not fool around for a while before I leave."

"Oh, that desperate! You are in business now. You can't afford to do that, can you? You have to watch your movements. Good times just don't come always. Just be watchful. By the way, what would you like to drink?" Rubin said more fondly.

"Anything cold!" she said.

"Like?" he asked.

"Diet coke! For the time being," she replied. "Are you extremely busy today?"

"Sort of. I'm expecting a call from Ris. My stuff, rubies Once that is ready I'm off to New York for good. My dad wants me back."

July had other things in her mind. She now had trouble putting her thoughts into action. What if he misunderstood or kicked her out of the room when she approached him? She just wanted to feel his body. She liked him so much and as seconds became hours her passions became irresistible, and she couldn't wait any longer watching his half-naked body. She had been thinking for sometime after the ruby deal. Just for one experience. It took all her courage to follow him, as he opened the refrigerator.

"Are you all right? You're sweating. Look, here is the diet coke. If you're not feeling well I have some pills for you," he said.

It took her a while to organize herself mentally. Then, it was quick.

"I'll come with you." July followed him to his bedroom. She couldn't wait any longer. Before her molten passion could crystallize into inaction, July took the bold initiative in grabbing his waist with her soft hands. She held him tight and both slumped into bed.

"July!" Rubin cried in disbelief.

"Just shutup," she said. "Give me a chance to warm you up. You'll be just fine. Trust me!"

"Listen to me. What are you doing?" he cried again.

Before he could complete the sentence, she had already plucked off his jump shorts and threw them on the floor.

"I want you, Rubin. I can hardly wait," she said, while holding his erection in her hand. "Now take off my clothes," she whispered, as she stared at his erection and his face in a high voltage shock and pleasure. He discreetly pulled down her skirt to have a glimpse.

With his hands now free, he unbuttoned her blouse, then the small clasp at the front of her bra. Her enormous brown nipples stood out of her light yellow breasts with full blush. She left his erection and grabbed his vibrating head close to her, and kissed him passionately giving him hardly any room to breathe. The warm build up was now getting ready to erupt anytime, as she swept his entire face with her hot lips. He quickly moved his hands to her bare marble white thighs, caressing and fondling. She just couldn't wait. She grabbed his thick and heavily veined erection again and plunged it to her clit, as he struggled.

It all happened within seconds of each other. As their breathing grew heavy with instantly eruptive tight muscles ready to explode anytime, Rubin felt this was enough. He just couldn't open his mouth and utter a single word, as the heat from each others body sank them back again to the place where they started. She wasn't ready to stop. She was enjoying his every inch of bare skin moaning lustily, as the thrusting took on its own intensity. She surrendered to her climax with ooh and aah, as they leaned on each completely exhausted. As they lay separated in bed, still with low moans Rubin looked at himself. He just couldn't believe his eyes how it all started and ended in such a short time.

She looked completely satisfied, as she moved her naked body closer to him.

"You are a strong woman. Where did you learn this?" he asked, tired and confused.

"Me? It's a secret. But I'm sure you didn't mind my interruption," she replied with a smile, which had a lot of meaning.

Rubin just laughed.

"Yeah, you bet. I was a bit nervous when you moved your hands all over my body. It was fantastic," he said, satisfied.

"So you did enjoy. I was a bit afraid you would stop and run away to call the police. I have to tell you this. I don't know where I got the courage to do this, but this one was really desperate. My instincts wouldn't refuse, and I was right. Believe me, there was no rehearsal of any sort to act like this. It was spontaneous. In the end, to be frank, I enjoyed it tremendously," she said plainly.

"I don't know what to say except that I know I was lying naked beside a naked woman, and I had my thing in yours, and yours in mine in such a short time," she interrupted. "Can I ask you a personal question? You have all the right to refuse or accept no ill feelings. Just be honest. That's all."

"What's it?" he asked curiously.

"If I ask you to marry me, will you?" She waited.

Rubin looked at her for a while. He took her hands to his lips and kissed gently.

"I will, with my body and soul. I will, July!" he said passionately.

"Oh, my God, I'm happy. Let's do it again," she replied quickly.

"Not now for heaven's sake. I'll die from a heart attack," he quipped.

Both laughed.

"I was just kidding. Let's go to the shower, and I'll wash you up for half an hour today."

"Really? For that entertainment, I can wait for a while. Now tell me how did they describe your ruby, when you opened the box," he said bluntly.

"Let's not talk about business now, Rubin. I know how you love to compare a ruby with all sort of things. I want to just relax and enjoy my day away from all that business. Just for one day. That's all," she reminded.

"I understand you, July. Pardon my ignorance. At least you woke me up," he said.

"I didn't mean anything, Rubin," she continued, "today I just want to keep business and love separate. I don't know how to explain. The thing I did to you today has been bothering me for some time, and I wanted to let it all go. It's your day too. You can do whatever you like with my body. It's yours. Try, experiment or whatever you might want to call it. It's for fun."

"I'm not that kind of person. You know that too well, don't you? Of course, I like you. You're clever. If you want me to do it, I will. Just tell me when to stop. I can control myself. But I'll never do the way you read in books or magazines. No fantasy stuff very simple! It's not real. We should not indulge ourselves like animals. It's not good for our health," he commented philosophically.

"I know that. Once in a while it's okay to go wild. We won't be doing this everyday. Don't intellectualize a sexy situation. See it as just feelings, like how gem dealers open and close a deal with all that heat and passion. When the deal is over, all the mistakes and clever moves are forgotten for good. Just see it that way. Make it simple and innocent. You see, when I was holding your erection, I just didn't know what to do. It was hot and my hand was also getting hot. I just didn't know for a second what to do. Can you believe it? That tells you how nervous I was. I saw the same when you were moving your hands to my clit. You had a hard time taking off my panties. The more you tried to pull, the quicker it stuck in my thighs. Anyway, in the end we somehow succeeded in accomplishing our mission the hard way. That's what I'm trying to say. Next time, we won't make this error again," she pleaded. Later, she couldn't stop giggling recalling the incident.

"Are you sure? We'll see," he said laughingly. They both walked together to the lavatory.

FORTY FIVE

After listening to Goldie's sincere advice, Sanders decided to visit Chin at a private hospital, on Lad Phrao Road. The traffic was heavy, but he had no other choice.

"Where is the frigging doctor?" Sanders rushed to the reception counter. This time he saw a new staff handsomely dressed and clean. She was as beautiful as Goldie. He couldn't resist asking her name. But something went wrong. He couldn't ask.

"Oh, please don't disturb him," she said cutely. "He is busy with a patient now."

"Okay fine," answered Sanders. "That's his job. I've a job for you now. Where is my wife? She is holed up somewhere in this building at my request, and I got a call from one nurse by the name Olla, reminding me that my wife would be living with her. What the hell is going on in this place?"

"Oh, pardon my ignorance, there must be a misunderstanding somewhere in the line of communication. I'm new here. Just started yesterday. Perhaps, Dr Tuchinda can answer that question. Is anything else I can do for you?" she asked politely. He couldn't ask further. The way she glanced at him reminded him of Goldie. She was just a photocopy.

"What's your name, dear?" Sanders asked, finally.

"Oh, please don't call me dear," she cried. "I'm married. My husband doesn't like that word. I am Tumy. Mrs Tumy!"

"Okay, Mrs Tumy, I don't see your husband anywhere. Why the hell are you worried? You must see it as a privilege when someone calls you dear. Well, if you don't like that word, I can afford to call someone else who deserves that status. Now pardon my inquisitive question. What does your husband do for a living?" Sanders waited patiently for the answer.

"He is a policeman. He is with me all the time," she added. "I love him so much. I just don't like to hurt him."

"Fucking policeman? Right here?" Sanders looked around. He saw nobody. "I think I have had enough of this lunatic place. Leave your policeman husband right there and find my wife, now. This place is full of nuts. I just didn't realize it till now."

"Please don't get angry with me," she said. "Be understanding and compassionate. I always help others and, of course, my husband too. What's your wife's name?"

"Frigging, Chin!" he uttered.

"Is that a name?" she asked innocently.

"Yes and no," Sanders said, remembering the blunder. "Just call her, Chin. Tell Melvine, her living husband wants to see her." He was shaking nervously and cursing everyone he could remember. Then came that familiar voice.

"Hi, I had been thinking of calling you," Dr Tuchinda said, as he walked towards Sanders frantically.

"I was about to do the same thing," Sanders replied. "What the hell is going on here? One Olla calls to tell me that Chin would be living with her from now onwards. Just now, before you came, your new staff, Mrs Tumy defends her policeman husband, because I called her dear by mistake. Is this a hospital or a lunatic asylum?"

"Perhaps, both," answered Dr Tuchinda jokingly. "We care and serve in its true sense. Now listen, Sanders. Your wife is showing some strange symptoms of abnormality. She thinks she is a goddess of some sort from a past life. She is demanding better treatment. That means, you have to pay extra if you want to entertain her request. What should I do? We have some policies not to entertain any strange patients in this hospital. It distracts the whole environment, in some cases, nursing staff and doctors too. You know the weak ones. She is persistent and punctual with her strange symptoms. Now it's up to you. You can donate her to the hospital for further research at no cost or you could take her home. If you need special services from us we could negotiate a long-term deal in each other's interest. Is this proposal appealing to you?"

"You're talking like an assembled gem. Are you telling me that my wife is a useless creep, and you wouldn't mind doing research on her if I permit? Is that right?" Sanders cried angrily.

"Precisely," said Dr Tuchinda. "She has successfully developed the symptoms I just mentioned; a candidate for intensive research. To be honest, she is useless. She will not have any desire for sex, and is deceptively suspicious of virtually anything which moves, acute brain shutdown, persistent craving to migrate to far away planets, instant belief that she is a God of some sort in captivity just to mention a few. These symptoms are seen only in extra-terrestrials or something similar. Even our best medical schools have difficulty understanding these symptoms. So it is a new case. Also a good reason for asking more funding from a research funding institution."

"Am I to believe that my wife is an E.T or stuff like that?" Sanders asked in bewilderment.

"Don't know," added Dr Tuchinda, "but her symptoms might have been concealed all these years for some strange reasons, and the time has come to reveal her true self. That identification has occurred in this now famous hospital, and I'm proud that I was part of it. It will just be a matter of time before the media and the general public picks up interest and who knows? Perhaps, a new movie might be on the roll."

"You're driving me nuts now," said Sanders. "I can't believe all this crap. I've a wife who is now identified by you as an E.T, and who knows what I will hear when I go to meet my daughter?"

"E. T's daughter! What else could that be?" Dr Tuchinda laughed loudly.

"Show me your medical degree now, Tuchinda. I need a second opinion on this strange diagnosis," Sanders said. He couldn't stomach Dr Tuchinda's joke.

"You will be the loser in the end," said Dr Tuchinda. "I checked with all the experts in every damn faculty I know, when I detected this symptom. They all have the same cautious approach. Guess what? Extensive research with generous funding. Now if you go out to contaminate my reputation, the damages you will be forced to pay will wipe out all your life's savings. It's no joke. I'm serious. So you have ample time to decide. Probably your wife may contaminate Olla too. Maybe, we will have to classify you as well. Just in case, you know if you should develop any of those symptoms."

"Oh my God, is this a curse?" Sanders asked, staring at Dr Tuchinda

"Oh, no. It's a blessing in disguise," added Dr Tuchinda. "First of its kind in this country. You must be proud of it till you develop the same symptoms. Who knows? Maybe, your name and, of course, your wife's too, might be in the next Time magazine or Newsweek issue. Instant celebrity! Free publicity. This could be your once in a lifetime chance to sell more rubies than you have ever sold. Look, our country has no short supply of freaks. They will buy anything, which has an E.T tag on it. A top quality ruby from a living E.T ruby dealer! Do you have any idea what that means? Think about the dormant mines opening up with your blessing and the profits you would be making for the next ten years or so till something else turns up, you know what I mean? Opportunity! This is yours, and you must be happy that it is happening to you in this lifetime for Christ's sake. Oh, look at you now. You are sweating, my friend. What can I get you to drink?"

"Just take me home," said Sanders. "I don't want to see her nor you too. I've had enough of this talk and information. Please, will you?"

"If you pay the bills!" That was a punctual reminder from Dr Tuchinda.

"How can you be so mean and rude?" Sanders said.

"Remember, Sanders, it's you who taught me," said Dr Tuchinda. "What? Never mix business and friendship. They should at all costs be separated. I'm telling you the same thing. I know there is a problem, not just a problem bloody big one. You know that. There is nothing to hide. It's now an open book."

"You have ruined my entire life with this diagnosis if I am to believe you. I've thugs from a different country chasing around me like bloodhounds. God knows what's happening with my only daughter? Now tell me; what do you want me to do?" Sanders asked.

"I'm asking you the same question," said Dr Tuchinda. "What do you want me to do? At the end of the day, it's all money. If she stays longer, someone has to pay the cost. If she doesn't want to stay, you have the right to take her away provided you pay the bills, and mine too, of course. You have identified the problem now. Why is it too difficult to understand?"

"Can I talk to my E.T wife at least?" Sanders asked hesitantly.

"Sure," replied Dr Tuchinda. "I can arrange that. You will have to wear a mask. Just to protect you from abrasive and unintentional moves."

"I don't care," said Sanders. "It doesn't make much difference now. I just want to see what she looks like? Then I'll decide what to do."

"Wishful thinking. Just follow me!"

FORTY SIX

It was a Friday evening. Gem dealers and their families, tourists and others, arrived at The Redd's to meet friends and have a good time. Friday's always brought special surprises.

Some loved to meet their husbands and share the experiences or give their friends the surprise of the day if their husbands were with their mia noi's (mistresses) and gems.

"Hi, Mike!" Miko and Tito walked to Mike's table, as he was glued to the tele watching the world cup soccer replay between Brazil and Denmark.

"Hey, look at you guys," said Mike. "Where have you been? I've been searching all around Bangkok. Everyone missed you for sometime. Welcome back. Be my guest."

"Thank you, Mike," replied Tito. "Working holiday."

"Who the hell cares? We all just got you guys back. That's more than enough. So how is business?" Mike asked, moving away from the tele to a corner table.

"Good and bad," answered Miko. "We thought of taking a low profile, and that's how it all worked out, good for a change. Can we get our regular table?"

"Sure," said Mike, waving them to their favorite number seven table. "It has been vacant since you guys disappeared. For some strange reason no one wanted to occupy table number seven. What did you do? Did you leave spell to make it difficult for future occupants? I'm kidding. Now, wait a minute. Who else was looking for you? Che, Jemma, Boron, and a few ladies especially Miko. Miko, I can tell you are a celebrity on your own in this part of the world. Women love you so much. What is the secret behind it?"

They all laughed heartily. "Give me a break, will you? Give us our usual drinks. Menu; give us some time. Who knows? Perhaps, some of these desperados might turn up. We missed the color and smell of this corner for sometime, didn't we?" Miko said to Mike, as they pulled up a chair.

"Oh, yeah. Look at who is talking to that bimbo. It's him, Che," Miko said. But Che was walking toward their table to greet them.

"Hey, Che, how are you doing?" Tito asked quickly.

"Look at you guys now," replied Che. "Oh man, at least I have someone to talk to. Business is really bad. Those frigging creditors and debtors are going bankrupt by the hour. Where have you been? Kabul? They have some nice rubies hidden behind those heavily mined mountains. It's true. Jegdalek! You remember?"

"Cool down, Che. How is your family?" Miko asked.

"I'm rehearsing for a divorce," answered Che reluctantly. "I've had enough already. Thank God, I don't have any kids. Otherwise, I would have to worry about those wretched species as well."

"What's the matter? Everything was going okay, wasn't it?" Miko asked, puzzled.

"When did I talk about her lately, do you remember? Then, I won't have to repeat the same thing all over again," Che quipped.

"You didn't tell us about that. Give us the latest." Both, Miko and Tito urged.

"I had a fight with her one day," Che continued. "If you want to know the reason then just don't laugh. Promise?"

"Promise. We won't laugh. Just listen," Tito said firmly.

"That particular day, I returned home very late from my office. I was so fucking tired and wanted to just open the door and sleep on the floor. Guess who was standing behind the door? My frigging wife in a voodoo costume, I almost stopped breathing, when I saw her frightening dress. That was part one. I couldn't speak a word. Instead, I fell on the couch. The next thing, I open my eyes, what do I see?"

"What? Tell me quick," Miko urged.

"Naked! My frigging wife standing naked in front of me," Che added. "Then, I looked at myself. Naked too! How the hell did that happen? When I fell on the couch, I was sure I had clothes. She did it. My desperate frigging wife peeled off my clothes like onions to do what? Before I could rub my eyes, she was already on top ready to pump. It took all my left over strength, and I threw her off the couch to the floor. I was so angry and frustrated by her aggressive and desperate action. I went to my room and locked the door from inside gulped a few sleeping pills and went off to sleep."

"That's it?" Miko asked.

"Nope," Che said. "The serious part evolved, when I woke up and came out of my room. I couldn't believe my eyes."

"What happened? Did she commit suicide?" Miko asked.

"Worse. Lawyer! She was waiting for me with a lawyer demanding a divorce. I went back to my room and emerged with a cricket bat. Before I could swing, they had all disappeared to a waiting car," Che said, staring at Miko expressionless.

"The result?" Tito quipped.

"I can't stand her any more," said Che. "I've had enough of this sexual kung fu. I work like a donkey the whole day trying to sell rubies, and when I get back home she wants only one thing from me. Bloody sex! No God, no prayer, nothing. I don't know what attracted me to like her that fateful day. Once in a while is okay. Not for God's sake everyday! I've never seen any woman, who is so addicted to sucking cock like her. A virtual liability! I'm sure she must be fucking around with other men, when I'm not at home. I think the best panacea is a quick divorce. We will see what happens next. I'll keep you updated."

"And the future? Any plans?" Miko asked.

"If the business isn't bringing any good money in, I'm thinking of absorbing religion," Che whispered.

"You are already a Catholic! What else do you need?" Miko said jokingly.

"I'm thinking of becoming a preacher," Che replied. "Less investment and good returns. I've the ability to speak well, of course, and the experience. Selling a ruby is no different from giving a gospel speech. We all talk so much everyday, and I think it is not that difficult to preach. I don't see any difference between preaching a gospel and selling a ruby. This time only the commodity is different. If successful, it could take me around the country, and perhaps the world. Who knows? I don't have to worry about sex and women anymore. If anyone approaches with a request, I would give him or her a free Bible, and a one way ticket back home. One soul is saved. What do you think? Is it a good idea?"

"Very strange," added Tito. "It's already overcrowded like any other business. You stick to what you know best. Preaching is a totally different ball game. It is not good for your personality. You have to start all over again. It's like a new career. No friends and support from the community, you know what I mean? I think religion is not the business for you. There is too much competition. That's the last thing in the world you want to do. Stay with rubies."

"And my wife? What do you suggest?" Che asked.

"Go for a good counseling. If that doesn't work, try the hospital. Maybe, she is just having an excess of those unwanted hormones, which are usually found in cats and dogs. If that doesn't work, what should I say, may be send her to me?" Miko suggested.

"What did you say? You will take my wife for what?" Che cried.

"Just to reason with her," Miko added. "That's what I meant. Maybe, she, you know what? We all need another round of drinks to freeze this thought."

"Mike, one more round. This time, Italian!"

"Campobello frascati?" he asked, holding the wine bottle.

"You are deceptively talking less today. What's the matter with you?" Che opened the conversation staring at Tito.

"I was just listening to your gospel. Very interesting! Something we are all familiar with. Family, work, sex, kids, money, relationship, religion, and all that left over crap. It's everywhere. Which home in the world is without problems?" Tito commented.

These social issues were a common topic at The Redd's every weekend, because they were part and parcel of gem dealer's daily lives. Even though they tried not to get too carried away by the allegations brought forward by their real wives about them in the absence of their mia noi's (mistresses), friends did a lot to bridge the gap and the lack of communication among the parties involved.

Anyone, who had offices on Silom, Mahesak, Surasak, and Surawong, knew more or less their families and personal affairs, because most of them either borrowed money or gems to settle disputes or other personal issues.

"Okay, we are friends, we like to share our feelings and mistakes. But I think with good reasoning and understanding and, of course, compromise, most of these problems can be worked out. What does your wife want? Sex. Give it to her when she needs it. That's one way of communicating. Maybe, that's what is lacking in your case. You are so busy making money you forgot her needs. I know this trade too well, and understand everything that you said. But they have difficulty understanding this intricate and often complicated environment outside their home. That's where dialogue and compromise comes in. Give some and take some. We are not angels or Gods. We are, what should I say?" Mike interrupted, moving to another table to meet his friends.

"Let's toast the wine," Miko said. After the clink of glasses, Che stared at Tito as if he hadn't seen him before. Tito looked different, and Che didn't know how to explain it in words after the drinks.

"Well, there is a point to what you are saying," continued Charlie. "I can't deny that. I'll think it all over again, before I do anything crazy. Did you watch that lady over there staring at us? Do you have any idea who the bimbo might be?"

"Nope," said Miko. "Tito, do you know her?"

"Nope. Don't bother. There's a lot of chaff around just wanting to waste our time and money. Just ignore her. Keep busy with your drinks. By the way, did you order anything to eat? What's special today on the menu?" Tito added, glancing at Che.

"I think I better go over to Mike and check it out. He knows what's good for us. What do you guys think?" Miko ushered.

"Mike, what's special today?"

"Everything! Today is my birthday. There is twentypercent discount on everything you eat and drink. Isn't that great?" Mike said happily with a broad smile like always. No wonder they thought it was crowded, as his friends kept coming to join the fun.

"Sure," said Miko. "Happy birthday to you, Mike. How old are you today, if I may ask?"

"Ninetyeight! Does it surprise you? Sure, it does. Divide ninetyeight by two. What is left is my real age." That was typical of Mike when it came to his age. He had done this before, and most of his friends kept forgetting all the time. And they realized their mistake only after hearing Mike's reply. Everyone laughed.

"Do you know the lady who is sitting over there? The purplish red dress?" Che asked curiously.

"Oh, you don't know her? She is a regular customer here. She comes here with her friends. What should I say, socialites? Is that the right word? Oh, look she is coming over. Just stay cool and relaxed, Miko," Mike reminded.

"Hi, Citrina," Mike said, extending his hand. Then came the surprise.

"Have we met before elsewhere? Are you Miko?" she asked, as if she knew him before. For Miko it turned out to be the mother of all surprises, as she kept looking at him intently.

"Sure I am," Miko said gently. He extended his hand to greet her and felt the warmth in her hands, as she pressed firmly.

"Call me, Citrina," she said. "Mike, can I borrow this gentlemen for a few hours?" She was too direct. Mike knew her, and he too looked perplexed at her comment.

"I'm with my partner, Tito," said Miko thoughtfully. "Would you excuse me for a sec?"

"Sure. I can wait," she replied quickly.

Miko walked to Tito's table and whispered, "Tito, that lady, do you see her? She is talking to Mike now. Her name is Citrina, and she has invited me to her table. What do you say? Before I could ask Mike about the special menu, she just walked over to invite me."

"I think you better go with her," Tito added. "It's okay. Just watch your words and deeds. If you smell a rat, I don't have to tell you what to do. Just take your time. I'll be around with Che."

The crowd was getting noisier as the music got louder. There were no complaints.

"Miko, you could have brought your partner as well. What's his name?" Citrina reminded him, as they walked to her table.

"He is busy with his client. It's okay," said Miko casually.

"I've ordered your specialty. Mike told me just now. So let me introduce you to our friends. Let's go to the table," she said.

Miko had never met the group of women before, but it seemed that they were enjoying their time at The Redd's, meeting new friends and renewing old relationships.

"Hi, everybody. This is my close friend Miko, a ruby dealer. He deals only in big stones." Miko sat agape at her introduction, and smiled quickly at the five women. All were well dressed in their late thirties and forties.

"Hi, Miko, can I ask you a personal question? Do you deal in synthetic rubies, I mean those really good ones? I love synthetics. You know why?" The woman was too direct, and he pondered how to answer her question.

"No. I don't," he said apologetically.

"They are cheap, attractive, and just as good as a natural ruby," she continued. "What's the difference?"

"There is a difference. Natural comes from the ground, while synthetics are created above the ground and carefully enhanced by men or women. There is a difference in price as well," Miko quipped.

"Sabby is a synthetic addict," Citrine interrupted. "Her husband is a synthetic ruby manufacturer. You shouldn't be surprised by her loyalty to her husband and product."

"Miko, my husband is in the computer business. No relationship with rubies or any stones. But I love rubies and my husband keeps buying them for me. You know why?" Another beautiful women raised the question for an immediate answer.

"I'm afraid, no," Miko replied.

"I just keep loving him. He works for Phil Win. Win's wife, Polly, is an avid ruby collector too. That's how I knew about rubies," said the woman. But the name Phil Win caught his attention immediately.

"Interesting, Citrina. You just opened up my mind," Miko said, expecting the next question.

"You know what? I heard a lot about you from other ladies," Citrina said to remind him that he was famous among her women's group.

"Really? That's a surprise. Did they tell you that explicitly?" Miko asked.

"Why are rubies so expensive? Whenever I ask my husband to buy one for me he says they are too expensive and are out of his reach. You know what? Instead he bought a 10carat cubic zirconia and showed me the brilliant flashes. He said rubies don't flash like cubic zirconia. Is it true?" The woman on his left asked.

"Calcy loves flashy stones," Citrina whispered. "She is wearing one, and look at those flashes. Her husband is a lawyer." Miko giggled at Citrina's remark. She was smart and quick.

"Comparing flashes of rubies and cubic zirconia would be like comparing apple and coconut. They are different chemically, physically and optically. They have different personalities, and that makes the difference in their values. Rubies, I mean really good ones are rare and difficult to find, while commercial qualities are not difficult. They are affordable and that's what you see in all the stores in this country. Cubic zirconia is altogether a different character. It does have flashes, but different make. They look beautiful too!" Miko said.

"Why do you like rubies? Is it easy to sell them like chocolates?" The women on his right asked.

"Alby's husband is the owner of Alby's chocolates," Citrina said. "She is an avid collector of all expensive artifacts."

"That's a good question," Miko answered. "I used to always

ask that question myself, but not now. To answer your question, they are beautiful, rare, durable, and that makes it easy to convince anyone who likes these qualities before they buy. We don't live that long anyway, as we grow older. But rubies stay young and younger all the time. They never get old, but we do. Top grades are difficult to find and, of course, to sell as well. I have to be selective in showing the top ones, when it comes to selling. You remember that biblical quote?"

"Which one? There are thousands of them," she said quickly.

"Don't cast pearls before swine!"

"Oooh! That was too much," Alby said. "I understand what you mean."

There was a deceptive silence first, and then everyone glanced at each other whether to continue. Citrina nodded. She had several things in her mind to ask him, but waited.

Meanwhile, Miko glanced at them, and then continued, "So inexpensive ones, lower grades are not difficult to sell. You might be able to sell them like chocolates. It's an altogether different quality. And that's what you see wherever you go, while looking in those shop windows. Really good ones you rarely see them like that. They are kept in special boxes to entertain the ones who can taste the quality and finally afford them. That's the difference."

"I think we need to eat something instead of talking," Citrina said. "Miko needs a break, am I right?"

He just smiled. He had a hard time sitting straight and talking with these beautiful women, all in their late thirties. For some strange reason women loved it, and they gave him a wink.

Citrina was watching him intently, as he ate slowly.

"What are you thinking?" Citrina asked, while squeezing his thigh. That sent a lightening chill through his spine, as he struggled to sit straight.

"Are you all right? Are you getting bored talking to us? You look a bit nervous. Drink this glass of wine," she said.

"I'm just fine," Miko replied smilingly. "Can I serve you those salads?"

"Oh, lovely," Citrina said thankfully. "I must introduce you to my husband. He would love to meet you. Who knows? He may want to introduce you to Phil Win. Phil might buy some pieces on his wife's behalf. What do you think?"

"Wishful thinking, Citrina," Miko replied.

While other ladies got busy with their pizza, spaghetti, and wine, Citrina felt a bit different and pondered what to ask, as time was running out.

"How would you like to share that experience when you have such an expensive piece in your hand? What's the, how should I say, feeling you go through when you explain, while trying to sell them, if I'm right?" Another fat women in her late thirties asked him.

"Amethyst's husband is a textile tycoon," Citrina whispered. "He just can't stay without them just like the air you breathe. You must meet him too."

"It's hard to put a number on every ruby," Miko added. "Each ruby demands special treatment, and thus the rewards. They keep coming and going all the time. The best I sold was a 15carat, a screaming red with a slight pinkish tint, eye clean and a well-cut ruby from Burma. The piece was sold to a private collector for a big amount. I can't disclose the price for proprietary reasons. When I've a piece like that in my hand, I just don't speak. The ruby does the speaking. Because it has a personality and those collectors who have a tradition of collecting pieces like that don't need to be lectured about quality and price. They know already. It's the ones who have never seen pieces like that before, who eventually become hesitant and ask all the wrong questions. When you hear that the best thing to do is just leave them alone. They won't buy. Instead, they would just be talking all sort of rubbish. Just wasting your time."

"I think we should meet together quite often to hear what Miko has to say. What do you think about this proposal?" Citrina said, glancing at her friends.

Everyone nodded. Citrina took the first initiative and paid his bill, while requesting him to wait. All the ladies walked toward him and shook his hands in appreciation of his time and comment, kissed him gently, and left one by one after paying their bills.

"Do you have to go back to your partner soon?" she asked, as they sat.

"Not really," Miko said. "He understands me better than anybodyelse."

"Why?"

"Because I've been working with him too long. He knows my every in and out. He is more or less like my father and mother. He just takes care of me," Miko answered affectionately.

"That's good. I won't take much of your time. Would you be interested in visiting my home? I've several homes in Bangkok and upcountry," she said, with a message. That statement alarmed him. She was after something. He looked at her, and her eyes had a lot to say.

"There shouldn't be any problem with that. You know where to contact me?" Miko said cautiously.

"No, I don't," she said, still staring at his face. He noticed that but pretended he was thinking something else.

"Good," she interrupted, "Why don't you give me your contact address and telephone number? Then we will have enough time to discuss it. I don't want my husband to know this. He might misunderstand. It's between us. That's all."

"I'll do what I can, Citrina," Miko said cautiously.

"I'm happy. I've been longing to meet you for sometime. Somehow it just didn't work. Today's my lucky day. Thank you, Miko. It was a pleasure meeting you and I enjoyed your wise opinion on rubies and related topics."

She shook his hand, and gently kissed him on his cheek, as he arose. Her impeccable personality attracted him a lot, as he stood watching her leave the table with her expensive Gucci handbag.

Tito and Che were still locked in intense discussions, as Miko took his seat to join them. The table looked wholesome with scattered beer bottles and pizza trays, as he pushed his elbow to rest his hand. "So, how did it go with those dames? Interesting?" Tito asked.

"Quite an interesting lot. All bloody rich and sexy!" Miko said, after a silent moment.

"Oooh, what did they do to you?" Che asked curiously.

"Just an opinion," Miko added. "That's all. The jackpot of the day was the lady, Citrina. Her husband is the number two in Phil Win's company. You know, that big company, which makes all that money making stuff. She mentioned Polly as well. I just pretended as if I was hearing about these big guys for the first time. There was even a lady whose husband created synthetic ruby. Quite an unusual bunch of rich ladies! Well, in the end, it looks like they enjoyed my company. I've an invitation to join them again at one of their get together places. I don't know where."

"Not a bad day," Tito interrupted. "I'm just trying to help Che out of hell."

"We better get back home," Miko said, glancing at his watch.

"Why don't you give a call to Chichi, and check how she is doing? Here is the mobile. Now go out and make the call. I don't want others staring at us," Tito reminded.

"Okay, I'm on my way out," Miko said, and left the table.

FORTY SEVEN

Hours dragged like days. Rubyhall had no intention of keeping Rubin waiting for the impossible. Lam's effort to fetch the 37carat ruby was getting him nowhere.

Rubyhall called Den. Lord wasn't making any commitment despite Den's intervention. Something was not right. So with no other options left at his disposal, Rubyhall called Rubin at the Oriental.

"Rubin!" Rubyhall continued. "We have a little problem with the 37carat piece. I will have to do something I haven't done in ages. You will get your 37carat piece just one week late. I'll have our men deliver it to your office in New York, at no extra cost."

"Why? What happened?" Rubin asked shockingly.

"It's a long dirty story, which you don't want to hear," Rubyhall added. "I just don't want to waste your time. I called David a few minutes ago, and told him you are on your way home tonight. You will see all the rubies in New York, in less than a week. Your dad has no problem with that. He needs you back urgently. Listen, you don't have to pay the bills at the Oriental. It's all taken care of. By the time you reach the receptionist, you will meet my secretary, Simi. She will give you an envelope. Your air ticket is in it. Your check out time is approaching. I must say, less than two hours. The limousine is waiting to take you to Don Muang International Airport. Don't forget to check once again the departure time."

"This is a real surprise, especially coming from you," Rubin said, glancing at his watch. In fact, he had other plans for the day, and now all had to be canceled.

"This time it had to happen this way," Rubyhall said apologetically. "Anyway, you will appreciate this arrangement. I think it's better for your health this way. You better leave the city, before something unfriendly happens to you. There is lot of rumors. I'll explain to you when you have reached home safely. That's all I can say. So don't waste your time. Forget about July. Is she still in your room?"

"No. She just left," Rubin said, expressionless.

"Good. Leave a message for her with the reception: Bon Voyage!" Rubyhall hung up the phone.

All of a sudden, like a warning, situations changed, and after glancing once again at his watch, Rubin rushed to pack his belongings. This was the first such experience for him.

Rubyhall's ambiguous statement regarding Rubin's health and safety rung in his ears repeatedly. Who would want to hurt him when his only dealing was with Rubyhall? Bangkok was considered a relatively safe city, especially Silom, and its environs.

He glanced once again at his watch. Everything was packed, and as he arrived at the reception, Rubyhall's secretary was waiting for him with an envelope.

"Everything is in," Simi said, affectionately. The limo was waiting for him outside the hotel. Rubin couldn't believe events happening at such a fast pace. When he came to Bangkok, he thought that he would be able to see all the rubies he wanted to buy. Now he was returning home with none. Rubyhall was going to deliver all the pieces in a week. He wondered what was going on at the Rubyhall's headquarters, something strange and serious. But he was no match to ask such questions. He believed in Rubyhall's promise. One week! Period!

He thought of July and their brief relationship.

Like a flash they met and conquered each other only to separate without knowing more. Her face and smile kept beaming back and forth, as the limo approached Don Muang International Airport.

He thought of calling her from the airport. Then, he remembered Rubyhall's remark. He didn't want any trouble, especially when departing.

While waiting at the lounge for his departure, a beautiful lady in a sarong approached him and said, "You must be Mr Rubin Rosenberg, right? Here is a message for you." She handed him a packet, and then disappeared.

He even forgot to ask who she was. There were several of them who looked pretty much the same if he decided to chase. She was gone. Rubin got back to his seat and checked the time once again. He had another twenty minutes to board the Thai Airways International flight. He looked around to see if anyone was watching him. Slowly he opened the packet wondering about its content. It was a message from Rubyhall wishing him a safe journey, and apologizing once again for the inconvenience.

As he boarded the plane, that same lady returned waving final goodbye to him.

FORTY EIGHT

The receptionist brought in one Bill Bose, after getting permission from Jeb Singthowala. The office was less busy, as Jeb welcomed Bose.

"Have a seat, Mr Bose. Can I get you anything to drink?" Jeb asked.

"No, Mr Jeb. I'm just fine," Bose said politely.

"Okay," continued Jeb. "I did go through your 37carat ruby. Perfect color; eye clean stone, and the cut, just right. Now, what is missing is your price. Do you have an asking price on this ruby?"

"You like it, don't you? That's good." Bose felt confident after Jeb's comment.

"Do you mind if I ask you some personal questions? You are under no obligation. If you think I am wrong, be open. I won't go further. You see different gem dealers have different styles. This is my style. It's a two way street. If you want to know anything about me be frank. I will be more than pleased to answer any of your questions," Jeb reasoned.

"I don't think that will be necessary," Bose added. "I already know who you are. Okay, what would you like to know about me?"

Jeb paused. He had already done his homework.

"Nothing much," Jeb said. "I'm just curious as to where you got this piece. Was this a cut piece when you bought it or did you buy it as a rough and then decided to cut?"

"I bought it as a rough and then got it cut," Bose answered promptly.

"Would you mind showing me the leftover from the rough, if you have it with you?" Jeb asked Bose in a nice way.

"Why are you asking this? No one has ever asked this before. What's the matter with the stone?" Bose replied, confused.

"Nothing unusual. If you don't have it with you, it's fine," Jeb said, relaxed.

"It had the crystal habits of a ruby," Bose reminded.

"So you know what I'm talking about, don't you?" Jeb said smilingly. Bose felt uneasy with Jeb's statement, but waited.

"Do you remember roughly the weight of your uncut ruby before being cut?" Jeb asked, expecting a quick reply.

"A hundred carat! We got a nice piece of 37carat, and a few small stones. We lost quite a lot," Bose replied.

"Where did you buy this rough?" Jeb asked.

"Of course, Burma. Where else can you get this color?" Bose said impatiently.

"Luc Yen, Vietnam! I've seen some stones from that mine of similar color," Jeb quipped. Bose paused. There was something wrong with the stone or price. And Jeb was slowly getting to that point.

"Interesting. Have you been to those mines?" Bose quipped.

"Yeah, several times," Jeb said. "I've never been an armchair dealer in my life. I always go to the source to compare everything including color, shape, and price. So I have an understanding of quality."

"I'm not surprised," Bose said.

"My question now is what makes you so sure this ruby came from Burma? You have never been to that part of the world. What's your sure bet for confirmation?"

That was too direct. Jeb was beginning to peel Bose like onions. His sharp and toxic tongue quite often hurt people both, friends and dealers.

"My friends don't cheat me," Bose said firmly. "I've tremendous amount of trust in them. This is not the first deal."

"That's the problem. I'll get back to that part later. Now, what would be the asking price for a piece of ruby like this?" Jeb said, looking directly into Bose's eyes.

Bose scratched his head feverishly, before looking straight into Jeb's eyes. There was a bit of nervousness, as he calibrated the numbers.

"What would you like to offer for this magnificent ruby?"

Jeb knew instantly Bose was using the reverse psychology to test the waters.

"Now before we waste too much of our precious time, I've only one question. What's your final price, which includes your profit? No room for bargaining. I know how much it is worth. But I want you to say that in one word or a sentence," Jeb said plainly.

That took Bose by surprise, a tactic, which didn't leave room for any sort of maneuver. He looked tense, as the build up from within released beads of sweat on his forehead. He tried to smile, but knew it didn't work out well. Finally, after intense contemplation, he uttered quietly, "One million dollars!"

Jeb stared at Bose without any emotion and asked, "Is that your final price?"

"I think so," Bose said quickly.

Jeb took his calculator and punched few numbers and double-checked again, before showing it to him. Bose's face turned white, as he read the numbers quietly.

"I calculated this way," Jeb added. "The weight of the stone is 37 carat. I will give this piece out of compassion two hundred dollars per carat. So if you multiply thirtyseven carat times two hundred, you should get seven thousand four hundred dollars, and I'm giving you a free one way ticket to Djibouti. Package deal. That's what it is worth. Nothing more, nothing less."

"Why are you so generous, Jeb?" Bose asked, puzzled.

"Because that's what I do when I see people make mistakes in their buying," Jeb continued. "I give them enough time to rethink in a vacation spot, where nobody bothers them. This is not the first time

I have done something like this. Countless recipients have enjoyed this privilege only to return punctually. You are not an exception."

"Are you sure, you didn't make a mistake in your judgment?" Bose asked nervously.

"Nope," Jeb replied. "You gave me enough time to study this 37carat ruby. I'm perfectly convinced of my judgment. You will make a good profit if you allow me to buy this ruby at my price."

"Where did I go wrong? There is a big difference in your price and mine," Bose said looking confused.

"That's the fun of the so-called price / quality mood swings," Jeb continued. "What do you think about this offer? You have nothing to lose. If you think you lost, then it is better to lose now before it is too late. Period."

"I don't understand your logic behind this calculation. Pardon me, if I'm a bit slow. Why so low?" Bose asked.

"Okay," Jeb said. "Let me share my thoughts with you. This ruby is definitely not from Burma, Vietnam, Thailand, or even from hell. This ruby is from another country, possibly the United States of America!"

"Do they have rubies in America? I didn't know that," Bose said, gasping for breath.

"What I meant to say is your ruby is a good quality synthetic made in that part of the world by some clever scientists in a lab. Whoever gave you this piece knew what they were doing. The problem was you. You just took it on faith, because it came from your beloved crooked friends. Another fact is that whenever you orbit with a piece of this size, you don't have to do so much talking and convincing. If you had taken a bit of your time getting it identified by an independent gem testing laboratory like the one in Switzerland, where an opinion on its identity or origin is given if requested. It's clear and an easy option. I wouldn't be talking like this today if you had that bit of information with your ruby. And, a ruby of this size should fetch a lot if it had been proven it came from Burma, many more times than the one million dollars you just quoted me.

That means your numbers were too low for a natural good quality ruby of this size," Jeb commented.

The telephone rang. It was his secretary. He reminded her not to take any calls for him for another half an hour. Jeb then hung up the phone turning his attention to Bose.

"That bad?" Bose asked.

"What really surprised me is the precise size of this stone. I mean, the 37 carat! There is another ruby of the same quality with a report from the Swiss lab in the hands of a ruby dealer. So there must be some sinister reason behind cutting the rough to this precise carat weight. They have used you as a go between to test the waters," Jeb said to Bose.

"I don't understand," Bose added.

"Well, you understand now that your new ruby is not the piece you represent. If you had been elsewhere, you would have been dead by now. The real ruby dealers take every transaction, opening and closing very seriously, because it affects a lot of people and their credibility. You cheated death today to be precise. I've an envelope for you. Before that, here is your ruby. Weigh the stone before you put it in your pocket. Double-check. I usually don't allow anyone to return in the guise of an error. Now open the envelope and read the instructions carefully," Jeb said calmly.

He waited for Bose's reaction.

"It's an air ticket to . . . ., where on earth is this place?"

"Djibouti! Your one way ticket. It's valid for a year. You have all the time in the world to rethink before you enter Silom. There are schools around the world where you can learn about identifying natural from synthetic. That's your only defense against ignorance. When we do business, we mean it. It's serious, no room for a mistake or error of any sort. Deceit of any sort will be punished severely without any mercy. Take your ruby and the envelope. Have a meaningful comeback," Jeb said to Bose in a friendly manner.

While leaving Jeb's office, Bose realized what a goof he was carrying a synthetic ruby instead of a natural one and that too without asking any questions. He wanted to kill Papov for using him as a guinea pig. Going back to Pattaya and telling Papov the truth was something he wasn't trained for, and he began to worry about it.

FORTY NINE

Polly opened her diary to mark an important appointment. There was a slight hint of a smile on her face, as she penned the names between the parallel lines of the page. Fond memories flashed through her mind, as she wrote the last words of their name. Their sweet voice, colorful personality, and that warm embrace permeated once again, as she struggled to sit straight before closing her personal diary. She sat for a while in deep thought as to what to do. There was a knock first, and the door opened.

Phil walked to her side with his files, which meant business. His business empire engulfed every nook and corner of the world wherever there was electricity making sure every home had a personal computer to fiddle with, either for fun or work.

"Our competitors are really nosing into our territory not knowing the dangerous landscape lying ahead. They are going to burn their money and people in this wretched poker game till their brains wake up from illusion," Phil said to Polly.

"Phil, what are you talking about? I was in bliss when you came in, and it's gone," Polly replied, turning her attention towards him.

"What sort of a bliss? How can you engage in bliss when we are fighting for survival? They are going to eat us alive. You must understand the whole concept. That's what I mean," Phil said, staring at his wife impatiently.

"You know something. We have more than enough to live on for several decades, if we live the way we do now. Let others also get a piece of this world. It's for everyone. Live and let live.

Why don't we put aside business for a while and think about the beautiful things in the world? Take some time to smell the roses. I know you don't have the time, but at least you can spare some time with me in this spacious room when I need you," Polly said, trying to reason with him.

"What beautiful things? You have more than enough to enjoy, and what more do you need. I know," Phil said, remembering something.

"You know what?" she asked.

"Rubies! I knew it the moment you mentioned beautiful things. What are you up to this time? Do you have an inventory of your collection so far?" Phil asked.

"No. I don't. Why should I? If I do anything like that the whole romance is gone. I want to keep it the way it is," Polly answered.

"You are nuts," Phil said, angrily. "Do you really see all these rubies you have bought so far?"

"How come you are so curious now when I have begged several times for your attention?" Polly asked quietly.

"Well, let me get to the point," Phil said. "I've a meeting with a group of people in traditional shield and spear from Dukuduku village, Kwazulu Natal!"

"Where on earth is this country? Never heard of such a place. A new discovery by our people?" she asked.

"It's neither new or old. The country has been on this planet before we were born. Africa! That's where it is. The whole continent is for heaven's sake untapped. Now what's your big problem?" Phil said, knowing her behavior.

"A 37carat, perfect, Burmese ruby, hot red, lightly included, and well cut," Polly added. "Miko and Tito are coming here to show me the piece. They know too well what I like and they always go the extra mile to obtain the rare ones for my enjoyment in privacy. That's the bliss I was talking about."

"Again? I'm sure it's not going to be that cheap. Okay, do

what you think is sensible and I'll talk to you later. I must go to the meeting," Phil said, glancing at his beloved wife.

Phil grabbed his files and planted a soft kiss on her lips, as he walked to the door.

FIFTY

"It's beautiful," Polly said, as she looked at her ruby necklace in front of the mirror. There was no one around to compliment her.

This was one of her hobbies, when she felt too bored with domestic responsibilities. She had an army of servants who took care of her mansion. Her two daughters Almandina and Spessartina embraced Buddhism thoroughly practicing the tenets much stricter than the average Buddhist. Their strict vegetarianism, refrainment from drugs, alcohol, sex, and other social activities took the Win family by surprise. The girls were not interested in their family's wealth, instead they engaged in some sort of meditation, which only they knew.

In the end, Polly turned to her friends to parade her collections when one arrived, and this time it was a 37carat ruby from Mogok, Burma. Polly never ventured out of Bangkok for one reason.

KIDNAPPING!

She was like a bird in a golden cage wanting to be free and gay, but was restricted to a very few selected known friends through careful appointments.

The color and brilliance of the ruby necklace was irresistible. She loved the piece all the time. She was enjoying the catwalk in her spacious room in style. The classical music in the background gave her the right mood and gravity, as she writhed her aerobic trained body to the tune. A lonely rich woman!

Phil had no interest in her pet hobby instead business came first. He yielded to all her requests without fail, and the 37carat ruby became another acquisition after the reminder slip showed up in front of his desk.

She put the gems back in the safe deposit box, but not before several rounds of scrutinizing the number of rubies in the necklace. Only she, Phil, and God knew the number combination. She checked the day's appointment. She chose to dress casually, an unusual tradition, but she had a reason. She felt restless and nervous about her image. Suddenly, she felt like pretending to be a teenager and dress like one. Her heart had another interpretation. There was a degree of constraint reminding her to be herself, despite the sudden behavioral metamorphosis.

There was a gentle knock on the door. It was her secretary, Nini.

"Mrs Win, Miko and Tito would like to see you."

"Okay, send them in," said Polly calmly. She glanced at her 25carat ruby ring her favorite when she had friends visiting her, and the cool flashes from the facets kept her always calm and alert. The power of ruby was always there to protect her. She checked her dress and the desk once again, as the door opened.

"Hi, Tito! Hi Miko!" She embraced them warmly.

"Hi, Polly! Nice to see you again," Tito said, sniffing the air.

"Take your seats and make yourself comfortable. Drinks?" she asked.

"No, thank you. We are just fine," Miko replied plainly.

"You can't say that," she added. "You are my guests. My friends brought some African punch for my opinion. I was too busy to try it. Why don't we try it together and see what it tastes like?"

"Maybe, after the business, Polly," Tito said. "If you want to see the ruby the way it is, it would be better to see it now. With the African punch, the ruby might look like an apple."

Everyone laughed heartily.

"You are the experts. After the business, we will try the punch," she answered.

"Tito has the ruby, Polly," said Miko, reminding her.

Polly waited patiently, as Tito opened a small black stone box in front of her.

"Oh my God, look at the stone. Is this from Mogok too?" Polly couldn't stand straight. The color was so hot and pleasant she needed more time to view.

"Yep," said Tito firmly.

"Why does God always put stones like these in Burma? I've asked this question several times, when colorful stones like these ended up in my safe," she said.

"Freak of nature, I suppose. Nothing to do with the people," Miko added. "I've the origin report from the Swiss laboratory. You may want to read it."

"Nay," Polly said. "I trust you both. Why this sudden request?"

"Just a friendly reminder. But look at the color first. It's superb, and with this size you see the color better. Very tiny inclusions and fair to good cut. It is a jackpot stone, Polly. When we saw this stone, we knew it had to be in your hands. You deserve it. God's lovely creation is in your hands now. An exclusive privilege," Miko said knowing her mood. She loved to hear such explanations, and Tito and Miko used information tidbits without fail to cheer her up before the buy.

"I'm very lucky," Polly answered. "My husband says that all the time. I don't know what I did in my past life. Maybe, I was too good to enjoy the fruits in this lifetime due to my meritorious karma."

"Well, if that's the case, you must continue the practice for mutual benefits, don't you think?" Miko looked at Tito.

"I'm sure we have met before in one of our past lives, Miko. I can identify you very well. Do you want me to say that?" Polly reminded, as a friendly comment.

"Nope," Tito said. "Please don't. Save that information for a future date."

"I was about to say that. Good, you identified my thoughts," she quipped.

She rolled the ruby in her palm, and walked around the room twisting and turning her arms to check the color contrasts, and with every turn she smiled broadly. She never bargained with them, because if it were initiated she knew from her husband and past experiences that there were different ways of losing the stone. She had this rule.

They knew it and she got the stones every time when a big piece was brought to her attention. Rubies never frightened her and all these years they were good to her. For some reason her husband's business boomed whenever she purchased a big and good one. Knowing this phenomenon, Phil never disappointed her. When she got carried away by the rubies Phil had a new client from some God forbidden place paying him back in long-term contracts at ten times the price of the ruby. That was his jackpot.

Now she took her seat and gazed at Miko and Tito.

"Do you have any story for this ruby, Tito?" she asked curiously.

Tito and Miko looked at each other in a quick surprise. It would look stupid to relate the chaotic experiences they had just survived. Instead, Miko took the initiative to quench her curiosity.

"I'm afraid not a good one," he added. "I don't think you want to hear it."

"That's what I like," Polly answered. "None of the rubies you sold me had a pleasant story. Why is it like that all the time?"

"That's the nature of rubies genesis," Tito said. "When a hot red ruby is sitting on my palm, I also thought about it several times. But I don't think there is much use worrying about what happened before we were even born. What we all should worry about is after it has taken up its residence in its right place. How long are they gonna stay? If the rubies think they want to continue their passionate journey above the ground, then they will move from hand to hand depending upon the times. History is full of such painful journeys. You could prevent that if you know how to handle them reverently. They are very conscious beauties, which very few people understand. Those who do understand their language know how to live with them without any side-effects and all that stuff."

"So that's the secret of this ruby?" she echoed her thoughts.

"More than that," Miko added. "It started its journey deep inside the jungles of Burma. The miner who found the rough screamed out of hell, when he spotted a red stone sitting in the dirt. When he plucked the rough from the dirty ground, his eyes almost popped out of their socket. It was a big one."

She interrupted. "Then what happened?"

"He wrapped it in a newspaper and hid the piece in his underwear to avoid suspicion. The guy was trigger-happy and foolish. The lifelong dream had come true after a stressful period of ten years. He knew where to sell."

"Bangkok, right?" Polly uttered unconsciously, "and then?"

"That meant a long journey to the town, and from there to Bangkok," Miko said. "Only his wife and brother knew about his new found luck. But his jealous brother killed him, while accompanying him to the Thai border. As he continued the journey, he refused to stop at one of the military checkpoints, so the Burmese soldier shot him. After searching the corpse, he found this ruby and headed to the Thai Burmese border town of Mae Sai, and this chap got shot while swapping the stone with a Thai by a Thai soldier, who mistook it for a drug transaction in the jungle. And the lucky Thai continued his journey to Chantaburi disguised as a Buddhist monk, and from there it has reached the right person to enjoy the beauty and rarity for the rest of its life."

"That's a very sad ending," she commented. "I pity the poor fellow. What happened to the Bangkok buyer? Is he still alive?"

"Very much so. He is still alive," replied Tito glancing at Miko.

"Lots of death with this ruby, aren't there?" she commented looking elsewhere.

"It's with all big stones everywhere in the world. The ruby is innocent all the time. Instead, it's the ignorant couriers who get into trouble and go through all the inconveniences. It's technically speaking avoidable if you just know how to do it," Miko said tactfully.

"So, at last, I'm the lucky woman to hold this ruby for the rest of my life," Polly said happily, after hearing the thrilling story.

"That's your destiny, Polly," Tito added, "and you deserve it."

GEMSICUTED!

243

"You are thinking like me," she replied, "and that's good. How should I pay you this time?"

"Like always," Miko said, "bank transfer. Here is the Swiss bank account number, and the price of the ruby." He gave her an envelope.

"That's all?" she asked. "Well, you all made my day with a good ending. Now let's celebrate this purchase with the African punch. What do you say?"

"As you wish, Polly," Tito said.

Meanwhile deep inside, they thanked Winston, Sanders, Jeb, and Baddy for making this event possible in the last minute, and the lucky jackpot lottery. All in one! They couldn't conceal their happiness, as they laughed with Polly's jokes, while drinking her favorite African punch.

The taste was horrible, but the ruby was gone, and the money was in.

FIFTY ONE

The more Takashi tried, the greater it became obvious, that getting a job in Thailand was certainly difficult. Lay off and unrest among the middle-class and poor became a daily occurrence. Even though the country and people were much friendlier than other countries in the region, the basic requirement of having a steady income and decent job to convince his parents and friends began to wane.

He knew his savings were going to disappear within a matter of time. Going back to America wasn't in his agenda at all, and the economic recovery in the region wasn't in the offing, even though predictions by the pundits suggested anywhere from five years to several decades depending on the severity and the political willingness to reform. Age-old tradition and bureaucracy weren't that easy to change.

With such a gloomy scenario lying ahead, Takashi began to ponder whether it was worth living in the first place. His only liability was to his parents, and being single and without any credible personal achievement, he theorized it was better to die as a loser than living.

After having traveled to several provinces in the North and Northeast of Thailand, the local population's simplicity and nature consciousness took him by surprise, even though he hated the countryside. There was no way he was going to live that way. He was born in a city, and remained addicted to living in a city no matter how severe the situation was. But the bottom line was how long.

While on his way back to Bangkok, he did stop at the province of Chantaburi. He couldn't believe his eyes at the number of rubies and sapphires moving from hand to hand with smiles, instead of guns. Though difficult to identify and value by just viewing, it stimulated an interest in gems. They were so small and portable, and he knew from others these beauties weren't that cheap. Yet, he thought for a second about how these people made money. If the investment was little, he thought of starting an all out new career to show his parents and friends that he was still standing on his own legs. That's when he thought of Lam.

Just for the sake of an experience, he bought a small ruby from a street dealer. There were so many of them carrying red stones, he assumed every red stone to be a ruby. The street dealers were more than happy to meet ignorant buyers because for reasons only they knew they took it for granted that the buyers never returned. And a Japanese look-alike meant easy money, because by tradition they were shy, and the street dealers took advantage of it. Then as if by a happy accident, he met one Yoshida, a Japanese buyer, who came regularly to Chantaburi to buy rubies. They got together while staying at the K.P. Grand hotel.

One thing led to another. When Takashi showed the ruby he bought for Yoshida's comment, the result shocked him. The gem identification kits Yoshida carried became a curiosity for Takashi.

Yoshida took Takashi to his room and showed how he identified the red stone. It was not a ruby instead it was a red glass. The gemological identification by Yoshida broke Takashi's heart.

Another loser! He cried in front of Yoshida for the loss of money and face. Whatever he touched was turning into garbage.

Yoshida tried to console Takashi that it was normal for any new person to be duped, but Takashi was in no mood to absorb Yoshida's reasoning. Instead, he saw himself as a qualified misfit.

That night, Yoshida and Takashi had dinner together, and Yoshida explained to Takashi how he came into the ruby business. But Takashi's mind was elsewhere after the red stone experience. For him, he saw the whole world as too unfair wherever he went.

Either someone was out to cheat him or never gave him an opportunity to prove himself. Always something went wrong.

The next day, he decided to leave for Bangkok, without even telling Yoshida, even though he was willing to help Takashi to locate the crook who sold him a red glass as a ruby. The dejection and failures one after another led him to the conclusion that he was no longer useful to the world, and to himself. He didn't know what to do next, but he had something brewing in his mind.

No sooner had he reached Bangkok, when he called Lam, he wasn't at home. He then decided to visit Tuna's Club & Restaurant for consolation. When he arrived at her place, she had gone to the bank for a few hours. Takashi saw these events as a bad omen. Silly, evil thoughts began to dominate him.

He left her place, and decided to roam at the Emporium, a huge department store on Sukhumvit Road. Kinokuniya Book Store caught his attention. A virtual selection of books from around the world neatly laid made it easier for a quick reference. As he strolled the store, from one subject to another, one book interested him.

The Book of Five Rings by Miyamoto Mushashi! He bought the book immediately.

Instead of going back to Tuna's place, he took a bus to Siam Square. From Siam Square he took another bus to Sanam Luang. Khao San Road was only a walking distance from Sanam Luang. After reaching his guesthouse, he decided to immerse himself in the book. From page to page, he read like in his school days absorbing every minute details and its practical use. He liked the message in the book, especially the author's interpretation of enlightenment and the paths to success.

After reading halfway through, he realized that putting into practice Miyamoto Musashi's methods meant discipline, insight, and self-reliance. All seemed easy to read and describe, but at this particular juncture, he needed a job and money to stay alive more than the attainment of enlightenment prescribed in the book. He felt depressed after reading arriving at a conclusion that it was difficult to attain success with so much competition and heartless people around.

Takashi pondered his next move. Without a job and money traveling here and there meant going bankrupt soon. The dreadful thought of calling home for help meant losing his face again. As the accumulation of worries peaked, his body became weak. He couldn't sleep.

After a while, he decided to call Jay again to see if he was at his home. There was still no answer. Instead, he decided to go again to Tuna's Club & Restaurant.

FIFTY TWO

Troublov waited patiently at the SV City Tower's Narai Pizzaria shop.

After ordering a vegetarian pizza and a salad, he moved to a corner seat so that he saw the people arriving and leaving. The shop was less crowded. The music was still on. He walked to the counter to fill in the bowl a balanced mixture of vegetables and fruits, a skill he had yet to learn compared to the young Thais. In a matter of minutes, he stood in awe the way they built pagodas in a salad bowl. After he had filled in, he returned to his seat watching the people carefully.

At this time, Sanders arrived at Narai with Goldie, carrying shopping bags from the Emporium, a place that she loved to frequent. She looked beautiful from a distance and no wonder, Troublov thought, Sanders was after her.

Now that was going to stop if everything went well according to his plan. He knew from the information he had, after Narai, she usually went to a manicure facility and then back to her condo on the twenty third floor.

Troublov ate slowly keeping a close watch on them, as they took the opposite end seat facing the main road. They were talking so much he heard their loud laughter. He had no other choice than to eat slowly or order another pizza. After glancing at his watch, he ate slowly. Goldie was still in a jovial mood with Sanders saying something, and then laughing, and then she saying something, and he laughing, it was going on and on. Others at the shop wondered what was the big deal, as both Sanders and Goldie ignored other's reaction. Troublov thought they were getting ready for something special.

After paying their bill, he saw them walking toward the elevator. He continued eating with his mind concentrated on them, and at the same time surveying the escape route.

Troublov didn't wait any longer. After paying his bill at the counter, he took a deep breath knowing the hurdles lying ahead. If anything went wrong during the course, he knew the price he had to pay, should he trip up.

He walked to the elevator with his backpack. The door opened, and he pressed the twentythird floor. From the information he had, the front door wasn't that strong. All he needed to do was to ready his battery operated screwdriver, and a palmtop sized gadget nicknamed ' Popov ', a tiny device that had the ability to break the security code given to him by Vladimir.

Whenever Sanders was with Goldie she was too careless. At least that was the information given to him by Vladimir. But he didn't want to take any more chances given the time he had to accomplish the job.

Troublov eyed the twentythird floor, when the red light flashed off. The door opened quietly. He wore a pair of black plastic gloves for efficiency, and walked to the room on the left. After remembering the condo number, his hands moved swiftly for the automatic screwdriver. But his sharp eyes noticed one thing. The door wasn't closed properly. Something was wrong. He pulled the door stealthily. The room was pitch black. He slipped on the night vision goggle.

Then he heard low whispers and high moaning in the next room. That was the last thing in the world he needed to watch, someone having a good time in bed. The rooms were well decorated with several antique jade collections, all behind the glass doors. A bronze statue of a naked woman caught his attention. He put his hands along the cleavage of the statue unconsciously, as if he remembered something. The closer he got to the bedroom, the weaker Troublov felt. His killer instinct was hemorrhaging away with each moan. Killing someone when they were having sex wasn't the skill he was neither trained at nor prepared for. He slowly opened the door for a better view. The incandescent light in the bedroom illuminating the two rolling naked bodies drove him crazy. The way they pumped each other urged Troublov to throw his crazy looking goggles and handgloves into his backpack and join them naked on their bed. His concentration level was so low he looked worried and desperate. He had two choices.

Either join them naked or kill both. With such a beautiful body lying in front, he felt like crying. Though he was trained to be strong and alert when it came to women, he couldn't exert the courage he usually had when with men. He had no problem killing Pavlov. This was the man who slaughtered Pavlov like a frog mercilessly. But Goldie was something altogether different. If he stood there any longer watching their pumping and moaning he had no other choice than watch sucking his own thumb or scream. His knees went weak.

Meanwhile, Sanders grabbed Goldie's pinkish red breasts and squeezed several times exciting her into a different level. The way he licked and sucked her knee and then inching his way to her marble thighs sent chills up and down her well-built body. She in turn leaned back allowing his cock to enter her. Both looked soaked in their own liquids and the more he played with her clit, the greater her enjoyment became driving Troublov to cry on quietly.

Now Goldie began to taste his cock in her mouth pulling his foreskin back and forth like peeling a banana, running her tongue around the bulged hot red head, before soaking them in her throat. This was something Troublov had never seen in his life before. She was so good in what she was doing, Sanders was just enjoying her skill.

Troublov glanced at his watch. It was approaching eleven. He didn't have the energy to kill either of them. Instead, he watched them enviously leaving the backpack on the floor and holding his own cock uptight. It was bulging beyond his control in his pants. Now she spread her legs wider for Sanders. Sanders sunk his head between her legs and tongued her clit and kept continuing, till she came thrusting back in force. After repositioning themselves, the same but slightly different posture yielded better results, as if both were enjoying the ride.

Troublov had no balls to watch further. As they continued their bedroom gymnastics, he walked slowly to the front door without the goggle and his backpack holding his cock intact. He wanted to kill himself for watching such a steamy scene. All the preparation he had for a fine execution went awry.

Before he could push the button for the elevator, he felt a gun pointed at his head. He turned around slowly.

"Vladimir! What are you doing here?" he cried faintly. It was too late. The answer was quick and precise.

Vladimir pulled the trigger, and the bullet tore through Troublov's brain, felling him to the ground noiselessly. He pulled Troublov's bleeding dead body to the front door of Goldie's condo, and then fled the scene.

FIFTY THREE

Lam returned home with a sunken feeling, after being tattooed and fired from the job by Rubyhall, and he had a month to leave his posh condo, when other details were settled. Marla received the news at first in shock and disbelief, followed by a deep sadness. For them the whole world was splitting apart, because of a 37carat ruby, and Rubyhall's inability to replace one immediately. Both sat in the living room speechless pondering their future. Finding a new job was close to impossible when the economy in the country and in the whole region was going down like a bungy dive. Fear and desperation ran through Lam's mind, while Marla kept wondering his thoughts. She was too scared to ignite his anger after watching him for the past several days. It was a difficult moment in her life.

For reason he couldn't explain, Lam was weighing several options. He had no intention of creating a miserable situation for Marla and his two girls. It was already taken care of.

The next phase was his future. This was a job he loved so much. But that has been plucked away by a 37carat ruby. He didn't realize until now how powerful rubies were, when it came to certain events. That thought reminded him of a tale told by Tom Chavalit about Aung San, the father of Aung San Suu Kyi, Burmese Nobel Peace prizewinner.

The Burmese soldiers killed him during a rally and the rumor was he forgot to wear the ruby he had worn everyday, leaving others on the stage unhurt.

The legend also had a different tale about rubies. The lucky owner was assured of peaceful life with all men, and a guarantee that his possessions would never be taken away from him, free from other damages. There was even a suggestion for the wearer to insert rubies into their flesh so that no sword, spear, or gun, could hurt them. For Jay, it was all wholesome bull looking at his own fate. It was legend and lore rather than fact, but events after a 37carat ruby came into the Bangkok market had brought him only misery rather than luck.

He began to hate rubies, and Rubyhall, of course. All his friends began to show disinterest in him after being fired by Rubyhall. They knew already, Lam had no more future. Working for someone else was close to impossible, because they had no interest in hiring a man of Jay's stature.

Jay had only two options. Either leave the country or start on his own. Both looked a distant possibility due to his age and competition. So there was nothing left, and the industry believed Rubyhall's version rather than his, because Rubyhall was more powerful and well known. He was just a shadow. This attitude disturbed him, even though he had contributed a lot to the organization, which the world and the industry didn't see. With this negative feelings accumulating incrementally by the second, he lost interest in everything, even his own existence. The only good friend he had was Tuna. She was a good listener and an understanding woman, and now his new friend, Harry Takashi, but for how long.

Without detailing further, he asked Marla to leave for Chiang Mai in a couple of day's time. She didn't understand his motive. He had a condo in her name, and had transferred all his bank deposits into her account. She refused at first to leave him but after his persistent reasoning, she decided to move to Chiang Mai with their two girls.

They were too young to understand the complicated events, and Lam was in no mood to explain them. He saw it as a relief once and for all from family commitments. Now it was just a few other important things. Some ideas were brewing in his mind, but he had no precise plans.

First, he decided to get out of his condo to be away from family. He loved to visit only one place, Tuna's Club and Restaurant!

The timing was consistent, as Takashi arrived at Tuna's Club & Restaurant just after Lam. It was already six, and the regulars had arrived to watch the replay of the world cup soccer. Some had already lost a lot after betting against France for Brazil and the winners decided to celebrate in style. There was disbelief and shock after Brazil's unexpected defeat, and Lam and Takashi had no problem joining the losers. The wine, which followed after the food kept the conversation going. As the gathering became too noisy, Lam winked at Takashi, and then led him to a corner seat, as if he had something to say. Takashi had no problem, because he had all the time in the world to listen to anyone as long as it had any mention of job or money. The rest was irrelevant, but still he insisted that he was listening. It was a clever disguise.

Lam had ideas, and he needed Takashi to accomplish his last goal knowing his pathetic situation. And he was right. Takashi too was thinking in a similar way, but due to the wine and beer, he nodded to Lam's ideas. He had no reason to think further. His life was falling apart. Surrendering in front of his parents without any achievement was the last thing in the world he could contemplate.

After paying the bills, they both got into a taxi and headed to a dirty-looking soi(lane). Lam knew the inhabitants of this dirty-looking soi (lane) somewhere close to Klong Toey.

Narong, a short and sturdy-looking man in his late forties, emerged from his apartment to welcome Lam and Takashi. Lam knew him through one of the gem brokers who frequented him while at Rubyhall's. Narong was the contact when it came to fake guns of any famous brand. Only he and a few policemen knew the original source of all the expensive guns reaching them at a cost.

Narong drove them to an unnamed apartment in Rangsit to show them the brands he had. Lam chose a Magnum .45. In fact, he bought two, one for him and Takashi. Takashi smiled unknowingly, while holding the gun in his hand. Lam was observing Takashi's reaction. He was trigger-happy looking like a fool. After collecting the money, Narong drove back to Sukhumvit, and dropped them in front of the Sheraton Grande hotel.

From there, they hailed a cab to his condo. Takashi accompanied Lam to his condo at the President Park for the first time. The two guns they bought were carefully concealed in a plastic bag. Takashi was really surprised by the size of his condo and the facilities inside. It looked a bit bigger than the one where he used to live, while working in Hong Kong.

It was just the two of them now. After hiding the guns in a safe place, Lam brought in more wine and beer to keep the mood at bay. He knew the time had come to implement the idea, which was unthinkable a few weeks ago. Now with Takashi in deep shit financially or otherwise there was no problem convincing him what to do. Lam needed an ally in that last moment to cheer him up for one more time.

Takashi too was having some serious thoughts, even though he was drunk. Though he had difficulty putting all those thoughts together into a meaningful sentence, he knew the purpose of the entertainment after seeing the guns. Someone had to die, and he had no idea who that was going to be. But he had no problem with that after he knew both had become some sort of losers, and perhaps this was one way to show the world they did something no matter how stupid the event might be. He glanced at Lam.

Everything looked blurred to him. Eventually, he slumped into the sofa. Lam looked at Takashi, and didn't feel like saying anything. His mind was clear, precise and determined, even though he was drinking as much as Takashi. The time had come to do something about it, and the images of his targets became more transparent and visible.

FIFTY FOUR

Ruth had been staying in a boarding school after the false pregnancy sign, and Chin's forced hospitalization.

After heeding to expert's recommendations, Sanders decided to send her far away from Bangkok's the so-called feel free environment. He believed the strict disciplinary environment in Singapore was the best panacea, while he sorted out issues regarding his divorce with Chin. He had lawyers working on it, and believed positively that at the right time Ruth would be able to return and stay with him or he could go to Singapore and visit her, whichever was convenient provided everything went well according to his plan.

Then came his special relationship with Goldie, as it was entering into a serious phase. He would have loved to officially marry Goldie and make it public and well known. Due to the entangled business interests she had with her inactive American husband and the commitments with several private, and government agencies the task became more difficult.

But they loved to continue the relationship the way it stood, irrespective of the pressures and commitments from elsewhere. Staying alone in different condos and villas around Bangkok, to avoid detection by the Russian gangs made him vulnerable and less free.

On the contrary, he would have loved to stay with Ruth and repair the damages done in their relationship, but for safety reasons he had to send her away, Chin was a confirmed lost case after the strange diagnosis by his controversial friend Dr Tuchinda. A carefully drafted divorce was the only way to put a full stop to avoid any further backlashes from her relatives and friends, who wanted a big share of his wealth.

But he had Jeb and Baddy standing behind to give him moral and financial support in case he had to flee the country knowing the unpredictable business landscape and the sliding economy in general.

The big blow came after they found Troublov's dead body in front of Goldie's condo, the night he was with her. The news flashed on the front page of the local daily newspapers alleging a coverup or some business dispute among the foreigners with Melvin's and Goldie's picture inset. The gem trade couldn't believe that Sanders was having such a relationship with a Russian blonde, who in turn according to the papers happened to be a Russian spy operating in Thailand. Some quarters were enjoying his downfall, while his friends worried about his future business prospects in Bangkok, especially in the gem circle.

People in the trade have gone through ups and downs due to economic cycles and other external factors for which they had no control, but not in a way Sanders was accused of after the Troublov murder. More and more juicy stories began to appear about their relationship and theories behind the suspicious environment. The Bangkok police released him on bail on condition that he would not leave the country till the investigation was complete.

Goldie too was going through a similar experience. She was devastated by the way her accusers in the media portrayed her. None of them expected that an incident such as this would have major implication on their career and personal life. She went into hiding to avoid any further attacks by the Troublov sympathizers who had a genuine reason to see both Sanders and Goldie disappear forever. They knew Troublov had come to the condo to kill both of them, but what they couldn't understand was the circumstances behind the trespassers mysterious murder.

The police found his duffel bag, goggles, and the gun left intact inside her condo.

So the search began for the murderer who shot Troublov and

dragged the corpse to the front door. Extramarital relationships were nothing new to the gem trade. Quite a lot of them did have that privilege, but due to his popularity and the volume of business Sanders did in the gem market, everyone expected him to be a big guy with a clean image.

Now that image had gone after the incident, and the responsibility to continue the business as usual fell upon Jeb and Baddy. They too had problems in their own way, but never became a media target. No one knew Sanders's whereabouts, except Jeb and Baddy.

It was shocking news for both, Tito and Miko as well. They called Jeb to offer their full support for Sanders, and since they were the targets by the Russians staying low profile became the best alternative. They knew the judicial system and the way it worked. In the end the true story never came out in its entirety. But it was an experience they couldn't stomach remembering the deal they had just sealed for the acquisition of that fateful and elusive 37 carat ruby. They praised all the Gods for making the sale possible. Now the ruby had gone to the right owner and the profits from the deal had also been shared according to the gentlemen's agreement. In fact they were looking for more deals, but now after the incident, they began to feel reluctant the way events were moving day by day.

They were too afraid to go and visit Jeb and Baddy personally to let them know how much they cared for them irrespective of what the public thought about them. Instead, Jeb reminded both, Tito and Miko, to stay out of this murky situation because they were the next targets according to the information he had from a reliable source.

After hearing the news, Tito closed their office in the Sita Building temporarily, and decided to stay at different places to avoid detection by the hungry avengers. They believed their killers, for whatever reason were still around for unfinished business. But no one had any clue as to who was behind this cold murder. The suspicion surrounded the Russian Mafia's in Pattaya and Bangkok, but that was too difficult to pin down. Obviously, the real culprits would have already left the country, but that was not the case.

Vladimir and Papov were closely watching the events from their offices in Bangkok and Pattaya, like the police investigation team asking themselves what on earth went wrong with Troublov when he was already inside the building. Only Vladimir remained close enough, and he had a reason to kill Troublov, because he saw a different Troublov, after seeing him walk toward the elevator with his hands on his cock.

He knew immediately Troublov didn't do the job. The old Troublov was so cool and focused when he killed Pavlov the way they had earlier planned, but not this time. Something had bothered him and that's what everybody wanted to know. The lawyers acting on behalf of Goldie and Sanders remained deadlocked as to how much information should be released to the investigating team, because lawfully their clients didn't do anything wrong.

Like close friends, they were having a good time. No one had a clue as to what prompted someone from outside to chase Troublov to gun him down, as he came out of the condo. Only Troublov knew the person, and as he was now dead. He couldn't help solve his own exit from this world.

But most important of all was the irreparable damage done to Sanders's and Goldie's businesses, and reviving them back to their original status was something they worried about at their safe hideout. Sanders had no idea how to relay the truth to Ruth who had been calling his office since the incident. Chin's family too wanted to know the whole truth if he had any part in this cold murder due to the alleged relationship with Goldie. The real guys having the last laugh were Ris Rubyhall and Winston Lord. They loved to see their competitor fade in disgrace and financial ruin, especially Lord, after he lost the ruby deal. He knew Sanders had a role in its acquisition and both, Tito and Miko, were part of that old game. Now they were wondering where Tito and Miko were hiding with all that profit they made from the deal.

After the unexpected incident both, Rubyhall's and Lord's fracture-filled friendship became stronger than ever, and they had a genuine reason to be that way to protect their market share. In reality both, Jeb and Baddy were down, but not out. They had no intention of abandoning their good old friend in such a disastrous situation. Business was as usual with their office open like any other day. The staff too, felt that this was the time they had to cooperate and pull through the rough ride instead of facing further consequences. So there was a genuine support within the organization. It was the negative publicity floating around, which made the old trust and connection difficult. For reasons they couldn't explain even Jeb's and Baddy's disgruntled wives began to show their full support for their husbands at this crucial moment, which meant a lot for both. So things were gradually getting back to normal, while the investigation was underway.

In the end, they knew both, Goldie and Sanders, had no part in Troublov's tragic murder rather his gang had a strong reason to silence him forever. Eventually, the whole world would forget the episode, like any other high profile scandals happening elsewhere in the world, it would fade away with time.

Sanders felt the terror and loneliness at his hideout at the O. P. Towers on Silom Road. Jeb had a unit in his name to entertain his friends, and he decided to keep Sanders there till it was safe to be taken elsewhere. He took care of Sanders well, but he felt unhappy at the events that led to all the chaos. It took him a while to realize the cause and the eventual effect that followed, though he didn't believe in any karmic beliefs like the Buddhists in the country. Now he was pondering that very possibility and his attitude began to change. He realized his fault and his inner voice began to sound louder warnings that it was not over.

It was just the beginning. He couldn't understand why such a thought was emerging from nowhere. He was never a religious person. Strange though deep inside his subconscious mind, the guilt feeling and the way he had treated Chin and their sour relationship, and other secret relationships he had with women in the past during the several buying trips in all the countries he had visited began to flashback.

He had no idea why it was coming back to him at this crucial juncture though he pushed hard to forget about it. It was coming back again. Now he really began to worry about the significance behind such thoughts. He was not dreaming. Something was wrong somewhere and he had no words to explain. The only consolation he thought of at the moment was in a matter of few minutes Jeb or Baddy were going to be at his side to update the latest. He missed the office and the busy environment he began to curse himself for all the mess.

But it was too late, and he seriously followed the advice of his friends. He began to wonder what Goldie was doing. It was a tragic fault to be with her that night, though he didn't see anything wrong in order to satisfy their sexual needs. Now he realized the pain of that sexual relationship alone. There was no sexual urge anymore. It was all gone. He desperately wanted to get back to work when the investigation was over.

RUBIES! A quiet call from within drove him crazy, as he walked up and down the room like a madman. Then a sudden numbness spread throughout his body, as he slumped to a nearby chair. He didn't know what was going on. He was getting weaker, as if he was going to die. The gravity pull coming from nowhere absorbed him into a tunnel engulfed in white light, indescribable pulling him towards a blissful phase.

"Noooooooooooooooooooo!" he cried in vain.

The gravity pull was beyond his control, and the more he resisted, the greater was the force. Sanders cried like a child pleading for freedom. Tears rolled down his cheeks waving his hands at the invisible force. He had no voice nor the strength left to plea. After one more last cry he fell unconscious.

When he regained his consciousness, he saw Jeb standing beside him with a glass of water and warm cloth. There was a sudden fright followed by that warm hug they always did when Jeb came with whatever news he had to share settled him in peace.

But Jeb was acting differently. He was not talking, instead gazing at Sanders like never before. He couldn't understand what was going on. He was too weak to speak after the frightful experience. Jeb paused.

"Goldie killed herself," he said cautiously.

Sanders went speechless after hearing the news. Now he realized what was going on for the past few minutes in the room. He didn't want to talk to anyone about his experience. Even the mention of her didn't make much difference anymore. He believed Goldie's soul was pulling him from somewhere, and since the force was so strong, he could have only imagined the pain of death.

With that thought still intact, he sobbed first, and then cried like a child in his chair remembering everything they did together, till that fateful night in a quick flash. Jeb watched Sanders helplessly knowing that no one could have helped her, as it was her decision to end her life with a gunshot. Probably, she knew that it was going to be difficult to hide for that long, when her killers were already in town in several guises, and escaping from their claws was close to impossible.

She had a good life with Sanders and there was nothing much to expect further, and the best alternative under the present circumstance remained to end her life once and for all to avoid their gunshot or a machete swing.

And now all the eyes were on Sanders, as he was the only suspect left. Any time he would be requested to explain the circumstances behind Goldie's sudden suicide even though he had given the police all that he knew and remembered during that fateful night. It was a sickening and boring experience answering the same questions several times, but he knew peace and tranquillity were already gone from his life from now onwards. With her death, a quiet and pleasant relationship had come to an end.

Jeb waited. He had more to share regarding the business, which was more important than Goldie's suicide. She was dead already, and they had no more part in that event. What he was more concerned about was Sanders's physical and mental health. His friends wanted to meet Sanders personally so that they could know the whole true story, instead of reading junk news everyday. They wanted to know if he was mentally stable and physically well to do business knowing the magnitude of the situation. He had several rubies with him and they wanted to know their fate, whether they could still keep them with him or should they take them back. Most of those transactions were verbal rather than in writing, especially with the big rubies from Burma and Vietnam. They wanted an immediate answer from Sanders before it was too late.

Like always, business and friendship separated in times of crisis. Jeb knew it was difficult to let Sanders know all his thoughts, but he had to make the move, as the business opportunities never waited that long due to the peculiar nature of the ruby business. Everyone had a deal or a deadline with someone and they needed the rubies back if he wasn't fit enough to survive the cutthroat competition.

Gradually Sanders woke up. He had to face the reality now. Hiding for that long was not good for the business or for his partners, and most important of all, he needed his friends back at any cost, because they were his suppliers. Hurting them in any sense meant, business closure or becoming a Buddhist monk for life. He didn't have that many choices left, but his friends were ready to help him if he told them the truth and that's exactly what Jeb and Baddy was expecting from Sanders. A safe place was arranged for such a meeting. But first, he needed Sanders's whole and truthful commitment regarding pending deal and that from now onwards it was going to be a different business relationship due to the sudden twist and turn of events. It was a difficult choice for Sanders, as he listened to Jeb carefully and quietly. He had no reasons to disagree, as he knew too well, they were working hard for the survival of the business as well as his well being.

Weighing all the possible options, they decided to conduct their secret meeting at the Holiday Inn with their friends after appearing at the Bangpongpang police station on Soi Suan Phru.

FIFTY FIVE

Chai was in an extremely happy mood, when he explained the 37carat ruby's potential to Marty and Pascal at Boonchu's office. Boonchu left his office to meet another client and promised to be back as soon as possible and they were allowed to use his office to work out the details of the peculiar looking 37carat ruby, as he recalled.

Meanwhile, Chai insisted that the $1.25 million dollars was the best deal in town, before absorbed by others in the trade. Marty couldn't resist. The color, luster, cut, and the brilliance flashes were such he didn't wanted to lose the piece. He remembered reading in of one the Christie's catalogues in Geneva, and there were several quotes from potential buyers, and one such quote by a London collector rang in his ears.

"If you like the piece just buy it. There are so many ways to lose a deal if you bargain on it."

But what Marty didn't realize was Geneva was no Bangkok. And both, Marty and Pascal forgot to remember some of the basic rules when it came to buying big pieces.

Identification report from an independent Gem Testing Laboratory!

It was a must and they didn't even bother asking Boonchu, after buying the rubies they liked from him. He too was waiting for them to ask, since he had the report in his custody, but waited to test their awareness. There was nothing to hide. But now it was an altogether different situation. Boonchu wasn't available for them now. He had gone to do his business elsewhere. Now they were left alone to make their own decision with no one looking over their shoulder.

And to the contrary, while they were contemplating, Chai had no doubt that they were going to buy. He read their face and mind like a book. And he knew if he couldn't pin them down now, then it was a lost case. A friend of his friend from Pattaya believed Bangkok as the best place to release such rubies as buyers both, experienced and novices came first to Bangkok, and then moved to other places, if they had no choice. Chai had already done his homework.

First, he wanted to sell the stone. Second, he was given a special account number in Hong Kong for the money transfer. Thirdly, he knew they had no idea about rubies other than their color and name. After some contemplation, Marty uttered the magic sentence.

"I'll buy the ruby. Is this your last price?" he said, glancing at Chai, and then at Pascal.

"Last price is 1.25 million, no discount. Already you have a fair price. Price is good. You can sell this piece in Switzerland double the price. Sure," Chai answered repeatedly without losing his confidence.

"Okay! How do you want the money?" Marty asked.

"Bank transfer to a Hong Kong bank. Here is the number," Chai said, while extracting a piece of paper from his leather bag. Pascal did the electronic transfer on a laptop computer with the assistance of her financial consultant in Switzerland. Chai meanwhile called his contact in Pattaya to call Hong Kong to confirm the money transfer. He waited for the reply. After the confirmation, he gave them the ruby. Chai rushed out of town to celebrate in style after a long drought. Marty was playing with the ruby in his hand as if it was for him. Pascal on the other hand was contemplating the profit they were going to make at one of the auction places after submission to a wider audience to bid.

Mount Kilimanjaro in Tanzania. That's where they wanted to spend their profit from the ruby deal, an already overdue vacation.

She smiled at Marty devouring the event happening. It was going to be an incredible experience.

Chai had already gone to Pattaya. Marty and Pascal waited for Boonchu. Boonchu arrived hurriedly a bit disappointed, and asked about Chai and the ruby. They told what happened, but Boonchu was so tired and confused after returning from a client, he suggested that they come to see him the next day morning so that his mind would be fresh to discuss the details. They understood the situation and left his office. Marty and Pascal rushed back to their hotel in a jovial mood after acquiring several rubies.

As Chai drove to Pattaya condominium situated on Wong Amat Beach, he had no idea what was awaiting him. To his amazement the traffic was moving much faster than expected. He too had several plans after collecting the commission. In fact, he wanted to travel to Alaska, and enjoy fishing with his Polish girlfriend. For him it turned out to be the jackpot of the day meeting Marty and Pascal, and wished more of these species turned up in Bangkok from somewhere. Big money always came with big rubies.

PATTAYA!

That's where his friend's friend had asked him to meet to discuss the final detail, the 5 percent commission. The receptionist at the condo handed him a message.

Though unusual, he didn't suspect anything wrong. He thanked the pretty girl, Thom, squeezing her big tits. She always enjoyed his treat because of the tips. After the ritual, he walked towards the beach.

He heard someone calling his name. Chai turned around to address the caller. Before he could open his mouth, a bullet hit his right brain crushing him instantly to the ground. He was dumped in a black plastic bag, and transferred to a waiting speedboat.

The next day, as expected Boonchu, was waiting for Marty and Pascal. They refused to turn up. That alarmed him.

Instead, he called the Holiday Inn to check their whereabouts. In fact, he wanted to give them the identification and origin report regarding the rubies he had sold earlier. The reply surprised him. They had already left the hotel that very same night for Switzerland.

He tried to call Chai on his mobile. There was no reply. He called his friends and asked if they knew about Chai's plans. They too declined. He really wanted to know the whereabouts of the 37carat ruby. Somehow his instincts alerted him that there was something wrong with the stone, either the identity or price. He was a bit too busy with his other commitments. But he knew if something went wrong with the ruby, they were going to call him or visit his office personally given the amount of money involved. He was patient and got busy preparing rubies for his next Chantaburi trip.

As he was grading his rubies, one by one brokers interrupted asking about Chai, because he had their rubies, and since he frequented Boonchu's office, they believed he knew Chai's itinerary.

He shrugged them off and continued with his grading. Now phone calls began to disturb him wanting to know more about Chai. This was very unusual. Even if these guys decided to take a vacation, someone always knew about their programs ahead so that there was no misunderstanding when it came to sales.

But this time he had not told anyone his plans except that his close friends knew he had a 37carat ruby, which belonged to someone in Pattaya. Boonchu couldn't help them in any way, because Chai hadn't told him anything in advance before he disappeared after the 37carat ruby sale. The only source remained Marty and Pascal, and they too had left the country without even giving him a call. He was a patient dealer so he waited for the truth to reveal itself in due course.

It was a Thursday evening, and Boonchu got ready for his trip to Chantaburi. He took inventory of his stock, sealed and packed them in his leather bag for the Friday early morning trip.

Then came the call. It was from Switzerland. It didn't sound pleasant at all by the way they were talking.

"SYNTHETIC! It can't be. Wait a minute! What are you going to do?" Boonchu asked Marty, as he was shouting and crying at the same time. He was talking about the

37carat ruby! After the call, Boonchu slumped in his chair in despair. The only person who could answer the question was Chai, and he was not in the gem market. There was something wrong. He couldn't concentrate.

Incidents like this never happened to him, because he always wanted his customers to return for repeat business. This event was extremely abnormal and disturbing. He waited till Friday morning or perhaps late evening to see if others had any news regarding Chai and his whereabouts. But the most alarming fact was that it was a bloody 37carat synthetic ruby. He couldn't understand who on earth had the intention to release the stone to destroy the reputation of the Bangkok gem market.

He wished Marty and Pascal were in Bangkok. He was helpless, as the ruby didn't belong to him. It was deliberate and well organized, and it didn't take him much time to theorize someone else was behind the ruby, and Chai happened to be the right guy for the wrong transaction, and the expensive victims? Poor Marty and Pascal!

He really wondered what they were thinking at this moment. Probably cursing the ruby, the ruby dealers, and finally everyone in Bangkok.

Even after getting back home, he couldn't cope with the thought that they had bought a synthetic ruby. His wife, Wan, and his three sons' numerous queries regarding this and that helped distract his attention to some extent, but it kept coming back punctually. Wan knew that he had to leave for Chantaburi the next day morning so she put the kids to sleep early wanting to know more about Marty and Pascal. In fact, she wanted to invite them for dinner if they were still in Bangkok. After hearing from Boonchu the true story, she sat wondering about their next move. It was a horrible and disturbing thought that it had happened in his office during his absence. But the biting problem was the bloody timing. In a split-second everything changed for good or bad in this business. And this one happened to be a bad one. A really bad one! They had no idea of the repercussions once the news was leaked to the gem market. Bonchu's name and reputation were on the ropes given the speed at which bad news traveled without even scanning the truth. That was the nature of most brokers and dealers of the Bangkok gem market. He had a hard time sleeping well.

Boonchu thought of all the contacts. Knowing the gravity of the situation, Wan sifted through all the name cards and friends he frequented at every possible entertainment facility. Like a stroke of luck, Wan got Chai's girlfriend's address. Moo, his trusted girlfriend, who worked at Bangkok Bank as a teller, mia noi (mistress) for sometime, knew more about Chai than the countless girlfriends he had in Bangkok.

Wan called her. The line was busy. She tried again. This time she got through, and the reply really surprised her. She said he was in Bangkok with some customers from a foreign country. Who else should know other than her? Wan didn't want her to know the real reason behind the call.

Boonchu too felt disappointed. He wished either Marty or Pascal would arrive at his office so that they could explain everything they knew about Chai and the ruby. There was nothing to say other than a sorry. He had neither clue nor history of the ruby other than its availability. Usually, he never put any rubies that quick for sale unless and until he had confirmed its identification and enhancement, if any. But this one event was so peculiar, and before he could really help them, the sale was already done with a quick money transfer.

With that sunken feeling, he went to the bedroom with Wan, hoping for better ideas when traveling to Chantaburi.

FIFTY SIX

Lord knew his position too well. The 37carat ruby had given him and others more than enough pain and cost several human lives. All that business animosity and greed were replaced by the human touch and reconciliation in earnest. More than anyone else, he wanted to get back to that old friendship he had with Rubyhall. The anguish which had been brewing in his mind after the failed London copper deal faded away soon after what he saw was happening to Sanders. Though problems like this were common among the gem dealers, but this one really shook him. Lord had no reasons to have an extramarital relationship. He was just happy and content with Ben the way it was.

Knowing Sanders and the way he and his partners did business, the group became everyones envy. They were so good in what they were doing, and all of a sudden a Russian women of dubious background pulling their reputation and business down to the ground became a stark reminder once again that friendship and business went separate ways irrespective of the deals they had done before. Now their suppliers wanted to know the real scoop, before doing any further business with Sanders and his partners. They were in a real hot spot. It was good news for Rubyhall and Lord, because events like this decreased the number of competitions tilting the balance in their favor.

Anyone who preferred consistency and reputation now didn't have that many choices other than Lord and Rubyhall. The international buyers now had an opportunity to reshuffle their affiliations when it came to special rubies, because consistency and a name were prerequisites for repeat business. At least that was Lord's prognosis, and instead of competing with Rubyhall for that huge share, he believed joining him was the best alternative.

CONSOLIDATION!

Lord had burnt his hands before with several partnerships for the sake of obtaining the most beautiful colored stone on earth, but the relationship with Rubyhall always had a charm of its own. Though everyone in the trade hated Rubyhall for obvious reasons, the international dealers and collectors loved to do business with him, and that's where the money was and he had a way of doing business with these people. That's what Lord lacked at times, while trying to win Rubyhall's clients. Something always went wrong. Either it was the quality or price or sometimes both. This was a specialty field and Rubyhall was the master in his craft. Even if he returned with an olive branch Lord knew too well Rubyhall wouldn't take it as it is. He would exercise all his tricks and games to test the waters, before revealing or even showing some of his expensive rubies.

But the events in Bangkok became a good boon to alter such perception, and knowing what was happening to Jay Lam, his expensive Mr Fixit, Lord knew he had a window of opportunity to do something about it. That was to fill the void of trust and confidence, his way.

After hearing that Lam had already been tattoed and fired from his ruby desk, it was Lord's best chance to soothe and win Rubyhall's special attention. He had no problem forgetting the past, but he had no idea if Rubyhall had such an attitude shift. The unbelievable gesture came when Rubyhall called after intense lobbying from Den. Lord knew Rubyhall must have had a reason to do that since the 37carat ruby scenario was now history. Rubyhall didn't mention anything about the ruby when Lord was called, except for a friendly reminder.

"It's important!" In this type of ruby business everything was important, and Lord didn't understand the reasons behind that simple reminder slip. The only way he was going to find out was by meeting Rubyhall at the Oriental's, Lord Jim's. They had several meetings during their hay days but this time Lord was cautious. He was willing to go the extra mile to win Rubyhall's trust at the earliest. His only concern was how long knowing Rubyhall's advancing age with no apparent heirs to succeed. And Lord needed Rubyhall's rubies knowing the stockpile of expensive and rarely seen qualities in his collection. That was his ultimate goal. The rest of his business interests were shared among Den, and a few investors from New York and London. He had structured them in a professional way, except his pet ruby business.

Rubyhall kept this one particular interest away from the hands of professional managers, because rubies and ruby deals where like toys for him. He could play any games as long as the players understood his rules. No one understood such rules except himself. That had been the reasons, with the exception of Lam, no one could work with him that long.

Now Lam being driven away permanently by Rubyhall's hand crafted moves, the gem market wondered what else he had up his sleeve. The market loved to hear half-truths and full-blown lies. And that's where money was made overnight or lost at the same time, because there was always a fool coming from somewhere either to listen or fall into a trap or they just didn't have the right source to double-check the information regarding the quality or the origin of rubies. It was always an impulse buy when it came to rubies, and Rubyhall took advantage of that weakness from his several years of experience in this colorful wild ruby trade.

"Thank goodness you are on time," Rubyhall said, as he welcomed Lord with that characteristic grand smile.

"Of course, I keep my time. When did I ever come late?" Lord added, jokingly.

"I remember once, when you had a fight with those tribesmen from Afghanistan over a parcel of rough rubies," Rubyhall said accurately.

He had a sharp memory, and Lord had to admit it as a matter of fact. Lord just smiled avoiding any further comment. He didn't want to ruin the day.

"That was not a fight," added Lord cleverly. "It was just a constructive disagreement over quality and, of course, keeping ones word. Yeah, now I agree, when that happened I was late. But it was never a habit."

"Let's cut if off," Rubyhall continued. "Nothing of much importance. Why I called you for this meeting is to discuss the future of our business after what has happened to Sanders and his partners, and our role as pioneers and all that nonsense."

Lord listened carefully. This was something really serious, but he had no clue as to what Rubyhall had in mind. He had a way of calibrating his talk with hesitation and deviation. "What's the matter Ris?" Lord asked politely.

"My wife has no interest in this business. All those big boys from London and New York know how to run my other business interests, but not this one. The ruby stuff. You are the one who knows all the in and out of this business, and perhaps I would like to listen to your ideas if you have any and, if not, I'm giving you enough time to generate a few," Rubyhall said plainly.

Knowing from Lam's experience, Lord wondered who on earth would ever wanted to work for Rubyhall. He recalled one such idea he floated during a similar meeting before the break up. Though it looked ludicrous at first, Lord just listened till Rubyhall finished the talk. He had ideas like relying on a very few quality people with brains perfectly calibrated and refined, who had the ability to think and act twenty years ahead, who never complained but worked like hell around the clock, fiercely loyal, dedicated with no family attachments and technical hangovers. Lam's experience was a stark example for Lord to avoid another repetition. Rubyhall believed that getting sucked into staff's marital, personal or spiritual situations halted smooth operation thus blocking creativity, productivity and of course money in all sort of ways. His suggestion of working with less than ten superior brains and attitudes helped to churn out millions with the assistance of clever computers. He knew computers never requested fringe benefits like humans nor did they have any conflicts or personal problems.

And to add to his strange theory, he believed the refined simulated superior human brains hardly had the time to spend all the money they got in stock options and cash in their present lifetime. So in the end they lived longer, the business grew dramatically, and the money stayed where it was recycled for further research and acquisitions. He even knew one or two things about artificial intelligence. Having known a bit about spectrophotometer, he believed that it could be used for communicating color with his clients around the world without any emotional handicaps in three-dimensional descriptions, far away from the stoneage perception of looking at gems under the table. He wanted to be known as the pioneer by the beginning of the next century with surgical precision, less overhead, and more productivity, thereby influencing the global ruby operation. Lord didn't have the knowledge or the guts to reply in any language, even if he had one. Now a recycled version was brewing in Rubyhall's evangelical mind.

"Do you think my opinion is important?" Lord quipped.

The reply was immediate. "You don't get my point, do you?" Rubyhall continued. "When we are gone like worms or fossils, someone else will have a perfect idea in a more acceptable way to finesse the next generation and the trade. I want this ruby business still to be centered in Bangkok, and that's why I need your help. It's for the future generation. Don't you understand?"

"Is this your vision? So far I am behind you, Ris. I think you need to put some compassion and human touch to all your ideas to make them realistic," Lord answered.

"Okay, I respect your opinion," Rubyhall added. "We all have different opinions on same issues. I can understand that. But think about it. Maybe, when you get back home other refined ideas might evolve from this rough one. Just don't give up. We will take a break for a while. The food must be getting cold now."

That was a meaningful reminder from Rubyhall, as they began to eat.

"What do you have here?" Lord said unconsciously.

"Everything that you like. Your favorites," Rubyhall said immediately.

Lord laughed heartily. "That's very thoughtful of you. I appreciate that, Ris. Let me pour some wine for you," he said sincerely.

"Jay is gone. He has too many problems. I thought for a while that he might take my place someday. It was just a thought, which popped from nowhere. I liked the guy when I poached him from the other company. He was intelligent and hardworking, but now something is missing. That something is very important to me, because that's what brings money, when I'm competing in this dog eat dog market. Now he knows about everything in my office. Do you agree with me?" Rubyhall asked.

Lord was in a catch-22 situation. He didn't know what to say other than feel sorry for the guy.

"Partly we were responsible for this mess, and he was the guinea pig. So generalization is not fair under the circumstance," Lord said, hesitantly.

Rubyhall stared at Lord for a while. Lord noticed the reaction, but remained calm and continued eating his food.

"Now another important issue is this Russian invasion," Rubyhall said thoughtfully. He then continued, "There must be concerted attempts in some quarters to frighten the trade and, of course, the dealers. I know the Russian Mafia is quite organized, and I have no previous experience with them to test the waters. What's your gut feeling?"

"If they exist, then they are serious. The Mafia's today are not illiterates. They are well informed daredevils," Lord answered quickly. He knew Rubyhall's comment had to do with Sanders's mess.

"But why Bangkok and rubies? We are no different from other taxpayers trying to make a living like anybody else in the open market. That's capitalism, right? Then why would someone want to shift the gravity to create chaos? If they attack our territory with whatever they have then everyone will be getting heat-treated and more. Why would anybody want to kill the goose which lays golden eggs everyday?" Rubyhall asked.

"The world is changing constantly, Ris," Lord said quickly. "They need a new enemy all the time. That's all."

"Really? That's bad. Not in Bangkok," Rubyhall replied.

"I'm really worried about Sanders and his friends," Lord said carefully to test Rubyhall, and his true intention of this meeting.

"Me too. That bloody 37carat ruby I was looking for is already in New York. I had to recut a 40carat ruby to keep my promise. I know it was my fault, but whatever happened has happened. I don't want to think about it again. The ruby is gone. I want to see what tomorrow is bringing. So I want you to forget about all the quarrels we had before. You are my partner from now onwards. I have a special client from Dubai, visiting Bangkok in a couple of day's time, and I want you to be with me during that period. You are going to see some beautiful rubies when this little rich guy comes to my office. From now onward, you will know a lot about my personal style in depth. That's why I invited you to let you know personally. My way, and you know that too well, don't you?" Rubyhall said laughingly, speaking his mind.

"I'm honored, Ris. Thank you," Lord replied shockingly. He didn't expect an announcement like this from Rubyhall knowing his style too well. He took his time when it came to important decisions, and probably Sanders's incident may have had an impact on Rubyhall's thoughts.

Rubyhall needed a strategic partnership, and Lord became his obvious choice.

FIFTY SEVEN

It was ten o'clock. Boonchu wasn't surprised at all when he received the call from Marty. He was already in Bangkok, and staying at some hotel the name he forgot to mention.

Marty really wanted to kill Chai, if he was still alive. Instead, Boonchu suggested that he come to his office so that he could explain the whole situation in a transparent way, before doing anything crazy. Bangkok was no Switzerland. Marty listened.

Since it was a Monday, Boonchu had several stones to be tested for identification at a Gem Testing Laboratory, before clearing the checks. He had bought quite a few good rubies both, single pieces and parcels, during the weekend Chantaburi trip. This was his livelihood so he was careful with every decision. Incidents like the one Marty was going through were not uncommon in Bangkok, but the way Marty bought the piece is what really surprised Boonchu. Obviously he got carried away by its color or price and till Chai's whereabouts were confirmed, Boonchu knew Marty would be thumbsucking for the rest of his life. This was no joke taking into account the amount involved.

So he waited for Marty to turn up to hear his side of the story, before suggesting a practical way out.

Meanwhile, Marty was staying at the Monarch Lee Gardens hotel this time for a genuine reason. At times he was superstitious when things went wrong, and it did go wrong while staying at the Holiday Inn. He was quite tired from the jet lag, and all the events surrounding this quick trip to Bangkok. Pascal wasn't in a mood to accompany him. She wanted him to settle the dispute by himself, and hated Bangkok.

All the rubies that were bought from Boonchu were perfect and natural, after testing at a Swiss laboratory. They were happy with the results, even though Boonchu had those very same reports ready for them. But they either forgot or were not in the mood to collect them. Before he could call them, they were gone. Marty just didn't have a clue what to do other than curse himself when he thought about that fateful day at Boonchu's office with Chai. He wanted a genuine answer from Chai as to why on earth he had to do such a stupid thing as sell a synthetic flux ruby, instead of a natural one. He had no answers till he met the crook, Chai, in flesh. That's what he was going to find out.

He decided to wear casual clothes and walked to the elevator. After reaching the ground floor, the door opened. There were several guests with their luggage waiting, as he came out.

Je-ez! Then, he recognized a face. He wiped his eyes again to make sure he was not daydreaming. It was Pius, the Swiss crook who bluffed him many years ago. He was with an Asian-looking woman with his luggage waiting for someone. Then a bellhop slipped a piece of paper to him. Marty could not care less. He knew what to do.

"Pius!" Marty called. Pius turned around, and became oxidized after seeing Marty's angry face. He didn't know what to do. He quickly glanced at his girlfriend to say something.

Then it was quick. Marty leaped at Pius strangling his neck using all his remaining strength. This was really unexpected, as a lot of guests in the lounge were watching the fight. Marty was saying something so loud and unclear, no one understood except perhaps Pius. But Pius gave Marty a tough resistance. Before the security personnel arrived, Pius got out of Marty's grip, and decided to run. He left his girlfriend and the luggage, and ran towards Silom Road. Marty followed him at the same speed. The guests enjoyed the fight for free, as they giggled and laughed, while his girlfriend slumped in a sofa not knowing what was going on.

She didn't know whether to cry or laugh. The staff decided to cool her down with a plain glass of water if she decided to run. No one knew the reasons behind this sudden happening. Marty was calling Pius every dirty word he remembered aloud, while chasing him through the soi's (lanes) Pius chose, not knowing his route. But the onlookers were having a good laugh with two farangs (foreigners) running in all directions. Now Pius was in Sathorn Road. He looked in all directions to avoid Marty. Then he saw a hospital. He read the name. Saint Louis Hospital! Marty was just behind him, as Pius ran over the bridge. The motorcycle taxi drivers who camped near the hospital seeing Pius and Marty running unnaturally thought they were thieves, and decided to take the law into their own hand. One fellow drove the bike in front of Pius, and hit him badly with his helmet. Pius fell to the ground immediately.

Before they tried the same on Marty, he hit back in a kung fu style felling the motorcycle intruder to the ground. His friends decided not to interfere with Marty by the way he looked. He was a really angry man. The traffic was bad on both lanes, and everyone watched the incident from their car for free. No one interfered. The police weren't around. Having seen a church and a hospital close by, Marty decided to take things into his own hand. He hit Pius several times with his fist on his face and chest for having eluded and costing him a lot.

Later, commonsense prevailed on the day. He carried Pius, who was unconscious by now to Saint Louis Hospital. The nurses were quick in action after seeing two farangs (foreigners) badly bruised. Marty needed only a minor treatment. But Pius had some bad head injuries after being diagnosed by the resident docs. Marty couldn't care less. He had several questions for Pius, once he was fit enough to talk.

Meanwhile the doctors wanted to know who was going to pay the bills after all the expensive tests they had conducted on Pius. After collecting Marty's credit card the hospital staff left. Marty waited patiently at Pius's bedside to make sure he didn't run away from the hospital again. Then he thought about Boonchu. But he was too scared to let Pius get away.

Then he saw a woman talking on her mobile nearby. Marty looked at Pius. He was asleep, and with all those stitches and bandages around his head and shoulder, he knew Pius wouldn't be able to run that fast. Marty approached the woman and asked to call a friend on her mobile. Seeing him and his friend in such a pathetic state she called for him, and waited. The line was busy. He had to wait for another half an hour. After hearing of the incident, Boonchu promised Marty to be at the Saint Louis hospital in less than an hour, after he had cleared the transactions with some gem brokers.

Marty looked satisfied, and thanked the woman for the call. She in turn promised him that she was around, and if he needed to call anyone he could use her mobile. Marty thanked her and moved his attention to Pius the crook. He couldn't believe his eyes about all that had happened in a short time. Marty had several questions for Pius, and he wasn't sure Pius was going to remember all of them when he regained consciousness. He looked bad and Marty wondered what his girlfriend might be doing now. Of course, not running like her boyfriend. He didn't know whom to thank.

GEMS AND CROOKS! Both operated side by side. He now realized that this business was not for everyone. Some did have a knack of surviving amongst the crooks, while others just disappeared in oblivion not wanting to return at all. He couldn't figure out how complex the people and the transactions were till he had to go through an unforgettable experience back in Switzerland, and now in Bangkok. Then he thought for a second. How did all the big dealers and jewelers survive the difficult times?

Synthetic rubies were already in the market since 1885, and were sold as natural from a fictitious mine near Geneva. The infamous GENEVA RUBY!

The ruby enthusiasts might have gone through a similar experience like him, but in a different way. With that thought, he moved his attention to the visiting doc and the nurse, who were doing some tests on Pius. After hearing from the docs that Pius's head injury wasn't that serious, Marty felt relieved. He wanted to know when Pius would wake up.

As they were discussing these matters, Pius opened his eyes slowly to see and feel the surroundings. The place didn't look like a five star hotel suite, and there were a lot of people in uniform talking strange languages. He blinked several times, and then saw Marty's blurred face. Pius closed his eyes immediately, but Marty was a bit quicker. Marty opened Pius's eyelid forcefully to say something. But the doctors reminded Marty that Pius needed rest.

Pius was conscious, but too weak to say anything. He knew the time had come to tell the truth, before taking more beatings from Marty. The way Marty had run puzzled Pius, and he was sure Marty wouldn't spare his life if he walked away from the hospital like a free man. Now the difficulty was how to put the confession in a way Marty could understand.

And then he thought of Corrine, his Malaysian girlfriend. This was his sixth collection in a matter of five months after he had promised her a fantastic vacation in Phuket for helping him during a sales pitch in Kuala Lumpur. Now that promise was ruined by this unexpected event, and he had no convincing answers for her.

Boonchu was shocked to see Marty and another foreigner in the intensive care unit of Saint Louis Hospital. He was relieved to see Marty back, but not the way he expected. After explaining to Boonchu what had happened, Marty said he was now after Chai. He couldn't care less if he lost his life, but wanted to know the truth. Boonchu understood the situation better than anybodyelse. The way Marty had pinned Pius down in Sathorn Road, was a stark and painful reminder for Chai. Marty was determined, but he was playing a dangerous game in a country where justice always came late.

And Boonchu knew it was not the right time to discuss business at the hospital. But he promised he would be back in less than two hours, since there was no one in his office.

Marty thanked Boonchu for coming and being a good listener and friend. And Marty reminded Boonchu that he was staying at Monarch Lee Garden's hotel. He had one more request regarding Pius's girlfriend. Marty wanted Boonchu to convey to the hotel personnel that Pius was safe in a hospital, and if possible wanted to know her full background. Boonchu promised to help Marty.

At last, Marty discovered a really good friend.

FIFTY EIGHT

There were altogether ten people at the Holiday Inn's Indian restaurant.

Jeb had booked the facility for the whole day so that they could dine and talk about the future business with their partners and suppliers. Sanders and Baddy remained quiet, but listened carefully about what Jeb had to deliver. This was their main source of income and by not telling the truth meant losing the important people in one stroke, and the consequence was incomprehensible. So every detail they wanted to know was briefed in a transparent way so that there was no ambiguity of any sort for them in the future.

After Sanders's acquittal things began to get better slowly. He was more focused as to what sort of future was lying ahead after Goldie's tragic death. Baddy helped him to talk to Ruth, who was worried as she couldn't get through the countless telephone calls reaching his office, while Chin remained holed up with her relatives wanting to know the full details, before they could sue further for more money from Sanders.

Sanders spoke to Ruth for the first time in a fatherly way, and urged her to be calm and courageous, till he sorted out the details. Then she could stay with him if she decided to do so. She remained quiet and noncommittal, but was happy to talk to him.

Getting back to his business became his utmost priority, and Jeb was doing a good job sorting out the details regarding the pending rubies both, rough and cut ones.

There were five miners / dealers from Mogok (Burma), two from Pailin (Cambodia), two from Luc Yen (Vietnam), and one from Chantaburi (Thailand). They were the bloodline for Melvin, Jeb, and Baddy, though they had other sources in Tunduru (Tanzania), John Saul (Kenya), Jegdalek (Afghanistan), and countless dealers without borders, who brought goods from other less known sources. But keeping the ten big guys became their priority because they were their only consistent source of supply to compete with people like Ris, Den, and Lord in the international market. It was difficult, but the profit sharing ratios Jeb and Sanders had worked out well ahead were working mutually beneficial, and the spicy Indian food kept the conversation moving in the right direction.

Due to the sudden economic downturn in the region, their immediate concern was how to protect the prices in a competitive market. They had no intention of dumping good quality rubies into the market at this particular time killing the trade itself. The buyers for such quality still remained in Switzerland, London, and New York. But the anonymous buyers were mostly Europeans, Americans, and a few Asians, living in China, Indonesia, Singapore, Brunie, Philippines, Japan, Korea, Malaysia, and Taiwan, using the three capitals as a conduit to collect them. In a difficult time the regulars trusted more in good quality big rubies than their own currencies. Good quality rubies above 5carat always fetched an attractive price, and the ones with discretionary incomes kept collecting them for investment rather than parading them in the streets and getting their heads chopped off. The traditional ruby miners knew the prices the international market was paying for their goods, but due to the typical political landscape and the stone age bureaucracy existent in their own country, they too had to be discreet in releasing such rubies to avoid the wrath of their corrupt government. They didn't want the government to know that such rubies of superior quality existed in their country to avoid paying tax and their government's fixed low price. That's where people like Sanders, Jeb, and Baddy, came in to fill the void doing it professionally or illegally sometimes depending on the situation, while taking care of their suppliers interest in whatever way they could. Because they too read the same newspapers, like the guys in Bangkok or elsewhere, and watched the same tele so hiding any details from them looked stupid and unwise.

The immediate priority was to get back the drained confidence, and to achieve the goal spindoctors from an advertising agency with international ties were hired by Jeb to release a carefully drafted script through some of the top jewelry and gem magazines in the world to confirm that they were back in business. That meant they were still in competition with Rubyhall's, Lord, and scores of other dealers.

Before they went on a large scale advertising campaign, they needed the miners full support and confidence. For the market that meant real business. The idea gained tacit support from the miners, but the real gamblers were Jeb, Sanders and Baddy. Working in the international market for a long time had given them the required experience irrespective of the unexpected economic downturn, but they were investing for a long-term scoop, and advertising was one such tool they used to achieve that goal. The main purpose was to let the market know that they were the guys with deep pockets and they could take the scandals and uncertainities without much difficulty.

Sometimes this trick worked, and the fact was they wanted Switzerland, London, and New York, to know that they were back in full swing. The miners from Mogok (Burma) had brought with them a few pieces of rough rubies concealed in their clothing to toast their friendship by giving one piece each to Sanders, Jeb, and Baddy.

It was unexpected, but the gesture meant they trusted them, and it was a new beginning after the brief interruption.

FIFTY NINE

Tito and Miko were still holed up at Chichi's mother's villa in Rangsit, waiting for the latest information from Jeb. It was an uncomfortable experience, but they didn't want to do anything stupid knowing that the thugs were still around.

Meanwhile, Citrina had been trying hard to call Miko, but the line always remained engaged. She felt that something was not right. But she was persistent and kept trying. This time the line was on.

"Miko!" she cried in despair. "What's going on at your office? I've been trying and trying, no answer. Can I talk to you now?" she asked.

"Thank you for calling. It's a long story. Our office is closed temporarily. What can I do for you?" Miko said plainly without elaborating much. He knew she had something in her mind.

"Where can I meet you privately? It's regarding rubies, and I would like to buy a few from you if possible," she said waiting for his reply.

There was a moment of silence, as he glanced at Tito for his opinion. He was talking on his mobile to Jeb. He recognized the call, but Tito looked serious, and he didn't want to disappoint Citrina at this particular juncture. It was a risk knowing the consequences, but Miko decided to do something about it.

"Where do you want me to meet?" Miko asked.

"Oh good, at my exclusive apartment on Srinakarin Road. You can't miss this one. Floraville! The place is not too far from Pattanakarn Road. It's very near to Jusco. I can pick you up if you want to be that way. It's safe," she assured.

"When?" he quipped.

"Tomorrow morning. Is that okay for you?" she asked.

"Fine. Give me the address. I will be there," he said.

Miko wrote the address and the telephone number on a piece of paper, and then hung up the phone to hear what Tito had to say. Chichi stood behind Tito wanting to know the full details about Sanders and Troublov.

"He is dead," uttered Tito aimlessly.

"Who?" Miko and ChiChi asked in confusion.

"Grigory Troublov, alias frigging Pierre Themiro," Tito answered quickly.

There was a sigh of relief, as Chichi rushed to the kitchen to prepare some food. Miko knowing the timing hesitated whether to tell him anything regarding Citrina and his visit to her apartment. But then again he thought even if he dodged Tito now, later he was going to know it fast and letting Tito know first was his best shot after the confirmed death of Grigory Troublov.

"Tomorrow, I will be visiting Citrina. She called me requesting to show her some rubies. Is that okay with you?" Miko waited for Tito's reply.

Tito looked at Miko in a suspicious way. Miko had never seen Tito staring at him in such a way before. But he was patient. He didn't want any trouble.

"Sanders is back. That means we can go back to our office and continue the old friendship and deals we had with them before. It's a good news," Tito said without replying to Miko's request. Miko knew immediately Tito had something else in his mind.

"Do you really want to meet her at her apartment?" Tito asked Miko again.

"Yeah. I think so. It's safe. She has been calling, and I haven't told anyone our problems. But she wants to see the rubies," Miko replied.

"Well, I wouldn't stop if you think her intentions are genuine, you know what I am saying? But to let you know now, Sanders has just told me to have a look at some of the rubies from Stanley

Chen. He is on his way to our place with Baddy. So I want you to be with me now. If everything goes well with the selection, you should be able to visit Citrina tomorrow," Tito said calmly. Tito had given the directions to Baddy to reach their camp.

Miko had no problems. He was happy that Baddy was accompanying Chen, who had a history of marital problem, but somehow had a way of getting rubies from God forbidden places. Now he wondered about the qualities of the rubies Stanley was carrying, but if Baddy was accompanying him there were reasons.

Tito wasn't elaborating much. And before Miko could rush to the kitchen for food, the doorbell rang.

Tito welcomed Baddy and Stanley to the study room. Miko brought in the soft drinks and cookies, while Chichi remained in the kitchen. She left them alone knowing the habits of these men in business. It was back to business after a few introductory 'how do you do's?'

"Look at this parcel of rubies. Where are they from Stanley?" Tito commented, opening the plastic bag.

"Cambodia! Good color, isn't it?" Stanley rubbed the stone parcel. Baddy remained calm and composed, waiting for Tito's comments.

"The colors are mixed. How do you want to sell? The whole or selection?" Tito asked glancing at Stanley and Baddy. As Baddy smiled, Stanley looked tense and undecided.

"Either you take the whole parcel or just leave it," Stanley quipped.

"What's the price for the parcel?" Miko interrupted.

Stanley scribbled his numbers on a piece of paper and slipped it through his fingers to Tito. Now Miko began to wonder why Baddy was quiet. He wasn't making any comment other than watch.

"What's this, the asking price or transaction price?" Tito asked.

"What? You don't like the numbers?" Stanley replied

quickly. That gesture brought a quick laughter from Baddy. Stanley had a way of replying. Very comic!

"Come on, Stanley. You know my taste and numbers. Why are we wasting our time?" Tito said plainly.

Stanley scribbled again on a piece of paper and slipped it through his fingers to Tito.

"I can't sell at this price, Stanley. My customers will never come back to me if I show this price. How is your wife?" Tito said.

"She is pregnant!" Stanley answered quickly. Baddy couldn't resist this time. He laughed loudly, joined by Miko. Stanley couldn't understand why they were laughing. Then he too began to laugh.

"You knocked her up again?" Miko asked.

"She asked for it. It was not my wish. What can I do? Every night when I'm back she is waiting for me at my bedside with everything flat open to enter. How can I resist? So I had to help her," Stanley replied. That comment brought another round of laughter, this time more forcefully. Chichi just arrived with some cakes and fruits but after seeing the environment, she decided to flee. Stanley continued, "Not good for the business, Tito. I can't see the colors properly when I help her in bed. Everything looks blurred. Gray! Why is it like that?"

"Maybe, you are getting old. How come you don't wear glasses?" Miko said, still laughing.

"I don't need that. All these years I had no problems. It's going to continue that way. Only after the night I help her, I have this hangover. Then I've problems seeing the colors," Stanley commented.

Everyone calmed down and got busy with the cakes and fruits. The rubies were still on the table waiting for a decision. Baddy wanted to get a feel of the price, as he had to be in Cambodia shortly.

"How about these colors in the Cambodian parcel? Can you see them?" Baddy asked for the first time since the bidding started.

"Oh sure, when I do business with you guys, I don't help her. I can't afford that mistake," Stanley answered honestly.

"So what's the real price?" Miko interrupted again.

"I can't come down," Stanley continued. "Then I lose money. You know how much I make from this parcel. The numbers are realistic for both of us. Make a good decision."

The game had already started.

"Still your price is high," Tito added. "It's a different world out there, Stanley. They are well informed. Those days have gone when they believed whatever I said. Today they bargain, and when that happens, my prices must be competitive. That's how I survive. If I can't get a competitive price, they go elsewhere. When that happens two times, three times, four times, they are gone. No come back. Then I've lost a customer, understand? I want to avoid that. You must help me to avoid that scenario. Now give me your realistic price, will you?"

Baddy nodded. He knew immediately Tito was closing in, in his own way. Stanley scribbled again on a piece of paper and slipped it through his fingers to Tito.

"Oh, cannot! Listen, I think I better leave you alone with the cakes and fruits. I don't want to waste your time either. What else do you have? Any good ones, single stones?" Tito asked deliberately.

"Sure," Stanley said. "How about this one? You won't believe this piece."

"Where on earth is this from?" Miko asked.

"Luc Yen, Vietnam! A 9carat piece! Do you like it? I know what you like. Your face and eyes are all screaming at the ruby at the same time. Take it," Stanley said purposely to hype the situation. Baddy too was glued to the ruby. All he wanted was to get a feel of numbers, the tricks and traps they played while negotiating a new parcel of rubies.

"What's your last price for this ruby?" Tito asked firmly.

"Tito, why do you want to cut me so soon? I'm roaming all over the streets to bring you the good ones, and then look at how you are killing me with your price. Give me your offer. Then I'll tell you if it is too high or low," Stanley answered glancing at Baddy. Instead, Baddy just kept smiling at him.

"Who owns this stone?" Miko asked.

"The owner wants to remain anonymous," Stanley said. "I think you will respect that decision. Why all this beating around the bush, Miko? If you guys like the ruby, then you should take it. Give me my price, and you will make your money in a unique way. I'm telling you pieces like this won't come every day. This one is different."

Everyone remained silent for sometime. They knew that too well what Stanley was up to with his so-called unique ruby.

"I know," Tito added. "Give me your last price."

Stanley scribbled his number again on a piece of paper and slipped it to Tito. After seeing the number, Tito said, "Okay, I will take it."

The deal was over.

"How about the Cambodian parcel? You can't leave it like that. Once it is gone it won't come back to me or to you either," Stanley reminded Tito keeping up the pressure. Baddy kept mum, watching their number play drinking diet coke.

"The problem is that it is too mixed. I'll have to sort and re-sort the whole bloody lot to fit my clients needs. Then it's gonna be a different pricing situation, and taking into account everything your numbers just don't make any sense to help me at any level. I'll have to leave it to you. I can afford to wait," Tito replied calmly.

"How can you say something like that, Tito? You are ruining my life. I've a family to feed. Now one more is coming soon anytime. Think about it. Do you want them to starve for the rest of their lives? Come on, you can't be that cruel to me," Stanley commented knowing Tito's mind.

"Who will pay me when I lose, uh? We all need to make money. I've no idea where you got the numbers from, but what I know is that I just can't make enough profit if I pay your price. It's as simple as that. Why this patriotic cry? Be more realistic. When I can make money with this parcel, then I'll buy. If I can't, I just tell the truth. We have known each for how long?" Tito said, staring at Stanley and Baddy.

"Fifteen years!"

"Is it too short? You must know more about me and my prices by this time," Tito added.

"Okay, don't cry. I know what you mean. I just can't afford to lose a friend," Stanley answered. He immediately scribbled his price on a piece of paper and gave it to Tito.

"Okay, I'll take it," Tito uttered.

"Thanks, Tito. You're my hero of the day. Do you want to see more?" Stanley asked.

"Hey, Stanley, looks like you have a lot of colors today. Is that right?" Baddy interrupted.

Miko and Baddy spread the rubies on a white tray checking their color. Meanwhile, Chichi arrived again with another tray of fruits and cakes to keep them merry.

"What did you buy?" she asked Tito. Tito showed the parcel he just bought to Chichi.

"Hmm, fair to good. How did the numbers go?" Chichi glanced at Miko this time.

"They were okay," Miko replied.

"What else do you have?" she turned her attention to Stanley.

"I've some rubies from Nepal and Russia. You want to see them?" he asked curiously.

"Hmm, what do they look like?" she asked.

"Like rubies from anywhere else. Pinkish red, purplish red, orangish red and hot red, if they reach that peak. But the ones I have, you can judge by yourself. No hurry," Stanley reminded her. After taking a few pieces in her hand, she said, "Not so good. Do you have any Burmese, Thai or Vietnamese?"

"Sure," he added. "No problem. Single stones or parcels?"

"Both. But first, show me singles stones: anything above 5carat," she said glancing at Tito. Instead, he signaled her to go ahead while he joined Baddy and Miko.

"How about this? The mother of all color, 8carat! If you have any Chinese clients they will swallow this piece with one gulp. What do you think?" Stanley asked patiently.

"Hmm, what's the price like?" she asked again.

Stanley Chen scribbled the number on a piece of paper for a bid.

"Why is it too high?" she reminded him.

"What do you mean too high? This is the market price. What's your bid price, Chichi?" he asked calmly.

"I want you to come down," she said. What do you think?"

"She is right, Stanley," Miko added. "Come down to a realistic level. Do you want to buy Tito?"

"Yeah, I have a client who can afford this color. But the price, Stanley, you have to make it affordable to quote. I mean, you must really help me," Tito said.

Chichi waited watching the games these men were playing against each other. She knew it too well. She wanted to see the outcome.

"What do you want me to do? I've already told you my problem. The market is already tight with money and the wrong goods. I'm just lucky that I've something that other's don't have. You must work out your numbers for our mutual benefit. I can't go further down. Believe me, this is the last price," Stanley cried.

"The last price? How many times have you told me that during the past fifteen years? When are you gonna stop this excuse?" Tito recalled.

Chichi laughed at both men.

"Give me a break. Okay, I will write down your last price. Let me see, if we have enough room for a last deal. My wife is waiting patiently," Tito said.

"How many more months left for the final exit?" Mike asked changing the subject.

"One more," Stanley said, while waiting for Tito's reply.

Instead, Stanley took the first initiative. He scribbled again, his transaction price on a piece of paper.

"Deal closed. Why did you have to haggle so long? We could have all finished earlier," Tito commented.

"Well, that's the fun of this business," Stanley said. "I don't want to end this bargaining so quickly. Then all the magic, mystery, and uncertainity is gone. I hate that. No big deal."

Everyone nodded.

"Okay, what next?" Stanley asked.

"Of course, the food," Chichi reminded glancing at everyone.

The mobile rang. "It's my wife. I got to go. She is having the pain. Okay, guys I'll be in your office tomorrow to settle the money and other issues."

"Wait for a sec," Baddy said. He drove Stanley to the hospital promising Tito that he would be returning soon.

SIXTY

"Mr Osman, this way please. Mr Rubyhall is waiting for you," said Lord, opening the door for Ali Osman, the Dubai tycoon, after Lord's meeting with Rubyhall was over.

"Thank you, Mr Lord. Are these slabs real lapis lazuli? This is an amazing office with such an artistic touch with all the ornamental stones," Osman commented.

"That's Ris's artistic angle, and he makes sure it's done perfectly. Well, there he is." Rubyhall walked hurriedly to greet Ali Osman.

"Hello, Mr Osman! Nice to see you."

"My assistants are not that many this time," Osman added. "Only two. I believe you have something interesting to show me this time. Last time, I was in a hurry with many business commitments, sorry for that. But this time, I have made it a priority that I should visit you to collect some nice rubies for my new wife, and the old one. Pretty young one this time, you know, and also beautiful." He chuckled.

"That's good. Are they accompanying you?" Rubyhall asked gently.

"Yeah. They are staying separately at the Sheraton hotel. We had a late night. I didn't bother to wake them up. They deserve their sleep. Okay, what do we have, Ris? All tops, I trust," Osman said firmly.

"All tops, as you requested," Rubyhall answered. "Your two pretty wives as you mentioned yesterday were twenty two and twenty four, right? I have two beautiful rubies from Burma, 22carat and 24carat! Excellent color with no orange or brown tint! Brilliance and luster is very good. Clarity, lightly included, just enough to prove it's natural, and untreated. Cut, believe it or not, excellent, with no excessive bulge. And most important of all, these two rubies were cut from the same rough. That itself tells a history to be remembered for the rest of their mortal life."

"Are they from Mogok (Burma)?" Osman asked curiously.

"Yes. I think you better have a look first," said Rubyhall, while opening his favorite black box. He took out the two stones and laid them on a white tray to observe them.

"Do you have a laboratory report stating their origin?" Osman interrupted.

"Yes. From the Swiss laboratory!" Rubyhall answered.

"Can you give me a black tray, please?" Osman requested.

"Sure. You want to see the color contrast, don't you?" Lord said quickly.

"Yeah," Osman added. "They look good as you said. Perhaps, I should name these rubies after my wives, you know." Everyone laughed.

"Of course, once taken and paid, I don't think there should be any problem with that. They will love and worship you with their body and soul for the rest of your life," said Rubyhall tactfully.

"I want to see these rubies in different light sources. Skylight, fluorescent, and incandescent light source. How do they look in these light sources, Ris?" Osman asked.

"I can guarantee you, they look the same red in all these light sources. You won't believe this. That's the truth, Mr Osman. Anyway, I have two light sources ready for you. Fluorescent and incandescent light source. Skylight, I think, Winston, can help you with that," said Rubyhall, glancing at Lord.

"I think you are right, Ris. Marvelous! How are things in Burma, I mean, your business interests?" Osman asked.

"They are quite okay with me, but with others it might be an altogether different story. We have established a relationship, which is mutually beneficial for the people and the country as a whole. But the outside world has seen it in a different way with all that human rights bull. The Burmese have an ancient culture, which is very simple, but too complicated for the shortsighted outsiders to understand. For us it took countless money, patience and politics to stabilize our interests. That's why we have been very successful irrespective of all that moronic negative publicity in this part of the world," said Rubyhall proudly.

"I believe so," Osman answered. "You are absolutely right. People in the West think of the other world with a narrow mind. Some of their arguments are right. I have no objections to that. As long as there is freedom of expression and noninterference, it should be okay, but definitely business and politics should go parallel. Am I right with my judgment?"

"Absolutely," said Rubyhall. "By the way, I have a rough ruby from Tanzania, translucent and good enough for carving. I was just thinking about you when I bought this piece. I can carve your face out of this rough. I have specialists in Idar-Oberstein (Germany) who would do an excellent job with this piece. Do you want to see the rough?" Rubyhall asked, after observing Osman's keen obsession of having one piece carved.

"Of course, I never thought about it, but it sounds to me like a good idea. My face carved out of ruby? My family would really like this piece to stay forever, like those famous rubies worn by the Moguls. The only difference is that I'll have to do it by myself with my own money. I think it's worth the money. At least they will remember me for the rest of their lives. Great!" Osman uttered.

"Okay, so you like the idea," said Rubyhall. "Now the price for the two rubies are in this envelope. Please open and sign it, if you are pleased with the rubies."

Ali Osman took the envelope and slowly opened it with reverence. He looked calm and steady, as he read the numbers scribbled on a gilt paper. Osman thought for a while, and then looked at Rubyhall once again, and signed the paper.

"How do you want me to pay? In cash or gold?" Osman asked.

"Not this time," said Rubyhall. "Direct to the Swiss bank account with instant confirmation."

"Okay," Osman answered. "I can do that for you now from my laptop computer." He asked one of his two assistants to switch on the laptop for him. Osman checked once again the account number from his palmtop, and then punched the code for the instant transfer.

"Okay, Ris, why don't you check with your bank?" Osman said.

Rubyhall got an instant reply from his bank, as he stood up to shake hands with Osman. "Everything settled, Mr Osman!"

Lord looked happy and content with the arrangement, and the pace at which the decision was made and executed. They all shared their good moment with a hearty laugh.

Suddenly there was a knock on the door, and before his assistants could reach the knob, the door slammed open.

"Everybody on the floor! Don't even try to move!"

Lam and Takashi moved swiftly to take up positions with their guns pointed at Rubyhall and then swept a full round to alert the foreigners not to act prematurely. Osman looked stunned first, and then froze with no sign of life on his face, as he saw how serious they were. Rubyhall and Lord stood shocked in disbelief at Lam and his accomplice.

Osman's two assistants laid face down on the floor inhaling the precious dust from the expensive Persian carpets anticipating their next move.

"What the hell are you doing here, Jay?" Lord shouted at Lam indignantly.

Lam slowly moved towards Rubyhall and Lord with his Magnum super .45 pointed at their forehead.

"Just visiting you both," answered Lam sarcastically. He continued, "I had no clue you were entertaining guests. But now I know. What do you want me to do with them?"

"Let them go, Jay. You are out of your mind," said Rubyhall angrily.

"Not this time," Lam answered. "This time it's real and precise."

"Oh, my God, please let us go," Osman cried. He was trembling with fear and pleaded with his closed palms.

"Who are you?" Lam asked.

"My name is Ali Osman. I'm from Dubai. Ris is a longtime friend of mine, and I'm here to buy rubies for my wives," said Osman quickly.

"How many wives do you have?" Lam became curious.

"Please don't ask! Do you have a problem with that?" Osman wasn't sure if he said it the right way. Lord interrupted. "It's none of your business, do not interfere with him, Lam," he added. "You must let him go. If you have any scores to settle it should be with us, not with our guests."

"Do you know this man, Ris?" Osman looked at Rubyhall.

"Yeah. He used to work for us," said Rubyhall. "I don't know why he is back."

"Don't drag out this conversation, Jay. Finish our job, and get out of this place before it's too late," said Takashi hurriedly, while watching others in the room.

"Yeah. Did you all hear that?" Lam said dryly.

"Please don't kill me. I've a big family and an army of employees to feed. Leave me alone. I'm a nice guy. What are you looking for? Job? I can give you a job, if you put your friend's gun down and leave us all alone. I can assure you, if you want to come with me to my country, please come. There is no crime, and it's small and beautiful as long as you obey the laws of the country. It's my promise. I can help to give you and your friend a new life," Osman said, glancing at Lam for mercy.

"Look at the fuck how he is talking, Takashi?" Lam said in a sarcastic way. This was no old Jay Lam.

"Don't believe what he says. He is just bluffing," answered Takashi, reminding Lam to act quickly, before it was too late.

"Are you bluffing, Osman?" Lam asked, calmly.

Rubyhall couldn't stand their presence any longer. "You should leave our guests alone," he added. "I repeat that again. You are standing on my property illegally. Trespassers are usually prosecuted, but in this case you will be executed without fail. I demand you leave or face the consequences."

Lam aimed his gun at Rubyhall first, and then shot at one of Osman's assistants. He screamed loudly in pain, and then slumped to the ground in preparation for his permanent sleep.

"You see, Ris, he is dead or at least he is dying," said Lam. "Do you think I'm bluffing with a toy gun? This is real. What I want is your life and yours?" Lam aimed the gun at Lord.

Osman fell to the ground with his two rubies crying heavily, as if he was about to die, while his other assistant laid face down glued to the floor not knowing what to do. They saw blood oozing from the wound of the dead assistant. Takashi was still behind them with his gun pointed at the rest.

"What do you want me to do, Osman?" Lam asked sarcastically.

"Kill the way you wish. All our lives are in your hands," said Osman hopelessly.

"At least you know the truth," Lam continued. "Okay, Ris, Winston, walk slowly to two chairs and sit quietly as I say. No tricks this time. I want to tell your guests once and for all the truth. That's all I want. Nothing more, nothing less."

"That means, I can still stay alive?" Osman pleaded, glancing at Lam.

Rubyhall shouted at Lam angrily. "What do you want from me, you loser?"

"The way you treated me, the way you dragged down my prosperous life, the way you destroyed my career, the way you almost made me insane, it has all accumulated now, Ris," Lam added. "Your fucking ruby craze has no limits, and I want to just stop it for the rest of your life. You can afford to lose everything with your second in command, another moron in the flesh. Do you have any idea how precious life is? It's priceless! A zillion times precious than the rubies you have in your safe. You have destroyed countless lives in this country and abroad without any consideration for human values, just to add fat on your ass and your friends in the name of God knows what. But the point is, I've lost every-thing because of you and the moron sitting beside you."

"Why is Osman standing? You should allow him to sit as well like us to listen your sermon," said Lord, poking fun at Lam.

"You have a point. Okay, Osman, you also sit close to them to listen to my sermon," said Lam firmly.

Takashi aimed his gun at Osman's second assistant, and shot two bullets piercing his brain into a hairy salad with blood spring-ing like geysers. Rubyhall fumed at Lam and Takashi helplessly.

"Kill them all," cried Takashi, looking at Rubyhall and his guests.

"Oh my God, not me. I'm innocent. I just happened to be here at the wrong time," said Osman. He was begging in the name of his young wife to let him go.

"So you bought rubies for the right women. Listen," Lam said. "Ris is very good in buying the right rubies for the right women. I used to buy rubies just like you bought on Rubyhall's behalf. I hate rubies now. It's the color of blood. That's what you are seeing on the floor. Am I right?" Lam asked furiously.

"I can't see anything except my family. I am confused. My wives are staying at the hotel. They will cry if you kill me, brother. I promise you a job and your friend, if that's what you are looking for. Believe me, I'm not lying. This is my word," said Osman, pleading.

"So now I've become your fucking brother, isn't that strange? And you, Ris? Winston? Why are you so deceptively quiet?" Lam asked frantically.

"What do you want from me, uh, rubies, money, what? Take it, if that's what you're looking for. Go and start a new life. For me, it doesn't make much difference. There will be a different way of seeing it that you're robbing me. Robbers will be robbers no mat-ter where they live either on earth, heaven or hell. Is that how you want to be recognized? What are you going to gain by killing us? Nothing! If money and rubies are not your concern, it's stupid and fruitless. If you think you have suddenly become enlightened with some age-old moral values, I really don't care much. Do you care about moral values, Winston?" Rubyhall glanced at Lord.

"Not an iota. You're simply wasting your time and ours for some crazy reasons. As Rubyhall said, if you want to take rubies and his money, you should accept the deal, and flee the country with your funny looking pal," said Lord thoughtfully.

"Hey, watch your mouth," Takashi said angrily. "I'll blow out your brains for the last time. What's funny with me, uh? I've everything like you have, except we have different names and different parents. Is that what you call funny? The way you sit and the way your watermelon sized eyes are bulging looks funny to me, you sonofabitch."

Lord was trying to use the reverse psychology by insulting Lam's pal, Takashi. It was a toss situation for both of them. When Rubyhall undertook Lam's demise so cleverly with his age-old experience in the trade, he had hidden motives, but now he was regretting and wondered what else was in the offing. Lam had nothing to lose. He didn't care about Rubyhall's rubies from around the world. That was for women most of the time.

Lam had worked with Rubyhall long enough to understand that not that many men went crazy like women for rubies. At least he knew that from his experience with Rubyhall.

Rubyhall and his gang of monopolist's succeeded in creating the so-called illusion and romance among women all around the world, then make bundles of money from their ignorance and stashed away the profits in invisible Swiss bank accounts. It was such an irresistible obsession no one could stop them. The color of money became an addiction.

Lord and Rubyhall didn't know what Lam had in mind. He was talking like Socrates with a gun. There was a much more civilized way to settle scores. The old fashioned way. That way to have a healthy and constructive debate rather than dictate. That way both parties came out without any blemish. The best definition of Ris Rubyhall: a victim of his own popularity.

Rubyhall urged Lam and his companion to drop their gun

letting off their steam. They had already killed Osman's two assistants. Calling the police at this juncture looked futile. But Takashi
had already read Rubyhall's mind.

Takashi couldn't wait any longer. "He is fucking thinking about
the police and all that nonsense. What are you waiting for, Jay?
Finish the job, before it's too late. You are just talking and talking
with these old men like in a pub. Get the fuck out of here, otherwise, I'm gonna do the job and leave you to watch," he reminded.

"Don't worry about that, Takashi," said Lam. "You are well
protected. No police will enter this lavish room, unless I permit
them. I need some more time, and then it's all over. I've never
talked like this before. This is one of my wish list and I want to do
it in style. I can afford to do that since they are in our captivity. So
just be patient, pal."

Osman had a lot to worry as Lam, Takashi, Rubyhall, and
Lord kept talking and talking about their problems, and he couldn't
understand why he should be involved. The high caliber gun in
Takashi's hand prevented Osman doing anything further. It was a
catch-22 situation.

"Where are the rubies you just bought from Rubyhall?" Lam
glanced at Osman.

"Jay, you're out of your mind," said Takashi impatiently. "This
is not the time for a chit-chat. You just forgot the whole purpose
of our mission. I can't understand what's going on?" There was an
immediate silence in the room.

"Here it is," said Osman. "Two rubies, one 22carat, and the
other 24carat. If you want them, then take them and let me go.
They are yours. I can tell a story to my wives and forget about the
whole episode. I just want to live longer. I've many things to do."

Meanwhile, Rubyhall was thinking what he could do at this
juncture. He looked helpless and confused, but still felt there was
room for a compromise. Lam's method of dragging out the issue
sent an alarming signal.

Lam looked determined and precise with his intention. It was
not the old Jay Lam. It was worse this time. Inch by inch that

frightening thought of dying from the bullets sent a chill through his spine.

Rubyhall remembered the conversation with Winston the other day about death and the overseas trip. The prophetic coincidence, and worst of all with his billionaire friend, Ali Osman, pleading for his own life all looked like a dream at first, but was becoming a reality. Instead of pleading guilty, his childhood urge for a fight first, and defeat later suddenly bloomed out of nowhere urging him to do something about it. If this was how he was destined to die violently, he wasn't ready to believe in such bull.

But the twist was his guest, Ali Osman. At no cost was he to become a casualty of inaction. Lord was thinking similarly, as he looked at Rubyhall.

"Hmm, they are good," said Lam, "the ones most women like. Lucky you, Osman, you can afford pieces like these. I've no interest in these speechless stones. They have no life. All that you hear from books and magazines are cleverly manipulated phrases by these parasite capitalists quoting tradition and geology, and all that nonsense. I'm returning them to you. Once upon a time I used to dream about these stones. Why? I was told they give peace of mind. Then I was told they speak a universal language of a thousand different tongues and every color flash coming from within displayed a power of its own, which no ordinary human understood, except for the few, who knew how to taste them by holding them in their special hands. It's all illusion. These mute stones don't bring any happiness to anybody; instead conflict and misery. History is full of such stories. In those days there were no TV or satellites like we have today to relay all the good or bad news. After you play with these stones for a while you will lose interest. You should keep them with you. They belong to you, because you paid for them."

"So that means you are going to kill me," cried Osman.

"Okay, pal," Lam said to Takashi. "Show time. Ris, Winston, but first, Ris."

There was some confusion around, as each of them looked

puzzled at the time and pace followed by the long boring sermon. Takashi wanted to finish the job quickly for good. Lam was still taking time. He had a sudden change of mind.

"Winston, you and Ris are both cross-fertilized for some reasons. I don't know if it was good, but one thing I know is, it was bad for me. You created the whole mess, right from the beginning with that 37carat ruby of yours, and now it has taken its residence in some safe vault. You pushed me to get involved, and then dramatically you made your peace with your foe. Now where do I stand in this whole drama? Nowhere! What did I get from this whole hand crafted mess? Misery, confusion, and mental breakdown! For some strange reasons, which I myself don't understand, I'm still alive to talk to you. Then you hired an assassin to do the dirty job; just like Pavlov had encountered his death. But I'm still alive. I'm sure, your men are still looking for me. Where do I stand in the conspiracy? Nowhere! As I said, I'm still lucky to be alive and know about all the behind the scene plots. And what do I want from you? You!"

Before Lord could open his mouth, Lam aimed the gun at Lord, with the right finger on the trigger. There was a moment of unforgivable silence, as both pairs of eyes locked into each other without even the muttering of a word. But that silence had several years of history, and that was coming to an end. Lam pulled the trigger and the bullet pierced through the right brain hemisphere splattering blood in all directions.

Lord slumped face down, his weight crushing him to the ground.

Rubyhall sat shell-shocked, and then looked at Lam angrily. He rushed to Lam like a thunderbolt for a physical match. His colossal Panda like body had all the physical stature to crush Lam to a pulp. But Takashi was a bit faster. He shot Rubyhall in the knee preventing that gruesome encounter. Rubyhall was mumbling in all foreign languages he had learned with time to curse Takashi, but he was helpless. He struggled hard to get on his knees to grab Lam, but Lam stayed out of reach.

Lam aimed the gun at Rubyhall, and looked straight into his eyes, and then squeezed his right finger on the trigger.

"Nooooooooooooooooooooooo!" Rubyhall screamed like a wooly mammoth, as the bullet pierced his brain spraying blood everywhere. With his swollen eyes and blood-stained suit, Rubyhall rose again from the ground to face Lam.

Lam shot him again and again, till Rubyhall completely slumped to the ground.

"You did it, pal," shouted Takashi. "Congratulations!"

Takashi rushed toward Lam to hug him.

"What are we gonna do with Osman?" Takashi asked firmly.

Osman had never seen so much blood in his life, as he sat like a statue watching his friends die like in some horror movies. He gazed at them, as if he was already dead. All the blood and water in his body had dehydrated into some chemical phase, he was pleading but couldn't utter.

"Let him go, Takashi," said Lam, consciously. "He is innocent. We have no business with him."

"Are you nuts? What do you think he is gonna do first? Pack his bag and wives to Dubai? Come on, you can't let him go. If you have problems with him, then I'll do it for you," said Takashi hurriedly.

"I said, let him go," said Lam firmly.

"Hey, this is not the old Jay. You look different. Why such a sudden change of mind?" Takashi asked, puzzled.

"I said, let him go," answered Lam firmly, again.

"You're fucking screwedup," cried Takashi, confused. "Look at you. You killed only two, and suddenly you feel like you conquered the world like Alexander the great."

Lam aimed his gun at Takashi, and locked his eyes into his.

"Hey, hey, what are you trying to do? Are you drunk with so much blood to kill me too? You shouldn't forget this. It's me who stood behind you, and now you're turning that same gun to my brains," said Takashi shockingly.

"We all need to go together," added Lam. "That's our destiny."

"How about Osman?" Takashi asked, again.

"He is not in this equation. He is an accidental witness. Our time has come. We must all go together," said Lam without any emotion.

As Takashi rushed to grab Lam, the bullet raced much faster to hit Takashi's forehead crushing him to the floor. Lam shot Takashi repeatedly.

Takashi was dead.

Osman had nothing to say other than to stare at Lam. He believed his end had come and closed his eyes tightly. He mumbled some last minute prayers he had learned at home to boost his consciousness, and then he heard a sudden gunshot. He thought he was dead, as he closed his eyes much tighter.

Instead, he was breathing heavily and faster than before. He was alive. He slowly opened his eyes. Osman couldn't believe his eyes.

Jay Lam had shot himself.

Osman sat shell-shocked, as he got a glimpse of his two assistants lying dead besides Takashi and Lam, while on the other side, Rubyhall and Lord, lying dead with blood flowing out of their wounds like an angry lava. Never in his life had he witnessed such a near death miss, and he just couldn't understand the logic of why he had to be spared. He opened his mouth wide enough to let out the built up scream, but he couldn't do it. He felt like crying first and then laughing, and doing both when he realized that he was still alive.

But first, he decided to call the hotel. He didn't want to leave the room to watch another blood bath; instead he preferred to stay in the room and call the police. As the thought subsided, the telephone rang.

A high voltage chill flashed through his spine, as he approached the table to pick up the phone. Osman hesitated first. He checked the rubies, and then put them in his underwear hurriedly.

"Hello!" The caller hung up the phone.

SIXTY ONE

Pius felt grateful and relieved by his sincere confession to Marty and Boonchu after his release from Saint Louis Hospital. He was on his own, as his Malaysian girlfriend fled the country with his luggage and belongings. He had nothing, except his clothes and a few dollars. He was poor again, and now he was at the mercy of Marty and Boonchu.

Forgetting his past became Pius's first priority, and he was willing to do anything for Marty and Boonchu, as long as they didn't hurt him again. Going back to Geneva was a remote possibility. After the incident, Marty decided to stay at Silom Inn and rented a room for Pius, till he figured out his next target, Chai. And he pondered whether it was a good idea of using a crook like Pius to catch Chai.

Pius had quite a lot of theories, and he suggested that Marty loan him some money to execute his plans. Giving money and trusting Pius was the last thing to do in the world, instead Marty listened taking his time.

But the news from Boonchu and his contacts was discouraging. No one knew exactly Chai's whereabouts, and all the speculations remained in and around Pattaya. Even the women whom he loved to associate with had given up their jobs and fled the place to avoid another wave of killings. They just didn't want to be the wrong target nor be questioned by any suspected groups knowing the violent landscape of relationships among opposing gangs busy procuring women and men for their special clients.

So with such a scenario progressing nowhere, Marty began to seriously ponder the purpose of his stay in Bangkok. He had already lost a lot of money buying the bloody 37 carat synthetic flux ruby, and taking care of Pius just for the sake of catching Chai looked stupid.

Marty hated himself for his carelessness, and instead of being patient and watchful, he walked into Boonchu's office with a final threat. He couldn't cope with the situation any longer. If Boonchu and his contacts were unable to track Chai's whereabouts, Marty was going to do something dreadful. Marty didn't elaborate, but the message was clear and specific. He gave Boonchu one more week to come up with the evidence, and after that he was going to act. No one had a clue except himself what Marty had in his mind. Boonchu knew the seriousness and the pain behind such decision. It was a catch-22 situation to abandon his business and go for Chai or wait patiently and get all the people involved to track his hideout, if that was the case. All his friends and relatives believed he wouldn't do such a thing, but they too hadn't a clue as to why on earth he had to disappear so quickly after the ruby sale.

Now the only suspicion remained if anyone killed Chai for the very same reason. After the news flash in the local dailies about a gem broker's suspicious disappearance, the last person to hand him a note was Lawan, who worked as a receptionist at the Pattaya condominium. She had slept with Chai several times and he always showered her with gifts and money. After reading the newspaper articles and the theories behind his mysterious disappearance, she began to fear for her life, because the last person to give her the note was Somboon, a friend of Chai.

She had done similar things before and there was nothing to be suspicious about, but now after what she had been reading for the past several days regarding a 37carat synthetic ruby, and the tale behind its acquisition she knew that one day she too might become a target.

Lawan had no idea of the number of men who had used her or any idea of the gemstones the news dailies were talking about. All she was interested was in money and she did anything for her clients as long they kept that standard. She had no reason to fear death because she was good to her clients.

Now a sudden chill flashed across her spine, as she thought about the consequences lying ahead. She had no idea what had happened to Chai after giving that fateful note to him. It didn't take much time for her to realize that some third parties might have killed Chai and dumped his body elsewhere. It was just a thought that beamed across her troubled mind. And she had every reason to believe, as several incidents such as these happened discreetly without much trace. The executioners were too organized and powerful with money and the right political connections.

It was a Tuesday morning, and like another day, she walked to her reception desk. There was a note for her. It was from Somboon. Suddenly she began to fear for her life though no one had any reasons to take her life. But consciously or unconsciously she felt something dreadful was going to happen. The question remained whether to go to his room or just flee like the others. But they knew her family and the usual hideouts, and escaping from their clutches was unthinkable. They would have caught her anyway. Going to another country had a remote chance. She had never been out of the country. She read the sentence in the note once again to see the difference in the wordings chosen. It was the same style. When Somboon wanted to have a good time with her, irrespective of the daily scores she always was there, and acting differently meant trouble. She decided to go to his room. It was a numberless room on the third floor, and she knew it by heart.

After a gentle knock, the door opened. There were two foreigners with Somboon. This was unexpected, as he always preferred to be alone when he needed her. But the foreigners wearing dark glasses frightened her. She tried to compose herself and stood beside Somboon waiting for his instruction. He was calm and gentle without showing any signs of stress or discomfort. After squeezing her breasts three times, a regular ritual whenever she was called in, brought a guarded laughter from the two foreigners. He did this when they were alone. The sudden change of habit really puzzled her, but she smiled at him and then sat on his lap so that he could do whatever he liked.

Lawan had never met the two foreigners before as they began to communicate in a strange rough language, while he played with her breasts. His hands were all over her body. They had other plans. She took his command seriously when Somboon said she was accompanying them in his BMW. She had no other choice than comply.

After getting dressed, Somboon said to Vladimir and Papov in Russian that she was the only link left who knew about Chai, and she was going to forget everything soon. They liked that statement.

Several buses kept arriving during the day, as tourists flocked to the beach for fun and other extracurricular activities. It was hard to distinguish their nationalities as there were many on the road busy having fun with a large number of Ka-toeys (transvestites). Lawan had never been out with Somboon in a car and the two foreigners were enjoying the ride watching his fingering on her, and at the same time driving like a Formula one race car driver to meet another Russian contact, Boris Luganov, at Montein Pattaya hotel.

As she was wondering what they were up to, Somboon picked up the speed to show his driving skills. Then a Ferrari crossed in front of them from nowhere hitting their car first with a big bang crushing other cars in the vicinity beyond recognition.

Since it was so unexpected, Papov and Vladimir had their skull smashed and limbs severed. Somboon and Lawan were confirmed dead with their body parts scattered around Pattaya Beach Road along with other metallic parts.

It so happened, the Ferrari belonged to a Thai politician and his son who along with his girlfriend were driving fast to join their friends at the Siam Bayshore hotel. As the police and the politicians family members arrived at the crash site busy sorting out the circumstances and other details, Boris Luganov counted his blessings.

He knew the consequences and decided to flee Pattaya for good to forget the event once and for all. His friends, Papov and Vladimir were dead and the time had come to take over and reengineer their discreet operations with another bait.

And that was only possible if he reached Bangkok safely.

SIXTY TWO

After paying the taxi fare, Miko had a glimpse of the building. Floraville looked gorgeous and exceptionally well designed for international guests, and Miko wondered where the money was coming from for Citrina to stay in such a posh place.

The receptionist had a message ready for him. She was well organized. He waited at the lounge, and in less than ten minutes, Citrina arrived in her casuals to greet him. He accompanied her to the elevator. She explained about the facilities, and if he was interested she was willing to take him on a guided tour. He was not interested.

As she kept talking, he forgot to note on which floor she was living. It was all at a quick pace, as she opened the door for him. The place was beyond description with oriental decorations, and the bright lighting made it all look as if he was in a mini grand palace. It was a three-bedroom suite with every convenience. He was too scared to ask if she was living alone in such a spacious facility. Instead, he observed her gestures and the real reasons behind the invitation. He couldn't believe how she managed to keep the place clean and tidy without the maids. The music was on as she emerged from one of the rooms with two glasses of fruit juice. He thanked her and waited.

There was an immediate silence, and then she smiled at him. Before he could open the briefcase, she said something different. That gesture took him by surprise.

"Why do you prefer to remain single, Miko?" she asked staring at him.

It was too direct and he had difficulty finding the right answer. Instead, he laughed and decided to make it look less serious.

"Oh, me? No particular reason," he answered plainly. "Why? Something wrong?" She didn't reply, instead she kept gazing at him. He felt that the woman was interested in gems and other special activities. He had heard from other dealers what the rich women in Bangkok did when their husbands were away for business. They had all the time in the world to do nothing, and out of boredom there was even the existence of a special club where they went for sex and couples swapping for experiments. His immediate guess took him in that direction by the way she looked and behaved.

"I have the rubies with me," Miko reminded, "and if you want to view them I can show you how to look for a good color. The rubies I have at present are from Burma and Afghanistan."

"Really? They have rubies in Afghanistan too? I didn't know that. Show me the piece," she said casually.

Miko opened the briefcase and picked five stone boxes, and put them on a white tray for her to view. He knew the incandescent room lighting enhanced the rubies and to make it clear, he advised her to have a look near the window so that she saw the difference in its color. Instead of giving her a tweezer, he held the ruby in a stone holder for her to avoid dropping the stone. He saw the excitement as she slipped the stone holder in between her fingers, and then moving toward the window to see if there was any difference. They looked the same red with a slight tint of pink. The absence of orange or brown made the rubies from special localities desirable for private collection and normal daily wears. The rubies were transparent with minimum inclusions thus making the brilliance flashes and the quality luster more desirable.

"I like both the rubies from Burma and Afghanistan. How much do they weigh?" she asked.

"Well, the Burmese ruby is 10.45carat, and the Afghani piece should be 8.01carat. I have more if you want to view them," he said, while checking once again the price and weight.

"Are they from the same localities?" she asked again curiously.

"Nope. I have five pieces, all in the range of 5 to 10carats. They are from John Saul(Kenya), Luc Yen(Vietnam), Bo Rai(Thailand), Mong Hsu(Burma), Ural (Russia)," Miko said holding his breath.

Miko put them all in a white tray so that she saw for herself the difference face-up (table-up) since that was the best position to view color in rubies. He waited for her decision, as she kept looking at them in a meditative mood. It was a hard choice for her, as they all looked so good and exceptionally beautiful in quality and of course, the size.

"I think I will go for three pieces now," she added, "the Burmese, Vietnamese and Kenyan. Do you have the prices?" she said calmly.

"Sure," Miko continued. "In fact, I have the origin report from New York and Switzerland for all the rubies I have here. The prices are . . . . .well, here it is." He handed her an envelope for her attention. She opened it, and then paused.

"How do you want me to make the payment?" she asked quickly.

"Here is our account in Singapore," Miko said, and then handed her a piece of paper. She glanced at them, and then nodded.

"The money should be in your account by early tomorrow. Is that okay with you?" she asked, and then signed a check.

"Thank you, Citrina," Miko said, and put the remaining stone boxes in his briefcase. She collected the three pieces and kept gazing at them again, while drinking the remaining fruit juice.

"Miko, I want to show you something. Can you just follow me?" she said, walking to an adjacent room. He had no choice other than follow her with his briefcase.

He remained composed as he entered her room, and then all of a sudden a remote control device locked the room. He stood lifeless not knowing what she was up to. He watched her putting the rubies in a safe deposit box and then walked toward him.

"I have to tell you something," she continued, "and I forgot to mention this first. There are many rich ladies who would love to buy rubies from you, if you would give something in return. You don't have to sell any of them to those filthy Europeans or Americans. You now what I mean?"

"I am afraid no," Miko said, puzzled. He had no idea what she was up to, but decided to see the end of it. She then took his briefcase and placed it on her dressing table. Miko waited. She then walked towards him and took his hand. He was shivering like a leaf, but she was so cool. Then she embraced him and stood like that for sometime whispering in his ears not to be afraid. She reminded him that she had no intention of hurting him, instead she wanted him to understand her deeply. Miko wasn't trained to respond to such requests, but he knew that the room was locked and doing anything stupid meant several things. Not only he was losing a customer, but the money and if anything went wrong his life too. He wasn't sure why she was doing this but the way she stood and rubbed his shoulders and neck meant she was experienced. She wasn't urging him to take off his clothes or hers, but she wanted him to stay close and to be a good listener. Suddenly, the music was on and she urged him to dance with her so that she could talk and feel his warmth. He complied with her request dancing like a novice, but she was good.

After a while, she talked about her husband and children who had only one thing on their minds. Business and money! She wanted something more from them. Her two children had no interest visiting her, as their father took care of them and their education in America, while he was always traveling making deals for Phil Win and his group of companies.

Miko didn't know what else to say other than feel sorry for her. She was like a lonely bird in a platinum cage wanting love and affection from anywhere, but selectively. Citrina wasn't an airhead bimbo. But she was taking one step at a time wanting to know his move and reactions. He remained noncommittal but a good listener by pressing her hair and back carefully. He was too scared and when she asked if he had been with a woman alone like this before, the ambiguous reply assured her that he was a novice or a rough gem. Now she had an upper hand in controlling him.

On the other hand Miko wondered when the music was going to stop so that he could go home and do some sensible work, as Tito and Sanders were preparing to get back to their old friendship and business. But she wasn't, as she kept explaining about this and that and all those story women always talk about. He responded carefully avoiding giving any wrong signals.

Everything seemed to be going well and then finally she raised his face and kissed him hard. They stood like that for sometime and she released him when the music stopped. After that she laughed loudly for so long, Miko wondered what in the world she was laughing about when he almost felt like dying from that deep kiss. She in turn laughed at him the way he looked. Immediately she grabbed a hand mirror from her dressing table for him so that he saw for himself how he looked. He too began laughing at his frightened face, and they both laughed till they dropped. It was an unforgettable experience for both, as they got back to their senses.

She didn't want to frighten him again. The next thing he knew was that the door opened and there was a maid waiting with two glasses of fruit juice. He couldn't believe his eyes, as he took one glass and walked to a nearby sofa.

Meanwhile, Citrina walked towards him with his briefcase assuring him that she didn't open it during the course. He laughed at her funny remark and remained silent. He checked the time. It was nearly noon. He wanted to get out of the place desperately. He waited.

She arrived from her room wearing jeans and a T-shirt to say something. She tried hard to persuade him to stay for lunch, but he declined politely reminding her of an important meeting with a client back at his office.

Later, she accompanied him to the ground floor. She hailed a cab for him. Before leaving, she reminded him to visit her again if he wanted to sell more rubies. He nodded. While sitting in a cab, he didn't have a clue regarding the right thing she just mentioned.

What a way to sell rubies! He said that a bit loudly. The driver looked back at Miko wondering whether he was drunk or mad. Instead, he smiled assuring the driver that he was fine.

SIXTY THREE

It was a Wednesday morning, and Boonchu arrived at his office a bit early to settle some outstanding accounts with two of his brokers, Seri and Tarin. They too had arrived in time so checking accounts and rubies with them and the ones on consignment were tallied with the receipts and other slips they often carried when going from office to office or upcountry.

At the same time, Boonchu was worrying what to tell Marty if he turned up on Friday, when he was already in Chantaburi for the weekend. And to add further confusion, his men had no reliable evidence to confirm that Chai was killed by the gangs or by the local Mafia's. The car crash at Pattaya did grab his attention but his men had no evidence to connect those incidents with Chai's sudden disappearance. With that sunken feeling he kept looking at the rubies and listening to the broker's comments at the same time.

Switching gemstones was a common hobby among the crooks who needed money, and Bangkok being the gem cutting center for natural, synthetic, imitation, and assembled gems, the availability and pilferage at the cutting factories became an excellent conduit to achieve that goal.

Even though there were many gem testing laboratories and a couple of gem schools to train people to differentiate naturals from synthetics, it was difficult to teach anyone how to avoid losing money in a foolish way, because in most cases people bought or sold rubies by impulse or excitement. Sometimes people just forgot to use their commonsense at the right time, and Marty's case was one such example. He got too excited and moved by the color and price of the ruby, only to regret like water over the dam situation. It was just too late. There were so many synthetics coming in every color shades and sizes from all over the world to Bangkok, especially from America and Russia. The age-old practice of making decisions by just looking under the sky or table remained intact, losing money, credibility and peace of mind all at the same time.

Salting parcels or single stones was easy or difficult at times depending upon to whom these dealers were showing the stones. One thing everyone knew about rubies were they were expensive and came only from Bangkok or Burma and the ignorant believed buying from the source helped them reap profits overnight. Tarin was quoting a similar story to Boonchu while sorting a parcel of rubies from Mong Hsu (Burma) and laughing at the stupidity of the foreigner who fell into the trap of a tout on Silom Road.

Boonchu didn't want Tarin to continue the conversation, instead he asked him to change the topic. He had enough of hearing such pathetic stories. Again the thought emerged what to tell Marty when he had nothing to share with him. With such a baggage of mistrust and impatience accumulating by the second, Boonchu knew Marty would think twice if and when he ever decided setting foot in Bangkok to buy rubies. The experience he had been going through was so painful and beyond explanation, Boonchu believed that he had lost one good customer for life.

As he was toying with such a thought, Marty arrived at his office as if he had something to say. Boonchu greeted Marty trying to conceal all what he was thinking just a few minutes ago. He had something important to say. He was leaving for Switzerland with one promise. Never again he was going to set foot in Bangkok even if anyone gave him a free ticket and a planeload of cash. He was going elsewhere. He didn't believe that Boonchu was in any position to help finding Chai given the time he was taking, and staying longer in Bangkok meant more worries and dreadful thoughts.

Personally, he liked Boonchu, but the system and the way in

which the traders worked weren't like in Switzerland. He blamed himself for his own spectacular demise.

When asked about Pius, Marty just laughed. Pius left in the morning with a note not to worry about him anymore since he had managed to make his peace with his Malaysian girlfriend. After borrowing some money from Marty, Pius fled Bangkok.

All these events seemed to happen so quickly, he had no one to blame except himself. Even though Seri and Tarin didn't understand a word about what Marty said, they felt his thoughts while remaining silent. Boonchu was speechless.

When asked what he was going to do if and when he got back to Switzerland, Marty had no convincing answers. Instead, he blamed the timing and people in general. Boonchu reminded him that rubies never cheated. It was the people involved who did the right or wrong thing, and he always guaranteed the rubies he sold to anyone. Otherwise, he wouldn't be sitting in his office comfortably. Marty had heard similar statements before so it was nothing new to him. But he still refused to answer Boonchu why he had come to his office.

"A final goodbye!" Marty said in a funny way.

"No final goodbye, Marty," Boonchu said. "I have also lost money before. But I never said goodbye to the ruby business. It was my mistake, and why should I blame the ruby. That's part of the game. No one wins all the time. But you must be patient. That's how you win the game."

"Yeah? It will take many years of work to recoup the money I lost with this fucking synthetic ruby, you understand? I know you are honest but look the way I lost money and peace of mind," Marty quipped.

"I can help you if you decide to stay where you are," Boonchu added, "because it is a fact you lost the money and ruby. I myself don't know where Chai is or his whereabouts. Let's assume he is dead, what next? We must think about the future and you are the only one who can decide what to do. Let bygones be bygones."

"Yeah? What are you suggesting?" Marty asked, puzzled.

"Start all over again, if you are ready. I can help you with the rubies, but first you should forget the past. If you keep worrying too much about it, then you won't be able to concentrate in your business. As you know, we make decisions fast, but carefully," Boonchu said with a smile.

Marty remained silent. Tarin and Seri were still grading the rubies and listening at the same time.

"Why are you so kind to me, Boonchu?" Marty asked, puzzled.

"Because I also lost money and misidentified rubies before. I understand the pain and sleep when someone loses money, especially one of my clients. You came to my office and gave me business. So in turn, I want to do the same thing," Boonchu replied calmly.

Marty was moved by Boonchu's assurance and tears began to roll down his cheeks not knowing what to say other than thanks. A NATURAL THAI!

"You know something," Boonchu continued. "I am going to Chantaburi tomorrow. You should come with me. I am sorry to ask this question? Do you have money?"

"Well," Marty hesitated for a while, and then said, "What do you mean?"

"Stay in Thailand. Be patient. You will make your money slowly. I will teach you what I know and then one day when you are ready, we go partnership. Fifty-fifty," Boonch said plainly. That was an offer he couldn't refuse.

"Are you serious?" Marty asked in disbelief.

"I don't joke when I do serious business. I can arrange everything for you, if you are ready. AMAZING THAILAND, isn't it?" Boonchu said, and then laughed. Both, Tarin and Seri who were listening also laughed. Marty had no other choice. He too laughed.

"I will tell you something. This is from my experience. If you want to learn more about rubies the best place is where there are gemstones," Boonchu said glancing at Seri who had a belly laugh. He continued, "Crooks are everywhere, am I right?"

"Is it true? I don't believe this. You must be joking," Marty answered.

"You don't believe me?" Boonchu asked.

"I didn't say that. You see I got cheated and I know the reasons. What else you can say?" Marty replied.

"Okay, you learned something today. Now get your bags from the hotel and stay with me. I have a condo unit empty. Come, let's go for lunch," Boonchu urged, and then walked to his safe deposit box to put some of the rubies back. For Marty it happened to be the best day since he arrived Bangkok.

SIXTY FOUR

Sanders was back in his office along with Baddy and Jeb having their early morning coffee break, and their chit-chat was suddenly interrupted by a call from Tito. Sanders took the call and instantly turned pale after hearing the news.

"Rubyhall and Lord are dead! In fact, they were gemsicuted," Sanders muttered.

Others took the news in a collective gasp of disbelief leaving their coffee mugs. Jeb was the second in line followed by Baddy. They were in a high voltage thermal shock.

They were just talking about the spectacular car crash in Pattaya that killed two Russians and Thais wondering about the timing. Jeb had a different version. He believed the crash had something to do with the Russian Mafia orchestration even though the police were still investigating the case. But no one expected this stop news, especially Rubyhall and Lord getting killed by Lam and a Japanese American. The whole gem industry was taken aback in disbelief by the way in which Rubyhall was killed. New York felt the tremor immediately with calls logged to all the major buying offices to confirm if it was true followed by London, Switzerland, Hong Kong and Singapore.

All the capitals were one way or other connected to Rubyhall's business empire and now all of a sudden getting killed by one his own men was hard to digest. David Rosenberg was admitted to a nearby hospital after hearing of Rubyhall's untimely and violent death, because one of the rubies he had just sent to New York happened to be a FRACTURE-FILLED RUBY from Burma, and now his client who bought the piece has filed a suit for damages. It couldn't have come at a worse time when the Dow Jones was taking a beating after the Russian crisis and the people were losing confidence in everything, especially rubies and bloody treatments, because someone was not disclosing the truth.

Gem brokers gathered at the seventh floor of MelJeb Towers wanting to see Sanders in the flesh after his long absence. He tried hard to keep his temper cool and calm as all sorts of crazy questions kept coming from the brokers. It was hard, but he needed them to get back to his normal business.

In the end, they looked more or less convinced and left one by one. Both, rough and cut gemstones began arriving through the brokers for inspection and bidding. It was getting noisier, and he loved the strange voices. His next move was to convince his international clients that everything was back to normal.

Sanders had a list of important names, and he began to call them one by one assuring the same old quality friendship and terms requesting to continue doing business with them. In fact, he was planning to visit them personally to repair the damages after all that had been written and speculated regarding his relationship with Goldie.

Then his next goal was to reconcile with Chin and Ruth. After asking for their forgiveness, he promised to be a good husband and father, and they seemed to accept him the way he was without any preconditions. The lawyers acting on behalf of Chin were told to go on a long vacation to Somalia.

She didn't need them any more.

She had learned her lessons the hard way and wanted her family back. So gradually he was making his peace, while Jeb and Baddy took care of the PR.

At times he wondered whether all these events were happening for the good.

Meanwhile, Chichi could hardly conceal her joy after hearing the news from Tito. The competition was over and the untimely death of Ris Rubyhall and Winston Lord has arrived as a blessing

326 JULIAN ROBOV

in disguise after all that chase and pain they had to go through to acquire the now famous 37carat ruby.

Now she had every reason to remind Tito and Miko to arrange that long awaited trip to LESOTHO (S.Africa), and she really meant it.

Miko had gone to MelJeb Towers to meet Sanders to reconcile pending deals. She had one more question for Tito after he hung up the phone.

"Do you believe in luck?" she asked.

"Why? What's the big problem?" he quipped.

"BEAUTY, DESTINY, AND LUCK ARE IN THE EYE AND MIND OF THE BEHOLDER. Look at that 37carat ruby. It is sitting safely in its right place. And we are the winners of the world's largest jackpot," she said, and then embraced him tightly.

"Do you think so?"

She then unwrapped a gem portrait immediately in front of him.

Trespassers will be gemsicuted or believe in gemstones

THE END